A Child of War

Désirée's Story~ Part One

D. Riesau-Moreno

Books by D. Riesau-Moreno

Désirée's Story ~ Series
A Child of War ~ Part One
Waiting in the Crescent City – Part Two-coming soon
Hiding as just Désirée – Part Three-coming soon
Ending Nightmares – Part Four-coming soon
Like Ashes in the Wind – Part Five-coming soon

A Child of War

Désirée's Story ~ Part One

D. Riesau-Moreno

Casa Moreno Publishing

A Child of War

Désirée's Story ~ Part One

Copyright © 2024 by D. Riesau-Moreno

All rights reserved.

Print version ISBN: 979-8-9916800-0-4

Published by

CASA MORENO PUBLISHING

Original Cover art by Trent Shadburne – Shadburne Creative

Cover layout by Anna Shadburne – Shadburne Creative

Dedication

for Desi
and lost girls everywhere

Contents

Chapter 1

May 1997 - Napa Valley

I hate Spring, the unpredictability of it. Oh, it arrives routinely every year, but with it comes an anxious anticipation, some surprise that will either delight or horrify. I can never relax until Spring has fully fledged into Summer.

May is always the hardest. Things happen in May that never occur during other times of the year, at least according to my experience. This May was no exception. The familiar discomfort had grabbed hold, and I tried shaking it off with a breath of fresh air out on the deck.

The ringing phone shouldn't have startled me, but it did, and when Ava came out to get me, my heart was already racing.

"Desi, there's a call for you. It's an overseas call for Désirée Pérot. That's you, right?" Curiosity filled Ava's eyes as she passed me the phone.

I could have ignored the call, pretended it was a wrong number, and gone on as I have for decades, hiding from my past, from the incessant memories that still haunt me when my defenses are down. But it was Spring, and something urged me to reach for the phone. As soon as I did, I knew I would have to face the questions brewing in Ava's eyes.

I hadn't heard the name Pérot in over fifty years, and the sound of it sent a chill down my spine. *Who could it be? Why now?*

With a trembling hand, I put the phone to my ear, then took a deep breath to steady myself. "Hello?"

"I have a call for Désirée Pérot. Is this *Madame* Pérot?" asked a cheery voice with a French accent.

"This is Désirée." I wouldn't say the other name.

"One moment, please."

The phone line clicked a few times, and then a familiar voice, shaky with age but unmistakable, spoke to me for the first time since February 1944.

"Désirée ? *Est-ce vraiment toi* ?"

Unsure how to respond, I moved farther down the deck, seeking more privacy, my eyes closing against the flood of memories escaping their long confinement.

"*Oui, c'est moi. Comment m'as-tu trouvé* ?" (Yes. It's me. How did you find me?)

Every moment of that twenty-minute phone call, every word exchanged contained a lifetime of suppressed fear, regret, and the overwhelming need for forgiveness. When it ended, I looked out over the rolling vineyards, still wet from last night's rain shower, relief sweeping over me like a long-needed breath, a cleansing sigh.

The surrounding fragrances filled my senses with each breath, the grapevines abundant with new life and the promise of sweet elixir, and the earthy smell of my kitchen garden. My mind instantly transported me back in time to another vineyard, another garden, to a life I lost long ago.

"Desi? Are you okay?" Ava asked, coming up behind me, stroking my back with a gentle touch.

"Yeah. I'm fine honey." My standard response fell out of my mouth as I shook myself back into the present, but rattled by the call, I added, "I just need a drink."

After handing Ava the phone, I headed inside, wondering if I had what I needed to make a Sidecar; cognac, a little Cointreau, and citrus. Noon on a Sunday wasn't too early for a drink, under the circumstances.

"Who was the call from?" Ava asked. "It seems to have upset you. I never knew you could speak French." She chatted nervously, following me into the kitchen, then busied herself with the laundry she'd been folding for me.

"Do you want one?" I asked, pulling the martini glasses from the cupboard and gathering the ingredients.

"Sure." Ava sat at the kitchen table, folding towels the way her mother taught her—I would have to refold them later—then she glanced up, her eyes still full of questions.

"I just realized something, Desi. I've never asked you about your family or where you're from."

It was a question couched as a statement, and completely true. I could hear regret and maybe a little shame in her voice. Jack and I had been married for over ten years.

"I have no family, except Jack, you and the other kids." I said, sliding the drink across the table to her.

She received the drink and the comment with a grimace, giving me a look that made me sorry for how harsh I sounded. I sat down across from her, took a sip of the Sidecar, then rubbed my eyes, and tried to collect my thoughts.

"What happened to them, to your family?"

"It was a long time ago, honey. Another life, another time," I said, pulling a cigarette from the case in my pocket, and lighting it with the old Zippo lighter I've had forever.

3

I hoped that would satisfy her, but knew the call had piqued her curiosity, and she wouldn't easily let it go. Of Jack's four adult children, I was closest to Ava, but that was the first time she asked about my life before her father.

"It's not idle curiosity, Desi. My kids are growing up, and I want to tell them our family stories. Your story is part of that family. Won't you tell me... please?"

I watched the sunlight dance through the lace curtains hanging in my kitchen window, took a long slow drink of my cocktail, then a drag from the cigarette, letting the smoke curl around my face before exhaling into the ceiling. For most of my life, I'd avoided speaking of my past, rarely offering any information, but that call opened a place inside me I had sealed decades ago, and I wasn't sure I could close the door again.

It's time to open all the boxes, Désirée. No need for secrets anymore.

Then I considered what telling the truth would mean and hesitated.

I took a deep breath, put out the cigarette, then tossed back the Sidecar.

"If I told you the entire story, we'd need a lot more of these," I said, holding up the half-filled shaker in silent question. "Honestly, Ava, I'm not ready to tell it, yet. It was a long time ago, and I've put it all behind me." I poured myself another drink and topped hers off.

Ava took a sip of her drink, her eyes searching mine for the answers to her questions and revealing her disappointment. I'd seen that look on other faces when I skirted my past, but old habits die hard, and I'd been hiding for a long time.

I might have gone on hiding, but for that phone call. That voice, slightly frail but crystal clear, kept repeating in my mind. *"It's time, Désirée, that we forgive each other, and ourselves."*

With a sigh, I looked across at Ava and relented.

4

"I'll tell you this for now. I was born in France in 1932. When I was eight years old, the Nazis came and killed my entire family, leaving me for dead. Some people found me, saved me. At the end of the war, I met an American soldier. He brought me to the States. I've been here ever since."

Her expression made me sorry that I told her, her eyes widening, then narrowing as my words evoked unimaginable images. Ava was a Baby-Boomer, born after the horrors of war were over.

She couldn't possibly understand what it had been like.

"Oh, my God! Did that really happen?" she asked, choking on her drink.

With eyes shut tight, I tried to stifle my angry reaction to her question. I didn't want to dive any deeper into that nightmare than I already had, so instead, I swept back the hair covering my forehead, revealing a long, thin scar at the hairline.

"This is the first gift the Nazis gave me," I said, letting her examine the scar I carried from the beginning.

Ava sat back in stunned silence, hands now cupping her mouth, eyes wide with imagined horror. "Dear God! How could a child survive something like that?"

Her question haunted me for days. There are probably millions of answers, countless stories of that horrible time in history. Mine is but one of them. I was lucky, but that's not how it felt at the time. To survive, I became who I had to be, but a lifetime of guilt and shame was the price of my survival.

That long-feared phone call unlocked my memories, and they began playing in my mind like a movie; one scene leading to the next, each moment vividly clear and visceral in its intensity.

"Our only path to forgiveness, Désirée, is to expose our darkest memories, bring them into the light. Then, we can finally let them go—like ashes in the wind."

Chapter 2

May 15, 1940

I've had many names over the years, but in the beginning, I was Désirée Marie Rondeau, the youngest of François and Claudette Rondeau's five children. We lived on a small farm nestled on the southern slope of the Stonne Plateau, about fifteen kilometers southeast of Stonne, in Northeastern France.

I was a happy child, living a simple life, sheltered and secure in the love of my family. Never in a million years could I have imagined how much my life could change in a heartbeat.

Maman and I were in the kitchen making my favorite dish for my birthday supper, *Potée Champenoise*. By eight years old, I'd already learned more about cooking than either of my older sisters, who were more interested in boys than anything else. I loved being in the kitchen with Maman, soaking up everything she would teach me. I loved the smells and sounds that filled our kitchen, letting them wash over me like a favorite melody, while Maman would chop and sauté the ingredients I helped prepare.

"Désirée, be a good girl and fetch some things from the garden. I'll need a bunch of parsley, and a few sprigs of rosemary. Snip a small bunch of chives, too."

"Oui, Maman." I said, grabbing my gardening knife and basket on my way out the door.

I needed no supervision, having watched Maman in the garden since infancy. learning the names of all the plants and how we used them. Picking the vegetables and herbs for our daily meals was a favorite chore because Maman's garden was a magical place, filled with the scent of fresh herbs mixing sweetly with the earthy aroma of well-tilled soil.

As I bent down to snip a few parsley shoots, I heard a sound rumbling in the distance. It sounded like thunder rolling through the sky, but there wasn't a cloud in sight. The same sound had been happening for the past few days, and Papa told me not to worry, but he and Maman were acting nervous since the 'thunder' noise started.

My sisters were working in the lower fields with my brothers, Jacque and Jean-Michel, and I wondered if they heard the noise too. Then Yvette's piercing shriek, followed by a scream that must have come from Anna, came echoing up the hillside. Their screams sent a jolt of fear charging through me, and I ran to Maman as she hurried out of the kitchen. I threw my arms around her legs, burying my face in the folds of her skirt.

Maman wrapped her arms around me, soothing my trembles, then bent down to whisper into my ear.

"Désirée, run to your hiding place under the porch. Like we practiced. Remember? Stay quiet and do not come out until I call for you. Do you understand?" Her eyes insisted on obedience.

"Oui, Maman. But why must I hide? What happened to Anna and Yvette? Where's Papa? Maman, I'm frightened. What's happening?" My body shook so hard, my teeth were rattling as I spoke.

"Désirée, do what I tell you. There is no time. I will explain all this later. Please hurry," she said, pushing me away from her, urging me to obey.

I ran to the end of the porch and down the steps, then squeezed through an opening in the lattice that encircled it. Under the porch floor, I crawled through the dirt to lay trembling beneath Maman's feet. Once she was sure I had settled beneath her, she tapped her foot three times on the floor above me.

"Shh. Stay quiet, ma petite. No matter what, stay quiet."

All I could see was the front yard and the tree-lined road leading to the lower fields. Papa was nowhere in sight. Then I remembered he'd gone to the vineyard on the far side of the farm, but I thought he must have heard the screams. I held my breath, waiting, unsure of what was coming.

A moment later, a group of men marched my brothers and sisters up the road toward the house. I'd seen soldiers before. Lots of French soldiers came to the farm over the past few months, but these men were different, their uniforms and helmets weren't like the others. Terrified, I lay there watching my siblings being pushed up the road at gunpoint, and it felt like an entire army had besieged my home.

From my hiding place, I could see fear on my sister's faces, their eyes wide with terror and dripping with tears, their mouths held tight. The soldiers kept saying something to them, but the words were strange and garbled. Anna, my oldest sister, pleaded with them to take what they needed and leave us in peace, but the soldiers didn't listen. They kept snarling something and pushing her forward with the ends of their rifles.

I lie hidden in the darkness beneath Maman's feet, shaking with fear and anger, watching in horror. Then Maman stepped down from the porch, approaching the soldiers.

"*Messieurs*, what can we do for you?" Maman spoke calmly, though I could hear the nervousness in her voice.

A tall, fair-haired soldier, who seemed in charge, responded with angry words we couldn't understand. He stepped ahead of the others, pointing his rifle at Maman, barking something at her and nudging her toward the group.

Maman joined her children in a huddle, trying to comfort her trembling daughters. Jean-Michel, the oldest at almost sixteen, stood tense and poised for action with clenched fists and tightened jaw, his fighting posture. Maman held onto his wrist to keep him in check. Jacque, who was only thirteen, had a red line of blood dripping down his bruised face.

A couple of soldiers stomped onto the porch above me and entered the house. Then crashing noises came from inside. It sounded like they were kicking doors open and tossing the furniture around. It felt like they were tearing my home apart.

The other soldiers pushed my family toward the edge of the porch until only their legs were visible, but I could hear them whisper. Maman whispered of Germans and war, and the fear I heard in her voice frightened me even more.

My mind was racing with panic. *Papa, where are you? Why haven't you come? Maybe he didn't hear the screams.*

I needed to find him. Silently, I crawled under the porch, squeezing through the lattice opening, then I sprinted down the hill toward the vineyard. Halfway there, I tumbled into Papa's arms, sobbing and mumbling. He held me tight, trying to calm me enough to understand what I was saying.

"Stay here," Papa ordered, then he took off running toward the house. But I was too afraid to stay behind, too scared for my family. I ran after him and entered the front yard just seconds behind him.

Now the rifles were pointed straight at Papa and me.

"Messieurs, please take what you need, but do not harm my family," Papa said, his arms outstretched to show he wasn't a threat.

I was certain the soldiers didn't understand, because their leader grew impatient with Papa's pleadings, snarling strange words at him, and pushing the rifle into Papa's chest. Then two other soldiers grabbed Yvette and Anna and started pulling the girls toward the house.

Papa lunged forward to stop them. A loud blast tore through the air, and Papa fell to the ground in a heap. Maman's scream filled my ears as I ran to Papa, but before I reached him, something smashed across my head, knocking me down.

My fall across Papa's body felt endlessly slow, as if I were falling through a long dark tunnel, towards an even darker pit.

A piercing pain forced me into consciousness, but I couldn't move. It felt like something was weighing me down, like being buried under sacks of flour. The sharp scent of blood was all around me. I tried to open my eyes but couldn't. Dried blood had sealed them shut. It was in my mouth; salty and bitter. I tried moving my arms up to clear it away, but something held them in place. Then the pain in my head forced me back into the pit.

Sometime later, the sound of weeping pierced through the intense pain searing in my head. The weights began lifting off my body. One by one, they disappeared until I felt the cool night air on my bare legs. I felt a softness beneath me and could smell Papa's musky aroma, coupled with the sharp scent of blood.

With the final weight removed, they found me, limp and almost lifeless, with a gash across my head. I moaned as they lifted me from Papa.

"Papa, Maman. It hurts."

"*Mon Dieu!* She's alive!" I heard someone say before I once again fell back into darkness.

Chapter 3

The Old Woman

L ight pierced through my dark dreams, pulling me toward consciousness. As I awoke, I kept my eyes closed, allowing my other senses to take in the surroundings.

I wasn't in my bed. The bed felt hard and lumpy, smelled of stale bed linens, and the pillow was flat and musty. The feel of a rough blanket, tucked tightly into the bed frame, sent my legs and arms kicking and fighting it away, trying to escape. I needed to escape... but I couldn't remember what I was escaping from.

A blast of searing pain shot through my head, sending me tumbling to the floor as I struggled out of the bed.

Maman, where are you?

Not daring yet to open my eyes until the pain faded enough to focus, I sat on my knees on the bare wood floor, wrapped in the blanket, quivering with pain, and filled with a paralyzing fear that something terrible had happened.

What happened? I can't remember. Maman, I need you.

The pain was too intense, so I curled up under the table, sobbing, and trying to remember.

The door creaking open startled me as an old woman came through holding a tray filled with a steaming bowl of something. She set the tray on the table, then noticed me lying half-hidden underneath.

"Maman, Papa?"

"Come out, child." She offered her hand to help me from the floor.

The pounding pain in my head made it hard to think, but I tried to remember if I knew her. I studied her face and searched my memories. Her eyes were dark brown pools with lines and wrinkles around the outside. Her mouth was a thin line nestled under a beak-like nose. She reminded me of the old crones from the fairy stories.

Then I remembered. I had seen her before, the last time I went to town with Papa. She was talking with him outside the church, so I took a chance and reached out my hand to her.

"You shouldn't be out of bed, child," she said, helping me back onto the small bed. A gnarled hand touched my cheek while the other lifted the bandage from my forehead to check my wound. "Your fever is down. That's good. It means you are healing, but this head wound still needs rest, so lay back down and sleep more. Here, drink this. It will help you rest." She lifted a cup of bittersweet liquid to my lips, encouraging me to drink. "Sleep now, *ma petite*. Sleep will help you heal."

Whatever she gave me began its effect almost immediately. I relaxed into the bed as she rearranged the linens and pillow, then tucked me back under the blanket. She sang a child's lullaby as she straightened up the small room, the sound of it soothing my troubled mind.

By the time the door closed, I had drifted back into my nightmare of pain and terror, trying to escape. Or was it to get help? I couldn't remember.

I woke to a dark room, except for the light beneath the closed door. Nightmares lingered around the edges of my mind, as pulsing shadows flickered in the darkness, adding to the constant throbbing behind my eyes.

Voices came from somewhere in the house. A man and woman spoke in muffled, angry tones. I wondered who they were.

Is it the nice old woman? But who is the man?

I waited, listened to their argument, not totally understanding what they were saying. The man spoke so fast I could only catch a word or two and the woman was shushing him. What I heard sent a chill down my back and a scream tearing from my throat.

"... the Rondeau family... all dead."

Seconds later, the old woman rushed through the door, flooding the room with light. She found me cowering in the corner, wrapped in the blanket, my body shaking uncontrollably.

"Come with me, child, out of the darkness," she said, reaching for my hand. "Henri, let's make a place near the fire."

His silhouette in the doorway was black and sinister, like the monsters in my nightmares, and I tucked myself deeper into the corner, cringing back as far as possible, tears filling my eyes.

"No, ma petite, no one will harm you," the old woman said. "Come, let me have your hand, child... Henri is big, yes. I see he frightens you, but he is a friend and would never harm you."

Even though I was terrified, I took her hand and let her lead me into the central room of the house.

Henri followed us, then bent down to add a log to the fire. He squatted there, waiting and watching me. Not much older than my brother, Jean-Michel, he was taller and more muscular, with dark hair and eyes. The scar snaking along his jawline might have made him scary to look at, but his eyes held an unmistakable kindness. His left arm had horrible scars, and his hand was missing two fingers. That *was* scary to look at.

"Where is Maman? Where is Papa? Why am I here?" I asked.

"Sit with me, child," said the old woman, patting the seat next to her.

Like the obedient child I was, I crawled up on the settee, wrapped myself in the blanket, and tried to create a shield against what I sensed was coming.

"I was a friend of your parents," the old woman began, "and my son, Henri, was a friend to your brother, Jean-Michel. Several days ago, we found you injured and brought you here to nurse your wounds. Do you remember anything?" She gave me the same look Maman would when she wanted to make sure I understood her.

"I can't remember... It was my birthday... Where's Maman? Where's Papa?" I was desperate for answers.

"You must be strong, child, stronger than you have ever been."

Why do I need to be strong? I wondered. *She was a friend?* Her words made no sense to me, and I felt more and more frightened.

"Several days ago, the Germans went to your farm and killed your family. They are all dead, child. War has come to France again. I am so sorry."

She waited, watching me, maybe even expected me to burst into hysterics, but I never did things like that, and the tears filling my eyes wouldn't fall. Only my trembling lip betrayed my feelings.

They're all dead?

The thought filled my mind, repeating like a drumbeat, over and over.

Maman and Papa, my brothers, my sisters. All gone? All dead?

I tried to still the shaking that threatened to shatter me into a million little pieces.

They're gone, and I'm alone.

All gone.

"They're gone." I said, my eyes stinging with unshed tears, and my breath catching in my throat.

Her expression showed the truth of those words clearer than anything else. She studied me for a moment. "Yes, they are, but you're alive, and you're strong. Lay your head here on my lap, child. I'll keep the darkness at bay for the night. When you're feeling better, we'll talk more. Rest now, ma petite."

Too overwhelmed and miserable to protest, I lay my bandaged head down upon her bony lap. Instinct told me I was safe for now, so I tried to relax against her legs, my mind still filled with shadowy images as the gentle motion of her hand on my head, stroking my hair, soothed me into a deep and dreamless slumber.

Time blurred. I had no sense of it. I was numb inside. The constant throbbing in my head forced me to hold back my tears. Crying wouldn't bring back my family, anyway. Only at night, when I was alone in my room, I would curl up beneath the blanket and sob into the pillow. The pain in my head was an echo of the pain in my heart.

Once the old woman judged me healed enough, I spent the daylight hours snuggled up on the settee by the fire, nursing the headache, a constant reminder of my loss. The medicine she gave me helped ease the pain, though it made me sleepy and tasted horrible. It was difficult to not gag on it every time she offered the dose.

I kept my distance and my silence around them both, responding only if spoken to, but beyond a polite "Oui, Madame," I did not speak.

But I wanted to know things. *What happened to my family? Why did this happen? What is going to happen now?* So I watched them, listening at every opportunity, trying to get the answers to my questions.

While I was healing, I overheard a lot of things. Some things made little sense, and other things I put away to think about later. One night, after Henri had come in, they spoke in hushed whispers about battles, Germans and Allies, and of families fleeing the war.

"Henri, you shouldn't have gone there. Someone might have seen you. It's still too dangerous," the old woman said. "You must be careful."

"Pfft!" Henri spat into the fire. "The filthy Nazis headed west once Stonne fell, and they haven't crossed Maginot's line east of us... so far. As for that other pig slime, the next time I see him I will show him my hammer... The talk is that France will fall. They all got it wrong and are running to the coast. Damn, we're all screwed," he grumbled.

That was frightening, but it still seemed remote, unimportant to me. I needed to know what happened to my family. A blackness filled the spot where that memory should be. I hoped I would hear them speak about it, but they never did, at least not when I was around to listen.

Sometimes, they would watch me, then exchange looks with one another, their eyes filled with sadness.

"Do I make you sad, Madame?" I asked, hoping it wasn't true, but fearing it was.

She stared at me, her eyes filled with questions. Her pinched expression seemed to hold a challenge, but one she was reluctant for me to accept. She must have seen my sincerity, because after releasing a deep sigh, she answered.

"No, child. Not you... but yes. Whenever a child crosses my threshold, they are a precious life God has placed in my hands. They come for help, and I do what I can for them. Sometimes it is not enough, or my help comes too late." Her eyes were full of tenderness and sadness.

"Will you tell me what happened to my family?" I hoped she would answer.

She sighed, shaking her head. "I wish I had the answer you seek, child, but I don't. You are the only one who knows what happened on your farm that day. You are the only survivor. Perhaps it's best you don't remember."

"But I want to know!"

She stared at me for a long time, her eyes searching mine. It felt like she was trying to decide how much information I could handle. My eyes pleaded for answers.

"Henri and I, and another friend, discovered your family. We thought you all were dead until we lifted your mother's body and heard you moan. When we brought you here, I wasn't sure you would live until I cleaned you up and tended your injuries. Henri and our friend laid your family to rest behind the house, on the hill facing the vineyard. The village grieved their loss."

I searched her face for any trace of lies and found only the sadness I'd seen before.

"Merci, Madame, for your kindness to my family and to me."

Shaking with tightly held grief, a crushing sadness filled my heart as I walked back to the little room.

Later that night, I thought about everything, sorted through it all in my mind. The old woman said *I* was the only one who knew what happened, except I couldn't remember.

Why can't I remember?! Why?

I always remembered everything, everything I learned or heard or saw. Papa said my mind was like a safe that stored everything away for future use. When I was three, he taught me how to sort it all into tiny boxes inside my mind, to keep it stored away, but instantly available.

I tried and tried, but the memory of that day wouldn't come. Trying to force it only made my head hurt.

If my nightmares were any part of the memory, I wasn't sure I wanted to remember. They were so black and frightening, and I would wake up shaking and cold, with my head pounding.

Maybe it's better if I don't remember.

I tried to think of anything to keep the nightmares from coming back, but the only images that came to me were of my family, Maman and Papa, my brothers and sisters, their faces clear in my mind. My throat would tighten as I realized I would never see them again. My eyes filled with stinging tears, and the pounding ache in my head would start again.

Stop it! Don't think about them! They're gone!

CRASH!

The noise startled me. It sounded like someone was smashing up furniture in the living room. Then shrill voices filtered through the noise. I crept to the door to listen.

The old woman and Henri were arguing again. Lately, they only spoke to each other in heated arguments, usually about the war.

"I've searched everywhere and found nothing," Henri grumbled. "If it's come, we wouldn't know. The Rondeaus were the contact. They knew the location."

I heard him pacing around the room as he spoke, his voice rising in frustration.

"Shh, you'll wake the child," the old woman said. "There still may be time."

"There is no time, Maman. We must act now before it is too late. You know we must move her before someone sees her. It's too dangerous for her to remain here much longer," he said, his voice deep with emotion.

"I know Henri. She is well enough to travel now. Is everything arranged?"

"Père André has assured me all will be ready. She must be at Saint Martin's rectory early Saturday morning. Have you told her?"

"No. Not yet. I prayed for more time, but it seems fate has other plans for this child."

"You must tell her, Maman. She must understand the danger, or all our lives could be at risk. You know this."

"Yes, Henri, I know. I have always known the risk," she said, sadness in her voice.

"I will speak with her in the morning. In the meantime, continue to search for that message. It must be somewhere close to the farm. Neither François nor Jean-Michel would have gone too near the village. Not after what François told me..."

They moved deeper into the house, their voices fading beyond my hearing. I stood for a moment, collecting my thoughts, then climbed back into bed.

Papa and Jean-Michel were contacts? Contacts for what?

Something the old woman said triggered a memory of Jean-Michel, and as I fell asleep, the memory filled my dream...

It was the day before my birthday. I'd gotten up early, before the rest of the family, too excited to stay in bed. I went to the kitchen for something to eat and to start breakfast for Maman. As I glanced out the back window, I saw Jean-Michel walking towards the woods, and I wondered where he was going so early.

I'd been pestering Jean-Michel for days about what he was going to give me for my birthday. He always gave me something unusual, but no amount of asking would make him answer.

"You must wait, Désirée," he said. "Now stop bothering me. I'm busy."

So that morning, I followed him, waiting until he reached the woods before running up the hill after him. Once I caught sight of him, I stayed out of sight, not wanting to make him angry, but too curious to turn back.

Not far into the woods but off the trail, Jean-Michel stopped, and stood there looking around and listening. Afraid he'd hear me, I stayed as still as I could, watching to see what he would do.

Jean-Michel took hold of a thicket of holly growing by the rocky outcrop, one of many that dotted the forest, and to my surprise, he pushed the holly away from the rock, revealing a dark opening.

A cave! How exciting!

He reached into the opening and pulled out a small metal box. Then he took a ribbon from his pocket, tied it to the handle of the box, then put the box back into the cave. He stood up, looked around again, pushed the holly bush back into place, completely hiding the little cave, then he walked back towards the farm.

Once he left, I came out of hiding, puzzled by the entire event. Jean-Michel was older, almost an adult, according to Maman, and adults were sometimes odd.

My burning curiosity prompted me to move the holly bush away from the cave to see what Jean-Michel had hidden in there. I hoped it was my birthday present, but there was only a low shelf at the back, with the metal box sitting on top. The cave wasn't even an actual cave; it was only a shallow depression under the rock.

I figured Jean-Michel was probably passing secret love notes with a girl from the village, and he'd be furious if he knew I'd seen him. I looked inside the box—though I knew I shouldn't—but sadly, it was empty.

"No presents here. No secret love notes, either."

After putting everything back the way it was, I ran back home, hoping the rest of the day wasn't as disappointing as this first adventure had been...

When my eyes opened, my breath caught in my throat. The dream felt so real, like I was home again. I wanted to go back, to stay where I was safe with my family, but I wasn't home, and I knew I'd never be home again.

My family is dead, and I can't go home.

That thought, and the memory of Jean-Michel's little cave, planted an idea and a fierce determination in my young mind.

I must be strong. I must be strong. I must be strong.

I kept repeating those words, like a chant or maybe a prayer. Over and over, they played across my mind until they finally lulled me to sleep.

Chapter 4

A good meal

I woke late the next day, having slept better than I had since arriving at the old woman's house. The ache in my head had dulled, and the sunlight no longer hurt my eyes. I almost felt like myself and decided it was time I did something useful instead of lying around.

When I climbed out of bed, I noticed a stack of clothes neatly folded on the table under the window: underwear, a chemise, a blouse and skirt, and a sweater. A pair of small shoes, with stockings inside them, lay underneath the table, and a coat hung on a hook beside the door.

These are my clothes.

I hadn't noticed them before. In fact, I didn't remember dressing at all since I'd been there. The past days felt like a foggy nightmare.

How long have I been here?

The old nightgown I wore was stale from too many days and nights of wear. I shook off the fog and pulled off the gown, then stood shivering in the chilly air, goosebumps rising along my arms.

"Start at the beginning," Maman always said whenever I was unsure of what to do.

Standing at the table, I washed myself with the cloth and basin of water the old woman had left. The water was cold but refreshing, and it helped clear away the darkness lingering around the edges of my mind. Then I dressed, making sure I buttoned my blouse and sweater correctly, and my skirt was on straight.

I must be strong.

Bending over to buckle up my shoes, I thought about what '*being strong*' meant.

I don't know. I'm just a little girl, my inner voice complained.

A stronger voice answered. *No, you're not! You're a big girl, you're eight years old now.*

But I don't know how to be strong. I don't know anything, the little voice whined.

Yes, you do! You know everything Maman taught you, the stronger voice insisted.

You know how to cook and how to clean the house and how to work in the garden.

You know lots of things!

You need to do something, so they won't send you away.

With a sigh, I looked around for something to tidy my unruly hair, but found nothing. There wasn't even a mirror to tell me if I'd really gotten my clothes on straight. I pulled the bandage from my head and gingerly touched the cut that snaked across my forehead. It felt bumpy and tender, but no blood smeared my fingers when I looked.

That's good. I hated the sight of blood. Especially my own.

I pulled the tangles out of my hair, brushing it behind my ears with my fingers, then left the room, my coat still hanging next to the door. After a quick stop in the toilet down the hall, I went looking for the old woman.

A moment later, I entered a cheery kitchen filled with light from the bank of windows. A wood stove stood on the inside wall, the oven heating for the day. The old woman stood at the counter under the windows, sorting through a basket of potatoes, and was grumbling about their size and inadequacy.

"Bonjour, Madame. May I help you?"

She glanced over her shoulder at me. "You must be feeling better, child. I see you found the clothes I left for you. Come, stand over here so I can check that wound."

She pulled me into the room and stood me on a short stool next to the counter by the windows. Holding my face in her gnarly hand, she examined my wound, peering closely and probing gently with her fingers. Apparently satisfied, she released my face, then went back to the potatoes.

"You'll carry a scar which may never fade completely, but it's healing well. You're fortunate it's at the hairline. It will be easy to cover," she said over her shoulder.

The way she was acting felt different, and it made me nervous. I needed to make the nervous feeling go away, so I asked again, "May I help you, Madame? Maman said I was a big help in the kitchen, much better than Anna or Yvette. Maman sa…"

Talking about Maman wasn't making me feel better. It was making it worse. So, I took an apron from the hook near the door, tied it around myself, and stepped back up to the counter. With the confidence of a seasoned kitchen helper, I began sorting the potatoes with the old woman, choosing the ones that were firm and free of blemishes, the way Maman taught me.

The old woman stopped working and watched me for a moment.

"When you're finished sorting those, clean the good ones with the rag, then put a half dozen aside for the meal and the rest in the bowl. Leave the small ones in the basket, and we'll see if they're good enough for planting. I'll be back in a moment," the old woman said, before walking out of the kitchen.

I went to work sorting and cleaning, happy to be doing something familiar. In the end, I had a large bowl filled with clean potatoes, six potatoes set aside for the meal, and a basket with enough seed potatoes for planting.

Ready to start the next task and begin preparing the meal, I lifted a skillet from its hook, placed it on the hot stove, chose a knife from the rack, then set to work chopping the potatoes the way Maman taught me. I found an onion and some garlic in another basket and chopped them up too.

Next to the stove was a container of fat, so I added some to the heating skillet. When I judged it hot enough, I tossed the potatoes, onions, and garlic into it, seasoning them with salt and pepper, stirring them briefly to let them sizzle around the edges. I covered the pan, and let the whole thing cook slowly, the way Maman always did it.

Savory aromas filled the kitchen by the time the old woman came back. She stood in the doorway, watching me tend the skillet. Briefly closing her eyes, she made a huffing sound, then walked straight to the counter and placed a basket of eggs on it.

"Show me what you can do with these, child." She stood back, her arms crossed, a challenging look in her eyes.

I glanced at her, then at the eggs. It only took a second for me to reply.

"Oui Madame. The meal should be ready in a half hour. Will that be too soon, Madame?"

"That will be fine. We will eat together when you're ready," she replied, then she left.

I was cracking the eggs into a bowl by the time the kitchen door closed.

Confident in my skill, I hurried to finish preparing the meal, having helped Maman make the same dish many times; an omelet made of savory potatoes and onions. I wanted to impress the old woman, to show her I could be helpful, and cooking something delicious was the one thing I knew I could do. Maman always said everything was better after a good meal. I hoped it would be true, but I had a nagging ache in my stomach, the kind that always made me feel like something terrible was about to happen.

To distract myself from the anxiety, I went searching the kitchen for plates and utensils to set the table, then finding napkins in a sideboard, I carefully set everything out. I found a loaf of bread wrapped in a bag, not fresh but not too stale, so I placed it on a small cutting board with a bread knife and took it to the table. Then I returned to the kitchen for the rest of the meal.

When I returned, clutching the cloth wrapped handle of the hot skillet, the old woman and Henri were sitting at the table talking. Surprise marked Henri's unshaven face when I came in, and I recognized a hint of pride, or maybe it was satisfaction in the old woman's eyes as she looked up. The ache in my stomach eased a bit.

"Henri, help her with that skillet."

"Merci, Madame, Monsieur. Bon appétit."

The old woman served us each a slice of the omelet, then bowed her head and gave a blessing for the meal. We mostly ate in silence, but occasionally punctuated by the same sounds Papa and my brothers would make when they liked what they were eating.

Henri must like the omelet.

He rewarded my efforts when he reached across the table for another serving. After he finished eating, he stood up, made a little bow in my direction, then left the room.

"You did well, child. It's clear you have kitchen skills. You'll need them in the months and years ahead," the old woman said. Her look and the tone of her voice brought on a resurgence of my stomachache.

"You're healed now, child, at least enough for you to travel," she continued. "I've done what I can for you and now must hand your care over to others. Henri brought some of your things from your farm," she said, pointing toward the front door where my satchel, a gift from Maman last Christmas, sat waiting.

"Madame? Have I done something bad? I promise I will be good, Madame. I promise I will do everything you ask. Please, Madame, please don't send me away." Tears filled my eyes, and it was hard to hold them back. My world was turning upside down again, and I didn't understand why.

"No, child, you've done nothing wrong. It is no longer safe for you here, and there are others who need my help. A friend will take you to the orphanage in Châlons-en-Marne. The nuns there will care for you."

"But why? Why can't I go ho...?" I stopped myself before I said the word, biting into my lower lip. I knew why I couldn't go home. There was no one left. My family was dead.

"But why, Madame? I'm safe here with you. Why can't I stay here? I don't understand." I was shaking, fear coursing through me.

"War is not a time for children. It is safer for you away from the fighting, in a place with other children. My friend, Père André, will be ready for you early tomorrow morning," the old woman said with finality, clearly expressed in her stiff posture and firm look.

I was desperate to change her mind. Being sent away felt more frightening than anything I could imagine. Then I remembered what I'd heard the previous night, what they said about my brother, Jean-Michel, and I remembered the little cave.

"I know where Jean-Michel's secret hiding place is," I blurted out.

Henri had just walked back into the room. He stood as still as stone, staring at me for the longest time, with a scowl on his face. "How do you know this?" he asked.

I looked at them, worried they'd be angry that I'd listened to them. But this was my chance to show them I could be helpful, that I knew something... if only they would let me stay and not send me away.

"Tell us, child," the old woman insisted.

"I followed him. He didn't know I was there. I stayed hidden because he would have been angry at me for bothering him. I wanted to see if he had hidden my birthday present in the little cave, but there was only an old rusty box," I ended in a whisper, fearing they wouldn't believe me.

"A cave, you say. Where is this cave?" Henri demanded. Then he turned to the old woman. "Maman, I have searched every cave in the area and found nothing. This is only a child's dream."

"We must be certain, Henri. There are too many lives at risk if this network fails. Where is this cave, child?"

"In the woods, close to our farm. I could take you there. Please don't send me away, Madame. I can help you. Please."

The old woman searched my face for signs of deception. What I hoped she saw was my desperate, hopeful plea for safety.

"Henri, take the child after dark and find Jean-Michel's secret hiding place." She stopped him with a raised hand before he could object. "It will be safe enough after dark. Go finish your work." She dismissed him, then spoke to me. "Clear the table, then come back and sit with me, child."

"Oui, Madame."

I set to work, carefully scraping and stacking the plates while stealing glances at her. Then I carried the stack to the kitchen, being extra careful not to spill anything. I was nervous and unsure if I'd changed her mind, but I hoped so.

When I returned, she was sitting next to the fireplace mending a seam on an old shirt, her eyes squinting through the pair of glasses perched on the end of her nose. She patted the seat next to her, and I dutifully sat down to await what was coming next.

"Child," she began, shaking her head and sighing, "There are things you must know, must understand before you leave here." My body tightened with renewed fear as I waited for her to continue. She must have seen she was frightening me.

"Your father and your brother, Jean-Michel, were working with some people, helping families escape the Germans, families with children like you, who have fled from their homes. The 'secret hiding place' you found may be very important. A family needs our help, but we don't know when. A message was to arrive the day your family died. Only your father and brother knew where to pick up the message. If it's there, we may still have time to help this family." She waited for me to absorb this new information before continuing. I stared back at her, wide-eyed and trembling.

"There is more, child. We aren't sure, but we believe someone betrayed your father. Someone sent the Germans to your farm looking for something. Do you remember anything about that day? Did you see anyone around the farm, any strangers?" she asked, staring at me, her eyes wrinkled around the edges, and her mouth held in a tight line.

I shook my head. "I can't remember that day. But a man came to the farm the day before I followed Jean-Michel to the little cave. Papa caught him

31

looking around inside the barn. I heard Papa tell him to leave and never come back. Papa was furious."

"What did the man look like?" the old woman asked, worry deepening the creases on her forehead.

"I'd seen him once before, the day I saw you and Papa talking outside the church. I was in the truck waiting for Papa, and I saw the man on the street corner, staring at you and Papa. When he saw me watching him, he walked away in a hurry. He was older than Papa, with white hair, and he had a walking stick with a silver top on it."

I didn't know if any of that was helpful, but when I saw her reaction, my heart started racing, and my trembles increased. She looked as if I had described a monster.

"Oh, child... that is what we feared," she said, closing her eyes, her head bowed. When she looked up, sadness filled her face. "When we found your family, and then discovered that you were alive, we decided I would hide you until you could travel. If the village knew you survived the attack, we feared that the man who betrayed your family might try to harm you... in case you'd seen something, knew something. We couldn't take that chance. When we buried your family, we marked the grave with all your names. As far as the village knows, the entire Rondeau family died that day." Her mending forgotten, the old woman leaned back into the settee, waiting for my reaction.

It was a lot to take in, and the worry on her face only fueled my fear about what would happen to me next. I clutched my hands together to calm my shaking as a memory suddenly flashed through my head...

I was standing next to an open grave two summers earlier. My brothers and father were lowering a small casket down into the deep hole they dug in the graveyard behind the parish church. Horrified by the thought of

Grand-Mère being covered up with all that dirt, even with the surrounding casket, I stood there looking down at her, shaking and miserable...

A shudder traveled through me as I imagined my family at the bottom of a huge grave, covered with dirt, worms crawling over them.

"May I see it?" I asked, needing to see something that would confirm all of this was real.

She narrowed her eyes at me, startled by the question. "See what, child?"

"The grave where you buried my family."

She sighed, shaking her head. "Oh, child, that wouldn't be wise. We cannot risk you being seen by anyone. I am sorry."

A single tear trickled down my cheek. She reached over to pat my clasped hands, trying to give what comfort she could, but I pulled my hands away, wiping the tears from my face. Then I stood up and ran from the room.

I threw myself onto the bed, crying inconsolably, until I finally fell asleep in utter exhaustion. I slept the rest of the day, waking occasionally from the nightmare with fitful tremors, only to fall back into the dark dream.

Chapter 5

Henri

T he sun had already set when I finally awoke to find the old woman standing next to the bed, gently touching my cheek, and urging me to wake.

"Come, girl. It's time to find the little cave."

I crawled out of bed, wiped the sleep from my eyes, and straightened my wrinkled clothing. After slipping on my shoes and donning my coat, I dutifully followed her into the living room.

Despite all I'd been told, I still held onto a tiny hope she would change her mind and allow me to stay.

Henri was waiting for us by the fireplace, a rifle leaning against the hearth next to him. He nodded as we entered, his gaze lingering on me, as if he were evaluating me like Papa would do when he bought a new animal for the farm. "Judging their soundness," Papa would say.

Henri nodded, then spoke to the old woman. "All is ready."

"Oui, Henri. It is time. Come here, child. We must cover your head. Your beautiful blonde hair will stand out in the moonlight."

She sat down on the settee, pulling me to stand before her as she draped a shawl of dark blue wool around me, covering me from head to toe. The shawl smelled of her with a hint of sage and lavender, and I drew the fabric together over my nose, inhaling deeply.

34

"Tonight, Henri will take you to the edge of the forest by your farm. From there, you must guide him to the little cave. Do you think you can find it in the moonlight?"

I nodded silently, my eyes now clear and alert.

"*Bien*. You are a brave girl. Never doubt your strength. When you leave with Henri tonight, you will not return. Regardless of whether you find the cave, Henri will take you to Père André. You will be in his care until you reach the orphanage in Châlons, where the good sisters will see to your care and education." She looked deep into my eyes and held them captive with her need to make me understand.

"Listen carefully to me, child. You *must* understand what I tell you now. When you leave this house, you must leave the name Rondeau behind—so no one can follow—so no one can harm you. You will have a new name. Père André will tell you more tomorrow. Do you understand?"

I trembled beneath the shawl, my eyes rooted to the old woman's. Nothing I could do would change what was about to happen. I was a powerless child.

Letting the last tremble roll through my body, I responded. "Oui, Madame."

The old woman looked up at Henri, tears threatening to break her fragile grasp on composure as she pulled me into a bony embrace, planting a tender kiss on my forehead. She slipped the satchel over my shoulder and gave me a final blessing.

"Be brave and strong and clever, Désirée. Your parents would be proud to have raised such a brave girl. May God be with you always." Then she stood up and handed me over to Henri. "Go now. The moon is nearly up. We'll speak tomorrow, Henri."

Henri grabbed the rifle, slung it over his left shoulder, then took me by the hand to lead me out into the night.

We walked in silence along a path leading away from the house, but before we'd gone too far, I turned to look back. I needed to see the house, wanted to remember what it looked like.

What I saw was a small glade surrounded by thick forest. The small house sat at the edge, now shadowed in darkness; the only thing identifying its presence among the trees was the faint light peeking out from behind the curtains. Henri's tug on my hand encouraged me to follow, and I turned away with a sigh.

I wasn't sure where I was. The forest was thick and dark, filled with noises that sent shivers down my arms. Comforted by Henri's presence, I clung to his big hand as we walked along a narrow deer trail through the shadowy forest.

We hadn't been walking that long, less than an hour by my estimate, when Henri stopped. I imagined it would take longer, but suddenly I was standing on the edge of the woods next to Papa's vineyard.

Henri stood perfectly still inside the tree line, listening and watching. When he deemed it safe, he bent down. "Do you know where you are now? Can you find your way from here?"

"Oui, Monsieur," I said, now confident in familiar territory.

I looked toward the vineyard, calculating where we were, then began walking along the rows of vines planted right outside the trees. These were my Papa's vines, tended with care, season after season. I could smell the soil, the fresh growth on the old vines, and reached out my hand to touch the new leaves.

Who will tend to them now? Who will harvest the grapes and make the wine? I wondered as I walked up the sloping vineyard, with Henri following close behind.

When I came to the top of the hill, I stopped. On the opposite side, at the bottom of the hill, I could see the outline of my house. I wanted to run down there, to make sure it was real, but Henri stopped me with a hand on my shoulder when I started towards the darkened house.

"No, we must not go there," he said, turning me away from the only home I had ever known.

There's no one there, anyway. They're all gone.

As we turned away, Henri took my hand and led me to where he buried my family.

There, sitting back on the hill overlooking the vineyard, was a large mound surrounded by seven small white crosses, shimmering in the moonlight with freshly planted flowers surrounding the grave. We stood there for a moment, both lost in our thoughts.

"Your brother was my friend. I'm so sorry. I wish…"

Maman, Papa, are you there?

I stared at the grave but couldn't speak. My throat tightened, my breath shuddered, tears flowed freely down my cheeks. Sorrow was overwhelming me….

I couldn't look at the grave anymore.

After saying a silent goodbye to my family, to my home, I took Henri by the hand, and led him into the woods and away from the sadness of that place.

I knew exactly where I was, knew every plant and tree around my home. I led Henri directly to the place where Jean-Michel had hidden the little box. It wasn't hard to find if you knew where to look.

"It's there, behind the holly bush," I said, pointing to the bush covering the rocky outcrop.

Henri looked around, apparently searching for signs of disturbance, and making sure we were alone. After examining the bush for traps, he pushed it aside to reveal the little cave.

"You were right. There is a cave. Let's see if this is what we hoped for."

He brought out the metal box and placed it on the ground by my feet. I noticed the ribbon Jean-Michel had tied to the handle was missing. When Henri opened the box, he found a piece of paper inside with the ribbon lying on top. He took the paper out and held it up in the moonlight to read.

"Thank God. There's still time," he said, stuffing the paper into his coat pocket. "Come. We must go. We have a long walk ahead of us." Leaving the box with the ribbon behind, he started walking back through the woods.

"Shouldn't we put it back?" I asked, concerned I'd be in trouble for disturbing Jean-Michel's secret place.

"We won't use this place again," Henri said, continuing down the path.

I didn't want to leave, didn't want to walk away from everything I'd ever known, but I had no choice.

There is no one left. You must leave.

I trailed behind him, but not before stopping to retrieve the ribbon, putting it safely away in my satchel.

At least I have something to remember them by.

We followed a deer trail through the woods, each holding our thoughts. Henri kept a steady, sure-footed pace, but walked slow enough for me to stay beside him while I gripped his hand, grateful for his presence in the darkness. I had never been in the forest at night before, never been so far from home, nor anywhere without my family.

Everything has changed. Nothing will ever be the same again.

These thoughts and more kept tumbling through my mind as we walked, and soon my natural curiosity overcame my shyness, and I broke the silence.

"Where are we going, Monsieur? How long will it take us to get there? Do you know what's going to happen to me? How far have we come?" I asked, hoping for some reassurance.

He stopped, leaning down with his finger to his lips. "Shh. We must be quiet. No one must hear us or see us." After that, I kept my questions to myself.

We'd been walking for a long time through the thick forest when suddenly a loud crashing noise in front of us brought Henri to an abrupt halt. He pulled me behind him, then peered around the trunk of an ancient fallen tree. Watching and listening, then slowly lifting his rifle, Henri was ready for whatever danger showed itself.

My heart beat hard and fast, like any small creature frightened of an unknown danger.

Then the sound of a wild pig grunting through the brush eased the tension, and Henri relaxed a little after the beast passed us by.

We continued walking through the forest and underbrush for what seemed like forever. Then, after crossing several open fields, we stepped onto a deeply rutted dirt road, empty of any other travelers as far as I could see, but Henri quickened his pace. He appeared nervous, looking around and listening for something. His nervousness only fueled my own.

We didn't stay on the road for long but cut across another field toward a stand of birch trees, their trunks softly glowing in the early morning light. A low wall skirted the trees, encircling a pasture on the other side. At the far end of the pasture sat an old stone barn and the shapes of cows huddled together, still dreaming cow dreams.

Henri lifted me over the wall and sat me down on it, then climbed over, looking around with the same worried look on his face he'd been wearing all night. After taking a deep breath, he relaxed a little. He leaned against the wall next to me, pulled a cigarette from his jacket and lit it, the brief glow of his match lighting up his unshaven and brooding face.

"Are we still in danger, monsieur?"

"No. We weren't followed, and the Germans are still to the north and west."

"Do we have much farther to go?" I asked, after taking a drink of water from the bottle he offered.

"No. It's there," he said, lifting his chin in the barn's direction across the pasture. He made no moves to get up, to take me there and unburden himself of me. He just leaned against the wall next to me, smoking his cigarette, brooding about something. After a while, he stood up, smashed the cigarette on the ground, then bent down to look me in the eye.

"I don't know how long this war will go on, but I promise you, when it's over, if I survive, I'll do whatever I can to find you. I owe that to your family, to your brother... to you." He looked at me for a long time before continuing. "You must survive this, Désirée. For your family's memory, you must promise me you will be strong and brave, and never forget their sacrifice. Do you understand? Can you promise me this?"

"Oui, Monsieur. I promise," I said behind trembling lips. The morning mist was seeping beneath the folds of the old woman's shawl, so I pulled it closer around myself, trying to still the shaking, determined to be as brave as I could be.

"Good. We must go. Père André is waiting for us."

I waited nervously for someone to answer Henri's rap on the door, and jumped back when the door pulled sharply open, the noise from inside breaking the silence of the long night.

A balding man in a black priest's robe greeted us. He wasn't as tall as Henri and was thin and wiry—very unlike the fat priest of my parish at home. His warm smile reached up to a pair of soft brown eyes, which peered down at me.

"You made it. I was getting worried. Well, you're here now. Let's have a look at you, child." The priest pulled me into the entryway, while Henri remained on the front step. "Stay here for a moment, while I speak with Henri."

I waited quietly as I looked around while they spoke in whispers, my fate once again in the hands of strangers. When their conversation finished, Henri kneeled in front of me, taking my hand in his.

"*Au revoir*, Désirée. Be well, be brave. Remember what I told you." Then he stood and walked away.

I hated the thought of him leaving and ran after him, throwing my arms around his waist and sobbing into his coat.

"Please don't leave me. Please!"

"No tears, ma petite," Henri said, stroking my back with a gentle touch. "You must be strong now. Père André will take you to a place where there are other children. You'll be safe there." He pulled my arms away and held me by the shoulders, looking down at me for a long time.

"Be brave, Désirée. Remember the promises we made. I will not forget." Then he walked away for good.

I wiped the tears from my face with the old woman's shawl as I watched him disappear.

Will I ever see you again?

Chapter 6

Not Alone

"Come with me, child. I want to talk with you before you meet the others," Père André said as he closed the door, then led me to the front parlor. "Here, warm yourself by the fire. You look chilled from your long walk."

I entered a small but cheerful room filled with overstuffed chairs covered in a floral print, and polished tables holding vases of spring flowers. A small fire crackled in the hearth, and I rubbed my hands together, grateful for the warmth.

"Look at me, child," he directed, pulling the shawl from my head, and laying it aside. Then he cupped my face in his hand, holding it still while he spoke.

"How old are you?"

"Eight, Père."

"Good, good. Everything is in order." He paused a moment, still holding onto my face.

"Your name is Désirée Pérot from Sedan, correct?" His eyes held mine in an intense gaze. "Désirée Pérot from Sedan. You lost your family in the fighting. All this is correct, yes?"

My new name is Pérot. I committed the name to memory as I stared up at him, then my next thought was, *I'm not Rondeau anymore.* Why I needed a new name was confusing, but the old woman's words echoed in my mind: '*so no one can follow, so no one can harm you.*' I had no choice but to believe her.

"Oui Père. I am Désirée Pérot."

He released me, then pinned a small envelope to the inside pocket of my coat.

"*Bon.* Are you hungry, Mademoiselle Pérot? I'm sure Madame Tierney will have something to fill you up before we depart." He stood and left the room in a rush, motioning for me to follow, so I gathered up my satchel and the old woman's shawl and scurried after him, feeling unsure, but not fearful.

The aroma of cooking food filled my nostrils as we entered a bright kitchen where a short, gray-haired woman stood at the stove, turning slabs of ham in a large skillet, while chattering away to no one in particular. Three children were sitting at the trestle table on one of two long benches. An older man wearing a beret stood by the outside door, smoking a pipe. They all looked over when Père André and I came in.

"Bonjour, *mes amis*," the priest announced to the room with a flourish. "Here is our new arrival, Mademoiselle Désirée. She will join us on our journey to Châlons. Make her welcome, *s'il vous plaît*. Pierre, have the truck loaded and ready when I return from morning prayers. We will leave within the hour." With a whirl of his black robe, he left the kitchen.

I remained frozen in place by the door, feeling very unsure and nervous.

More strangers. Be strong, be brave, like Henri said, I reminded myself.

The woman broke the spell, taking me by the hand, and clucking like a mother hen about children being dragged out in the dead of night and other things that made no sense. She settled me onto the empty bench at the table across from the other children, my meager possessions neatly laid beside me.

"Désirée, such a beautiful name," she continued in an endless stream of conversation. "Let me introduce you to your fellow travelers and to myself, of course. I am Madame Tierney, housekeeper for the good priest here at Saint Martins. This distinguished gentleman, wasting my time, as usual, is Monsieur Pierre, who will escort all of you to La Maison in Châlons," she said, pointing to the old man.

"Here we have Mademoiselle Janine," she said, pointing to the girl with long black wavy hair, who looked like she was ten or eleven. "And these two are Mademoiselle Margot and her brother Monsieur Jon." She patted the small boy's head, then clucked her way back to the stove, leaving us children to ourselves.

I looked from one child to the other, wondering what horrible fate had brought them there, wondering if their families were dead like mine. The younger of the girls looked like she was younger than me, maybe six or seven. She had her arm around her little brother, who didn't look older than four, his face shyly peeking out from his sister's shoulder. They both had wide, frightened eyes, with hollow looks on their faces. The older girl stared back at me, her expression hard to read; angry or hurt, maybe.

We took each other's measure, as children are wont to do, none of us saying a word.

"Eat up, children. You may not eat again before arriving in Châlons," Madame Tierney said, placing four steaming bowls of potatoes with ham and four glasses of fresh milk in front of us. We all shifted our attention to our meals.

My stomach growled like it hadn't eaten in days. Then I remembered cooking for the old woman and Henri the day before. That felt like forever ago.

Since waking up in the old woman's house, everything felt like a dream. But when I looked up from my bowl, and took in the looks on the faces of the children sitting across from me, I was certain this wasn't a dream, at least not one I would ever wake up from.

I also realized I wasn't alone. I wasn't the only child who lost everything, and somehow that was comforting. I was not alone.

A short while later, Père André returned and herded us all outside to get ready for the journey. An old truck, loaded with crates and sacks, waited for us outside the house.

"Make yourselves as comfortable as you can, children," Père André instructed. "We have a long road ahead of us. With God's grace, we'll reach Châlons by nightfall."

Père André climbed into the truck, while Pierre got in behind the steering wheel and started the engine.

"Merci, Madame Tierney, for your gracious assistance. Au revoir," Père André called back to her.

As the truck rolled down the road, we settled ourselves for the trip, and except for the endless whimpering of young Jon, we held our silence, each still shy or frightened or both.

Wrapped in the old woman's shawl, I found a place in the corner, laying my head against a sack of potatoes with the earthy smell under my cheek, familiar and soothing. I watched the clouds move across the morning sky until finally exhaustion, and the rhythmic motion of the wheels along the road lulled me to sleep.

After hours under the old woman's shawl, I woke up hot and sweaty. Throwing off the shawl, I stretched my arms and legs as much as space allowed and looked around for something to quench my thirst. A half-filled bottle of water was sitting on a box next to me, so I took a deep drink, then set the bottle aside, noticing the older girl, Janine, watching me.

"I saved it for you. Jon and Margot would have finished it if I hadn't," she said.

She was sitting across from me, her legs pulled up close to her body. The younger children were asleep, curled up next to her. Margot held Jon tucked neatly in her arms as he sucked his thumb, his small shoulders shuddering with each breath.

"*Merci*. Do you know where we are?"

"Not really. Somewhere between Saint Martins and Châlons. The priest says we'll stop in the next town."

Gradually letting go of our shyness, Janine and I started talking.

"What happened to you, Janine? Why are *you* with Père André?" I asked.

Her eyes still held the hurt I had seen earlier, but they softened a little as she told her story.

"We lived in Sedan. Papa had gone to fight with the army against the Germans. Maman and I kept the café open as long as we could. When we heard the Germans were coming, we packed up a cart and hurried away with some other families." She cleared her throat and wiped her nose with the sleeve of her coat before continuing.

"After we crossed the bridge, bombs started falling all around us.... Something hit Maman, and she fell. There was so much noise with explosions and gunfire all around us. Everyone ran, but Maman didn't get up. She was dead... and I had to leave her. I had to run away." Janine paused again to catch her breath, as if she'd been running. "After that, I walked for a few days with some people I didn't know, but then Père André found me." Tears rolled down her face as she finished her story, but she sniffled and wiped them away, straightening her shoulders.

This horrifying story was the first time I'd heard about the war, what it really was, what it really did to people. Tears stung my eyes as I tried to hold them back, afraid of losing control.

"I think that's what he does... Père André," she explained. "He's a traveling priest who rescues lost children like us."

Janine waited for me to share my story, but I had turned away. Hearing her story made me sad and I couldn't help feeling my own loss.

"What happened to you, Désirée?" she finally asked.

When I looked up, Père André gave me a quick glance through the open cab window, a silent warning in his eyes. I'd never been prone to lying, but his look and the old woman's warnings stayed vivid in my memory, so I simply said, "I don't know. I don't remember." It was the truth. I didn't remember what happened.

Janine stared at me with her brow furrowed, clearly waiting for me to continue.

"I got hurt," I said, reaching up to touch the wound on my forehead. "I don't remember how. Some people took care of me. They took me to Père André, because the Germans killed my whole family," I said, ending in a whisper.

I hoped that would be enough, and it seemed to be because Janine just stared at me with a sad look on her face. When I glanced up, Père André gave me a brief nod.

Turning away from them both, I studied the landscape we were traveling through; low rolling hills covered with grapevines, row upon row as far as the eye could see. I watched as the rows on either side of the road merged, then narrowed to a point in the distance.

The sound of wild geese increased as the rows of grapevines receded in the afternoon sunshine. The flock flew overhead, forming a perfect counterpoint to the receding vines. Fat bellies beneath their beating wings, their insistent honking rending the air with a discordant noise. I always loved seeing geese fly overhead, their arrival each year signaling the change of seasons.

What change are you bringing now? I silently asked the birds, thinking it wouldn't be one I would choose for myself.

I'm a lost child, and there's no one left to find me. There is no one to go home to.

The noise of the birds startled Margot and Jon awake, their eyes wide with wonder as the geese flew overhead.

"I'm hungry," Jon announced.

The truck slowed to a stop at a more significant roadway, cutting across the landscape from east to west. A line of heavily loaded cars and trucks with frightened faces peering out of the windows advanced slowly down the eastbound lane.

Père André looked back at us through the cab window, then spoke to Pierre. "Let's hope our luck holds out. I'm eager to speak with Père Thomas at the cathedral in Courtisols. We need to know what to expect in Châlons."

Pierre silently nodded, then pulled the truck onto the westbound roadway.

The road into Courtisols skirted a small river, curving around but heading west. When we finally entered the town, its size amazed me. It was so much larger than my little village, which only had one road. This town felt bigger than any I had been in before; people, cars, and trucks jamming the streets, everywhere a bustle of anxious activity.

Père André called down to a young soldier as our truck went by. "What news of the front, my son?" But the stony-eyed soldier either didn't hear or ignored him.

Everywhere I looked, every face we passed held deep emotion; anxious, angry, nervous faces. At one intersection, a traffic jam halted our progress, trucks, cars and carts jammed up in four directions. Entire families loaded into their cars with whatever they could take were apparently heading away from where they thought the Germans would be. Every face I saw was full of fear and confusion. Trucks filled with soldiers rolled by, presumably heading toward the German army. It seemed to me some of those soldiers looked like they hoped for a different destination.

I couldn't understand any of this. *Why are the Germans coming to France and killing people? Why is this happening?* War made no sense to me, and with each unhappy, nervous face we passed, my nervousness increased.

We crossed a short bridge as the river turned north, and the road continued west, straight into the L'Epine square. There stood the most massive building I had ever seen, La Basilique de Notre Dame de L'Epine. Pierre guided the truck around the square to the side of the church, stopping outside an entrance. Anxious energy filled the air as people hurried in and out of the church.

Père André climbed out of the truck, calling back instructions as he hurried inside. "Pierre, stay with the truck. Children do as Pierre tells you. I'll return shortly."

I couldn't take my eyes off the church. Ornate carvings hung from the enormous building, which stood with two tall spires, one slightly taller than the other, both reaching into the clouds. I tilted my head back as far as I could to see the top, making myself dizzy. Stone carvings of monsters of all kinds hung from the walls and perched on every surface of the cathedral. The overall effect stunned and fascinated me.

I wondered what the inside would look like, with the afternoon light shining through the enormous stained-glass windows.

Do you live in there, God?

I thought He must, for it was the grandest church I could imagine.

I wanted to go inside to light a candle for my family and ask God why this was happening. But, as I looked at the anxious faces coming out of the church door, I thought there probably were no answers inside that church, for me or anyone else.

Père André appeared a short time later, with a young girl in tow. She was maybe nine years old, with mousy brown hair and she wore a woman's coat several sizes too large for her slight frame. She held the garment tightly around herself like a lifeline.

"Quickly, quickly climb up, my child. We must hurry along if we are to reach Châlons by dark," he said to the young girl, helping her onto the back of the truck.

"*Mes enfants*, our new companion is Mademoiselle Rachel. She will join you at La Maison, which with any luck we'll reach by suppertime. Settle in, and we'll be on our way," Père André said as he got in the truck.

Pierre drove the truck around the church and back onto the road, heading west.

I took a last look at the church as it receded behind us, the late afternoon sun shining on those tall spires and the stained-glass windows.

If you're not in there, God, where are you?

Chapter 7

La Maison

"They haven't crossed the German border," Père André informed Pierre. "And they haven't breached Maginot yet, but I fear it won't hold for long. The Germans are moving from the north towards Paris. Rumor is, they may be there within a week, perhaps more. The government is evacuating to the south. Bordeaux, he said."

The sun was setting when our slow progress through the jammed streets of Châlons finally came to a stop. The south entrance to the Cathedral Saint Etienne was on our right, another enormous church with elaborate stonework over the side entrance and a tall bell tower.

Directly across from the church stood a large four storied building taking up almost half of the block. Rows of tall windows lined each of the upper floors, and three tall windows flanked either side of the entrance, marked by a large blue door.

"We have arrived, children," Père André announced. He climbed down, making his way to the blue door, but as he was about to ring the bell, the door opened wide. Two nuns greeted him, both dressed in full habit, wearing winged white hats that reminded me of the geese I'd seen earlier.

"Bonsoir, Révérende Mère. Bonsoir, Sœur Marguerite. We have arrived, as you can see. Merci, merci, for your help and charity to these lost children." Then he spoke to us children in the back of the truck.

"Come, mes enfants. Time to rest with the good sisters. Come, come and meet Révérende Mère." He urged us out of the truck to stand facing the nuns.

We all hurried to follow his instructions, happy to escape the confines of the truck. Jon was whining and pulling on his sister's dress. Margot was just as unhappy, but trying to be brave for her little brother. Janine stood the tallest of all of us, her head held high and her arm around Margot's shoulder in support. Rachel, still wrapped in the big coat, her head bowed, was unwilling to look at anyone. I was glad the journey was finally over and hoped I could find a bowl of soup and a bed somewhere inside that big house.

I slipped my satchel over my shoulder and swung the old woman's shawl around me, then stood in front of the blue door wondering what was inside, and what would happen next.

"...... and this is Mademoiselle Désirée Pérot," Père André said.

Hearing my new name, I looked up into the greenest eyes I'd ever seen. They were the color of the forest in the afternoon sun. The face was long and thin with a sharp nose above a slightly pinched mouth and pointed chin, but the sparkle of those green eyes softened the overall effect, and I relaxed under her gaze.

"Bonsoir Révérende Mère."

"Bon. Sœur Marguerite, please take the children to the kitchen for some nourishment. I'll be in shortly." She addressed the men while the rest of us were being shuffled into the house.

"Pierre, you can unload the truck in the back. You know the way. Merci." She paused, looking at each of us as we passed. "Père André, you know we cannot take the boy. We must make some other arrangements. I will make inquiries. The Bishop has asked to speak with you as soon as you are available. Père Phillipe awaits you at the rectory." Then she followed us into the house, closing the door behind her.

The entryway opened into a long hallway flowing left and right, with a staircase on either end. Light from an overhead chandelier illuminated the space. Sœur Marguerite led us down another hallway towards the back of the house. We passed several doors and then entered a large dining room with a long table surrounded by lots of chairs. A fireplace dominated one end of the room, and the outside wall was mostly windows and tall glass doors, apparently leading to a courtyard.

I lost count of how many doors we passed. All the beautiful paintings filling the walls kept my eyes captivated. Everything about the house was fascinating, like it was out of a fairy tale. Then I heard familiar sounds coming from an open door at the far end of the dining room.

"Come in, come in," a cheerful voice greeted us as we shyly followed Sœur Marguerite into the kitchen. The voice belonged to a woman in a simple black dress with an apron tied around her ample middle, a kerchief covering her head.

"I am Sœur Louise Claire. You have met Sœur Marguerite and Révérende Mère, the others you will meet in time. Welcome children, you are safe now, here at La Maison. We have soup and bread for you, but first, we must wash." One by one, she guided us to the deep sink by an outside door to wash our hands.

As I washed the dust from my hands and face, I looked through the window over the sink and watched Pierre pull the truck into the courtyard. A boy and an older man came out of the building on the far side of the yard to greet him. The two men embraced like old friends do, then talked for a moment before setting to work. The boy glanced toward the kitchen window and caught me watching him. He waved, then grabbed a sack of potatoes, slung it over his shoulder and headed towards the kitchen door.

"That is Alex Guerin, the oldest son of Monsieur Dariel Guerin, the groundskeeper for the Cathedral and the Bishop's gardens. The family lives there, in the carriage house." Sœur Marguerite said, seeing who had caught my eye as she opened the outside door.

"Merci, Alex. You know where to store them downstairs."

The boy nodded, heading directly down a flight of stairs just across from the door. When he came back up, Révérende Mère had come into the kitchen.

"Merci, Alex. Please tell your father I would like to speak with him. After the truck is unloaded will be fine."

The boy nodded again and went out to continue his work and give his father the message.

Janine, Rachel, Margot, Jon, and I sat at a kitchen worktable, each of us nervous and silently waiting for the promised soup and whatever was going to happen next. All except Jon, who was whining and resisting any comfort from his sister or Janine. A stern look from Révérende Mère quieted him down to muffled whimpers into his sister's lap.

"Shh, *mon fils*, we will eat, but first we must give thanks."

Révérende Mère made the sign of the cross and bowed her head, waiting for us to do the same.

"Blessed Mother, to you I assign these children, which God has entrusted to us. Help us keep them safe in body and soul. Guide our hands as we teach them your loving ways."

"Bless us, O Lord, as we face the trials ahead. Bless this food and all the hands that prepared it. In the name of the Father and the Son and the Holy Spirit. Amen." She crossed herself again, then smiled at each of us. "Sœur Louise Claire, s'il vous plaît, let's get these children fed."

In almost no time, bowls of steaming soup and chunks of crusty bread appeared in front of us, and the only sounds heard were the clink of spoons and crunching bread as we happily filled our bellies. While we were eating, I watched the two men and Alex finish unloading the bags and boxes into the basement below.

When they finished, the men stood quietly, talking with Révérende Mère. Monsieur Guerin left the kitchen, only to return a moment later with a woman carrying a young child on her hip.

"Bonsoir, Madame Guerin," Révérende Mère said. "God bless you for your kindness. This is the boy I spoke with your husband about."

Révérende Mère glanced at Jon, who was finishing his last bite of bread. He dunked it into the bowl, then stuffed it into his mouth, soup and crumbs dribbling down his face. He sensed the attention of the room on him, and lifted his head from his bowl, eyes wide and curious.

"Jon, this is Madame Guerin and her sons, Alex and little Robert. You will go with them...."

"No!"

The scream didn't come from Jon, as I expected, but from Margot. She held onto her brother as tightly as she could, Jon wiggling in her grasp, clearly not understanding why she was so upset.

Révérende Mère and Sœur Marguerite gently pulled the boy away from his sister, trying to soothe her fears amid her noisy protests.

"Margot, my child, he is not going far, only across the courtyard to live with Madame Guerin and her boys. You can see him every day if you wish. Come now, no more tears," Révérende Mère said, wiping the tears from Margot's unhappy face.

"But why can't he stay with me?" Margot pleaded.

"Because this house is for women only. Our Order dictates that men must not live in our homes. We host them, of course, and work with them every day, but they must sleep elsewhere. Madame Guerin will take good care of Jon."

"But why...?" Margot started again, then Janine put her arm around the girl and whispered something in her ear, which seemed to calm her.

"Come, little man," Alex said, stepping in to take Jon in hand with his little brother slung over his shoulder, the toddler laughing wildly at the game. "Let's go find the men's sleeping quarters," Alex said, marching Jon out the back door.

With that, Jon instantly became part of the Guerin family, leaving the rest of us to wonder what our fate would be.

My exhaustion from the long trip to Châlons and the midnight walk with Henri had totally drained any patience I might have had. I hated the uncertainty, and needed to know if this house would be my home, or if I was to be sent somewhere else... like Jon.

"Révérende Mère, are you going to send us away too?" I asked.

She looked down at me, her green eyes searching my face. I looked back, seeking honesty.

"No, my child. This is your home now. We are the Sisters of Charity and have opened our doors to care for orphaned and lost girls, however they come to us, and for however long they choose to stay."

"Will we be nuns like you?" was my next question.

A beautiful smile bloomed across her face. "That is for God and each of you to decide... when you are older. For now, it's time for prayers and for bed. Tomorrow, we will talk about what the immediate future holds." She bid us all goodnight as Sœur Marguerite led us up the back stairs.

"Here we are," Sœur Marguerite said, escorting us into a large dormitory room on the third floor. A small fire burned in the hearth, giving the room a warm glow, lighting the faces of a group of girls sitting in front of it. One girl stood up when we entered.

"Sœur Marguerite. I told the others they could stay up to greet the new girls. I hope that was all right." She was a pretty girl, about twelve or thirteen years old, with dark blonde hair and soft features. Despite what she said, she had the look of someone confident in herself and her decisions.

"Of course, Annalise. I'm sure you were all curious. Let me introduce you."

Sœur Marguerite introduced us to everyone, but by then, all I could think about was how exhausted I was. All I wanted was to climb into bed and sleep till morning. I headed toward an empty bed across from the hearth, intending to crawl into it.

"Not *that* one," said a stern voice behind me. Annalise was shaking her head, looking at me as if I had made some grievous error.

"*I* assign the beds, and *yours* is over there," she said, pointing to another bed farther away from the hearth.

I wondered why it made a difference to her. All the empty beds were the same as far as I could see, and there was plenty to accommodate everyone. With a shrug, I gathered up my things and moved to the bed she assigned, too tired to complain. I stored my satchel under the bed and left the old woman's shawl neatly folded on the pillow.

They took us on a quick tour of our new living quarters, and after we had all washed and readied ourselves for bed, Annalise directed us to kneel by our beds and bow our heads. Sœur Marguerite led us in a simple nighttime prayer, then bid us all goodnight.

I pulled the blanket up to my chin and stared at the beamed ceiling overhead, listening to the surrounding noises; the crackle of the fire as it burned down, Rachel's muffled crying, her face buried in the coat she'd let no one else touch, and the soft whispers of Annalise and one of the other

59

girls. I took a deep breath then released it, a peacefulness finally quieting my mind, then the rhythmic sounds of the sleeping girls lulled me to my rest.

My final thought before drifting off was of the geese, and I realized they *had* given me a sign. They had led me to the nuns with the wide white hats that looked like wings. I think I fell asleep smiling.

Chapter 8

Elise Montclair du Châlons

I woke before sunrise, snuggled in the little bed with the old woman's shawl around me. Thankfully, the nightmares had not disturbed my rest, and I awoke refreshed.

Curious about the house and the nuns, who they were and what they did there, I also wondered what my new life would be like. I was determined to do my very best, so they wouldn't send me away again.

Normally restless in the morning, I wanted to get up and explore the house, but I wasn't sure if that was allowed.

No one said we couldn't.

Quiet as a mouse, I slipped out of bed and tiptoed to the bathroom. After washing up and dressing, I tiptoed through the dorm room, careful not to wake the sleeping girls.

The kitchen was empty, the stove cold, and the only available light was coming from the windows, as night gave way to dawn.

I was hungry, as usual first thing in the morning, but only found a small heel of crusty bread leftover from the night before. I took it despite its hardness and continued through the door leading to the front of the house.

It was the paintings that drew me. One had caught my eye as we passed through the night before, and I wanted a closer look at it. A large portrait of a young woman hung above the fireplace in the dining room, the look in her eyes commanded the room. She wore an old-fashioned dark blue dress with a high collar, puff shouldered sleeves and fitted bodice. Something about her face reminded me of someone, but I didn't know who.

I continued wandering through the house, munching on the bread, and studying the artwork. They were mostly religious, but there were landscapes of vineyards and a photograph of a family, father, mother, son, and daughter. The girl in the photograph was the same as the portrait of the young woman in the blue dress.

"You're up early," said a voice behind me. Sœur Louise Claire stood in the doorway to the kitchen, tying on an apron.

"I woke up. Maman said I was always an early riser. I wanted to look at the paintings," I said, glancing up at the nun to see if I was in trouble.

Sœur Louise Claire gazed around at the artwork. "They are beautiful, are they not? Oh, to have such talent, to paint such beautiful images. It is a gift from God. Do you like to paint, Désirée?"

"No, I don't think so. I just wanted to look at them again, like the one over the fireplace of the girl in the blue dress. Do you know who she is?"

"Oui, my child. That is Madame Elise Montclair du Châlons, when she was much younger, of course. She is our benefactor here at La Maison de la Charité. Come," she said, leading me into the kitchen. "I see you're a curious child, and an early riser as well. Follow me, and we'll get the kitchen warmed up. Then perhaps I'll tell you the story of Madame Elise."

I followed her into the kitchen, excited to hear the story, and hopefully to get something more to eat to quiet my rumbling stomach. Sœur Louise Claire directed me to a stool at the worktable, then busied herself with what appeared to be her regular morning routine, warming the oven, putting a kettle on to boil. It all reminded me of sitting in my kitchen at home, watching Maman do all the same things to prepare for the daily meals. It surprised me to have the same safe feeling in this new place that I'd known at home.

While Sœur Louise Claire worked, she talked, and I quietly listened, especially after being given a bowl of fresh yogurt with fruit. The nun told me the story, as she understood it, of Elise Montclair du Châlons...

"Elise Montclair was the only daughter of a wealthy family here in Châlons-en-Marne; landowners, winemakers, a very well established family in the province. When Elise was a young woman, she went to our motherhouse in Paris to become a novice."

"Then the Great War began, and she trained as a nurse, eventually working in the army battlefield hospitals. During the war, she traveled around the edges of the battles, helping wherever needed. She saved many children who lost their families in the fighting. If there was no one to care for them, she sent them to the orphanage in Paris."

"Elise Montclair never took her vows with the Sisters of Charity and at the end of the war, she returned to Châlons. Her mother and brother had died from the influenza epidemic, and her father was ailing from a heart condition. Elise stayed in Châlons to care for him and to run the family estates."

"After her father passed away, she continued to run the family business for a while, but her heart yearned to resume her work with the poor and displaced. She sold the winery and wine business and then gifted her family home, along with the other properties, to the Sisters of Charity. Her only condition was that this house become a home and school for orphaned girls."

"What happened to her?" I asked when she finished the story.

"No one knows. She simply left everything behind... Some say she continued her work with the poor in the countryside, some say she went to Poland to work with the Sisters there, others say she married and went to live in the north somewhere. No one knows for sure. But there are others doing the work she started long ago... Père André is one of them. We've been able to help many girls, like you, Désirée, because of the generosity of Madame Elise."

I looked up at her in amazement, suddenly realizing who the young woman in the portrait reminded me of. The old woman who cared for me after my family died, who saved me and then sent me away, was Elise Montclair du Châlons.

Then I remembered what she said...

"The good sisters at the orphanage in Châlons will care for you, keep you safe."

Sœur Louise Claire continued to talk as she worked and spoke more candidly than any adult I'd met so far. As I listened, I learned about La Maison and the school, and about the other children. When our talk turned to chores, I asked if I could help in the kitchen.

"Révérende Mère approves all the work assignments. We'll need to speak with her about it," she told me. "Do you know much about cooking, Désirée?" she asked with her eyebrows raised.

My eyes flashed open wide. "Maman taught me. She said I learned much more than Anna or Yvette ever did. Maman said... oh," I stopped as my eyes filled with unbidden tears. I bit my bottom lip to keep from crying.

"I know, child," Sœur Louise Claire said, gently patting my back. "It's hard to lose the people you love... but it's always good to remember them. That way, they'll stay in your heart."

I looked up, grateful for her understanding. "Mm... Maman said I could be a talented chef one day. I don't know about that anymore... but I do like to cook."

Sœur Marguerite hurried down the back stairs and into the kitchen, a panicked look on her face. She stopped short when she saw me sitting at the worktable with Sœur Louise Claire.

"Oh... there you are. When Annalise said you were missing, well, I didn't know what to think," she said, the wings of her hat bouncing with her agitation.

"Désirée has been here with me, Sœur Marguerite. We've been having a very nice chat, haven't we, child?" Sœur Louise Claire said, turning to me with a wink and a smile.

"Oui, Sœur."

"Well, the other girls are ready, and Révérende Mère is waiting," Sœur Marguerite said just as Révérende Mère came into the kitchen behind her.

"It's all right, Sœur Marguerite. I'll take charge of the girl. You take the others over and get them settled. We'll join you shortly." Révérende Mère shifted her gaze in my direction, taking in the state of my attire with a critical eye.

"Come with me, child. We must get you changed for mass."

I followed her up the back stairs to the dormitory, the room now empty of its inhabitants and in perfect order, all the beds neatly made, except mine. I would need to make it before Annalise came back, or I would surely hear about it.

"Come over here, Désirée," Révérende Mère said. "Take off those things so we can get them cleaned and put away for you. All our girls wear uniforms." She sorted through a wardrobe, pulling out several dark blue dresses in varying sizes. Finally settling on one, she held it up to me. "Here, I believe this will do. Put this on."

I removed my old clothes, noticing for the first time how messy I must look. My wrinkled clothes, stockings and shoes were a mess from the long journey the day before.

"Is this your coat, Désirée?" She held up my coat, then noticed the envelope pinned to the inside. After she read the note, she looked down at me with a curious look on her face.

"Oui, Révérende Mère. Père André put that in my coat."

I pulled the dress over my head, pushing my arms through the sleeves. The fabric was soft, and I liked the little white collar around the neckline.

"Did you know Madame Elise?" I asked, struggling with the buttons.

Révérende Mère stared down at me, her eyes narrowing. "Where did you hear that name, child?" she asked, a wrinkle creasing her forehead.

"Sœur Louise Claire told me the story of Madame Elise, and how this was her home when she was a girl."

Révérende Mère closed her eyes for a moment. "I knew her briefly, a long time ago in Paris, when I was a novice. She was a very kind and generous woman."

She guided me to the seat at the dressing table and began brushing the tangles from my blonde waves, watching me in the mirror with increased interest.

"I think so too." I smiled up at her.

"How old are you, Désirée?"

"Eight, Révérende Mère."

"Hmm...... well..."

Just then, the bells from the church rang out. Révérende Mère shook her head as if to clear her thoughts, then finished pinning a small lace handkerchief to the top of my head.

"Let's hurry, Désirée, or we'll be late, and then we both will be in trouble."

She took me by the hand and led me down the back stairs into the kitchen and through the house to the front door. We were across the street and walking through the church door before the last bell rang out from the tower.

Chapter 9

Mass

O nce inside the church, Révérende Mère slowed her pace, walking down the right side of the nave to the rows occupied by the girls and nuns from La Maison. Two nuns I hadn't met sat next to Sœur Marguerite and two older girls. The younger girls were in the row in front of the nuns. Révérende Mère directed me to a seat at the end next to Rachel, then sat down in the pew behind me.

My eyes filled with beautiful, amazing sights. Towering pillars of shining white marble and massive arched ceilings so high I had to lean my head back as far as I could to see them. The tall stained-glass windows told stories from the Bible in a dazzling array of color and light. It all took my breath away.

As soon as we sat down, a deep sound filled the cavernous church. I looked to see where it was coming from and spied the giant pipe organ filling the gallery above the main entrance at the back, its large brass pipes masking the stained glass behind it. The music built with a resonance I felt inside my body, and then the chanting voices joined in, clear and beautiful, adding a magical feeling to the music surrounding me.

I sat quietly, taking it all in and feeling very small. Everything was so big, so much bigger than I ever imagined things could be. I missed my simple little parish church with the fat priest, who'd always hand me a sweet he'd pull from his robe pocket after mass. My life was so simple then, I wondered if it would ever be simple again.

It was the longest mass I'd ever been to, and when it was over, Révérende Mère led us all down the center aisle and out the massive door under the giant pipe organ, the music echoing through the church as we exited.

The nuns lined us up in two neat rows on the step outside the church door and directed us to stand quietly. So we stood there, waiting for something. I wanted to ask someone what we were waiting for, but thought better of it. It seemed to me even the nuns were fidgety, standing there waiting.

After what seemed like forever, several priests came out the church door in a flurry of black, looking like a flock of crows. They were the same priests from the mass processional, but they'd all changed into black robes with white collars and were wearing the little black caps that priests wear, except one of them had on a dark rose-colored cap. He was the one who approached Révérende Mère while the other priests waited behind him.

"Révérende Mère, I see you have new charges," he said, offering her a hand that wore the biggest ring I'd ever seen. Révérende Mère bent to kiss the ring as he continued. "I spoke with Père André last night regarding his work and what we might expect in the coming months. I'd like to have your thoughts about this as well."

"Of course, Your Excellency, at your convenience. Perhaps you'd care to join us for supper this evening?" Révérende Mère offered.

It seemed to me as if she had said those words before. It sounded like when Maman would *invite* Papa to Sunday dinner, and everyone knew that's where Papa would be, anyway.

"Please allow me to introduce you to our new girls... Girls, may I present His Excellency, The Most Reverend Joseph-Marie Tissier, Bishop of Châlons."

I wasn't sure what a Bishop was but supposed he must be someone important. I did a little curtsy when it was my turn to be introduced to him and even kissed his big ring as instructed, though I thought that was silly.

After that, the nuns and priests all said 'Bonjour', then we were all herded down the steps of the church, heading toward home, I hoped. My stomach was rumbling with each step.

"Sœur Bernadette, you and Sœur Anne-Marie take the girls down to the park for a stroll in the sunshine. It will do them good to be outside for a while. I'll see you all later. Sœur Marguerite, you're with me," Révérende Mère said. Then the two of them were off, walking up the street toward the house.

Janine distracted me by tugging on my arm to walk with her.

"Where were you this morning?" she asked. "That girl, Annalise, had a fit when she found out you weren't in your bed."

"I woke up early, so I went downstairs... No one said I couldn't," I said, feeling defensive.

"Well, you'd better watch out for her. She thinks she's the boss of all the girls, so you'd better pay attention. I think she could make things hard on us if she wanted to."

Janine was older than me, and even though I'd only known her for a day, it seemed like much longer. She was someone who'd been through as much or more than I had. That made her a kind of sister in my mind.

We walked across the street, heading south, next to a wall surrounding a large garden. I wanted to go inside and look around, but the others had moved down the street, so I had to follow.

"Stay in line and keep up," Annalise said, snapping at us over her shoulder, so we hurried to catch up.

I made a point of noticing the surrounding landmarks, wanting to make sure I could find my way back to La Maison, if I was ever on my own. The street we were walking down was next to the river Marne, which wound its way south and flowed past the park.

We weren't the only strollers taking in the morning sunshine. There were lots of people around. But what most caught my attention were the groups of men standing around talking or arguing, and all of them appeared worried.

On our way into the park, I overheard an old man say, "If we can hold them at Reims and Compiègne... if not, Paris will fall within days." The men quieted as soon as they saw us passing by. One of them tipped his hat to us, which I thought was nice. Papa always did that.

After a turn through the park, I was ready to go back to La Maison and get things settled, to find out what I'd be doing there, what they expected of me. I knew there must be rules, though I hadn't heard of any yet. Thankfully, the two nuns leading the group circled around and headed back towards the church, the wings of their hats flapping in the breeze and the rest of us following along, like goslings waddling behind their mothers, back to the nest.

Chapter 10

The Rules

When we returned to La Maison, it was to the rear of the building, walking up the street behind the house and then into the courtyard.

Jon was out in front of the opened carriage house door, playing with little Robert, who seemed more interested in knocking down what Jon was building, rather than helping him build it. Jon seemed happy and when he saw his sister, he ran to give her a hug, then quickly returned to his play. Madame Guerin waved to us from the doorway as we walked by, and the nuns stopped to talk with her.

Margot's face fell after her brother had gone back to play with Robert, clearly sad he seemed so happy without her. She looked miserable, so I took her hand and gave it a little squeeze, then whispered in her ear. "Let's go see if we can help Sœur Louise Claire in the kitchen. Maybe she'll give us a treat before dinner."

I hurried ahead of the others to the kitchen door, Margot in tow, and went straight to the kitchen where I thought we'd find Sœur Louise Claire preparing the mid-day meal. Instead, we found a strange man standing by the worktable, his hat in his hand, nervously shifting it from one hand to the other. He looked up as we entered, startled and wary, his eyes seeming to search for an escape route, as if we had caught him where he shouldn't be. Then Sœur Louise Claire came up from the basement carrying a box filled with food.

"Oh, you're back. Good. Help me with that sack I left on the steps there below," she instructed, as she carried the box to the worktable. I went down the steps to the basement and found the sack sitting at the bottom and brought it upstairs, placing it on the table next to the box of food.

Curious about who the man was and why she was giving him food, I stood out of the way with Margot while the nun finished her business.

"We're happy to help Monsieur Jacobi. Please tell your wife she can come to me anytime," Sœur Louise Claire said.

"Merci, Sœur," the man replied, donning his hat and hefting the box and sack into his arms. He exited through the kitchen door, nodding to the other nuns and girls as he went out.

"Sœur Louise Claire, was that drunkard Eli Jacobi leaving with our food?" Sœur Bernadette asked as the group filed into the kitchen.

Sœur Bernadette was the oldest of all the nuns, small and a bit bent over like Grand-Mère, and she had a sharp tongue which I didn't want to be on the receiving end of. I already noticed Sœur Bernadette made it her business to keep everyone in line.

"Oui. It was," Sœur Louise Claire said. "Madame Jacobi is ill, and the children need nourishment. It was little enough, and their need is great. What harm can it do to share what we have with those in need?"

"Humph," the older nun grumbled, "Let's hope Madame Jacobi gets what you've sent, and he doesn't sell or trade it all for wine."

"Sœur Anne-Marie, take the girls upstairs to settle in and change for dinner, s'il vous plaît. Sœur Bernadette, I'm sure there's something you must prepare for tomorrow's lessons," said Révérende Mère, who was standing in the doorway taking in the scene. When she spoke, everyone immediately moved to do her bidding. She wasn't mean or anything, but she had a way that made you want to please her rather than cross her.

The exchange between the nuns was interesting, confirming what I already felt about them. Sœur Louise Claire was kind and generous, and Sœur Bernadette was harsh, with a mean spirit wanting everyone to follow the rules, which I realized I didn't know yet.

I followed the rest of the girls up to the dormitory, heading straight to my bed to put it in order. The warning Janine had given me earlier about Annalise still echoed in my ears. As I was pulling the blanket up and smoothing it like the other beds, Annalise came over to inspect my work.

She had a stern look on her face, reminding me of my sister Yvette. "Hmm... It doesn't look like you've had to make your own bed very often. Well, you'll get used to it. Make sure the corners are neat and even on both sides, the way the other beds are. Sœur Bernadette doesn't like our room to be messy... so... being the oldest, I make sure everyone keeps it neat." She watched with a critical eye as I finished making the bed, and after a few adjustments, she grudgingly nodded her approval.

"We *do not* leave our room before we make our beds and put everything away," Annalise said, the tone of her voice harsher than I thought necessary.

I could tell she was working herself up to something because she looked just like Yvette would when she was trying to be in control of everything. Having had four older siblings who always bossed me around about nearly everything, I prepared myself for a lecture from this older girl, who clearly thought of herself as the leader.

"You're new and don't know how things are yet, and you're little, so I can't really expect you to act like you know... but we *do not* wander around the house in the morning while everyone is sleeping. You should stay in your bed until it's time to get up," she said, pointing her finger at me as if I were a baby.

Annalise seemed pleased with her reasonable lecture, and with a raised eyebrow in my direction, she went to join the others, who'd gone to the dressing room to change.

Everything is different now. Nothing will ever be how it was before.

I knew I'd have to get used to it, to follow the rules and behave like the other girls, if for no other reason than to avoid problems with Annalise.

We changed out of the Sunday dresses into simple muslin dresses and pinafores, and then the novice, Therese, took us new girls on a tour of the house. When the tour was over, she led us to the hallway outside Révérende Mère's office, where she instructed us to sit on the bench until called in.

Révérende Mère called Margot first, who looked scared as she went in, unsure of what to expect. None of us knew what was going to happen. The four of us were orphans with no family to go home to, and this strange new house and all the people in it were all any of us had. My stomach flipped over a few times.

Margot came out of the office a short time later with a smile on her face and a lightness to her step, which helped me relax a bit. Rachel went in next. She hadn't really talked much to anyone, and she didn't look happy as she stepped inside. When she came out a few minutes later, she seemed more at ease, not smiling like Margot, but not as sad as she'd been.

I expected to be next, but Révérende Mère called Janine's name, so I sat alone on the bench, wondering what they were talking about. I remembered the warnings the old woman and Henri gave me about my family name and hoped I wouldn't have to tell a lie to Révérende Mère. Then the office door opened, and Janine came out.

"You're next," she said. "Don't worry, she doesn't bite. You'll see."

I stepped into the office and looked around. It was a large room with bookshelves covering one entire wall and a large desk sitting in front of it, with two leather chairs facing the desk. A couch faced a fireplace on the opposite wall, and a side table with chairs sat under the tall windows overlooking the Cathedral across the street.

"Come in, Désirée, and take a seat," Révérende Mère said, leading me to a leather chair across from her. "I wanted to take a moment with each of you, to welcome you and answer your questions."

She sat at her desk, shuffling some papers out of her way. One was the note that Père André pinned in my coat, and as she moved it, she read it again, then looked up at me, her green eyes thoughtful and curious.

"It seems you've had a difficult time over the past few weeks," she said, moving the note aside. "I know you must be sad and frightened, but I want you to know you are safe here. Nothing can harm you now, Désirée," she assured me.

"That's what I thought before all this happened," I said before she could go on. "I thought I was safe at home... then everything changed... and I don't know why." I clasped my hands together in my lap, looking down at them, and wondering if I would ever really feel safe again.

Révérende Mère came around the desk and sat in the chair next to me, taking my hands in hers. "None of us know why this is happening, or what will happen next. We are all in God's hands, child. The best we can do is to help each other and pray the war will not last for long." She regarded me for a moment, assessing me as adults always did.

"Before this is over, there will be more children, like you and the other girls, who'll come to us for help and shelter. We must all do our part to help each other. Do you think you can help, Désirée?"

"Oui, Révérende Mère," I said, trying to hold back my tears.

"Good. All right now. You're eight years old. Have you been to school yet?"

"No Révérende Mère. Maman taught me to read and write and to do my sums. She said I could start school in the fall... but now...."

"No matter. There are several local girls your age who attend our school. You'll be in a class with them and with Margot. You'll start school in the morning with Sœur Anne-Marie, who teaches the younger children. Now, as to the chores we'll ask you to do, I've heard from Sœur Louise Claire you've asked to help in the kitchen. Is this correct?"

My eyes lit up at the question. "Oui, Révérende Mère. At home, I would help Maman every day in the kitchen *and* in the garden. Maman taught me everything about cooking and about growing food. If you let me work in the kitchen, I promise I'll work really hard and do everything you ask."

I was so excited. I knew if I could be in the kitchen every day, then I'd be happier than almost anywhere else.

"Well, I don't believe we've ever had a girl so young working in the kitchen, nor one so enthusiastic about work. Let me think about it." She looked at me with a curious expression on her face, like she wasn't sure I was as I appeared. Then she raised her eyes towards the ceiling, holding her chin in her hand and tapping one long finger against her lips.

With a decisiveness that surprised me, she said, "I think we'll try it and see how you do. Sœur Louise Claire can undoubtedly use some help with the meal today, so let's you and I go speak with her about it."

Happiness surged through me as I jumped off my chair and threw my arms around her. "Oh, merci Révérende Mère, Merci beaucoup. I promise I will do everything that Sœur Louise Claire tells me. I promise. Merci, merci."

And with that, my new life at La Maison de la Charité began.

Chapter 11

Annalise

O ver the next few days, life at La Maison became as normal as it could be, especially considering all the anxiety swirling around me, the feeling of impending doom that permeated throughout the household.

I missed my old life but tried not to think about it because when I did, it only made me sad and it made my head hurt.

Instead, I threw all my attention into learning everything I could about my new home and the people I was living with. Fourteen people lived in that house. La Maison was home to eight orphan girls, including me. Annalise was the oldest at twelve, Sylvie was eleven, Janine was ten, Karin and Rachel were both nine, Giselle was eight, and Margot was six. Two novices, both sixteen years old, and four nuns, supervised and cared for the orphan girls. We all lived together in that big house, and it wasn't much different from home, except there were no boys.

I learned the rules quickly, and almost everyone was helpful when I didn't know something, which was usually some rule I hadn't had to follow in my old life, like raising my hand when I wanted to say something at the dinner table. Annalise even imposed this rule in the dormitory when all the girls would gather at night for story-time. She'd scold me as if I were a baby when I forgot and spoke out of turn.

"I told you, Désirée, you're not to talk unless called on. That's the rule. Now sit down and be quiet." She'd stand there scowling at me until I looked away.

I'd had older sisters and brothers and knew what battles I could win.

It wasn't long before I realized Annalise didn't like me, but I didn't understand why. I tried being as nice as I could, but nothing seemed to work with the older girl. She always seemed unhappy with me, no matter what I did. But there were lots of new things to help distract me from any trouble Annalise sent my way.

My first venture in a school classroom was exciting, and I wanted to do well. The youngest group, five- and six-year-olds, spent most of the day playing and learning the alphabet and numbers, things Maman taught me when I was three. The older group, seven- and eight-year-olds, worked on rudimentary reading and doing simple math problems. At first, it was fun helping the others learn what had come so easily to me, but after a couple days I knew, and thankfully Sœur Anne-Marie realized, I wouldn't learn anything new in her class.

She found me in the library one afternoon, reading a book one of the older girls had left behind on the table. The room wasn't off-limits, but the younger girls rarely went in there, and I found it a quiet refuge from the constant squealing. I had fallen in love with reading from the very first book Maman put into my hands, and that library held more books than I had ever seen before.

"Désirée? What are you doing?" Sœur Anne Marie asked as she came into the library to straighten up after class was over for the day.

"Reading."

"What are you reading?"

She came over to sit down next to me, flipped the cover over to see the title, and then looked at me with a tilt of her head and a curious expression on her face.

"You can read this?" She looked at me like she couldn't quite believe what she was seeing.

"Oui, Sœur. We had this book at home, and I was reading it with Papa. *The Three Musketeers* was one of his favorites. He liked it when I read to him." I glanced up at the nun, hoping I had done nothing wrong. As far as I knew, none of the other girls ever went in there to read. "I hope it was all right for me to read in here."

"Of course. What is a library for, if not for reading? I'm just surprised you can read at this level. Would you read aloud for me?"

I read to the end of the chapter, as I'd done with Papa, then I stopped and looked up at her. "Would you like me to keep reading?"

"No, Désirée. But I think perhaps we should speak with Révérende Mère about moving you into the class with the older girls. What do you think?" Sœur Anne Marie smiled down at me, amazement and understanding lighting her eyes.

"Sometimes it is boring reading children's books and doing simple sums all the time." I hoped I wasn't being too rude.

"I'll speak with Révérende Mère this evening," Sœur Anne Marie said, then she left me to my reading.

Moving to the older class was better in a lot of ways, but it created more problems too. The biggest one was Annalise. She became visibly annoyed that Révérende Mère promoted me into the same classroom as her, though not in the same group. She tried to ignore me and encouraged the other girls to do the same.

Annalise also seemed to resent that I was working in the kitchen and had a certain amount of responsibility and freedom the work there required. She just couldn't accept the changes gracefully and made her opinion known to all the other girls.

"I don't know why *she's* allowed. She's only eight and has only been here a little while. Révérende Mère is giving her everything she asks for. It's not right, not fair to the rest of us," Annalise complained to the others the day I joined the older classroom.

Janine put her arm around my shoulder and led me away from Annalise's negativity. "Don't pay any attention to her Désirée. She thinks she's the boss of everyone, but she isn't. Just try to stay out of her way. That's what I'm doing."

I did my best to stay out of Annalise's way, but living in the same room, sharing the same space with her, seemed to be enough to annoy her, no matter how nice I tried to be.

Eventually, I became accustomed to the rhythm of the house and the moods of the people. I found peace in familiar tasks and places, gravitating towards those who offered comfort and what I hoped would be safety.

Mornings were always happy times. I rose earlier than the others to help Sœur Louise Claire in the kitchen. We'd share a bit of bread and a glass of milk while preparing the morning meal for the house, and we'd talk about everything. Sœur Louise Claire was always willing to speak with me and answer almost every question I asked.

After a difficult encounter with Annalise the night before, I asked the nun for help with the older girl.

"She doesn't like me. I make her mad all the time, but I don't know why or what I need to do to make her happy." I had never met anyone who didn't like me and wasn't sure how to handle it.

Sœur Louise Claire gave me an understanding look, then her dark eyebrows raised almost high enough to touch the edge of the short white veil banding across her forehead. It was an expression I was becoming familiar with. It meant she had a definite opinion about something. Sometimes she would say what she was thinking and other times she wouldn't.

"It's simple jealousy."

"Jealousy? I don't understand. Why would Annalise be jealous of me?" I was more confused than ever.

"Do you know anything about Annalise, about her life before she came to La Maison?"

I shook my head. "No. She never talks about herself, or if she does, it's with the other girls when I'm not around."

"You're right, she rarely speaks of her life before coming here, but it plays a large part in explaining why she is the way she is." Sœur Louise Claire sighed, a compassionate look in her eyes.

"Annalise came to us almost five years ago when she was a little younger than you. She'd been at the orphanage in Paris for a few months before coming to us. Before that, she lived on the streets of Paris in one of the worst parts of the city. That's where the sisters found her; alone, sick with a fever, and malnourished. Annalise had no one to care for her, beyond throwing her a few scraps to keep her fed. When she was five years old, her mother sent her out on the streets to beg for food, for money, for survival. The sisters found her living on the streets a month after her mother died.

Annalise has never known what you have known, a family who loved you and cared for you."

I worked while listening, peeling potatoes into a large bowl. Annalise's life before La Maison was sad, but all the girls had a tragic story to tell. Even my story was sad, what little I remembered. The nun's explanation still confused me.

"We all have lost something, all the girls here. I don't understand why she would be jealous of something I don't have anymore."

"That's just it. You *had* what she has always wanted. From the moment you arrived, we could all see you were a well-loved child who had never known hardship. Your self-confidence, your curiosity, your ability to be strong in the face of all you've lost, it all speaks of a life surrounded by love. That is what Annalise wants the most, to be loved, although it's the one thing she doesn't know how to achieve. The best advice I can give you is to be kind to her, even when you don't feel like it. Shower her with kindness, and then see what happens. If nothing else, it will make you feel better." She gave me a friendly pat on the back.

That might be hard. But I was willing to try anything to make life at La Maison easier.

That morning, I paid extra attention to Annalise, adding an extra spoonful of fruit to her bowl of yogurt. Annalise loved fruit. The gesture earned me a raised eyebrow, but no thank you.

Keep trying

And then my world flipped upside down again.

Chapter 12

The nightmares are real

It happened later that day, after school. I'd gone with Alex and his father to the Bishop's garden on the corner to collect the herbs for the soup Sœur Louise Claire was making for supper. I loved going there, not only because it gave me a chance to get away from Annalise for a while, but because it was where I could work in the soil, harvesting herbs for the kitchen at La Maison, like I'd done at home with Maman.

After I finished my collecting, I left the herbs waiting in the basket next to me while I continued weeding the bed around the plants. I was kneeling along one of the far beds, digging out a stubborn weed hiding behind the rosemary bush, when a rumbling noise began. It wasn't loud, but I could feel it coming closer, the vibration traveling up my body from my knees on the ground.

What is that? I looked around for Monsieur Guerin or Alex, but I didn't see either of them. *Maybe they went to the work shed.*

The noise was getting louder, something big was coming from across the river, and it was moving in my direction.

I looked around again and still didn't see Alex or his father, so I went to look for them in the courtyard between the garden and the Bishop's House. The noise was loud by then, a roaring that filled the space between the tall buildings, reverberating against the stone and pulsing through my body.

As I approached the gate to the courtyard, I saw them rolling up the street; a kind of truck I had never seen before, huge with no windows and a big pipe sticking out the front of it. Then truckloads of soldiers rolled by with lots of other cars following as they drove up the Rue de la Marne towards the City Hall.

I stood mesmerized, watching through the gate, not daring to go out to look for Alex. Then a truck turned onto the Place Saint Etienne, in front of the Bishop's House, and another two cars followed behind it, coming right towards me. My heart was racing, and the vibration became a shaking I couldn't control. I couldn't move or look away.

As the truck passed the entrance to the courtyard, I breathed a sigh of relief, but it lasted less than a heartbeat. The two cars behind it turned into the courtyard right in front of me, and eight soldiers got out. Four of them headed into the Bishop's House while the others stood guard at the door. Then I saw soldiers with rifles standing by the street entrance to the courtyard, one of them giving orders to the others.

Something about them, something about the sound of their voices, frightened me beyond reason.

Terrified, I hid like any frightened animal, tucking myself behind one of the large citrus tree planters that sat along the wall, next to the garden gate. I shut my eyes tight, covering my mouth with my hand, trying to control my rapid breathing, trying to stop the shaking.

Then a memory flashed across my mind, and I remembered the day my nightmare began, all the horrible details filling the empty places in my memory.

My farm and the kitchen garden, my birthday, collecting herbs for Maman... Anna's scream. Hiding under the porch, and the soldiers with rifles pointed at Mama, my sisters, and my brothers... Soldier's voices, hard and demanding, saying words I didn't understand. Then running to the vineyard to find Papa... Rifles pointed at Papa and me... Soldiers grabbing Anna and Yvette, Papa, trying to stop them. BANG! Maman screaming, Papa falling, blood pouring from his head. Trying to help Papa. SMASH! Blackness, nothing... All gone... All gone... All gone.

I couldn't move, wouldn't move, terrified they would find me, certain they would kill me like they killed my family.

The last rays of the sun were shining on the top of the wall, which concealed the garden from the street beyond, and I knew it would be dark soon. I had heard no soldiers for a while, their harsh voices loud and garbled, bringing back the terror of the day when everything changed. It was getting cold, and I knew I couldn't stay hidden forever.

"Have you searched the work shed? She must be hiding somewhere. Look again, Alex, please."

Révérende Mère sounded worried, but I was still too frightened to emerge from my hiding place behind the planter.

Alex came through the gate, walking towards the shed, softly calling my name.

"Désirée, Désirée, come out. Let me take you home."

I'd been curled up hiding for so long my legs were cramping, and the trembling started again. I must have made a noise because a moment later, Alex and Révérende Mère were pulling me out from my hiding place and wrapping me in a blanket.

Révérende Mère lifted me into her arms and carried me out of the garden, Alex cooing comforting sounds and patting my back as he walked beside us. The German guards posted at the entrance to the Bishop's House stopped us.

"Halt!"

Révérende Mère stopped and turned, regarding him with calm attention.

"Monsieur, we've found the missing child and must take her home to get her warm and fed. With your permission."

Another soldier came out of the Bishop's House walking directly towards us. He was different from the others. Compared to the gray green of the guards, his uniform was darker, neater, with gold buttons down the front of the jacket and gold braids and bars around the stiff collar. He wore a different hat too; not the soup pot helmet like the other soldiers, but a dark gray cap with more gold braids on it. When he approached us, the guard drew up to attention, clicking his heels together and lifting his arm straight forward and up into the air.

"*Heil* Hitler!" the guard yelled.

The fancy soldier must have been in charge, because he dismissed the guard with a word and gesture.

"I see you have found your lost child, Madame. Where was she hiding, I wonder?" he asked in his heavy, harsh-sounding accent.

"She was behind the lemon tree planter, tucked against the wall in the garden. The girl is frightened, Kommandant. I would like to take her home, with your permission," Révérende Mère said in a tone which usually brooked no opposition.

I wrapped my arms around her neck, burying my head under the white wing of her cornette, trying to hide as much as possible from the man's eyes.

"Ah, yes. But let's have a look at the child. She appears young to be out on her own."

He reached over to remove the blanket in order to see me better. "Such a beautiful little thing."

I moaned at his touch, pulling away from him.

"Kommandant, the child is frightened. I must take her home. My girls are waiting and worried about her welfare. With your permission." She turned away from him, Alex walking silently beside her.

"Yes, take her home, Madame. But I would caution you to keep better track of your charges in the future."

Révérende Mère carried me straight to her office, where she deposited me onto the couch facing the hearth. She thanked Alex for his help and asked him to send in Sœur Louise Claire.

Despite the warmth of the room, I pulled the blanket closer around me, hoping to hide from everything that frightened me, including the wrath of Révérende Mère, which I suspected she would direct at me for causing so much trouble.

I couldn't stop shaking, couldn't stop thinking about the soldiers and what they did to my family, what they would do to me if they found me, knew who I was. I held my eyes closed tight, wishing it all would go away, that it was all a horrible dream. The sound of Révérende Mère moving around the room dispelled that hopeful notion, and I sat sobbing into the folds of the blanket.

"Oh, thank God!" Sœur Louise Claire cried as she came into the room carrying a tray filled with cups and a pot of something. "Is she unharmed?"

"Oui, Sœur, she's unharmed, just frightened. Thank you for the tea. You may tell the others she's all right and I'll speak with everyone at supper.

There will be new rules we must follow from now on. You may go. I need to speak with the child alone. I'll bring her in when we've finished."

"Of course, Révérende Mère. When Alex came back without her, I thought, well, I don't know what I thought. I was just so worried." Sœur Louise Claire sounded worried, but also relieved.

"Go on, Sœur. We'll speak later," Révérende Mère said, then she closed the door.

"Come out, child. There's nothing to fear now." She sat down next to me, pulling the blanket away from my face. "You must tell me why you hid, why you didn't come when Alex and Monsieur Guerin called for you."

My tear-filled eyes rose to meet her concerned gaze, bright green eyes willing me to compose myself, to be strong. Sobs racked my body, catching my breath in fits and starts, but I forced myself to answer, my voice weak and shaking.

"I heard them coming... then I saw them, the soldiers, so many... I watched them from the garden, at the gate... then they came into the courtyard, and I heard them talking... and I remembered. I remembered what happened to my family."

The terror of that day flashed through my mind again, and I shook uncontrollably, my eyes darting around the room, seeking another place to hide.

Révérende Mère gathered me into her arms, holding me close, the way Maman would whenever I was frightened. She told me everything would be all right, like Maman would, and it helped a little, but I knew nothing would ever be all right again.

"Whatever it is you remember, Désirée, has already happened and the memory of it cannot harm you," Révérende Mère said, gently stroking my back.

"It was my birthday... when the soldiers came to our farm." Breathless and shaking, I forced all the memories out, bit by bit, and as I finished, I collapsed back into her arms, sobbing and grieving for my lost family all over again.

She let me cry, rocking me in her arms, whispering calming words in a language I didn't understand, but was comforting even so. I cried until I had nothing left.

"When I saw the soldiers... I... I thought if they found me, they would kill me, like they killed my family. So, I hid from them. I heard Alex and Monsieur Guerin call for me, but I heard the soldiers, too. They scared me, Révérende Mère. I'm still scared."

I looked up at the nun hoping this woman, so much like my mother, could make it all better, make all the bad things go away.

"Désirée, listen to me carefully," she said, wrapping her arm around my shoulders. "When Madame Elise sent you to us—and yes, I know who the old woman is—When she sent you here, it was because she knew this would be the safest place for you. Here you are under our protection. I will not allow anyone to harm you or any of my girls. The Germans are not looking for a little girl. They're here to take control of France, and for now, all of us must learn to deal with that."

She held me, stroking my back until my sobs and trembles subsided, then she reached into the folds of her habit and pulled out a handkerchief to wipe the tears from my face.

"I know this is hard, but you must put your grief away. Now we must all gather our strength to face what lies ahead. I won't lie to you, child, there will be hard times ahead. There always are during a war. But if we're strong and true to each other, we can survive this." She searched my face for understanding.

"Come now, you must be hungry. Do you think you can face the others?" she asked. "Everyone was worried about you. Sœur Louise Claire was ready to take on the entire German Army to bring you home."

"Oui, Révérende Mère. I... I think I'm better now. Bu... but what if they ask me why I was hiding? What should I tell them?" I asked, my bottom lip still trembling.

"Tell them the truth. Say the soldiers frightened you. I'm sure you'll find all the girls were frightened. You needn't say anything about your family, nor about your time with the old woman. It's best not to speak of that to anyone. Do you understand?"

"Oui, Révérende Mère. That's what she said, but I had to tell you. I had to. Was I wrong?" I worried that by telling what happened to my family and me, I had put the old woman in danger and maybe Révérende Mère, too.

"No, child. You weren't wrong to tell me, but you shouldn't speak of this again." She took me by the hand, leading me out of the office to face the rest of the household.

Chapter 13

Trouble ahead

Révérende Mère stood at the head of the dining table to address the assembled household.

"Considering today's events, it is necessary for me to make some changes to ensure the safety of each of you. As of today, you are not to leave the property without my permission. Outside this property, one of our sisters or a priest from Saint Etienne must always accompany you. Be courteous to the Germans, but do not engage any soldier in conversation. If you are with an adult, this will not be a problem. The soldiers will, most likely, direct their inquiries to the adults and not to a child." She looked down the long table at each girl, making sure her instructions were both understood and acknowledged.

"I am charged with your welfare, and I fully intend to keep faith with that charge. What happened today with Désirée must not happen again to any of you. La Maison de la Charité is a sanctuary, and with God's grace, it will remain so."

She glanced around the table again, and this time I felt her gaze hold mine longer than she did the others. I could feel the stares of the rest of the girls at the table, too. Annalise's eyes shot daggers at me.

Lowering my head, I clasped my hands tightly together while my usually fair face flushed red with shame and regret.

"Sœur Louise Claire, we are all undoubtedly hungry after such an eventful day. What delicious dish have you made for us this evening?" Révérende Mère asked, trying to lighten the mood in the room.

"Oh, well, I'm not sure how delicious it will be. I was missing the creativity of my helper today, so I added a bit of everything," Sœur Louise Claire said with a wink and nod in my direction.

"I'm sure she'll be there tomorrow, but let's serve whatever you've created."

According to the girls at La Maison, Sœur Louise Claire's attempts at culinary creativity were modestly successful. Her best efforts were soups, which, in my experience, were simple to create and difficult to mess up. That is what she served, a soup with everything; chicken with lots of different vegetables in a thick broth. What it lacked were fresh herbs, which would have enhanced the richness of the broth and brightened the flavor of the vegetables.

Then I remembered why the soup had no herbs. The basket of freshly picked herbs lay in the Bishop's garden, forgotten when the Germans came.

I ate my meal in silence, ashamed of causing so much trouble for everyone, especially Sœur Louise Claire, who was always so kind to me. I promised myself I'd do nothing to make her or Révérende Mère worry about me ever again.

In fact, never going outside again sounded like a good idea to me, but I knew that would be impossible.

Who will collect the herbs from the Bishop's Garden if I don't go get them?

You must be brave and strong, and clever. The old woman whispered inside my head.

I know, but I'm scared.

After the meal, all the girls retired to the dormitory, with me heading straight to the bathroom to bathe and dress for bed. Still shaken by the horrible memories, I wanted to avoid talking with anyone.

Janine, Margot, and Karin were all sitting on my bed when I returned. Margot and Karin jumped up when they saw me coming. Janine sat there waiting with a worried look on her face.

"Are you okay?" Janine asked.

"Yes, I think so. I'm not hurt. I just got scared, so I hid," I said, trying to shrug off the memory.

"Do you want to talk about it? It's all right if you don't. I understand."

"Well, *I* think she owes us all an explanation," Annalise said, coming up to stand next to Karin, the other girls huddling behind her, except for Rachel.

"She caused the entire house to be in an uproar for hours, and *she's* the reason we can't leave the house now. I want to know why." Annalise stood there with her hands on her hips and a big scowl on her face.

"Leave her alone, Annalise," Janine said, her voice low and deliberate.

"I WANT her to tell us."

"I said, LEAVE HER ALONE!" Janine rose from her seat, her eyes flashing fire.

As far as I knew, none of the girls had ever spoken to Annalise that way, and it was clear from her expression that it was an unfamiliar experience, one she didn't much like.

"Well... Humph." Annalise spun on her heel and walked away.

Janine had already turned her back to Annalise, as if there was nothing further to say. Then she looked at me with renewed concern.

"It's all right, you don't have to. They scared me too... when I saw them on the street. The noise of all the trucks and tanks... it reminded me of... well, they scared me too, so I understand."

I felt so grateful to her, not only because she stood up for me with Annalise, but because she shared her own fear. My tears began falling again as I remembered what she told me about her mother.

"I remembered what happened to my family. When I heard them talking, I remembered, and it frightened me." My voice was small, almost a whisper, but my wet eyes met hers in understanding.

"I know, I remembered too. Sometimes I wish I could forget." Janine wrapped her arms around me, giving me a big hug. "We missed your special touch with the soup tonight," she said, getting up to go to her own bed.

Margot and Karin both gave me hugs, then went to their beds. Everyone else had settled down for the night, apparently not wanting to talk after the confrontation with Annalise and Janine, each lost in their own fears and memories.

I climbed into bed, pulling the blankets up to my chin, and rolled onto my side to slip my hand under the pillow. Grasping the old woman's shawl, I drew it from its hiding place, holding it close, rubbing my fingers along the fine weave, back and forth, back and forth, trying to calm my mind, trying to find comfort.

I had struggled so hard to remember that day, but now the memory kept flashing through my mind, just like the nightmares, only now the monsters had faces. They were real. It was like having to re-live it all over again. All I wanted now was to forget.

I wrapped the shawl around myself and dragged the other blanket over my head, trying to shut everything out, trying to force the frightening memory away, to push it as far down into the dark parts of my mind as I could.

Forget that day. Forget that day.

Chapter 14

June 13, 1940

T he next morning, all I wanted to do was to stay in bed under the old woman's shawl and never come out, ever again, but I knew that wasn't an option.

Reluctantly, I got up and made my bed, quickly dressed and slipped out of the room in stocking feet, shoes in hand. I needed to go down to the kitchen to face the day.

At the bottom of the stairs, I stopped to put on my shoes, being mindful of the clacking noise they made on the wooden stairs early in the morning. As I sat on the step, I heard Sœur Louise Claire moving around in the kitchen, talking with someone.

Normally, it was only the two of us for the first hour of the morning, but she was talking with Révérende Mère, so I listened, even though I knew it wasn't polite. I just wanted to know... well, I wasn't sure what I wanted to know, but I listened anyway.

"If the reports I've heard coming out of Poland are even half true... Blessed Mother, help us." The lilting accent of Révérende Mère sounded tired and worried.

"The Bishop's influence may protect us, but if they come, they'll take whatever they want. I don't want anyone to interfere when they do. We must prepare ourselves, Sœur, be ready to help when it's needed. Food will be an issue, it always is, especially if this goes on for years. I want you to take another inventory. And let's get Monsieur Guerin to gather up the pots and barrels from the storehouse. We'll plant them this year in the courtyard."

She was thinking out loud, checking off lists in her mind to prepare for something... Maman used to do that. I could hear Sœur Louise Claire at the worktable, chopping something and occasionally adding a 'Oui Mère' to Révérende Mère's suggestions.

I stepped off the stairs and walked into the kitchen, determined to face the day as bravely as I could. "Bonjour, Révérende Mère. Bonjour, Sœur."

"Oh. Bonjour, Désirée. How are you feeling this morning?" Sœur Louise Claire asked, worry still marking her face.

"Bonjour, Désirée. I hope you're feeling better today." Révérende Mère looked me over for signs of the frightened little thing from the day before.

"I'm better now. Merci," I said, trying to convince myself, as much as them. "Sœur, I'm sorry about yesterday, about making you worry so much, and about forgetting the basket of herbs. I think it must still be there, in the garden."

"Oh, dear child, don't worry about that. Monsieur Guerin will bring it back for us."

Révérende Mère stood to leave. "I've asked Sœur Marguerite to inform the girls we will not be having school today, Désirée. Everyone is to stay inside. I will speak to you all later... Merci, Sœur, for the coffee. I'll be in my office if I'm needed."

She looked tired, like she hadn't slept, her usual light step now slow and deliberate.

"I'm sorry, Sœur. I wish I could have been braver... but... I was so scared," I said after Révérende Mère had gone.

"No more of that now, child. It's all behind us. Let's get the food on the table for everyone. We'll be a bit more casual today, though I'm sure Sœur Marguerite will find a task to keep everyone busy. You and I will take inventory downstairs after breakfast." She worked as she talked, as usual, the worry of the previous day forgotten, replaced with more pressing concerns.

I moved slower than usual through the morning tasks, laying out the plates and knives, rolls and jam, conveniently placing everything on the sideboard in the dining room.

My eyes kept turning to the portrait of Madame Elise hanging on the wall behind me. It felt like the old woman was watching me. The image was of a much younger woman, but the eyes were the same eyes I remembered waking up to... after that horrible day. I tried to shake out the memory, not wanting to think about it anymore.

"Be brave and strong and clever." The old woman's voice kept repeating in my head, but the frightened child inside kept protesting.

But I'm just a little girl, and I'm scared.

I shut my eyes tight, trying to silence the dialogue, but the old woman's voice was persistent.

"Be brave and strong and clever."

Then I heard another voice, this one younger, with a funny lilt to the accent.

"They're not looking for a child."

Could that really be true?

I hoped it was. Otherwise, I didn't think I would ever go outside again.

Then I realized I had never fully explored the house and all five floors.

There must be lots of hiding places in this house. I decided I would explore the house after helping with the inventory, whatever that was.

Now that I had a plan, I finished laying out the breakfast, then hurried back to the kitchen.

Sœur Louise Claire and I spent the morning down in the basement, counting and sorting, not only the food stored there but all the other things, too. The space was immense, easily the entire area of the house from front to back. The third had once been the original kitchen. A large black wood stove sat on the back wall next to a fireplace with an oven built into the side. The massive worktable, scarred by years of service, stood across the room, stacked with boxes and bins of vegetables and canned goods.

We counted everything. My job was to write the names and counts of each item. Once Sœur Louise Claire was satisfied with the legibility and accuracy of my list, she left me to it. Occasionally she'd say something about what she was counting, thinking out loud, and I jotted down a note by the item in question, so she would remember later.

We continued through the old kitchen and into the storerooms. Two large rooms were on either side of a long hallway; one dedicated to storing linens, one for sewing and mending clothes, one had shelves of china and stemware, boxes of silverware and serving pieces, candelabras with lots of places for candles. I'd never seen such beautiful things before.

Racks of wine bottles filled the last room, row upon row of wine bottles lying peacefully on their sides. Sœur Louise Claire explained the wine was from the Montclair winery. Monsieur Montclair had been a lover of excellent wine, and several bottles remained from when the family flourished in Châlons.

"I heard Monsieur Montclair and Bishop Tissier were good friends, and the two of them would share a bottle or two at Sunday supper. Révérende Mère usually brings up a bottle when Bishop Tissier comes for supper."

As we moved around the vast spaces, I kept a lookout for places to hide—should the need arise. Unfortunately, almost all the walls were bare brick or stone, which left few places to hide, except behind the stacks of boxes or barrels. Even the storerooms offered few undetectable places.

We finished the inventory around mid-morning. After reviewing my neatly written lists, Sœur Louise Claire dismissed me with her thanks.

With no class to go to, I continued my exploration of the house. As long as the monsters were in France, I would never feel safe, and I wanted to find a secure place to hide.

My upstairs search started in a storage closet on the second floor, the third, if you counted the basement. They used the closet to store linens and collect dirty laundry. Wood paneling covered the walls from floor to ceiling. A light bulb hung from the ceiling, lit by pulling a long string. I didn't pull the string, but left the door ajar, allowing in light from the window across the hallway. I tried to stay as quiet as possible in my exploration of the closet, not wanting to be discovered.

"What are you doing?" a young voice said behind me.

When I heard her, I bumped my head on the shelf I was searching under.

"Oww." I looked around to see who it was. "Oh. It's you," I said, surprised to see Rachel standing in the doorway.

"You're looking for hiding places, aren't you?" She peeked into the closet. "There's nowhere to hide in there. I've already checked."

"You have? Why?"

"You're not the only one who wanted to hide yesterday. We were all scared." Rachel's plain face still showed signs of the sadness I'd seen since the first day I met her.

"What happened to you, Rachel? I mean, what happened to your family?" I really wanted to know why this sad girl had come to La Maison.

At first, I didn't think she would answer. Rachel had been the quietest of all the girls in the house, never giggling or laughing. She looked long and hard at me, seeming to gauge my trustworthiness. When she answered, she whispered, as if she didn't even want the walls to hear her.

"My father went to the army to fight the Germans and keep them out of France. We hadn't heard from him for a long time. Then Maman got a letter from a friend in Poland, where her family lives. They said the Germans forced all the Jews to live together in ghettos and were taking some away to work in camps. They said the Germans sent Maman's family to a camp. Maman was frightened that it would happen here too, so she talked to the priest about sending me away, to be safe." Rachel stared straight at me, almost daring me to dismiss her story. I stared back at her, trying to make sense of the things she said.

"I don't understand. Who are the Jews? What is a ghetto?" I asked, wanting to be sure I understood.

"You don't know about Jews?" Her deep brown eyes widened in disbelief.

I shook my head.

"Jews are people who practice the Jewish religion, which is almost the same as the Catholic religion, except for Jesus. The Jewish people don't believe Jesus was the Messiah."

I was astonished. I thought everyone believed Jesus was the Son of God. A thousand questions flew through my head, but the one I asked was, "Why do you need to hide from the Germans?"

"Maman told me to find a good hiding place, wherever I was, because of what the Germans are doing to Jews," she said, once more looking around the closet.

I decided having a partner to explore the house would make the search go faster. It was a big house, and Rachel seemed to want the same thing, so I told her what I'd found so far.

"You're probably right, there's no place to hide in here... except... maybe... there's a place along the wall somewhere." I ran my hands along the wood paneling at the back of the middle shelf, searching for a hidden cupboard door.

"I found something this morning, in the basement. It's a kind of hole in the wall with ropes hanging down. And I found another opening above it in the kitchen by the sideboard. I think the hole might go from the basement to the attic." It excited me to talk with Rachel about it.

"Let me see if I can find it." Rachel looked behind the linens and towels, but the paneled wall did not reveal any door.

Then I saw it. The shelf on the right, next to the door, was different. It was deeper and taller than the rest of the shelves. The paneling at the back didn't have a handle attached that would pull a door open, but I found two small holes at the bottom, right above the shelf, where the handle must have attached. The paneling camouflaged the door, but I could see the outlines of it.

"Oh. Look." I grabbed the edge of the door with my fingers, pulling it forward, then lifted it up. Inside was an empty wooden box with two ropes dangling next to it. It didn't have a front or back and was open to the brick walls of the shaft. The box was roomy enough for a child to hide in.

Rachel and I looked at each other, then back to the opening inside the wall of the closet, each thinking we'd found the perfect place to hide.

"Let's keep this a secret, just between us. Agreed?" Rachel said, her voice barely audible, even though no one else was around.

"Agreed." I was already pulling the paneled door back into place and setting the shelves to rights again. Once everything was back in order, we closed the closet door and went upstairs to the dormitory.

Rachel and I spent the rest of my free time sitting cross-legged on my bed, getting to know each other. Our mutual curiosity had finally overcome our shyness, and soon we were talking freely.

I wanted to know more about the Jews, so Rachel told me about her parents. They were both teachers. Her mother was from a wealthy family in Poland, and her father was from Paris. They met at the university in Paris, fell in love and got married. Both their families objected to the marriage because he was Catholic and she was Jewish.

"But why wouldn't their families be happy if they loved each other?" I asked, unfamiliar with this kind of family dynamic.

"Because Christians have always hated the Jews." Her look dared me to deny it.

"Why? Is there something wrong with Jews?" I genuinely wanted to understand. I sorted through all my memories, everything Maman or Papa had said about Jesus or religion, but could find nothing that would confirm or deny Rachel's statement.

She stared at me with a look that said she didn't believe the question was sincere, almost an angry face. Then her look softened, as if she'd remembered something.

"No. There's nothing wrong with being Jewish... Father said the Jewish people were the same as everyone else. They just do some things a little differently, and that makes some people uncomfortable." She stared at me for a long time, her sad eyes seeming to search mine for understanding.

She'd given me a lot to think about. I didn't know anyone that was mean or cruel just because someone did things differently. That sounded stupid to me. There was so much in this big world that I didn't know or understand yet.

I smiled, thankful I had a new friend. "My papa always said we should treat people the way we want to be treated." That always made sense to me.

Rachel returned the smile, seeming to want to talk more. Perhaps she needed a friend, too. The two of us sat cross-legged on my bed, sharing stories and finding a moment's comfort in each other's company.

"My parents said it was important for everyone to know their history," she said, resting her chin on her upturned fist. "They sent me to regular school *and* to a Jewish school, plus I went to the synagogue on Saturday with Maman and to Mass on Sunday with Father. Maman said we led a very rich life, though we never had much money."

"I didn't go to regular school. Before I mean. I only went to Mass on Sunday. Maman taught me how to read and write when I was little, and then how to do sums when I was five. I was going to go to real school in the fall. Maman even bought a satchel for me to put books in for... Oh, I forgot about..."

I jumped off the bed and scrambled to the floor to pull the small storage box out from underneath. My old clothes were put there after being washed, and my other things were there too, but I hadn't even thought about them since I arrived at La Maison.

My satchel was at the bottom of the box, under the folded clothes. I lifted it out, placing it on the bed, then climbed up to sit facing Rachel once again.

"What is it?" she asked.

"It's the satchel Maman gave me for school. Henri brought it to me the day I went to Père André. I never looked to see what he put inside." My voice faded to a whisper as I opened the satchel.

The ribbon I saved from Jean-Michel's metal box sat on top, and I set it aside to search further. I found a pair of socks, underclothes, a sweater, and a nightgown. Under the clothes was a small handmade cloth doll, the one my grand-mère made for me when I was a baby. It had been sitting on my dresser at home. Underneath the doll was a folded piece of paper. I pulled it from the bottom, unfolding it across my lap.

"Oh........." I cried, covering my mouth with my hand. My eyes immediately filled with tears as I stared at the image on the paper. It was a drawing of my family; Papa, Maman, Jean-Michel, Jacque, Anna, and Yvette, with me standing in front of them, our farm in the background. I made it last winter and gave it to my parents for Christmas. Maman pinned it to one of the kitchen cupboard doors; a drawing I made in a much happier time was now all I would ever have of them. A flood of emotions hit me hard, and my tears were unstoppable as I tried to catch my breath.

Right then, Annalise and Sylvie came into the dormitory. Janine and the rest of the girls followed a few steps behind them. As they were walking by, Annalise stopped when she noticed I was crying.

"What are you crying about now? You're such a baby." Annalise said with her usual air of superiority. Then she spied the drawing on my lap, snatching it up before I could stop her.

"What's this? Oh, it's a baby drawing. Look." She waved the picture around to show the other girls.

Janine reached over Sylvie's shoulder, slipping the drawing away from Annalise, then placed it back on my lap.

"No, Annalise, you're wrong. It's a drawing of her family, the family that was murdered by the Germans. So, leave her alone. Please."

Janine spoke calmly, yet every girl felt the impact of what she said. Even Annalise relaxed her angry posture, seeming to understand the magnitude of my loss, but unable to show sympathy, she simply walked away.

Janine came over to me to give me another hug, like the one she'd given me the night before. "You should put that away to keep it safe. You're lucky to have it. I wish I had a picture of my mother," she said, tears filling her dark eyes.

The afternoon bells rang out, signaling what would normally be the end of classes and the start of chores for all the girls. But today, they completed the chores early, so the rest of the afternoon would be free time for everyone except me. At the sound of the bells, I jumped off the bed, carefully placing the drawing, doll, and clothes back into the satchel, then storing it back into the box under the bed.

As I stood up, I offered a silent prayer of thanks to Henri for his kindness.

"I've got to go help in the kitchen." I wiped the tears from my eyes and hugged Janine and Rachel before running from the room.

Chapter 15

Being brave

L ife continued as normal, well as normal as it could be, since the Germans landed on our doorstep. But everything felt different to me, like a dark cloud had blown in and settled overhead.

I hadn't gone outside since the Germans arrived, but soon realized if I wanted to keep my position in the kitchen with Sœur Louise Claire, I would have to get over my fear. Besides collecting herbs from the garden, one of my chores was accompanying her to the shops for supplies. I'd gone twice before the Germans came and loved the opportunity it gave me to hear the latest news and see more of the city. Missing these outings just because I was afraid wasn't what I wanted, but when I thought about the Germans, my fear would take over and I'd want to run and hide.

I need to be brave. But how?

"Breathe slowly. Relax, ma petite. Be calm," Papa would say that whenever I was frightened and confused.

Breathe. Relax. Be calm.

I kept repeating it over and over, hoping I could push the fear away.

My first test came on a Friday, the week after the Germans arrived. Sœur Louise Claire stood by the back door waiting as I hung up my apron and put on my sweater.

"Are you sure, Désirée?" she asked, looking a little worried. "You don't have to go with me if you don't want to. Though it will only be a quick walk to the pharmacy and to the bakery, then to the post office and then home. If you don't want to go, I'm sure I can get Karin or Giselle to go today." I heard a challenge in her tone.

I slipped on my Calm face to answer. "Oh no Sœur, I'm fine. I want to help. Really."

My heart pounded in my chest in anticipation of the moment I'd see them again, but I grabbed the large basket from the counter and followed her out the back door.

It wasn't far, only a few blocks, but my nerves rattled with each step we took, each step that led us further from the safety of La Maison.

At first, we didn't see any soldiers, but we'd been walking on the small side streets and through the church grounds until we reached the Rue de la Marne.

It was usually a busy street, lined with cafés and shops, but now, even though it was late afternoon on a Friday, the traffic on the street was much lighter than the last time I was there. The people riding by on bicycles kept their eyes straight ahead. Local people, who would normally gather at the sidewalk cafés for an afternoon refreshment and conversation with friends, were mostly absent. Instead, pairs of German soldiers stood around while small groups of German soldiers sat at the café tables, drinking and talking with their fellows, like it was the most natural thing in the world to come into someone's home and take over.

"Are you all right, Désirée?" Sœur Louise Claire asked as we approached the pharmacy, our first destination. Two soldiers had come out of the shop and were standing on the sidewalk in front of the pharmacy door, talking and laughing about something.

I checked my face in the dress shop window we were passing, to make sure the fear I felt inside didn't show. "I think I'm going to be."

It surprised me to say that, but it was true. As scared as I was, I was also angry, and that surprised me even more.

We had to skirt around the soldiers to enter the pharmacy, and as we passed, one of them said something to Sœur Louise Claire in their strange language. When the nun told him she didn't understand, holding her palms up and shaking her head, he tried again in a mix of French and German while he smiled and pointed to me. Sœur Louise Claire said she was sorry, but she didn't understand.

As I stood in the open doorway of the shop, my heart was beating so hard it felt like it would burst out of my chest, but my face and body remained relaxed while the exchange between the nun and the soldier took place.

The other soldier laughed at his friend's attempt to be understood. With a friendly shove to his companions' back, they both tipped their helmets to the nun, then continued down the boulevard towards the City Hall.

"Oh... well, that was... well, I couldn't understand what he was saying at all," Sœur Louise Claire said to Monsieur Breton, who'd come out from behind the counter when we finally entered and closed the door.

"He was saying what a beautiful child you had with you. Désirée seemed to remind him of his own daughter. They meant no harm, Sœur," Monsieur Breton said.

Surprised the pharmacist could understand the strange language, I asked, "Do you speak their language, Monsieur?"

"Oui. I find it helpful to speak more than just French. You never know who'll come into the shop," he said, lifting his chin toward the receding soldiers.

"They seemed harmless enough, but you should take care of your girls, Sœur. One never knows what a soldier will do. Though I doubt Désirée will have any trouble with them."

I wondered what he meant by that. *Could what Révérende Mère said be true? Those soldiers didn't seem to want to hurt me.* When I thought about it, they even seemed nice, or at least they weren't being mean or cruel. But I still didn't trust them.

It seemed like a good idea to learn a few German words or phrases, and I thought about asking the pharmacist if he would teach me.

While Monsieur Breton and Sœur Louise Claire conducted their business, I wandered through the shop, making a mental list of the words and phrases that might be helpful:

My Name is.

Yes, sir.

No, sir.

I don't understand.

I don't know.

Those were some things I thought I might have to say if they ever questioned me. But thinking about that possibility gave me the shivers.

"Did you see them, Désirée?" a voice broke through my musings.

Juliette had come out from the back of the shop where she helped her grandfather after school. She was older than me and we'd never really spoken before, even though we saw each other at school, so the question caught me off guard.

"I did. They were leaving as we came in. Did you see them?"

"I saw them come in and talk with Grand-Père about something. I didn't understand everything, only a few words, but don't you think they're so handsome? Their uniforms are so much nicer than the ones our soldiers wear. Don't you think?"

Juliette chattered on about the German soldiers until I wanted to scream at her.

DON'T YOU KNOW THEY'RE MONSTERS, YOU STUPID GIRL!?

That's what I wanted to say, but of course, I didn't do that. Instead, I asked, "Can you teach me some of their words?"

"Sure, I can. I only know a few, but I can ask Grand-Père to teach me and then I can teach you. Oh, it will be such fun, Désirée. Then we can talk with them, too." Juliette spoke with so much enthusiasm it made me nervous.

I didn't think this silly girl had any idea who the Germans really were, and something warned me to be careful about what I said to her. So, I simply agreed it would be fun to learn a few German words, though I already had a bad feeling about the idea.

"Désirée? I need the basket, child. My goodness, you're very distracted today." Sœur Louise Claire had been calling my name without response until her voice finally broke through the haze of thoughts going through my head.

"Oui, Sœur. I am a little. I'm sorry." I handed the basket up to Monsieur Breton behind the counter, then an idea popped into my head, and I acted on it.

"Monsieur, how do you say I don't understand in German?" It seemed an important enough phrase to not wait to learn.

The old pharmacist peered over the top of his wire-rimmed glasses at me with the same expression so many adults seemed to give me, like I'd said or done something surprising.

"*Ich verstehe nicht,*" he said, smiling down at me.

He repeated the phrase a few times, then had me repeat it back to him. The words felt strange in my mouth, like the sounds wanted to squish together and be crisp, all at the same time. After a few attempts, Monsieur Breton gave my pronunciation his approval. Juliette and Sœur Louise Claire even gave the strange words a try, the girl with far more enthusiasm than the nun.

"Merci, Monsieur Breton. That was most instructive," Sœur Louise Claire said. "I will remind Révérende Mère about the meeting. Au revoir, Monsieur, au revoir, Juliette." She took up the basket, now filled with her purchases, then headed for the door as I thanked the pharmacist and Juliette and followed her out onto the street.

"Dear me, that was strange. I would have thought you wouldn't want anything to do with the Germans after what happened. Why did you ask him to teach you that, Désirée?" Sœur Louise Claire asked once we were alone.

We walked up the boulevard toward the end of the block where several German soldiers sat at the outside tables, enjoying the late afternoon sunshine and a drink at the Bistro de Ville. Other soldiers stood close by with their rifles draped across their shoulders, apparently standing guard.

I took a breath, settled my face again, then I answered her.

"That's why." I pointed to the soldiers in front of us. "They don't look like they're leaving soon. I just thought knowing how to say, I don't understand, might be helpful," I whispered as we passed by the soldiers on our way around the corner.

"You might be right, Désirée, you might be right. Let's get to Monsieur Denier's. I'm interested in what he has to say about all this, and perhaps he has a couple of chocolate croissants left. I could do with a treat today."

The tempting aromas of baked bread wafting through the air greeted us as we stepped inside the boulangerie and ran right into Alex, his arms filled with long loaves.

"Désirée! I'm glad to see you. You too, Sœur," he added shyly. "Maman sent me for more bread. She says Robert and Jon should be twice as big as they are with all the bread they eat. Are you coming back to the garden, Désirée? Papa says he misses your help. I don't have nearly as tender a touch as you. He says my pruning is more like plowing."

"You do have enormous hands, Alex," I said, laughing at his joke.

Alex and I stood out of the way and talked while Sœur Louise Claire conducted her business with Madame Denier across the counter. We talked about Jon and Robert, about school, and, of course, about the Germans. I kept one ear open to hear what the adults were saying, not wanting to miss any important information. But my attention didn't yield me anything useful, only more talk of a big meeting with the Mayor, the Bishop and some businesspeople.

I wondered what they would all be talking about and prayed it would be to tell the Germans to go back home and leave us all alone. I hoped that would be true, but didn't really think it would.

"... then I heard they were moving south towards Tours and our soldiers are still fighting in some places. I also heard it's all but over, and there'll be a surrender. Surrender! Can you believe it?" Alex whispered. It seemed even he felt the need to keep his voice low when talking about the Germans. It was something lately I noticed in all the adults.

"I want them all to go home and leave us alone." I knew it was a childish thing to say, but I was a child, after all. Alex had become like a big brother to me, never teasing me about being silly or young. He'd just mess my hair up like Jean-Michel used to do.

"You're a funny girl, Désirée," he said, reaching over with his free hand to muss my hair. "Remember, I said I'd take you fishing the next time we go? Do you still want to? Papa, George, and I are going tomorrow morning."

I'd gone fishing with my papa and my brothers lots of times. Anna and Yvette would go sometimes, but not as often as me. I loved the excitement of hooking a fish on the line, and then the joy of bringing it home to Maman for supper. This was a chance I didn't want to miss.

"Of course, but I must ask permission."

"Great! I'll tell Papa we'll need another pole and he can clear it with Révérende Mère. Hey, that reminds me, why are we pulling out all the old pots and barrels from the warehouse?"

"I'm not exactly sure, but Révérende Mère probably has a plan for them." I was curious myself what those reasons could be.

Sœur Louise Claire finished her chat with Madame Denier and rejoined Alex and me, her basket filled with bags of rolls and loaves of bread, and three chocolate croissants sitting on top.

"Let's go, children. I still need to stop at the post office. Here, each of you take a croissant. We can enjoy them on the way."

We didn't need to be invited twice, each greedily snatching up a croissant. Sœur Louise Claire took the last pastry before hefting the basket onto her arm and leading us out the door.

We stopped on the sidewalk for a moment, enjoying our treats in the building's shade and looking to see if the German soldiers were still on the corner. They were still there, sitting at the bistro, drinking and talking. It appeared like they were celebrating something, which only fueled my anger.

I quickly glanced at my reflection in the window to make sure I didn't look as angry as I felt inside. Consciously relaxing my expression, I tried to think calming thoughts, then remembered about fishing with Alex and decided I would ask while the nun was happily consuming her treat.

"Sœur? Alex invited me to go fishing with him and Monsieur Guerin and George tomorrow morning. Would it be all right if I went with them? I'll get my work done first. I promise."

I really wanted to go, imagined myself by a river, sitting along the bank, fishing while the sunshine danced on the water, like I used to do with Papa. If I could catch a fish or two, that would make it even better. I'd show Sœur Louise Claire how Maman prepared the fish with toasted almonds and lemon. I could almost taste the delicate flesh and the crispy skin, a burst of lemon juice squeezed on top at the end.

"Mm. That's delicious," the nun said, licking bits of chocolate off her fingers.

"May I go with them, Sœur?" I asked again, wondering if the nun had read my mind somehow.

"I'll have to check with Révérende Mère when we get home. It seems to me she said something about Monsieur Guerin earlier."

We continued down the street to the large four-story building, taking up the whole next block from front to back. It was almost as large as the Cathedral, but not quite. The carving above the entrance said Télégraphes ~ Postes ~ Telephones, and like so much in this big new world I was living in, the idea of needing such a large building to handle mail seemed amazing.

How much mail could there be? I wondered.

"Alex, will you stay with Désirée while I go pick up something for Révérende Mère? The two of you can wait for me inside. I'll only be a moment." Sœur Louise Claire asked as she handed me the basket.

"Of course, Sœur. We need to plan our fishing strategy for tomorrow, anyway." Alex followed us up the steps to the post office.

The entrance of the building opened into a tall, wide room, brightly lit with light from the windows and a chandelier hanging from the high ceiling. Sœur Louise Claire disappeared through a windowed door on the right, while Alex and I settled ourselves on a bench outside the door. A calendar hung above our heads declaring the date; Friday 21 June 1940.

Across the lobby, a bank of phone booths lined the wall. One booth hosted a German soldier lounging half inside. He was talking to someone with animated gestures. Then I noticed the other soldiers; two inside the main entrance on either side of the door and another two standing at a hall entrance leading toward the back of the building.

Alex must have noticed them too, because he nudged me with his elbow and raised his chin in their direction. The soldiers didn't pay us any attention beyond an occasional glance at the bread we were holding. It didn't matter. Their presence alone made me angry, but I made sure my face didn't show it.

A few moments later, Sœur Louise Claire came out the door and, without a word, she gestured for us to follow her. As we reached the front door, it swung open with the momentum of the three men coming in: two German officers and a distinguished looking older man. Sœur Louise Claire stepped back as they pushed their way into the lobby, Alex and I peaking around her wide frame.

The soldier in the phone booth broke off his conversation and stood at attention when he saw the German officers come into the lobby. The other soldiers did the same. As the three men made their way across the tile floor, the older gentleman directed the officers to the hallway where another man nervously greeted them, introducing himself as the person in charge of the Post Office. I wondered who the older man was, and why he was being so friendly with the Germans.

Sœur Louise Claire watched them as they passed, her lips pursed, her eyebrows raised to the band of her cornette. Then she hurried to the entrance, signaling for us to follow. Alex and I looked at each other with the silent communication of children, each wondering what was going on but holding our tongues.

Before we reached the door, the old gentleman called out for Sœur Louise Claire to stop. "Sœur, a moment, s'il vous plaît."

She didn't turn around right away, she just stood there facing the door, huffing. I could tell something was wrong. The nun had never acted that way before. When she finally turned around, her face was tense and her lips tight.

"Oui, Monsieur Maire, what can I do for you?" she asked, though it seemed to me she didn't want to do anything for him.

It was so unlike Sœur Louise Claire to be rude or unkind, and I worried something bad was going to happen. I glanced at the soldiers who were at the entrance, standing at attention, and saw nothing to show they were interested in what was happening with the old man and the nun.

"Sœur, be so kind as to tell Révérende Mère we require her presence this evening. Eight o'clock at City Hall. I've made several calls to her today and could not reach her. I certainly hope she's not avoiding me. That would not do at all, I'm sure. Tell her Bishop Tissier will be there. That should pique her interest," the old man said.

Something about the way he spoke bothered me, like he expected to be obeyed in all things, but feared he wouldn't be. Since the Germans arrived,

I became sensitive to the way adults around me acted, being all too aware my fate was in the hands of those adults.

Sœur Louise Claire regarded the old man for a moment, her thoughts a mystery, her eyes speaking her disapproval, but of what, I wondered.

"I will give her your message. Good day, Monsieur Maire." she said curtly. Then she ushered us out the door, leaving the old man standing alone in the lobby.

Alex and I followed her out onto the street and around the corner, not saying a word but silently communicating to each other our curiosity about what we had witnessed. I wanted to ask Sœur Louise Claire what was wrong, but Alex put his finger to his lips and shook his head to let me know now was not the time for questions. So, I followed behind the nun's swaying black habit and flapping white wings, down the street towards La Maison, wondering what could have upset her and if that would change her decision to let me go fishing.

Chapter 16

A sad day for France

Robert and Jon attacked Alex from both sides as soon as we entered the courtyard. Both little boys tried climbing his legs to snatch the bread that he was holding out of reach of their grubby little hands.

"Maman! Come and take this bread before I use one to fight off these bandits!" he called to his mother, who was taking sheets off a line by the carriage house.

"Settle down, you two or I won't give you the treat I brought you," Alex told the little boys as he handed the loaves to his mother.

"What did you bring us, Alex?" Jon asked, trying to be patient but bouncing up and down eagerly.

"Tweet, tweet! Awex, tweet, tweet!" Little Robert cried, pulling on Alex's leg.

Alex pulled a chocolate croissant from his pocket, tearing it in half and then handing a piece to each boy. "Here. You must share, or Maman will say I spoiled your supper," he said, wiping the crumbs from his hands onto his pant legs.

"How did you do that? I saw you eat your croissant," I asked in amazement.

A smile lit up his face. "It's not magic, just who you know. George gave me one before you came into the boulangerie. I was going to eat it on the way home. Then Sœur gave me another... *et Voila*! A treat for the little bandits and I'm a hero," he said with a shrug.

"Lucky for you, your best friend is the baker's son, you mean. Merci, Alex. I hope I can go tomorrow."

I hurried to catch up with Sœur Louise Claire, who was standing at the backdoor, taking deep breaths, her shoulders rising and falling. "Are you all right, Sœur?" I asked, stroking her arm.

"Don't worry about me, child. I just needed to ask God for forgiveness. I shouldn't let that man annoy me like that, but sometimes it's hard, especially today."

What she meant was unclear, but I knew the old man in the post office had upset her, and that gave me an uncomfortable feeling. There wasn't much I could do except to help put things away and begin preparing the evening meal, so I grabbed my apron and went to the sink to wash my hands.

"Sœur? Who was the old man at the Post Office?" I asked, not wanting to upset her again but also thinking I needed to understand things better.

"Him? He is our mayor. The Mayor of Châlons-en-Marne, and the head of the city council. How fortunate we all are, no?" she said, rolling her eyes. "Pay no attention to me, child. Let's get these things put away and get started on the meal."

Sœur Louise Claire unloaded the purchases from the basket onto the worktable. "Here, Désirée, you run up and take this to Sœur Marguerite, and this one to Sœur Bernadette. They've both been eager for these to come in. You can tell them that Monsieur Breton is unsure when he'll be able to get more, so they should make it last." She handed me two small packages, specifying which went to which nun, then resumed putting the rest of the things away in their proper place.

"Oui, Sœur. I'll be right back to help you."

I almost collided into Sœur Marguerite at the top of the stairs on my way up.

"Oh... Sœur Marguerite. I was coming to find you," I said, a little out of breath. I handed her the package from my right hand and hurried with the message. "Monsieur Breton said he wasn't sure when he would get more, so you need to make it last." I gave her a little curtsy, then went in search of Sœur Bernadette.

"Merci Désirée. I will. Merci," Sœur Marguerite called back to me.

Sœur Bernadette was usually in her room in the afternoon, always retreating there for a rest before supper. I assumed it was because she was so old, but also suspected she hid in there to get away from the giggling and squealing girls. She was a cranky old woman, and I usually avoided her, but now I had to interrupt her 'quiet time' and thought it probably wouldn't matter I was bringing her something she wanted.

Nervous about knocking on her door and tempted to leave the package on the floor outside, I struggled to decide what to do, but then I remembered about the message.

I tapped on the heavy wooden door: tap, tap, tap.

No answer.

I knocked again, a little harder: Knock, knock, KNOCK.

The door swung open, and Sœur Bernadette stood in the doorway with a look that would freeze stone.

"What could be so important as to disturb my prayers?"

"Ah...... Sœur asked me to bring you this and tell you there won't be more soon andyoushouldmakeitlast." I hurried through the last bit, shoved the package into the old nun's hands and beat a hasty retreat down

122

the stairs, hoping to avoid any repercussions from the message. But all I heard was a "Humph" sound.

When I returned to the kitchen, Sœur Louise Claire was standing at the counter by the sink, furiously chopping slabs of ham into small pieces. I could tell she'd been crying; her shoulders were shaking each time she snuffled her tears away.

"Sœur? What can I do to help you?" I timidly asked, touching her lightly on the back.

She stopped chopping, took a deep breath as she wiped her hands on the apron. With a handkerchief she pulled from a hidden pocket, she gingerly wiped her eyes dry and shook her head.

"I'll be fine. Why don't you start on the leeks and onions? I've shed enough tears for the day. You do that and I'll finish with the ham and get the oven heated."

We were making Quiche Lorraine for supper that evening. I had mentioned the recipe Maman often made for the family, and how easy and delicious it was, and Sœur Louise Claire agreed to make it for the evening meal. The pastry crusts were already chilling in the refrigerator, along with a large bowl of shredded Gruyere.

Making quick work of the leeks and onions, I ended with two piles of uniformly cut vegetables ready to be sauteed. Then I removed the pastry crusts from the refrigerator and pricked the bottoms and sides, then laid a smaller tin pie plate in each, filling the tins with dried beans to weigh them down.

When the pie shells went in the oven, I kept a close watch on them, while Sœur Louise Claire started frying the ham, onions, and leeks. Once slightly browned, I pulled the shells from the oven, then reduced the oven heat for the next step in the recipe.

The egg and cream mixture came next; two dozen eggs in a large bowl, add cream and milk, whisking it all together with some freshly chopped tarragon in at the end.

Once she seasoned the meat and vegetables with salt, pepper and a little cayenne, everything was ready. We filled the baked shells in layers; ham and vegetables, cheese, some egg mixture, then carefully put the filled pie shells back into the oven to bake for almost an hour.

The only thing left to do for the evening meal was make a simple lettuce salad and slice the bread, and nothing needed doing immediately, so we sat and chatted for a while. I hoped she was in a better mood than earlier because her unhappiness made me nervous.

"Sœur? When we were at the pharmacy, Monsieur Breton said something I didn't understand. He said I wouldn't have any trouble with the Germans. What did he mean? Am I different from the other girls?"

The Germans we saw earlier didn't act like the monsters from my memory, and that worried me. They acted friendly, nice even. Then the pharmacist's comment confused me even more. I didn't want to be special to the Germans. I wanted to be invisible to them.

"Don't pay any attention to Monsieur Breton, Désirée. He has his own ideas about how things should be. You just do as Révérende Mère tells you, and you'll be fine."

It wasn't much of an explanation, but I didn't think I would get much more from her on the subject, and right then Révérende Mère came in through the back door, her arms filled with baskets of what looked to me like old clothes.

"Good, you're back," she said, dropping the baskets on the floor by the basement stairs. "Désirée, take these to the mending room, then go fetch the other baskets from the car. They're in the back seat. Merci." Then she collapsed at the worktable with a sigh.

"Oui, Révérende Mère." I jumped up off my seat and hurried out to obey.

I didn't want to miss asking Révérende Mère about fishing with Alex, so I did as she asked as quickly as possible. As I walked back into the kitchen with two baskets slung on my arms, the two nuns were talking about the meeting Sœur Louise Claire needed to remind the Révérende Mère to attend.

"Saints preserve us," Révérende Mère said in that funny, lilting accent. "it's all I've heard about all afternoon. I suppose I'll have to be there. I'll call the Bishop, to arrange a ride with him."

I hurried downstairs to the room dedicated to sewing and mending and unloaded the baskets into the corner. It took me a couple of trips back and forth to get it all downstairs, but I soon headed back up to the kitchen. When I walked in, I busied myself with simple tasks, not wanting to disturb the nuns, who were sipping on cups of coffee and talking.

"Well, you know how Monsieur Breton can be, Révérende Mère. But I thought it best to tell you," Sœur Louise Claire was saying as I came in. "The strange thing was, she asked him how to say, I don't understand, in German. Didn't you, Désirée? And he taught us how. Isn't that right, child?" Sœur Louise Claire asked on her way to check on the baking quiches.

"Oui, Sœur," I said, confirming her story. I hoped I hadn't got either of us in trouble with Révérende Mère, who was giving me one of those funny looks I seemed to get a lot of.

"So, Désirée, it appears you've gotten over your fear of the Germans. Is that correct?" she asked, her green eyes holding me in place.

"Not really, Révérende Mère. Hmm, it's only that... Well, I didn't want to stay inside all the time, so I tried to look like I wasn't so afraid when I saw them. Like this..." I said, demonstrating my Calm face for them.

She smiled and shook her head at me. "You certainly are full of surprises. Do you remember how to say it?"

"*Ich verstehe nicht.*" I recited the phrase as best I could.

"*Gut,*" Révérende Mère replied in the same language, "But say it in French first, if you must say it at all. I think it's best if the Germans believe you do not speak their language."

Sœur Louise Claire was chuckling as she often did when I said or did something she thought was funny. It seemed like a good time to ask if I could go fishing in the morning, so I plucked up my courage, but Révérende Mère seemed to read my mind.

"Sœur Louise Claire tells me Alex invited you to go fishing with him and George tomorrow, and from the look on your face, I can see you would like to go. Well, fishing isn't an activity many of my girls would choose. However, being a country girl myself, I understand the fascination. You have my permission. But a word of warning; you are always to stay with Alex, no wandering off. Is that understood?"

"Oui, Révérende Mère. I understand, merci." Excitement bubbled inside me at the possibilities of what the next day would bring.

Révérende Mère rose from her stool and stretched with a deep sigh. "Whatever the two of you have created tonight smells heavenly. I'll be in my office until supper."

After she left the kitchen, Sœur Louise Claire looked over at me with a smile and a shake of her head. "You are such a funny child. Now go get the table ready for supper."

With the aroma of Mama's Quiche Lorraine filling my senses, I happily obeyed.

Chapter 17

Three things to remember

D awn broke the following morning, all rosy and pink, with just enough cloud cover to keep the fish from spotting you on the shore. I thought it was a good omen. Papa always said a red dawn meant good fishing. I dressed and ran downstairs to get my chores done before I was to meet up with Alex and his father. We confirmed the arrangements before supper the night before.

The first surprise of the day came when I found Révérende Mère waiting for me in the kitchen, dressed in a simple, dark blue habit and short veil. I wondered if Révérende Mère ever went to sleep. She was always up and dressed, no matter the time of day.

"Good, you're up. We need to get an early start."

"Aren't I going with Monsieur Guerin and Alex?" I asked, my disappointment clear.

"There's been a change of plans. You'll be riding with me to the farms. None of that now, child," she said, giving me a stern look when I complained.

"You'll get to fish later, but we've more important things to tend to first. Get something to eat. We'll be leaving soon." Révérende Mère finished her cup of coffee and headed out the back door.

"Don't worry about the chores, Désirée. I'll get one of the other girls to help this morning. There's a basket by the door with a bit of something for later," Sœur Louise Claire said, handing me a bowl of yogurt with fruit. "Hurry now. You don't want to keep Révérende Mère waiting."

The change of plans didn't really bother me, but it seemed strange that Révérende Mère would choose me to go with her, and not one of the older girls.

It won't be so bad spending time with her.

Maybe I can ask her some questions.

I quickly finished my breakfast and took the bowl to the sink to wash. "Sœur, why does Révérende Mère want me to go with her today? Is there something I'm supposed to do?" I asked as I dried my hands, then headed for the back door.

Sœur Louise Claire smiled with a gentle look in her eyes. "I'm sure Révérende Mère has her reasons. Just be yourself, Désirée, and enjoy the sunshine if it ever comes out. Run along now. I'll see you tonight."

I still didn't know why, but soon forgot about it when I saw Alex and George packing shovels and a wheelbarrow into the back of the truck. Révérende Mère was talking with Monsieur Guerin, so I put the basket in the backseat of the idling car, then went to join the boys.

"Bonjour George. Bonjour Alex. What are the shovels for? I thought we were going fishing today," I asked, as the boys settled themselves in the back of the truck.

"Bonjour, Désirée," George greeted me shyly. Even though he was Alex's best friend, they were nothing alike. Alex was charming and easygoing, but George was shy, usually letting Alex take the lead.

"We are, but Papa says we have work to do first, but even that should be fun." Alex was always an optimist. He reached behind him and pulled out a small pair of overalls, tossing them down to me.

"Here. Maman says you should put these on when we're fishing. I guess she wants to keep the fish stains off your regular clothes," he said, grinning down at me.

"Merci. I forgot how messy fishing can be." I held up the overalls. They were too long and too wide through the middle, but they were better than nothing. "These should work fine."

"Come, Désirée. We need to leave," Révérende Mère called out.

I waved to Alex and George, then hurried to the car and wondered what other surprises the day would bring.

Révérende Mère drove out of the courtyard and headed south, then west toward the river, the truck with Monsieur Guerin and the boys trailing closely behind. German soldiers stopped us at the river, questioning Révérende Mère and examining her papers, but after a few tense moments, they allowed us to pass.

I wanted to ask her what we were going to do and why I was going with her, but she seemed lost in her own thoughts. There was a tension in the air I didn't understand, and it made the silence in the car uneasy.

"You're probably wondering why I wanted you to come with me today," Révérende Mère said, once again reading my thoughts.

How does she do that?

"You're a farm girl, are you not?"

"Oui."

"I must inspect our farms today, and you are the only farm girl currently with us, so it seemed sensible for you to come with me, since you were going fishing with the boys, anyway."

"Farms? We have farms?" I asked, my voice brimming with excitement. I missed my family farm so much, missed the freedom of being outside every day and the smell of the fields and vineyards.

129

"We do, and we need to visit them today to make sure everything is going well for the season."

It seemed a good time to ask a question or two, so I ventured one related to the farms. "Why did Alex bring the wheelbarrow and shovels?"

"Those are for the soil. We're going to load soil from each farm onto the truck today. Shovels and a wheelbarrow are essential, don't you think?"

"Soil? Oh, so that's why Monsieur Guerin pulled the pots and barrels out of the warehouse. Alex asked me about it yesterday. We're going to make a garden in the courtyard, aren't we?"

"Clever girl. That's exactly what we're going to do. We're going to grow as much as we can, in as many places as we can."

"But why? If we have farms to grow food, why do we need to grow more?"

Révérende Mère looked over at me, then blew out a long, slow breath, and returned her gaze to the road ahead.

"You've never been hungry, have you? Hunger is a terrible thing, Désirée. I've seen what it can do." She sighed again, shaking her head, seemingly to release a terrible memory.

"The courtyard garden is my small way of making sure we have what we need. Remember when I told you that because of the war, we all will need to help each other? The courtyard garden will be a way for you to help. You are the farm girl, after all."

That gave me a lot to think about as we passed through the outskirts of the city. The farther we traveled, the buildings shrank in size and closeness to one another, until only fields and hedgerows were visible, rolling away into the distance.

As we drove through the countryside, Révérende Mère told me about the farms owned by the Sisters of Charity. For several generations, the same families had worked the farms, each growing a different crop. One grew wheat and other grains, one grew beets and root vegetables, another had orchards and grew cabbage and other greens, and they all had chickens and dairy cows. The Sisters also owned a vineyard with grapes that would become the next vintage of champagne.

Révérende Mère explained that everything grown on the farms provided the income, and much of the food, for the orphanage and school, as well as providing an income for the families who worked on the farms. It was a relationship started by the Montclair family generations ago, and Révérende Mère said there'd been no reason to change anything when Madame Elise gifted the properties to the Sisters of Charity.

The farms were much larger than my farm, the fields many times larger than Papa's fields. The houses were larger too, with multiple out-buildings and barns for the animals and equipment. Even though they were bigger, like everything else I'd seen since leaving home, they were each still so familiar, the sights and sounds, and especially the smells. Each farm we went to smelled like home.

We only stopped for a short time at each farm, only long enough for Révérende Mère to speak with the family. She inspected each property, talked about the season's progress and discussed the difficulties the families were experiencing, which were a lot, considering the Germans were everywhere.

While I tagged along behind her, the boys and Monsieur Guerin were loading wheelbarrows full of soil into the back of the truck. I watched them load soil from the outside row at the end of a field. Alex and George were laughing and occasionally tossing dirt clods at each other; an activity I longed to join. But Révérende Mère had made it clear that any playtime would have to wait. So, I followed behind her, smiled and said 'Bonjour' to everyone. Mostly, I observed and listened as we toured the farms, remembering my home and once again feeling the rhythm of life in the country.

We had our mid-day meal with the family at the third farm, after the truck was full of soil and Révérende Mère had completed the inspection. By the time we left and headed north to the last stop for the day, the vineyard by the river Marne, I had almost lost control of my deeply ingrained obedience.

My feet held tightly together, tapped on the floorboard to a beat playing inside my head. It was my attempt to distract myself from the tension which had built up around us all day. It wasn't anything I had said or done making everything so tense; it was the Germans.

We heard the same story over and over; the men were missing, French soldiers either killed in battle or taken as prisoners, and the Germans had swept through each farm and taken whatever they wanted. The families worried how they'd be able to finish the season if the men did not return. Old men and grandmothers, women with babies and children under the age of sixteen, all waiting to get word of their loved ones. When would their men return home? What would they do if they didn't? Those were the questions on everyone's mind, and they looked to Révérende Mère for the answers.

Something about Révérende Mère seemed to calm the fears of even the most distraught widow. She had a gentle understanding, and a strength of purpose, which kept faith alive in those around her. I felt it myself, knew she would do everything possible to help the families, like she helped me.

"Tell me, Désirée," Révérende Mère said, silencing the tapping feet beside her with a touch to my knee. "What have you learned today that you didn't know before the day began?"

I thought about the question for a moment. It felt like she was seeking something more than just the similarities and differences between my family farm and the large farms we visited. They were basically the same, but there was something different, something missing with the people.

When I remembered my home, it was of happy times with my family, laughing and working together, a joyfulness in almost every memory. The families I met that day left me feeling sad. Each person touched by the same fear and sadness, brought on by the same monster that had destroyed my family.

I took a deep breath and released it with a sigh before answering.

"I learned the Germans have hurt a lot more people than just me and my family. And I learned the people hate them but are afraid of them too. They're afraid of what might happen if they say or do something wrong."

Révérende Mère gave me one of those looks, her green eyes flashing in the afternoon sunshine. "You didn't know this before?"

"No, not really. I mean, I knew there were others, but those families are like mine, the way they live. They still have their homes and each other, except for those who aren't there anymore, but the people are afraid and angry and sad. Just like me."

"All true, child. And sadly, there are many families like them, all over France right now. You need to understand three things, Désirée. First, that sadness is something you must learn to endure. Second, that fear will always stop you, if you allow it. And third, that anger can both fuel your determination and derail it with recklessness." She waited a moment, then asked, "Do you understand?"

"I think so. Madame Elise told me I needed to be brave and strong and clever. I didn't know what she meant, but now I think I'm beginning to."

A smile bloomed across Révérende Mère's face as she guided the car down a tree-lined road. The truck followed behind for a while, then turned into a work yard in front of several large buildings. Révérende Mère continued up the road a short way, then stopped in front of a beautiful stone house with steps leading up to the entrance.

"This was the Montclair's château estate. Monsieur Montclair was quite the wine connoisseur, and the grapes from this vineyard are highly prized. Let's hope we find all is well here, at least."

An older man and his wife greeted us at the bottom of the steps. Révérende Mère's warm response made it clear this was a favorite place. She introduced me to the couple, then released me to Alex, who'd run up from the work yard to fetch me.

"You've done well today, Désirée. Go have a bit of fun now. Take the basket with you and don't wander off. We'll be leaving for home at sunset." Révérende Mère said. Then she walked up the steps and disappeared into the château.

As I turned to go with Alex, the vista I saw took my breath away. Rows of grapevines grew down the gently sloping hill and nestled into the folds of the river, fed by the water and protected by the trees growing along the banks.

"Oh! How beautiful! It's like a dream," I said, breathing in the warm summer air, rich with the scent of growing vines.

"Oh, right. I guess it is. It's a good place for fishing, that's for sure."

Alex handed me the overalls and took the basket from me. "Here, put these on and I'll race you to the river. George is down there already."

The overalls were big for me, but I climbed into them, stuffing my work dress down into the wide waistband. Alex helped me hitch up the straps over my shoulders and roll up the pant legs, so I wouldn't trip over them.

"Hmm. These were mine a few years ago. Ready - Set - Go." He took off running down the road, laughing as he ran.

"Wait for me," I called, chasing him down the hill, laughing and playing like a child once again.

Chapter 18

Fishing

Alex, George and I spent the rest of the day lazing along the banks of the River Marne, talking and eating and fishing for the sweet fat trout that hid in the bends of the river. It would have been a perfect day, but for the Germans.

They were the only thing Alex and George wanted to talk about, speaking in whispers, even though I was the only one around to hear. They talked endlessly about what they'd do to *les Boches* if only they were older and allowed the freedom to carry out their plans. Both boys were twelve, still too young to be anything but obedient. They made their plans, anyway, once even asking me for my opinion.

"Do you think our plan will work, Désirée?" George asked after detailing his sabotage plan for the third time.

"I think... I don't want to think about them today," I said with a shrug. I would not let the Germans ruin what could be a perfect day, like they'd ruined everything else. Mostly I ignored the boys' talk of revenge, and instead played at the edge of the water, daydreamed in the afternoon sunshine, and fished.

By the end of the day, I was filthy, exhausted and bubbling with happiness. It was the best fishing day I ever had. I landed four large trout, with a little help from the boys, and was excited to bring them back to Sœur

Louise Claire. Even Alex and George had been successful, each landing three trout.

We kneeled side by side next to the river, cleaned the fish, and wrapped them in wet grass and grape leaves for the trip home. I placed mine in the basket, now empty of the food Sœur Louise Claire had sent.

"I can't wait to show Révérende Mère and Sœur these fish. Merci, Alex, for inviting me. This was the best day."

When I got back to the car, I proudly held the basket while Révérende Mère stood on the steps of the château, saying goodbye to the old couple. She took one look at me and laughed.

"It appears you've had a successful afternoon on the river," she said, peeking into the basket I held up to her with pride. "Four! Congratulations!"

She took another long look at me, then insisted I shed the filthy overalls before getting into the car. She said it was to keep the seats clean, but then she fussed over my dress and hair, like she'd done that first Sunday before mass. It seemed strange to make such a fuss about how I looked when we were going straight home, but I didn't object.

Once I cleaned myself up to her satisfaction, I sat quietly in the front seat of the car while she offered her thanks and bid a final 'Adieu' to the old couple.

We left the château at sunset, Révérende Mère leading the way in the car, the truck with the boys following close behind. The road we traveled skirted the river, passing through several small villages, and I relaxed into the seat with the basket held on my lap, too tired to give the landscape much notice. But I noticed a tension in Révérende Mère next to me; her hands gripping the steering wheel, her attention on high alert each time we passed through a village. She didn't seem to want to talk, so I closed my eyes, reliving the wonderful moments of the day, and trying to ignore the nervous beating of my heart.

We'd been driving for a while when the car slowed, then came to a stop behind another car on the outskirts of Châlons. A guard station, with a long bar blocking the road ahead, sat next to the road. Several German soldiers and French Police were standing guard, apparently stopping vehicles entering the city.

"Stay still, Désirée," Révérende Mère said. "There's a checkpoint up ahead. They will search the car and truck. Do as I tell you and don't speak."

The people ahead of us returned to their car and drove away after the guard raised the bar. When the car passed, the guard lowered the bar again, the other soldiers standing at attention behind it.

Révérende Mère pulled our car to a stop in front of the barrier and waited, her hands still tightly gripping the steering wheel. The German soldiers stared at us through the windshield as one of the French Police walked around the car to speak to Révérende Mère. A German officer stood in the guardhouse's doorway, apparently to observe the proceedings.

"Bonsoir Révérende Mère," said the Police officer. "Forgive the inconvenience. There's been some trouble at the train station. Our orders are to search all vehicles going into the city and question the occupants. Exit the car, s'il vous plaît." Then he took hold of the handle, opening the door for Révérende Mère.

"Get out of the car, Désirée. Stand quietly and wait for me," she said, giving me a look that brooked no argument. Then she got out and walked to the front of the car to speak with the men.

I was nervous, standing on the side of the road; the basket forgotten in my hands. I heard Révérende Mère explained where we'd been and what we'd been doing all day. She repeated her explanation to the German officer, who immediately sent two soldiers to search the truck.

From where I stood, I could see and hear what was happening with Monsieur Guerin, Alex and George. The soldiers ordered them all out of the truck, aiming their rifles at them. When George was climbing down, a soldier yanked him by the collar and threw him to the ground in a heap. Alex and Monsieur Guerin helped him to his feet, and the three of them stood silently on the roadside. One soldier held them at gunpoint while the other searched the truck, poking his bayonet deep into the soil in the back.

The look I saw on Alex's face was the same look I saw on my brother, Jean-Michel's face when he stood in front of our house on that horrible day, and it terrified me to think something might happen to Alex. So, I walked towards them, hoping I could distract Alex from trying any of the stupid plans he thought up earlier. I knew the Germans were monsters, but I walked towards them, anyway.

"Halt!" the soldier guarding the boys yelled, pointing his weapon at me.

I stopped a few meters away.

He said something I didn't understand, but then it became clear he wanted my basket.

I backed away, unwilling to relinquish my prize.

"No! You can't have them!" I yelled, backing farther away the closer he came.

Hearing my cries, Révérende Mère hurried over, the German officer by her side.

"What's this Désirée? I told you to stay still."

"Who is this? Let's see what you have in here, *kleiner Liebling*," the German officer said as he reached for my basket.

"No! They're my fish. I caught them, and I'm going to cook them for Sœur Louise Claire," I said, scowling up at him and clinging to the basket.

The German officer looked down at me, his expression amused rather than angry.

"So, you can cook as well as fish. *Gut.* And you look like a perfect little Aryan child, as well. Perhaps you'll come and cook for me one day." He smiled as he looked me over from head to toe.

My eyes flashed defiance as I glared up at him, my hands still tightly gripping the basket.

I'm not Aryan! I'm French and I will never cook for you! I thought, but I didn't say it out loud.

What's Aryan?

"Give him the basket, Désirée," Révérende Mère instructed.

"But…"

"Now, s'il vous plaît," she ordered.

Reluctantly, I handed over the basket to the German officer, who immediately stood at attention, clicked his polished boot heels together, then nodded his head sharply down at me. He then addressed Révérende Mère, handing back the papers she had offered for his examination.

"Bonne nuit, Madame. Thank you for your patience… and for the fish," he said with a smugness I hated. Then he signaled the soldiers to raise the bar and stood aside as we got back into our vehicles and drove away.

When we drove into the courtyard at the back of La Maison, I broke the silence that had filled the space between us since the encounter with the Germans. I had fumed the entire way home, my anger and frustration almost too much for me to bear.

"I hate them. They ruin everything," I said, tears falling down my face as we pulled into the courtyard.

"I'm sorry about your fish, Désirée, but it was a small price to pay to avoid any unnecessary conflict."

"I still hate them."

"There are times to fight, and times to walk away. A basket of fish isn't something to fight for. You need to be smarter when you're around them. Do you remember what I said about anger?" she asked, locking her eyes to mine with a look that was both stern and gentle at the same time.

I sat there frustrated and angry, knowing she wanted obedience and understanding, but I couldn't forget what they had taken from me. It wasn't just the fish—though it made me so mad to think of the Germans eating my hard-won prize—it was everything else they had taken from me; my home, my family, the life I should have had. I knew I was powerless to do anything but obey, but I vowed someday I would make them pay for all of it.

"Oui, Révérende Mère. I remember."

I remember it all, and someday, I will make them pay.

Chapter 19

The Kommandant

By the end of summer 1940, the courtyard garden was lush with growing things, though it was a struggle to get it started. At first, Révérende Mère met with resistance, residents who didn't like the idea of working in the dirt. But she would accept no opposition to her plan. With everyone lending a hand, the courtyard quickly became a lush oasis, bursting with an abundance of pots, planters, and half barrels, each teeming with crops that would contribute to the food stores for the house.

The courtyard garden flourished under the tender care of the children of La Maison and the diligent supervision of Révérende Mère. It even inspired others in the community to create their own small gardens, and in doing so, take back a bit of control of their lives.

As the garden flourished, the house filled up with an almost steady stream of lost children. Père Andre arrived the week after the fish incident with four new girls and two young boys. Then the following week, more children arrived by train from the mother house in Paris, accompanied by three new nuns. The week after that, another group from Reims arrived with more children and two more novices. Then there were the local children, the ones abandoned after the Germans killed or imprisoned their parents. Someone would bring them to La Maison, or they'd find their way to the big house with the blue door, known to be a refuge and sanctuary for children. Révérende Mère turned no one away, not even the boys.

More than half of the new girls were younger than four years old, two of them just babies. The rest were my age or older. Twenty-one girls, four novices and eight nuns now lived together at La Maison.

Révérende Mère arranged with the priests to open the seminary as a home and school for orphan boys who came seeking shelter. By the end of the summer, the seminary house was jam-packed with almost as many boys as there were girls at La Maison.

The last Sunday in September, I was in the kitchen helping Sœur Louise Claire with the evening meal for the Bishop. Normally, the extra work it took to get the meal 'just right' wouldn't send the nun into a frenzy, but that day I could feel the tension in every move she made and wondered what was wrong.

"They should be here soon," Sœur Marguerite announced as she popped her head into the kitchen.

"They? You mean it's true?" Sœur Louise Claire asked, horror clearly showing on her face.

"Oui, it's true. I heard it from Père Phillipe this morning. He said the Bishops' House is in an uproar. Révérende Mère says it's likely he'll come tonight," Sœur Marguerite explained. Then she saw me drying dishes at the counter.

"Désirée, did you make the Lemon Tarts the Bishop is so fond of?" Sœur Marguerite was fussing more than usual over the details of the Bishop's regular dinner visit.

"Oui, Sœur. There on the sideboard, by the dessert plates."

"Good girl."

Then the doorbell rang, and Sœur Marguerite hurried to answer it, but I could see through the opened doorway that Révérende Mère was already there to greet her guests.

"Bonsoir Your Excellency. Thank you for joining us this evening." Révérende Mère greeted Bishop Tissier, holding the door open wide as he and his secretary, Père Phillipe, came in.

Bishop Tissier stood in the entry, shedding his long cape onto the bench by the door. "Merci, Révérende Mère, Merci. As you can see, I've brought a guest this evening. I hope you'll indulge my whim with your hospitality," he said, as a Nazi officer stepped up to the door.

"Bonsoir Madame. Forgive the intrusion." He clicked his heels together and bowed his head.

With a barely perceptible shift of posture, Révérende Mère welcomed him. "Of course, Kommandant. Welcome, please come in."

The Kommandant walked into the house, followed by a young soldier who stayed close, but out of the way.

"Merci, Madame. I thought I'd take this opportunity to pay you a visit, since we are neighbors now. Bishop Tissier has told me of your work. I'd like to meet the girls living in this orphanage. Or is it a school, or perhaps both? Doesn't matter. Bring them down."

The surprise guest was the same Nazi officer who'd taken my fish. He was speaking to Révérende Mère in the same nasty way he had that night; like he was in charge of everything, even La Maison. That thought sent alarm bells ringing through my head.

Sœur Louise Claire was also listening at the kitchen door when she realized I was there behind her.

"Leave that child and run upstairs now. When they send the girls downstairs, hold a baby in your arms, and try to stay behind the others," she said, shooing me up the back stairs.

"Why?"

"Do as I say, Désirée. Go on, hurry."

I ran upstairs, still confused about why she wanted me to hold a baby. I didn't really enjoy caring for the babies. They were sticky and cried all the time. But when I lined up with the other girls being led down the front stairs, I gathered up a sleeping baby and cradled it to my shoulder, being careful not to wake it.

I followed the girls into the dining room, staying at the end and sheltering behind Sœur Marguerite, who'd led us in and organized us into two neat rows along the wall. Révérende Mère, Bishop Tissier, Père Phillipe and the Nazi officers stood at the long table, two bottles of wine and six glasses waiting in front of them.

When we filed into the room, the Kommandant was still talking. "As I said, Madame, the morality of my men, and that of the local population, is of the utmost importance to the Fuhrer and therefore to me. I will not tolerate the... How do you say *ausschweifung*?"

"Debauchery," the Révérende Mère responded flatly.

"*Ja*, debauchery. I will not have it in my ranks. The men can have their fun in Paris if they must, but not here, under my command," the Kommandant said to the room.

"A commendable sentiment, Kommandant." Révérende Mère's face was an unreadable mask.

"The move to the new headquarters will help to curtail some of it. However, I require your assistance, Madame. I want two of your girls to serve at my weekly staff dinners."

A gasp from Therese earned her a stern look from Révérende Mère.

The Kommandant walked around the table, continuing his lecture.

"The women currently working there are totally unsuitable for this task. I find French women too distracting for my men, and the priests won't do at all. No, two young girls would be better. Perhaps I can find one who might remind the men of their families at home and what we're here to accomplish."

He walked up the line of girls as he spoke, looking closely at some and completely ignoring others, his gaze always lingering longer on the girls with fair complexions and blonde hair. When he got to the end of the line, he turned around to retrace his steps, then stopped when he spotted me, standing half hidden behind Sœur Marguerite.

He took me by the elbow and brought me forward to stand in front of him. Then, without saying a word, he took the baby from my arms and unceremoniously handed the infant to Sœur Marguerite, whose discomfort around babies was only slightly less than my own. By then, the baby had awoken and was making an awful racket. Sœur Marguerite passed the child to Sœur Louise Claire, who reluctantly took it away.

When the room was quiet once more, the Kommandant bent down, looking directly at me.

"Ja. It is you. The little Aryan Fish girl," he said, then he spoke to the other officer. "*Erinnerst du dich an Bruener? Das ist die kleine Dresden-Puppe, von der ich dir erzählt habe.*"

The soldier glanced at me, then sharply nodded his head. "*Jawohl. Sie sieht aus wie eine Dresdner Puppe.*"

I held my expression still, a mask holding the turmoil inside me tightly in check. Then would not be the time to make a scene, but I screamed inside my head as I heard the Kommandant's next announcement.

"This girl is perfect. Exactly what I was looking for."

"Kommandant, s'il vous plaît. She is too young, barely eight years old." Révérende Mère argued.

"Ah, but Madame, she was not too young last June when you took her on the inspection tour of your farms. Nor too young to help harvest your vineyards, I imagine," he said, dismissing the nun and her objections. Then he shifted his steely gaze back to me.

"I seem to recall you telling me you were going to cook those fish. Pity I didn't let you. The fool of a cook ruined them. I wonder, *kleiner Liebling*, how would you have prepared them?"

He acted as if he were a special guest, and we all should be happy to entertain and indulge him. It made me so angry and terrified it was difficult to control my feelings. I wasn't sure if I really had to answer him, but knew I didn't want to. He singled me out and used that word again. Aryan. I didn't know what it meant and hated being called something I didn't understand.

"Answer him, Désirée," Révérende Mère said.

Fixing my gaze on the portrait of Madame Elise, hanging directly behind the Kommandant, I pulled whatever strength I could from it. It was all I could do to keep my voice steady and loud enough to be heard while feeling the stares of everyone in the room. Stoically, I recited the simplified steps of preparing Maman's Crusted Trout with Lemon.

When I finished, I kept my eyes riveted to those of Madame Elise. The Kommandant took my face in his hand and forced my eyes to meet his. He wasn't rough, but his touch sent a ripple of dread shooting down my spine.

"Where did you learn such skills, *kleiner Liebling*? Where were you born?" he asked, holding me captive with his stare.

"In the north Monsieur. Maman taught me."

"She will do perfectly, Madame," the Kommandant announced, finally releasing my face from his grasp. Then he walked down the line of girls once more, stopping to regard Annalise for a moment, but then he rejected her for the younger and blonder Giselle. "This one will do as well."

Once his selection was complete, he dismissed the rest of the girls with a wave of his hand, except for Giselle and me. He ordered us to serve the evening meal as a demonstration of our skills.

Révérende Mère's eyes gave silent instructions to the nuns as they guided the rest of the frightened girls back upstairs. She then turned back to her supper guests, looking for the Bishop's support to curtail any further depredation to her household, but the old priest had shifted his attention to the bottles of wine waiting on the table.

"Sœur Marguerite, take the girls to the kitchen. They can assist Sœur Louise Claire with the meal service this evening. I'm sure our guests are hungry by now," Révérende Mère instructed.

We retreated to the kitchen where Sœur Louise Claire was waiting to console us, and to help instruct us in the proper way to serve the meal.

"Révérende Mère and I will both be there with you," Sœur Marguerite assured us. "Try not to be frightened, girls. If you don't remember something, look at me. I'll try to help." Then she returned to the dining room.

"Hush child. We've no time for tears." Sœur Louise Claire told Giselle as she tied a fresh apron around the girl's waist.

"But why do I have to? Annalise or Janine know what to do, not me. Why did he pick me? What if I make a mistake? What will happen, Sœur?" Giselle cried.

"Keep your eyes on me, Giselle. Do what I do," I said, with a lot more confidence than I felt.

How hard can it be?

I felt bad for her. Giselle wasn't a kitchen helper. She had found her talents best suited to taking care of the younger children, especially the babies. Giselle had lived most of her life with the nuns at La Maison, and because of that, she had no truly bad experiences. The poor girl did not know what the Germans were capable of.

Sœur Louise Claire gave us a few minutes of basic instruction in formal food service, then sent us out with the first of four courses, waiting at the kitchen door to help if needed.

By the end of the meal, Giselle and I stood by the dining room wall, trembling with exhaustion and fear. The Kommandant approved our performance, then ordered Révérende Mère to deliver us to the kitchen at his headquarters each Monday and Thursday afternoon, to serve during his staff dinners. No amount of discussion, reasoning, or cajoling from Révérende Mère, or Bishop Tissier, would change the man's mind.

"But, to allay your fears Madame, I will have my assistant, *Leutnant* Bruener, escort the girls back to your doorstep at the end of the evening," the Kommandant assured her.

"Make no mistake, Madame, this is an honor and an opportunity for these girls to show their worth to the Reich. So far, I've restrained my hand regarding you and your home. Don't make me regret that decision," he said, his voice both charming and threatening. Then he rose from his seat. "My compliments to your cook. Thank you for a pleasant evening. I look forward to our next meeting."

He clicked his heels together, dipping his head in a formal bow before departing with Leutnant Bruener, leaving the Bishop and Père Phillipe to deal with the tempest obviously brewing inside Révérende Mère.

"Your Excellency, this is intolerable. We cannot let him use these girls in this way. They are innocents and have nothing to do with this conflict. The church must protect them. You must do something," Révérende Mère said as soon as the front door closed.

Bishop Tissier was an old man, and I could see from the slump of his shoulders he had no interest in pursuing any conflict between Révérende Mère and the Kommandant. He held her gaze for a moment, then lifted his glass to finish the last of his wine, and with a sigh of satisfaction, gently placed the glass on the table.

"There is nothing I can do, Révérende Mère. I am sorry, but I must not create any controversy or bring undue attention. The Kommandant has the cooperation of the new *Magistrat*, and I must think of the welfare of the entire diocese. You should be grateful he needs you and your farms. This could have gone far worse." He rose from his chair. "Merci, Révérende Mère, for your understanding. Please give my thanks to Sœur Louise Claire for the delicious meal. Père Phillipe, I believe it's time to depart. Révérende Mère, we'll speak again."

Sœur Marguerite escorted the two priests to the door, bid them goodnight, then returned to the dining room where Révérende Mère was sitting at the table, brooding over the events of the evening. Both nuns seemed to have forgotten Giselle and me, still standing silently along the wall and awaiting instruction.

"Révérende Mère, may we be excused?" I asked timidly.

She raised her head in surprise, clearly having forgotten we were waiting for her, for her reassurance.

"I am so sorry, girls. I..." she stopped and sighed, shaking her head.

"You did well tonight, both of you. Tomorrow Sœur Louise Claire and Sœur Marguerite will work with you again, to prepare you. Go to bed now and get some rest." She rose from her seat to give each of us a kiss on the forehead as she sent us off to bed.

Giselle was happy to escape the room and ran up the back stairs to the dormitory. I stood there for a moment, troubled by the events of the evening, by everything I heard.

"Révérende Mère? You told me they weren't looking for m... a little girl. That wasn't true. He came here looking for girls, and he picked me, first," I said, my eyes full of tears.

Révérende Mère faced me, the truth of my accusation stinging in her expression.

"What I told you is still true, Désirée," she said, holding my gaze. "He picked you because of how you look, not who you are. You and Giselle look like girls from Germany, with your blonde hair and blue eyes. You remind him of his home. That's why he picked you both, and for no other reason."

"But I don't want to be a German girl, Révérende Mère. I'm a French girl." I whined, thoroughly exhausted and frightened by then.

"I know, Désirée, but you must pretend to be as he sees you. And you must hide what's in your heart. If you behave as he expects you to, like an obedient girl who looks like his home, he'll not see the girl you are. Go to bed now. We will talk in the morning," she said, placing another kiss on my brow.

"This is your fault. That Nazi picked Giselle because of you. This wouldn't have happened if you never came here," Annalise snarled as I walked into the dormitory. Giselle was sitting on her bed, being consoled and obviously shaken by what had happened.

"He picked us because we look like German girls," I said defensively, then added. "I'm sorry, Giselle."

Being around the Germans terrified me as much as it did her, so I was sorry about what happened to us, but I didn't understand how it could be my fault.

"You should be. Since you came here, everything has changed. Why can't you be like the rest of us? You're always showing off, like you did with that stupid fish recipe."

Normally, this would be the time Janine would step in and stop Annalise from doing any actual damage, but Janine had already pulled the blanket over her head. Even Rachel had covered her head. Right then, I didn't have the energy or even the courage to stand up to Annalise. Nothing I could say would change what happened.

"I'm sorry Giselle. I'm sorry, Annalise. I really am."

I knew Annalise wouldn't let it go. Giselle was like a little sister to her, and Annalise was fiercely protective. She turned away from me, returning to comfort Giselle as they both settled down for the night.

Soon the dormitory quieted into the normal sounds of sleeping children, all except for me. I lay wrapped in the old woman's shawl, as I had nearly every night since coming to La Maison. Trembling with exhaustion, my troubled mind raced with everything I heard and learned that night. I wasn't sure what it all meant, especially the part about the Aryan race.

For most of the evening, the Kommandant had lectured the room about the superiority of the Germanic Aryan race and the inferiority of other races, especially the Jews. It was obvious he didn't like the Jews, calling them filthy animals.

I didn't understand why he hated people because of their race. Papa taught me that a person's behavior would be the measure of how they're treated; if you're a good person who treats others well, then you'll have a lot of friends, or, if you're mean or a bad person, then no one will like you. It seemed so simple, so basic. That a person was bad because of their race made no sense to me. Then I remembered what Rachel told me about her family in Poland, and shivers ran down my back.

The other thing making me nervous was that the Kommandant had called me an Aryan girl. I knew this label would create a bigger problem for me, setting me apart from the other children. I didn't want to look Aryan. I wanted to be like everyone else.

I realized that how I looked to them, to the Kommandant, was what might keep me safe, if only I could pretend well enough. Révérende Mère was right, I had to pretend to be the German girl the Kommandant thought I was and hide who I really am behind a pretend mask, the way I hid my fear of them.

He doesn't know who I am; I told myself, praying it was true.

He didn't come to find ME.

He didn't see ME; he only saw a girl who looks German.

As I struggled to find sleep, a final thought came to me.

Désirée Rondeau is dead.

I must pretend to be whoever I must be, so I can be safe, so I can survive.

Remember: be brave, be strong, be clever.

That night, the nightmares came back.

Chapter 20

Insurance

We walked into the large kitchen at the back of what used to be the Bishop's House until the Nazis converted it into their headquarters. Révérende Mère had Giselle and me on either side of her, clinging to our hands. It felt to me like we were the lambs, and she was reluctantly leading us to the slaughter.

"Bonjour Madame. I am Révérende Mère of..."

"Come in," the woman ordered, waving her hand in a not-too-friendly greeting. "I know who you are. *Herr* Steigler told me to expect you." She was a tall, imposing creature in a prim black dress, the tight bun at the back of her head emphasizing her sharp features. "They look sturdy enough. Are they trained?" she asked, looking down at Giselle and me with an arched brow.

"They are, though neither girl speaks German. Your instructions must be in French. They will both do as you ask." Révérende Mère gave our hands a gentle squeeze.

"I'm sure they will," the woman said as she handed each of us a freshly starched apron. "Leutnant Bruener will return them to you at the end of the evening, per Herr Steigler's orders. Now, Madame, I have much to do to prepare them for this evening. Bonjour Madame. Follow me, girls," she said, dismissing the nun and turning to lead us to our fate.

Révérende Mère gave us a blessing and watched as we reluctantly followed the woman through the door leading into the depths of the Kommandant's new headquarters.

"I am *Frau* Möller. I have worked for Herr Steigler for many years. I know what he likes, and what he doesn't like. You will learn this, or be sorry you didn't," she said with dark cruel eyes staring down at us.

Giselle and I stood silently with our eyes glued to the lecturing woman, both of us struggling to still our fear. As Frau Möller continued her instruction, I listened to not just what she was saying, but how she was speaking. After a while I was sure she was German, though her accent didn't give it away; her French sounded practically normal. It was more in the way she acted; rigid like hardened wood, very unlike most French women, who were softer when around children.

By the end of the lecture, I knew there would be no chance of making Frau Möller an ally and friend the way I had with Sœur Louise Claire. Frau Möller didn't seem to like children.

The rules were simple:

Be on time, be clean and groomed, which meant braided hair, clean hands, and a clean dress.

Do not speak unless spoken to directly.

Do exactly as instructed at all times.

Disobedience will be punished.

And pretend to be a German girl, I reminded myself, though I wasn't exactly sure how to do that.

Of all the things Révérende Mère said to us that morning, 'Stand straight.' was what stuck in my mind, which at the time, didn't seem that important. Mastering my fear seemed much more urgent. But I soon realized my posture would become a sort of security blanket in a situation I was powerless to control. My body was the only thing I *could* control, so

I quickly learned to master any fidgety movements and nervous energy. To display such childish traits would earn a slap or a pinch from Frau Möller, who was quick and ruthless in her punishment.

The work wasn't difficult; dinner service and clean up afterwards, but it was who we served that made us both tremble inside.

Six Nazi officers, including the Kommandant, attended the staff dinners. They paid little or no attention to us, except for that first night.

There wasn't a formal introduction, but as Giselle and I stood waiting for the signal to begin service, the Kommandant was announcing something, and each man at the table reacted differently. He raised his hand, halting any outbursts, then allowed each man to have his say.

Eventually I knew each of them by name and reputation, but that first night I secretly gave a few of them nicknames, which were easier for me to remember.

I named *Hauptmann* Rolph Klein, *Le Charmeur,* because of his striking good looks and dazzling smile. He reminded me of the photos I'd seen of movie stars in the magazines my sisters would read. He was the first to speak, and from his tone and the muffled laughter of the other officers, he wasn't happy about the change. His tone was pleasant enough, but something about the way he looked at the Kommandant sent alarm bells ringing through my head, though I wasn't sure why.

Le Charmeur wasn't the only one who triggered alarms for me. The one I named *Le Loup* kept looking at us with an odd smile on his face, which gave me an uneasy feeling. He was Hauptmann Stefan Wolff, and I sensed he was someone we should avoid.

Le Soldat Jouet was the youngest and most junior officer of the group. He was Leutnant Fritz Bruener, and he served directly under the Kommandant as his assistant. He said little the first night, just took notes for the Kommandant and said 'Jawohl mein Herr' a lot.

Somehow, we made it through the night with nothing more serious than a few slaps and pinches from Frau Möller, usually for spilling something or rattling the plates too much. Frau Möller gave us a last lecture at the end of the evening, with a stern warning she wouldn't be as lenient the next time.

It was Le Soldat Jouet's duty to take us back to La Maison at the end of the evening. As we walked through the darkened street, I could tell he was trying to be friendly, to ease the trauma we'd just been through.

"I have girls, sisters, like you in my house. Me wish war finish soon. Go home to sisters," Le Soldat Jouet said in broken French, smiling a toothy smile. He wasn't much different from Jean-Michel, though he looked older. He had a gentle way, but a clear sense of his duty, as his behavior showed around the other officers during the evening. Even though he wasn't as frightening as the others, he was still a Nazi and no friend to me.

That first walk back to La Maison was one of the few times I ventured to ask him anything. "Monsieur, why did the Kommandant want us to serve his dinners?"

The question took him by surprise, and he stopped to look at me for a moment, his homely face filled with pity he couldn't, or wouldn't, disguise.

"You are *Versicherung*. I not know the word. So your mother obeys the Kommandant's orders. Obey and nothing bad will happen."

I didn't know what versicherung meant, but I didn't believe the last part. Nothing but bad things had happened since the Germans had come to France, and I didn't think being obedient would make it better. The Kommandant was obviously someone not to be crossed. Even his own men

157

seemed unwilling to challenge him. I didn't want to find out what would happen if he ever became angry.

Révérende Mère was waiting on the front step of La Maison, silhouetted by the light from the open doorway, her hands tucked into the sleeves of her habit. She didn't move when she saw us approach, apparently waiting for the soldier to bring us home as promised. When we reached the front door, she stepped down onto the sidewalk and took our hands, gently pulling us to her side.

"Merci Monsieur. Bonne nuit," she said, guiding us into the house and closing the door.

"Are you alright? Did they hurt you? Tell me everything that happened, girls." She led us into her office.

"Révérende Mère, I don't want to go back there." Giselle cried, her pent-up emotions finally finding release. "They pinched me and slapped me. Please don't make me go back," she cried, then collapsed into a puddle of tears on the couch.

"Is this true, Désirée? Did they punish you?" she asked, her green eyes flashing fire.

"Not the soldiers. They didn't touch us. It was Frau Möller. If we did something wrong, like dropping a plate or spilling food, or if we didn't move fast enough or stand straight enough, she would slap us or pinch our arms," I said, rubbing the sore spot on my arm.

"Tell me everything, Désirée."

"Frau Möller has four rules: Be on time and neatly groomed, no talking unless spoken to, always do exactly as told, and she'll punish us if we disobey. It was hard because she wanted everything to be perfect, but

Giselle and I were the only ones serving, and the soldiers scared us. Only the soldiers were there with us. Frau Möller waited in the other room, watching from the doorway. Whenever we went to take in the dirty plates and get the next course, she would be there waiting to punish us for what we did wrong. She said she wouldn't be as lenient next time." My pent-up tension finally released in a shiver that ran through my body.

Révérende Mère looked us over for any physical damage, then asked, "Did the soldiers speak to either of you?"

"No, Révérende Mère. They didn't speak to us at all. Except for the one who brought us home, he told us he had sisters, and he wished the war would end so he could go home."

Révérende Mère gathered us both into her arms and hugged us as tightly as she dared, then gave us both a kiss.

"Run to the kitchen, girls. Sœur Louise Claire has some warm milk that will ease your rest tonight," she said, releasing us, then she returned to her desk.

"Révérende Mère?" My voice seemed to startle her when she found me still standing in the doorway.

"Yes, Désirée. Do you need something?"

"I was wondering if you know what *versicherung* means." I asked, hoping I pronounced it correctly.

"You heard that word tonight? From whom?" she asked, concern obviously building in her voice again.

"The soldier who walked us home. I asked him why the Kommandant wanted Giselle and me to serve his dinner. He said we were *versicherung* so you would follow the Kommandant orders. He said nothing bad would happen if we obey. I don't really believe the last part, though."

Révérende Mère closed her eyes and lowered her head into her hands. It took her a moment to compose herself enough to answer.

"The word means insurance," she said, releasing a deep sigh. "The Kommandant believes he can force me to obey his commands by insisting you and Giselle work for him. He needs to control me and what we have, and he's willing to use my girls to accomplish this goal. I'm sorry, Désirée, but that is the truth of it."

"I want you to know, Désirée, I will do everything I can to keep you, Giselle, and the rest of the girls out of harm's way. For now, it seems the Kommandant has been true to his word and you both have returned unharmed, relatively. The next time, you must both work hard to avoid Frau Möller's punishment."

She held my gaze for a long time, her eyes brooding and weary.

"It's alright, Révérende Mère. I thought that's what it was. Don't worry. We'll do better next time. Neither of us wants to be pinched again. Bonne nuit, Révérende Mère."

As I walked away, I heard the nun drop to her knees and whisper a prayer in her lilting accent, "Jesus, Mary, and Joseph, save us from this nightmare."

Chapter 21

Language skills

Monday and Thursday, Monday and Thursday, week after week, month after month. Those days were waking nightmares for Giselle and me. Révérende Mère tried everything she could to get us released from the Kommandant's service, but nothing made any difference. We were only children and had no choice but to obey. I dreamed of running away, but there was nowhere in France to hide anymore. The Nazis were everywhere.

Eventually, Giselle and I learned our jobs and performed them with as much precision as possible, avoiding the worst of Frau Möller's punishment. But it was rare we returned to La Maison without having received at least one hard pinch or slap.

Frau Möller was one of the worst parts of having to work for the Nazis. It seemed nothing could please her. She never smiled, never laughed, nor even spoke kindly to anyone, except Le Soldat Jouet. He was the only one she seemed to like even a little, other than the Kommandant, who she appeared devoted to.

We started referring to her as *La Dame Noire*, the Dark Lady, because she always wore black and wore her dark hair pulled back into a tight bun. She reminded us of the witches from the old stories.

Most of the soldiers ignored us. We were just children, after all. The only exception was Kommandant Steigler. He took particular interest in our progress, always watching us and commenting to Frau Möller at the end of the evening, which sometimes earned us a final pinch.

For me, the very worst part was not La Dame Noire, nor even my fear of the Nazis—I'd mastered my fear by pretending to be what they wanted—No, it wasn't fear that bothered me; it was not being able to understand what they were saying.

At first, I struggled with their harsh words and phrases, the sound of it so foreign to my ear. I knew they were deciding the fate of everything around me, and I couldn't understand what they were saying.

Eventually, I started really listening to them, listening to their words and observing their reactions. Bit by bit, I could put a meaning to a word or phrase; *Guten Abend* meant good evening. The officers would all say this when they came in for dinner. *Danke* meant thank you, *Gute Nacht* meant good night.

At first it was simple things like that, but week by week, month by month, I understood them, not everything but a word and phrase here and there. I even secreted away a French and German dictionary I found in the library of La Maison. I studied the German words and their French translations, page by page, committing it all to memory. It was the only thing I could do that felt like defiance.

I told no one, instinctively knowing it was dangerous. I got good at pretending I didn't understand them until I started understanding things that were hard not to react to.

After months of working for them, the soldiers no longer took any notice of us. We became ornamental servant girls, there to remind them of home and nothing more. They became more arrogant in their control of everything, and therefore less cautious about what they said when we were around.

"*Was sind Ihre Befehle für die Gefangenen?* (What are your orders for the prisoners?)" Le Charmeur asked at the end of dinner in early January 1941.

The previous day, Alex told me the Nazis had rounded up several local men accused of sabotaging the railroad tracks outside of Châlons a few days earlier. Their families were petitioning the Magistrat for their release, insisting their family members were innocent. But it was no use. The Magistrat would not intervene. Their fate was in the hands of Kommandant Steigler.

"*Führen Sie die Anführer aus, und schicken Sie den Rest in die Arbeitslager.* (Execute the leaders and send the rest to the work camps.)" was the Kommandant's answer. He was so cold, giving no thought of the lives he was taking. It was just another order he expected to be obeyed.

As I refreshed his wineglass, I willed my hands to stillness and bit the inside of my bottom lip to prevent any sound from escaping when I heard him pass the sentence. Nothing I could do would make any difference to the fate of those men.

"*Danke, Désirée,*" the Kommandant said, smiling at me as I carefully lifted the wine bottle away from his glass. "Clear the table and then you both may go."

We quickly, but methodically, did as instructed, eager to be gone from them and back to the safety of La Maison, at least for a little while.

It was always easier for Giselle to switch back and forth between the Nazis and La Maison. When we were with them, she'd do her best to do what

163

they asked, but never without a timid terror she couldn't hide. When she returned home to La Maison, Annalise would sweep her up and spend an hour consoling her. Giselle would cry about how frightened she was and how they punished her more than they did me, which was true.

For me, it wasn't as easy. I had no shoulder to cry on. Working for the Nazis had changed my relationship with the other girls, especially Janine and Rachel. They were still friendly, but both girls had become cautious around me, apparently afraid of being noticed by the Nazis if they got too close.

It felt like I had to wear a different pretend mask for everyone, always pretending to be someone I wasn't. With the Nazis, I pretended to be the obedient 'German' child. For Révérende Mère, I was the brave orphan girl. With Sœur Louise Claire, I was the clever kitchen helper. I was Alex's funny little sister. And with Annalise, I was always sorry, because for her, everything bad was my fault.

During those months, I began losing any idea of who I really was. My entire focus was always on pleasing the person in front of me in whatever way necessary. Désirée Rondeau was dead. I hardly thought of her anymore. Everything the old woman and Révérende Mère had said about being safe at La Maison was a lie. No one was safe from the Nazis anymore.

I was sure of one thing; I was the only person I could count on, and I needed to survive, no matter what happened.

In March 1941, at the end of the farewell dinner for a few of his staff, who were being reassigned, the Kommandant sent Giselle to the kitchen to clean up, and he took me into his office with Le Soldat Jouet. I thought he was going to punish me for something, but I didn't know for what.

"Come over here, Désirée."

I reluctantly obeyed, moving to stand in front of him by his desk. He pulled a folder from the drawer and from it took out two charts with photos. One photo had just eyes of different colors and the other of several children's faces with different color eyes and hair. He held the charts up next to my face, apparently comparing me to the images. I didn't know why he did that, and it made me very uncomfortable.

"Exactly as I thought. There is no mistake. She is perfect. You see Bruener? She has exactly the right traits," he said, holding the chart up to my face again, so the junior officer could see.

"Jawohl, mein herr," Le Soldat Jouet responded.

"Ask Frau Möller to come in. I have a task for her."

A moment later, La Dame Noire entered the Kommandant's office with suspicion in her eyes when she saw me standing next to him.

"Frau Möller, I have a special task for you. Frau Steigler will arrive on Friday's train from Munich, and I need your help in making my new home ready for her."

"Of course, Herr Steigler." I could tell by La Dame Noire's expression that what he said did not thrill her.

"There's another matter, Frau Möller. I've decided to take Désirée into my home, to raise her as a proper German girl." He stroked my back as he spoke and it was torture trying to keep my body still, trying to curb my reaction to what he said.

"Her work with you these past months has shown that she is, as I originally thought, a true Aryan child. I believe it's my duty to make sure she lives up to that potential. Take the girl to the dressmaker in town tomorrow and find her some suitable garments. I want her properly dressed and ready for my wife when she arrives. Danke, Frau Möller. Bruener can take them back now." He dismissed us both with a wave of his hand.

"Jawhol, mein Herr," she said, but the scowl on her face clearly expressed her feelings about the order.

When we left the Kommandant's office, it was all I could do to walk calmly, and not go screaming out of the building. I hadn't understood every word, but I understood his wife was coming, and he was planning on making me a German girl. I couldn't breathe.

A hard pinch on my arm by La Dame Noire as we returned to the kitchen forced me to wince, releasing a solitary tear.

"It seems your fortunes have changed, girl," La Dame Noire said with a sneer. "Hurry and finish. Leutnant Bruener is here to take you back." Then she spoke with Le Soldat Jouet before releasing us. "Tell the nun the girl Désirée must be ready for me in the morning. I'll fetch her at nine sharp. If the nun has questions, tell her to speak with Kommandant Steigler."

Le Soldat Jouet delivered us back to La Maison a short time later. He gave the message to Révérende Mère, clicked his heels together, pivoted, and walked away, leaving her stunned.

Giselle and I hurried into the house; she running to the comforting arms of Annalise, and me marching straight into Révérende Mère's office.

"I can't, Révérende Mère, I won't do it. I'm not German, I'm French," I screamed.

"What is this about, Désirée? Why is that woman coming for you in the morning?"

"His wife is coming on Friday, and he wants me to live with them in his new house. He wants to make me German. I can't, I can't, I won't!" My pent-up anger and defiance spilled out at last.

"How do you know this, Désirée? What did he say to you?"

"Nothing... I... I mean I heard him tell La Dame Noire, Frau Möller, he was going to take me to his new house and for her to take me to get some clothes, so I'd be ready for his wife when she arrives. I don't *want* to live with them, Révérende Mère. Please don't let him take me." I cried, frustrated and angry, tears pouring down my cheeks.

Révérende Mère looked at me sternly. "You heard them speaking? Were they speaking in German or French?"

My eyes flashed open, and I knew my secret was out. Révérende Mère would know they spoke only German to each other.

She took a deep breath, shaking her head as she released it. "How long have you understood them, Désirée?"

A little shiver went through my tired body. "For a few months, Révérende Mère," I confessed, sniffling away my tears.

Révérende Mère shook her head again, worry filling those green eyes. "I'll speak with the Kommandant. There's no need to say anything about this to the others yet. Let me handle it. Go to bed now. We'll talk in the morning." The look of worry and hopelessness I saw in her eyes confirmed what I already knew. Neither of us had any choice but to obey the Kommandant's orders.

Later, I wrapped the old woman's shawl around me, seeking whatever comfort it would give, and tried to quiet my mind enough to go to sleep. I made a vow to myself that no matter what happened, I would never become a German. The adults could control everything else about my life, but what was in my heart was mine alone, and I would always be French in my heart.

Chapter 22

Final days

There were no formalities, no pleasantries exchanged, nor promises made. La Dame Noire arrived at the door of La Maison at precisely nine the following morning and waited on the sidewalk for Révérende Mère to present me.

"*Komm mit mir, Mädchen.*" La Dame Noire took my hand, obviously not caring if I understood her and expecting to be obeyed.

I was powerless to do anything but put on my Aryan girl mask and go with her, if not willingly, then at least obediently.

In a different world and a different life, that morning might have been a fairy-tale adventure for an eight-year-old girl. New clothes, new shoes and stockings and being fussed over by the dressmaker and her assistant like I was a princess. Only I wasn't a princess, and the look of horror and pity in the seamstress's eyes reminded me this wasn't a fairytale.

"Have these things delivered to this address by Thursday morning," La Dame Noire instructed the dressmaker curtly, handing her a piece of paper.

The woman looked up, stunned when she read the address. "To this address, Madame?" she asked.

"Oui. That is correct. Is there a problem?"

"No, Madame, no problem," the dressmaker quickly answered. "Merci, Madame. I will have them for you on Thursday morning."

"Merci. Come, child," La Dame Noire said.

I followed her out of the shop and back to La Maison.

I was silent on the way back, but she was not. She muttered to herself in German the entire time. Obviously upset by the turn of events, she said things like, "Why did he have to send for her?" and "I'm the one who has helped him from the beginning," and "This is a mistake, he must see that." She didn't know I could understand her, and based on her mood, might not even have cared if she had known. It was apparent that trouble was brewing between the Kommandant and this woman, and I was in the crossfire.

She left me at the front door with a final order, "Be ready on Thursday, girl."

When I went in, I could hear loud voices coming from Révérende Mère's office down the hallway. It sounded like Sœur Louise Claire and Sœur Marguerite were arguing with her.

"We can't allow this, Révérende Mère. She's been through so much already." Sœur Louise Claire said.

"Isn't there something the Bishop can do?" Sœur Marguerite asked.

"I've already tried. He said he won't intervene, and I must not make trouble. The Kommandant has made it clear that La Maison, the work we do and the children we help, have no value to him. If I fight him about this, it will put everything and everyone here at risk. I'm sorry Sœurs, there's nothing I can do. Any legal adoption will take time to go through channels, but that will not stop him from taking her," Révérende Mère said, her own distress apparent in her voice.

I didn't wait to hear more. Misery and hopelessness overwhelmed me as I ran through the house and out to the courtyard garden to be alone with my tears.

It didn't take long for the news to find its way to the girls at La Maison. By the end of the day, the dressmaker's assistant had told her younger sister, who was friends with Annalise, and that was all it took for my life to sink into even deeper misery.

I overheard Annalise tell a group of girls about it as they came into the dining room for dinner that night.

"You see. I told you she wasn't like us. She's a *Boche*, like the rest of them. I'll be happy to see her leave. She's been nothing but trouble since she arrived." Annalise sneered in my direction.

"If I were you, Annalise, I'd be careful about what I say about Désirée. If the Kommandant is really going to adopt her, he probably won't like hearing the things you say about her," Janine warned, stepping around the older girl.

"I'm not scared of them. The Boche will be gone soon, and so will she," Annalise announced with bravado, turning her back to Janine.

I couldn't face any of them. Nothing I could do would change anything. It felt like I had some terrible disease they all could catch if they came too close, and I didn't want to contaminate them. They kept their distance, most too scared they might be the next girl taken by the Nazis.

I spent my last days at La Maison avoiding them and sleepwalking through my chores. It was especially hard working with Sœur Louise Claire because she had been like a mother to me since I arrived, and I couldn't bear the thought of not being with her every day.

Neither of us could talk about it. There was nothing to say. We silently did our work, struggling to hold back our tears. When I couldn't hold them back any longer, I ran from her, out to the courtyard garden, to cry in solitude among the bean towers and cabbage pots flourishing there.

Why? Why?! Why?!! When there were no divine answers offered, I collapsed between the pots, sobbing into my hands.

"Désirée? Are you alright?" Alex asked, sitting down next to me and pulling me into his arms, allowing my misery to soak the front of his shirt.

"Ah, petite sœur. Cry as much as you need to. I'm here, I'm here," he said, soothing my distress.

"I know you're scared, Désirée. Who wouldn't be? But you've been working for him for a long time and the worst thing that's happened to you is a slap or two from La Dame Noire. I bet that won't happen again once his wife arrives." Alex was always seeing the bright side of the darkest moments.

"But he wants to make me German. He said I have perfect Aryan traits, whatever that means." My sobs were turning to frustration. "I'll *never* become like them, no matter what they do to me."

"That's the spirit. Now listen, this is not the end for us. The house he's taken is only a few blocks away, across from Le Petit Jard. We heard they took away the entire Kuklinski family on Monday night. No one knows where. But the next day, we saw the Boches going through the house, throwing out anything personal. Frau Möller was there."

"He told her to get his new house ready for his wife," I said between sniffles.

Alex held my shoulders and looked straight at me, worry and wonder filling his face. "You speak German now, don't you?"

"No, I don't speak it, but I understand a lot." Alex was the only person I really trusted anymore. "It's awful, Alex. Knowing what they say, what they do to people. Sometimes I wish I didn't understand."

"Be careful, Désirée. Don't let him know you understand until he expects you to."

"I know, Alex, I'm careful."

We spent our last hours together making plans about how we would stay in touch. Neither of us thought they'd allow me to come back to La Maison, but Alex had a plan.

"Don't give up," he said, giving me a hug. "Don't forget this either." He reached up and swept his hair back, then tugged on his left ear twice, our new secret signal.

"I won't forget, Alex. Merci, mon ami," I said, holding on to the hope that I wouldn't lose him too.

On Thursday afternoon, I sat in Révérende Mère's office for the last time, waiting to be taken away. I packed what few things I owned into the satchel Maman had given me so long ago; the little doll, a piece of ribbon, the folded drawing of my family (hidden beneath the lining at the bottom), and the old woman's shawl. My clothes I left behind, to be added to the pile for the other orphans. I clung to the strap of my satchel, to the last pieces of my old life, hoping they wouldn't take that away too.

There were no more tears left to shed, nothing to do but wait.

When the silence and the waiting became unbearable, Révérende Mère spoke. "Merci, Désirée, for being such a brave girl. You must continue to be brave and strong and clever, just as Madame Elise told you. That's how you'll survive, how we all will survive. Madame Elise was right in that, at least. I'm sorry I couldn't protect you from this."

"I know, Révérende Mère," was all I could manage.

Moments later the doorbell rang, announcing their arrival and marking the end of my life at La Maison.

When Révérende Mère led me out of the house, Le Soldat Jouet and La Dame Noire were waiting by a big black car with two Nazi flags flying above the idling engine. Le Soldat Jouet stood at attention, his expression unreadable, while La Dame Noire stepped forward to take me in hand. Her face wasn't hiding how she felt, and I had a sinking feeling my life was going to get a lot worse.

"Come with me," was all she said as she grabbed my hand and pulled me into the waiting car.

Chapter 23

La Dame Noire

L a Dame Noire escorted me directly into the Kommandant's study upon arrival at what would be my home for the next three years. She gave my back a nudge as I reluctantly entered the room to stand in front of him.

"Ah, you're here. Good," he said, looking up from the papers spread out on the desk in front of him. He took his time inspecting me, his thoughts unreadable.

"Good," he said again, eyes softening with resolve. "Frau Möller will take you to your room and help you settle in, then you and I will have a little supper together before my staff meeting tonight. Won't that be nice?" he asked, a gentle smile lighting his face.

Most of the time I wasn't sure if he expected an answer, but to be safe I responded with a quiet, "Oui, Monsieur."

"Frau Möller, please take her up and see she has what she needs. I'll see you later, Désirée." Dismissing us both, he waved Le Soldat Jouet forward, who'd been standing at the door to the study. The young soldier clicked his heels together and bowed his head to me as I passed.

I followed La Dame Noire up the stairs to a large sunny room at the front of the house. A tall window looked out onto the street and across to Le Petit Jard on the other side. It was a beautiful room, decorated in pale pastel colors and delicate furniture, made for a young girl. A writing desk with a vase of roses sat next to the door, and a beautiful gold-framed mirror hung above it, reflecting the late afternoon light. The bed had a canopy with pale yellow drapes tied at the corners and a beautiful doll lay against the pillows.

La Dame Noire showed me around the room; the wardrobe filled with the things she ordered a few days earlier, the personal bathroom, and even where they kept the soap and linens.

"Bathe and put these on," she brusquely instructed, laying a cream-colored dress and matching sweater on the bed, then added fresh stockings and a pair of slippers.

"I'll come for you in an hour. Be ready, girl." She spun on her heel and left, closing the door firmly behind her.

As I stood in the middle of the stolen room, shaking with suppressed fear, I knew another girl had occupied the room only days before. Her presence lingered there. She and her family were missing, taken away by the Nazis. No one knew where. Taken by the whim of the same man who had taken me. I had only one choice: to obey.

An hour later, after being carefully inspected by La Dame Noire, she took me to the dining room.

"Come in, come in, *liebling*. Let me see your new dress. Beautiful, yes. Perfect, for a perfect little girl." The Kommandant twirled his hand around, which meant I should turn around for his inspection and praise. His tone was light and charming, not at all like the serious and commanding tone he usually had, and that made me nervous.

"Sit here next to me, Désirée, so we can get better acquainted," he said, then he addressed La Dame Noire, who was waiting behind him. "Please bring in our supper, then you may go, Frau Möller. I won't need your services tonight. We'll speak in the morning. Danke."

La Dame Noire is being dismissed.

A tremble flashed through me when I saw the anger behind her eyes as she stared at me over his shoulder before leaving the room. That look scared me more than anything.

I had a hard time controlling my trembles during that first meal alone with the Kommandant. He spent most of the time telling me what a lucky girl I was, and what a wonderful life I was being given, and that I should always strive to be worthy of this gift. The rest of the time he spoke of his wife, Frau Steigler, Katarina, who he hadn't seen since the war started. He was sure I would love her as much as he did. He never asked me about myself, he just expected me to comply and be grateful.

"Merci, Monsieur," I dutifully responded at the end of the meal.

"From now on you must say *Danke mein Herr*. Tomorrow you will start learning proper German. *Gute Nacht*, Désirée. Go to bed now. I'll see you in the morning."

"*Donka mine hair. Gutanot*," I echoed, my childish attempt seeming to please him.

Late that night, I awoke startled by La Dame Noire. She was standing next to my bed, panting, the smell of stale wine and cigarettes wafting over me.

"This is your fault," she said in German, then she sat down hard on the bed next to me, grabbing my arm and squeezing. "Your fault... You think you're safe? Not safe, not now... Why couldn't you have been like the other one, stupid and afraid? He wouldn't have noticed you. He had forgotten her, forgotten them both before he saw you."

She was drunk and rambling, squeezing my arm harder and harder. I was afraid to cry out, afraid she'd reach up and kill me in her drunken rage.

"He'll see... He'll see when she comes that this was a mistake. He'll see it was me, has always been me... I'm the one who helped him, not her." Her frustration and anger reached a fevered peak as she gripped my arm like a vise, like she was strangling someone.

I cried out when the pain became unbearable. The sound seemed to bring her to her senses, because she scrambled away from me and stood there panting and shaking, then she walked out.

All I could do was wrap myself up in the old woman's shawl and cry myself back to sleep, not knowing if I'd be alive or dead in the morning.

The sound of the door opening and someone moving around the room woke me. I could tell by the light through the folds of the shawl covering my head that it was morning, and realized I was still alive. I was alive, but every bit as terrified as I was the night before, my eyes still leaking tears that hadn't stopped all night.

"Wake up, girl."

She sounded different from the night before, almost sorry, but she still frightened me, and I pulled the covers tighter over my head.

"None of that, now. Herr Steigler will not like waiting for a petulant girl. Hurry and get dressed," she said while laying out the clothes from yesterday.

That sounded more like the La Dame Noire of the past months, stern and demanding. I expected her to pull me from the bed, but all she did was stand there silently watching me, then she left.

I ran to the bathroom to wash the tears away, my thoughts racing and unfocused.

Don't let them see you cry! I told my red-eyed reflection in the mirror above the sink.

Pretend to be what he wants.

Should I tell him about La Dame Noire? About what she said?

NO!!! She'll kill you!

I dressed, made the bed, then checked my reflection in the mirror above the dressing table. I looked different, like a German girl, I hoped.

Kommandant Steigler was chatting with Le Soldat Jouet at the dining table when I walked in. The scene seemed so normal, so casual, like a family breakfast, and that took me by surprise.

"*Guten Morgen*, Désirée." He seemed to be in a cheerful mood, especially after I repeated his greeting in my childish German.

"*Gootinmorgin, mine hair.*"

"*Das ist gut. Ist sie nicht klug, Bruener?*"

"*Jawohl, mein Herr*," Le Soldat Jouet replied between bites of sausage. He said that a lot.

"Sit down Désirée. Have some breakfast. Here, some eggs and sausages. Do you like sausages?" the Kommandant asked, as if he actually cared if I did or not.

"Oui. Merci, Monsieur. I mean, Ya. Donka mine hair."

That seemed to please him, but then his attention shifted to Le Soldat Jouet.

"I'll be leaving for the station soon. I want you to stay here. The girl is not to leave the house under any circumstances," he ordered in German.

"Jawohl, mein Herr."

"And inform Frau Möller, I noted her absence this morning," he added.

"Jawohl, mein Herr."

I ate quietly as they talked, pretending I didn't understand them, which I realized was going to be harder now that I was around them all the time. I had to be careful to only react or respond to things they expected me to understand. It was terrifying to think what could happen if they knew I'd been understanding them for months.

Be clever, Désirée, be clever. Be a little girl who doesn't understand.

The Kommandant tossed back the remains of his coffee, folded the newspaper he'd been reading, and stood up to leave when La Dame Noire appeared in the doorway.

"Herr Steigler? May I have a word before you leave?" she asked, her tone respectful, but I heard a little uncertainty in the question.

He didn't acknowledge her immediately, instead he reached down and took one of my hands and patted the back of it, speaking to me in French. "I will see you later, my dear. Bruener will be here with you until my return." Then he switched to German when he spoke to La Dame Noire. "I don't have time for this now, Frau Möller. I'll speak with you later," he said, passing her on the way out the door.

Well, that was interesting. It looks like La Dame Noire isn't as important as she thinks she is.

I kept my head down so she wouldn't see I noticed their exchange.

She stared at the closed door, lost in her own thoughts, her body tense with what I could only assume was anger. The noise of Le Soldat Jouet's fork clanging against his plate brought her attention back to the room. She caught my eye before I could look away, held it with a silent warning, then abruptly left the house.

Once she left, I excused myself and retreated to my room, hoping she wouldn't return before the Kommandant came back. Right then, La Dame Noire felt like my biggest threat.

I spent the morning by the bedroom window, looking across to Le Petit Jard, hoping to see Alex standing among the trees, tugging on his ear. I didn't see him, which left me feeling lost and abandoned.

Don't forget me Alex, please.

'Don't give up Désirée', I heard his voice in my head.

Don't forget me, I begged him again.

Chapter 24

Katarina

J ust after mid-day, I heard the Kommandant return, the escalating voices of a man and woman filling the entry beneath my room. I listened at my bedroom door, wondering why they were arguing, and terrified what their argument might mean for me.

"I've already told you, Anton. I'm not staying. The only reason I agreed to come here was for Karl." The woman sounded irritated with an old quarrel.

"If you care about Karl, Katarina, then you must do your duty. You're my wife and Karl's mother and it's time you acted like it. Your place is here with me, not in Salzburg teaching privileged girls how to dance on their toes." He sounded frustrated, like he'd been trying to convince her of something unsuccessfully.

"Duty. That's rich coming from you. Is that what you told yourself when you sent Karl to become part of that hateful Hitler Youth program? Or when you took Leda away? That it was your duty?"

"Enough! I will hear no more about this. Karl knows where his duty lies, and so should you."

I was listening intently when a soft knock on the other side of the door startled me. I jumped away before it opened, and sat down at the desk, book in hand, pretending to read.

"Fraulien Désirée, come with me," Le Soldat Jouet said after he opened the door, his expression as stoic as always, as if he couldn't hear what was going on below.

I followed him down the stairs and into the living room at the front of the house. The Kommandant and his wife were facing away from each other, like two fighters taking a breather between rounds.

I stood in the doorway, waiting for them to notice me. It was his wife who saw me first, and the look on her face was a look I'll never forget. She stared at me for the longest time in wide-eyed, shocked silence; first confusion and then profound sadness and then horror showed plainly on her face.

"Anton, who is this child? What is she doing here?" she asked, her voice trembling.

"Come in, child," he said, pulling me into the room. "Say hello to Frau Steigler."

"Bonjour Madame," I said, too scared to even attempt it in German. She continued staring at me like I was a ghost or something equally horrible.

"I found this little pearl lost among the rabble and knew I had to rescue her. Look at her Katarina. Isn't she perfect?" He seemed so pleased with himself, like I was a special gift he was presenting to her.

"Found her? What do you mean you found her, Anton? Why is she here?" her voice rising again.

"You lost a child, Katarina, and I know the loss has grieved you as much as it has me. This child needs a mother. It's a perfect solution to two problems."

"*Lost?* You think I lost Leda? How dare you say that? You took her from me, Anton. You and that creature, Möller!" she shrieked.

I never heard anyone speak to him that way before, and by the look on his face, he didn't like it. I sat down on a couch by the hearth, hoping they would ignore me, forget I was there.

"That's enough Katarina, I'll hear no more of Frau Möller," he said, a warning behind his eyes. "Just look at her, Kat," his tone softening once again. "Isn't she perfect? She has all the traits of a true Aryan child. This is what our daughter should have been, not an aberration."

"Is that what you thought? That Leda was an aberration?"

He weighed his response before he answered. "The Reich requires strong, whole children to ensure our future as leaders in the new world, not deformities and useless mouths draining our resources."

"Oh, Anton... I can't do this... I shouldn't have come. Send her back to her family." She shook her head, turning away from us both.

"She has no family. I found her in an orphanage. But if you insist on being rid of her, my dear, your wish is my command."

He walked over to the telephone sitting on the side table and dialed a number.

"This is Kommandant Steigler. Have a truck sent to my home. I have an item for disposal."

Disposal? He's going to kill me because she doesn't want me!

It was all I could do to stay still, to pretend I didn't understand.

"No! Anton, you can't!" she screamed, rushing to take the phone from him.

He calmly told the phone to hold a moment, then said, "I assure you Katarina, I can. Resources are precious and we shouldn't waste them on unnecessary mouths."

"Please no, Anton, no. I'll keep her... I'll keep her." Her shoulders slumped in resignation.

"Good. I knew you'd see it my way," he said smugly. "Cancel that order," he told the phone, giving his wife a steely smile.

"There's some business I must attend to at headquarters. I'll return before dinner. Settle in Katarina, get to know the child. I'm sure you'll find her a charming little addition to our household. Bruener will bring your things from the station." He leaned over, kissing her on the cheek, then he left with Le Soldat Jouet.

We were both shy.

Me, because I was afraid; afraid if she didn't like me, she would change her mind and send me away for disposal, and because I wasn't supposed to know that.

I imagined she was shy because she didn't want to be there, and because every time she looked at me, a deep sadness she couldn't hide filled her eyes.

Katarina Steigler was the most beautiful woman I had ever seen, elegant and poised. Her golden blonde hair fell in waves down to her shoulders, and her eyes were as blue as the summer sky. She stood tall and lean with a kind of core strength that reminded me of Révérende Mère.

"What is your name, child?" she asked in perfect French, a gentle smile lighting her face as she sat down next to me.

"Désirée, Madame."

"That's a beautiful name. How old are you, Désirée?"

"Eight, Madame."

"Eight," she repeated with a sigh. "Yes, that would make sense."

She stared at me for a long time, touching my hair and stroking my face, then she seemed to decide something.

"Well, Désirée, it appears the two of us are in the same boat. I suppose we should get to know one another. But first, let's find something to eat. I'm starving. How about you?" she asked, holding out her hand. "Where's the kitchen?"

At that moment I saw a small glimmer of hope, so I took the hand of Katarina Steigler.

Chapter 25

Tante Elsa

"Why don't you know where the kitchen is? How long have you been here?" Katarina asked as we wandered through the house in search of sustenance.

"They brought me here yesterday, Madame. I haven't been in this part of the house before."

We soon found the kitchen at the end of the hall, at the back of the house. It was a cheery kitchen with large windows, lots of cupboards and all the modern conveniences. I sat at a small round table with a cushioned bench tucked into the alcove of a bay window, which looked out to the walled-in courtyard outside. I nervously watched her while she set about heating water for tea, then gathering cheese, bread and fruit for our snack.

"Tell me, Désirée, how did you come to be here with my husband?" Katarina asked, taking the seat next to me at the table.

I had to be careful because I didn't know her, and even though she saved me from disposal, she was still his wife and a German. I would only say what he would confirm.

"The Kommandant came to La Maison last September and chose me and another girl to serve during his staff dinners. Then they brought me here yesterday. Am I going to work for you now, Madame?"

"No Désirée. That's not why you're here." She sighed and shook her head. "Tell me about the orphanage. How long had you been there?"

"Only for a few months before the Kommandant came."

"A few months? That means you arrived at the beginning of the war. What happened to your family? Why were you with the nuns?"

This was dangerous territory, and I wasn't sure how to answer without lying to her, so I just stuck to the simple truth, hoping it would be enough.

"My family died when the war started, and then a priest took me to La Maison." I struggled to still the quiver in my lower lip and hold back the tears threatening to fall. It was still hard talking about my family without feeling the deep loss.

She looked at me for a long time before she spoke again, her voice soft and sorrowful.

"I am so sorry, Désirée. This must be so sad and frightening for you. This war is wrong for a lot of reasons. We shouldn't be here."

She was staring out the bay window, not really looking at anything, and I realized she didn't mean the two of us shouldn't be there, though that was true enough, but that the Germans shouldn't be in France.

"I know this must be hard for you—it's hard for me too—but we both must make the best of it. It's just... you look so much like her." Tears trickled down her cheeks as she spoke, then she pulled me into a tight embrace.

"Ow!" I cried, feeling a sharp pain shoot down my bruised arm. I rubbed it gingerly.

"What is it, child? Are you hurt?"

"No Madame. I'm all right," I said, scooting away from her.

"You're hurt. Let me see." She pulled me towards her to remove the sweater covering the deep purple marks encircling my arm above the elbow.

"Did Anton... did my husband do this to you?" she asked, a horror-stricken look on her face.

"No, Madame, it wasn't him."

"Who then? Who did this to you? This bruise looks new."

Tears filled my eyes again, and I struggled to hold them back. I was afraid to say anything, afraid to tell her about La Dame Noire, afraid of everything.

"Oh, dear child, come here. It's all right, it's all right now. I won't let anyone harm you. You must tell me who did this, so I can protect you." She cradled me as she stroked my hair.

"La Dame Noire," I said, sniffling away my tears.

"Who is La Dame Noire? Is she a nun at the orphanage?"

I sat up to look at her. "Oh no, Madame. They wouldn't hurt any of the girls. It was Frau Möller. She was angry with me, but I don't know why."

"Frau Möller?!" From her tone, it was clear the name was distasteful. Katarina took a deep breath, releasing it with a heavy sigh. Her expression became harder and angrier as she examined the bruises on my arm.

"Don't worry about Frau Möller anymore, Désirée. I won't let her hurt you ever again. I promise," she said, her blue eyes blazing.

At that moment, I didn't believe her, but I pretended I did.

We sat at the table sipping tea and snacking on the bread and cheese and apparently waiting for something.

"*Tante* Elsa and the luggage should be here any minute. She'll get everything sorted out in no time at all. You'll see." She seemed to think this would reassure me.

"Who's Tante Elsa?"

"She's my aunt, my father's youngest sister. She took care of me when my mother died. I was about your age. Tante Elsa has been my closest companion my whole life."

Please don't let her be like La Dame Noire, I silently prayed.

A short time later, Tante Elsa and all the luggage arrived from the station, with the help of Le Soldat Jouet. When she came in, I saw the same look of shocked surprise on the older woman's face as I'd seen on Katarina's.

"Tante Elsa, this is Désirée. Anton has... brought her here to live with us," Katarina explained, the sad look still haunting her eyes.

Recovering her composure, Tante Elsa greeted me with a warm smile and a friendly handshake.

"Bonjour Mademoiselle Désirée. What a delightful surprise." She spoke in flawless French, then immediately switched to German when she saw Le Soldat Jouet coming through the door overloaded with luggage.

"Be careful, you big oaf! Don't you dare drop that phonograph, as much trouble as we had getting it here?"

Tante Else quickly unpacked, putting everything away, then went through the house from top to bottom, arranging and rearranging things and noting the layout. I followed her through the house, discovering all the different rooms and making my own mental note of all the exits and places to hide. Eventually, we ended up in the kitchen, where she looked through the cupboards, making a list of items she would need.

Just as Katarina had said, Tante Elsa took charge of everything, and it wasn't long before dinner was on the stove. Madame Breton, Juliette's mother, had arrived at the back door promptly at 4 o'clock, explaining she had orders to cook and clean for the Kommandant's wife.

I was so happy to see a familiar face, but also uncomfortable, unsure how Madame Breton would see me now that the Kommandant had taken me from La Maison. She had always been friendly and kind whenever I'd gone to the pharmacy with Sœur Louise Claire.

Am I different now? Will she still see Désirée, the French girl?

Madame Breton didn't speak to me at all except to say Bonjour or Bonsoir, but I could feel a wariness that I'd never felt from her before.

When dinner was almost ready, Katarina came into the kitchen, excited about something.

"Tante Elsa, Serge said he has arranged everything. Oh, I didn't realize we had a guest," she said, noticing Madame Breton standing at the stove.

"Kat, this is Madame Breton. Anton has arranged for her to cook and clean for us while we are here. Madame Breton, this is Madame Steigler." Tante Elsa's eyebrows raised in an expression I didn't quite understand.

"I'm very pleased to meet you, Madame Breton. Thank you for coming. We're grateful for your help in this new... place. Come, please sit with me for a moment. I'd like to ask you a few questions, if you don't mind. Would you like a cup of coffee? Tante Elsa, do we have any coffee prepared?"

"*Ja, natürlich.* Sit. I'll bring it over," Tante Elsa said. It amazed me at how effortlessly the older woman switched from German to French, mixing the two languages seamlessly.

Madame Breton appeared shy, unsure, and undoubtedly suspicious of her new German employer's friendliness, but she sat at the kitchen table as instructed.

"Oui, Madame. I will answer if I can," she said, wrapping her hands around the cup of coffee Tante Elsa had placed in front of her.

"Merci Madame. All this must feel rather strange, but I want to assure you I will do everything within my power to create a pleasant environment for all of us. Were arrangements made regarding your schedule and wages?"

Katarina was friendly, not demanding an answer, just gently inquiring. She was so beautiful, at least to me, and I thought it strange Madame Breton didn't relax under the gaze of those sky-blue eyes.

"No Madame. I was told by the other woman to come last evening to prepare dinner for the Kommandant, then to return today at four o'clock. Which I have done," Madame Breton said, with a wary expression.

"The 'other' woman is Möller," Katarina told Tante Elsa, a look of disdain on her beautiful face.

"Frau Möller will no longer have any further business with this family," Katarina told Madame Breton. "Your instructions will come from Tante Elsa or myself from now on. Should you agree to stay, of course."

I remembered the things La Dame Noire said in her drunken state the night before and wasn't sure she would leave so easily.

"Oui, Madame. I understand," Madame Breton responded.

"Well then, I will pay you directly for your services. Whatever the standard rate for cooking and housekeeping is, I will pay. Is that agreeable?" Katarina asked.

"Oui, Madame." Madame Breton seemed shocked by the question, her eyes widening, then narrowing with suspicion.

"As for your schedule, let's agree you'll come daily when I'm in Châlons, which will not be all the time. While we are in Paris, your services here will be minimal. Tante Elsa will inform you from week to week." Katarina paused, lifting both hands in the air. "All this must be uncomfortable for you, though that's probably too polite a word given the circumstances. But I want you to know, Madame, I am not here to take advantage of you or anyone else. I wonder, do you know the people who lived here before?" she asked, almost timidly.

Madame Breton looked up, startled, clearly unsure how to answer the question. I was certain she knew what had happened only days before, but she seemed reluctant to tell this stranger the truth. After all, Katarina was the wife of the man who ordered the family's removal.

"Oui, Madame. The Kuklinski family lived here."

"I want to pay them for the use of their home. Do you know how I can get in touch with them?" Katarina asked.

"No, Madame," was the stoic response.

Katarina looked at her for a moment, then sighed. "Well, if you know anyone who can help with this, please let me know. Speak only to me about this. Understand?"

"Oui, Madame. I understand." Madame Breton still looked cautious, but now curious as well.

Once supper was ready, Tante Elsa sent Madame Breton home and the three of us relaxed in the front room listening to music, waiting for the Kommandant's return. I sat on the floor by the phonograph, looking through the box of records they'd brought from Germany, while the two women chatted quietly across the room on the sofa. To anyone looking in, the scene might have appeared like a normal family waiting for Father to come home for supper. But we were strangers sitting in a stolen house, pretending everything was normal.

It felt like something big was about to happen, and this was just the calm before the storm.

We heard the front door open but waited for the Kommandant to find us rather than going to greet him. He came into the living room looking very pleased with himself, like a big tomcat, who had a mouse under one paw and a bird under the other.

And then the storm hit.

It wasn't violent or loud, more like the coldest arctic blast imaginable. Katarina didn't direct her frigid assault on him, though I was certain he could feel it, but rather at the woman behind him, La Dame Noire.

Tante Elsa immediately rose to greet him, "*Hallo,* nephew. It's nice to see you again."

"Elsa. I didn't expect you, but it's lovely to see you, too. You look wonderful, of course," he said, bending to kiss the older woman's cheek.

"Ja, ja. You should know by now, Anton, I go wherever Kat goes." Then she held out her hand to me. "Komm mit mir, Désirée."

She led me out of the room and past La Dame Noire, whose eyes held mine for half a second, just long enough to pierce my mind with a silent warning.

We didn't go to the kitchen as expected. Instead, Tante Elsa led us into the dining room, and then stood next to the closed sliding door which led to the living room, obviously wanting to hear what was being said between her niece and the Kommandant. She seemed to forget about me as the argument on the opposite side of the door raged on.

"Send that woman away, Anton. I will not have her near me," Katarina snapped, the icy steel of her conviction crystal clear.

"Katarina, be reasonable. Frau Möller has been a tremendous help to me since I've been here, and to us. She has prepared the way for your arrival." He sounded like he was trying to convince her, rather than order her, which surprised me.

"I'm sure she has."

That sounded venomous, and I wondered what she meant.

"You brought me here to fulfill my duty as your wife and Karl's mother. If that's what you want, Anton, I will do it, but I *will not* have that woman here. You must send her away. I don't care where, just make it far enough

193

that I never have to see her again. That's *my price,* Anton. Her or me. If you don't send her away, I will return to Salzburg on the next train."

My heart stopped beating when I heard that, and I had to turn away from Tante Elsa to hide my reaction. *She'll leave if he doesn't send La Dame Noire away. What will happen to me then?*

Silence filled the space on the other side of the door. After an endless moment, we heard him let out a heavy breath of resignation.

He must have moved away, because we couldn't hear what he said to La Dame Noire, but we heard the front door open and close a moment later.

I could breathe again.

Tante Elsa looked down at me, put her finger to her lips, then wiggled it so I would silently follow her. Once we entered the kitchen, we both let out sighs of relief.

"That was long overdue," she said, though not really to me because she said it in German.

I pretended ignorance and asked, "Madame? May I help with the meal?"

She looked at me for a long time, her expression held the same sadness Katarina showed me earlier. Reaching down, she cupped my face gently in her hand.

"You look so much like her... hm..." she said in her native tongue, then she smiled, and answered me in mine. "Do you like to cook, Désirée?"

Chapter 26

A mother's love

With the Steiglers, I was living in a bubble of privilege and abundance, a life I could never have imagined. Katarina kept me insulated and protected from the sea of deep despair, hunger and seething anger growing outside that bubble.

I survived by always pretending, always guarding my thoughts. I became what they needed me to be, and at some point, I found the one thing I'd missed and needed the most: a mother's love.

Katarina kept her promise and sent La Dame Noire away. And after that first act of defiance toward the Kommandant, I thought maybe I could trust her. If I could be what *she* wanted, what *she* needed, I might survive the war. I was alone. The security of La Maison, however weak it had been, had vanished. But Katarina kept her promise, and that was a start.

She set the stage for the make-believe life we would all live, filling the walls of the stolen house with light and music and laughter. We each played our parts instinctively; Katarina, the dutiful wife and loving mother, the Kommandant, the devoted husband, Tante Elsa, the doting aunt, and me, the perfect child. It felt like each of us needed to please the others for our own reasons.

The first order of business was teaching me to speak German.

"She must learn to speak properly, Kat," the Kommandant insisted. "I want her speaking only German from now on, especially when addressing any German person."

It was a rule neither Katarina nor Tante Elsa was very strict about unless the Kommandant was at home or when we were around any soldiers. She made a game of teaching me German, using poetry, music and dancing to make her lessons fun.

Katarina was fluent in six languages, though her favorite was French, so when the Kommandant would leave the house, we would ignore the rules. "One can never have too many languages, ma petite," she said.

"Do you see Katarina?" the Kommandant said after I recited my latest lesson nearly perfectly. "She is exactly as I told you, a perfect Aryan child; beautiful and smart. She'll be speaking like a true German in no time."

"Yes, Anton, you were right. She's a very smart little girl," Katarina replied, giving me a tender smile.

For me, however, this new ability created a whole new set of problems. My innocent ignorance was no longer an option. No matter what I heard, my reaction had to be what they expected. By observing them, I would gauge how I should react. I learned to play the part of their clever, grateful daughter, because I had no other choice if I wanted to survive.

Whenever any soldiers were around, my guard was up, but it was different when they left for the day and there was only Katarina, Tante Elsa, and me. After breakfast Katarina would walk the Kommandant to the door, exchange a few loving words and a kiss, then close the door behind him with a sigh and a wicked grin.

Her smile was like lights being turned on in a darkened room, or a window opening to allow in a fresh breeze. Katarina would allow no darkness to penetrate her world, nor duty to impede her quest for happiness. Instead, we played games and laughed and danced, and in time shed our doubts as we relaxed in each other's company.

Katarina taught me language and music, geography and history. She told me stories of the places she'd been, and the things she'd done. She attempted to teach me ballet, though I was never very good at it. It didn't matter; I did whatever she asked of me, not because I needed to, but because with her it didn't feel like pretending. It felt like me.

When I wasn't with Katarina, I sought Tante Elsa's company. Most often, I'd find her in the kitchen at the little table with a book and a cup of coffee in front of her. We would sit and talk, the same way I had with Sœur Louise Claire. Sometimes she would tell me stories in German and ask me to translate the story back to her as a test of my understanding.

"You have a keen ability with language, Désirée. German is not usually so easy to learn." Tante Elsa always seemed amazed, and maybe a little suspicious, that I picked up the language so swiftly.

"I've been hearing it for almost a year. I guess I learned a few words." I didn't want to tell her, or anyone, about my memory. Papa told me I shouldn't tell because people wouldn't understand. They might become suspicious of me because I remember everything.

Chapter 27

Alex

After a couple of weeks living in the stolen house, still learning how to be around the Steiglers, a surprise visitor came to call.

Katarina and I were lounging in the living room, having just finished the morning language lesson, when the phone and the doorbell rang at the same time.

"You get the door, Désirée. I'll get the phone. Ask whoever it is to wait. I'll only be a moment," Katarina said.

Révérende Mère was standing behind the guard outside the house.

"Fraulien Désirée. *Die Nonne ist hier, um mit Frau Steigler zu sprechen,*" the guard said, speaking slowly so I would understand.

"Danke mein Herr." I held open the door for the nun, who waited patiently on the sidewalk. "Bonjour, Révérende Mère. Please come in. Frau Steigler will be with you in a moment."

My heart was beating hard inside my chest. I didn't know what her presence meant, but I was so happy to see her I almost threw my arms around her after the door closed. But I didn't. Part of me still hurt from how she let the Kommandant take me away, even though I knew she couldn't have stopped him.

"How are you, Désirée?" she asked. "You're looking well," she decided.

Does it really matter how I am? Is what I wanted to say, but I already knew the answer, so I just said, "I'm fine, Révérende Mère."

"Bonjour. So sorry to keep you waiting," Katarina said, gliding into the entry. She always seemed to glide, or dance, rather than simply walk.

"Bonjour, Madame Steigler. I am Révérende Mère for the Sisters of Charity. Perhaps your husband has mentioned me."

"Yes, of course. Please come in. I'm happy you've come. Would you care for some coffee or tea? Désirée, my dear, go tell Tante Elsa we need some refreshments for our guest."

She led Révérende Mère into the living room while I raced to the kitchen to give Tante Elsa the message.

I didn't want to miss what they would talk about, but Tante Elsa kept me busy in the kitchen putting the refreshment tray together. When I returned, they were sitting on the sofa talking quietly.

"So many," Katarina said, shaking her head. "If there's anything I can do, Madame. Or should I address you as Révérende Mère?" she asked, handing the nun a cup of coffee.

"Sœur Valerie will be fine Madame. Merci." Révérende Mère replied, taking a sip from her cup. "I saw you dance once, years ago in Paris, with *Le Ballets Russes*. You were exquisite to watch. Had I not committed to my calling, I might have dreamed of being a ballerina after seeing your performance." Her green eyes sparkled with remembered dreams, a whimsical smile lighting her face.

"Merci. That's very kind of you to say. It's been quite a few years since I took the stage, though it never quite leaves you. Please, call me Katarina. No need to be formal with me."

They allowed me to sit and listen while they talked, mostly about me, and what I'd been doing at La Maison, and how the Kommandant found me there. Révérende Mère spent the next hour chatting companionably with Katarina, and by the time she left, they had decided my fate.

First, I wouldn't be returning to La Maison. The Kommandant and Katarina would file for legal adoption. They never asked me if that's what I wanted, and I already knew Révérende Mère wouldn't fight them about it. I had no choice but to accept what was happening.

Katarina informed Révérende Mère I wouldn't be returning to school but would have tutors under Tante Elsa's supervision.

"I wonder, could you recommend someone who would come once a week to do the outside chores? One of your older girls perhaps," Katarina asked.

Révérende Mère looked at me, smiled, and then suggested Alex Guerin, assuring Katarina of his trustworthiness. "Alex is a very responsible boy. I'm sure he would be happy to work for you. I'll speak with his parents tonight."

After everything that happened, that was the best news I could have heard. Alex was coming.

He arrived at the door the following Thursday afternoon, a time conveniently arranged when the Kommandant attended his regular staff dinners. When I answered the door, he stood there tugging on his ear with the biggest smile on his face.

"Bonjour, Désirée. Révérende Mère said there was work for me here." His dark eyebrows arched slightly with his conspiratorial grin.

"Bonjour, Alex." I couldn't stop smiling. It felt like I was getting back a piece of my life.

"Bonjour. You must be the boy Sœur Valarie mentioned. Come in, please," Katarina said, coming up behind me. She led him down the hall into the kitchen. My excitement was nearly uncontainable as I followed them.

"Tante Elsa, this is Alex Guerin, the boy Sœur Valarie recommended for the outside chores," Katarina said.

Tante Elsa greeted him with a warm handshake. "I'm very pleased to meet you, Alex. Thank you for coming. Désirée has told us you work with your father as groundskeepers for the cathedral. We don't have as much to care for here, but I like things to be tidy, so I appreciate your help. Does Thursday, at four o'clock, work for you?" she asked, giving Alex a thorough looking over while she spoke.

"Thursdays are perfect, Madame. I'm here to do whatever you ask." He looked around at the three of us, giving us another toothy smile, his boyish charm and good nature instantly winning them over.

Once they got to know Alex, Katarina and Tante Elsa had no problem with Alex and I spending time together in the courtyard behind the house whenever he came.

We always talked as we worked, just as we had before. He would ask me how I was, and I would tell him I was fine, then he'd muss up my hair and laugh. When I would ask about his family, and everyone at La Maison, he'd tell me stories about the little boys and sometimes about the nuns.

He never said much about the girls unless I pressed him, and even then, it felt like a touchy subject.

"Janine said to say hello, from her and Rachel. As for the others, don't mind them, Désirée. They're scared to death or too stupid to realize you had no choice. I know why you didn't complain or say anything, and I won't forget it. I promise."

"Why do you care, Alex? Why does what happens to me matter to you?" I felt so defeated, abandoned by everyone but him.

"Because if I turned my back on you, I couldn't live with myself. You're my little sister. I won't walk away, and I won't let you give up."

Alex never let me forget who I really was.

Sometimes I'd see him in the park across the street, casually leaning against a tree, his bicycle resting next to him. He would sweep his hair back and tug his ear when he saw me at the window.

That signal would remind me he hadn't forgotten me, even when everyone else had decided I was a traitor or as good as dead, and therefore untouchable. At least that's what it felt like. Alex always made sure I knew he hadn't forgotten me, but whenever I saw him, it was like a bittersweet pill I had to swallow, reminding me of who I really was, but also everything I lost.

Inside the pretend life I was living, the attention and ultimately the love Katarina and Tante Elsa lavished on me became intoxicating, and in that first year, sometimes I almost forgot who I'd been before.

Chapter 28

Paris

"As lovely as it is here, Anton, if my duty is to help you and Karl, then allow me to use my influence to do so. Paris is where I can be more effective. Not all the time, of course, but enough so I can make a difference for you both. I've rented the suite at the George V. It's close enough, but not on top of the crowd. I wanted an elegant place where we can host parties for the Reich, but private enough to have family dinners when Karl comes to Paris. The George V is perfect, don't you think, darling?"

Katarina knew exactly how to get what she wanted from him; loving deference coupled with a beautiful charm he couldn't resist. The more I watched them together, the more I realized how much he loved and valued her, almost more than he did his position or his duty. He would do almost anything she asked once she convinced him she wouldn't leave.

I also realized he had used their son, Karl, as bait to get her to come to France, but I was the net to keep her here. He must have known that once she saw me, she wouldn't walk away, but I didn't understand why.

Katarina said I would accompany her to Paris whenever she went there. She said it was part of my education and that everyone should experience Paris, especially if you're French.

The first time we went, the trip on the train from Châlons mesmerized me, and then the size of the city stunned me. If I thought Châlons was big, and I did, then Paris was gigantic. It seemed to go on forever, an endless maze of streets and buildings with the River Seine running through it. I never felt so insignificant as I did on that first trip to Paris.

Fearing the Kommandant would dispose of me on a whim, I imagined running away once we got to Paris. I hoped I might find someone who would help me escape from him. But, as the train finally pulled into the *Gare du Nord*, fear of being alone in that enormous city settled in the pit of my stomach, and all thoughts of running away vanished.

A driver met us at the station and took us directly to the hotel, a twenty-minute ride through the streets of Paris. By the time we arrived, I knew my imprisonment was complete. German soldiers were everywhere, on almost every street we traveled, and the giant Nazi flags and banners flew from every building they occupied. From what I could see, the Nazis had completely taken over Paris.

"Welcome back to the George V, Madame Lang," a distinguished man at the front desk greeted us. "It's good to have you back in Paris again. We have arranged everything, per your instructions."

"Merci, Cédric. Good to see you again. It's been far too long. Your family is doing well, I hope?" Katarina asked, her eyes scanning the lobby while she maintained her elegant composure. A few Nazi officers seated in the lobby watched with admiring looks as Katarina spoke to the hotel manager.

"We're all doing well, Madame. Merci," he replied with a humble bow.

"That's good to hear. You remember my aunt, Elsa Lang. And this is my daughter, Désirée, who'll accompany us when we're in Paris. Say hello to Monsieur Boucher, my dear."

"Bonjour, monsieur."

Now, everyone here will think I'm German! The thought horrified me.

"Allow me to escort you to your suite, Madame. I hope you find the accommodations to your satisfaction. Right this way."

We followed him through the lobby and into an elevator which took us to the seventh floor. He led us down a long hallway and into a large two-bedroom suite with a third adjoining bedroom. It was dazzling, beautiful, full of light from the tall windows reflecting off the multitude of gilded mirrors hanging everywhere. The living space was opulent but comfortable, with sofas, chairs and tables, a dining area and even a small kitchen. There was a small office tucked into a bay of tall windows with a door leading onto the balcony outside. The view was breathtaking; the city of Paris laid out in front of us with the Eiffel Tower on the right.

I had been nowhere like it before, never imagined myself living in such luxury, but that suite at the George V was to become my home in Paris. For almost three years, I lived above the fray, insulated and protected in my gilded cage, half the time in Paris, the other half in Châlons.

Paris became the backdrop of my education. Through the eyes of Katarina Lang, renown ballerina of Le Ballets Russes, and wife of Nazi SS Officer Anton Steigler, I learned about my country, its history, art and architecture, its culture.

Katarina and I would spend the mornings exploring, walking down the Champs-Élysées to the Jardin des Tuileries, haunting the halls of the

Louvre, where she would describe the artwork which had hung there before, but now was sadly missing.

We strolled through the Place de la Concorde, the place where the French people guillotined King Louis XVI, Marie Antoinette, and a lot of other aristocrats after the Revolution. Katarina remarked how little men had changed since then.

We visited the palaces and museums of Paris, shopped in the finest stores, and lunched at sidewalk cafés, sipping coffee and hot cocoa. We even climbed the Eiffel Tower together, racing up the last steps to stand side by side, dazzled by the view of Paris at our feet.

Katarina hired a tutor for me; Fräulein Heller, one of the many German women who'd come to Paris to work for the Reich. Fräulein Heller provided lessons in language (German, French, and Spanish) as well as classical history, geography, and mathematics.

But mostly, Tante Elsa and Katarina taught me how to be a proper young German girl, wrapping me in their gentle protection, shielding me (they thought) from the real horrors around me.

At night Katarina would go out to some social event with the Nazi elite. I rarely accompanied her to those events, only going to the occasional daytime luncheon. It seemed to me she was insulating me from the Nazis as much as she was from the occupied French.

Sometimes she would entertain her theatre friends in our suite, and when they came, the place would fill with music, dancing and laughter.

Everywhere we went in Paris, everyone welcomed and fell in love with Katarina Lang, including me.

In July 1942, we spent a week in Versailles, visiting an old friend from Katarina's dancing days. The Nazis had taken control of the Château de Versailles, like they had everything else, but Katarina made a call to get us inside for a tour to see what remained.

We walked hand in hand through the palace and gardens as she told me stories of the kings and queens of France from long ago and how they lived. It was like walking through history, so vivid were her descriptions, even though little remained. To me it was like walking through a real life fairy-tale, made all the better because Katarina made the tale come alive.

We left Versailles after lunch, bidding our hosts goodbye and heading back into Paris. It wasn't very far, less than an hour by car. We were heading north, next to the river just south of the Eiffel Tower, when our car came to a stop. A line of busses filled with people were blocking the road in front of us. French Police and German soldiers were supervising the unloading of the busses, herding the people into the Vélodrome d'Hiver.

"Are they going to watch the cyclists race?" I asked Katarina as the confusing scene played out in front of us. She had taken me there once to watch a bicycle race, but the scene in front of me didn't look right. Some people going inside were carrying suitcases. Families with children were being hustled into the stadium, and they didn't look happy to be there.

The bus in front of us pulled forward, allowing our car enough room to drive past, and a soldier waved us through when he saw the little Nazi flags on the front of our car. As we passed by, I looked out the back window just as a boy jumped out of the bus. He darted past the policeman and around the front of the bus, making a mad dash across the street towards the river.

I watched in stunned horror as one of the German soldiers casually lifted his rifle and shot the boy in the back before he reached the other side of the street.

The boy fell hard, his jacket flying open as he hit the ground face down. I could see the big yellow star on his jacket change color as blood seeped out of his lifeless body onto the street.

"Turn around, my love," Katarina said, pulling me down to face forward again. "We'll be home soon."

I didn't sleep very well that night. It took forever to fall asleep, and then dreams of the dead boy with the yellow star haunted me.

It confused me why Katarina and Tante Elsa said nothing when it happened. I knew they must have heard the gunshot; the car window had been partially open for fresh air. But neither woman reacted at all, except to tell me to turn around. The murder of the boy didn't seem to bother them.

I couldn't ask them why. I had to play my part, always taking my cues from them.

Katarina went to dinner with Karl that night, and I woke when she came in late, upset about something.

She always seemed a little sad after her visits with Karl, and when we boarded the train for Châlons early the following morning, she seemed especially distracted. She spent the first half of the trip writing letters while Tante Elsa did her needlework. I kept myself busy practicing my handwriting in the little notebook Katarina had given me.

"Désirée, *meine Süße*, go to the dining car for a little tea or something and do your work there for a while. I need to speak with Tante Elsa alone. Danke, *Liebes*," Katarina said, putting her writing aside.

They usually sent me away when they wanted to talk privately. I lamented the days when they thought I couldn't understand and would speak freely in front of me. Being multi-lingual had its disadvantages. But on that occasion, I was happy to escape the stuffy cabin.

"May I go to the back of the train?" I asked, wanting to be outside, to feel the sun and wind on my face.

"You may, but be careful and be back by the time we arrive in Châlons."

It was a warm July day and the thought of drinking anything hot didn't appeal to me. Instead, I walked through the train to the very last car to spend the rest of the trip leaning against the metal railing at the back and watching the countryside recede away from me.

The track hugged the river Marne for much of the way, winding through endless fields and tree-topped hills with an occasional village or town to break up the monotonous beauty.

I hoped the fresh air would help clear away the image of the dead boy, but it was useless. Those brief seconds repeated over and over in my mind; the casualness of how the soldier pointed his rifle at the boy, the sound of the shot, the boy falling, and that bright yellow star turning red with blood. As I stood at the back of the train, I realized that what happened to the boy had happened to me, but I had survived.

Why me? Why did I live and not that boy? The thought tormented me.

I felt horrible, sad, frightened, and guilty. There was no one to share my feelings with. I needed to play the part they'd given me. That was how I would survive, hiding my feelings away, deep inside, like so many other things.

Not yet willing to step back into the pretend life, I lingered at the back of the train as it pulled into the station at Châlons. The train passed several boxcars sitting on one of the other rail lines on the outskirts of the station. As we rolled by, I saw faces straining to look out the small high windows and hands reaching through the bars. I stood there transfixed, trying to make sense of what I was seeing. Then I heard someone call my name.

"Désirée! Désirée!" It sounded like it was coming from the boxcars, then I heard it again.

"Désirée. Come, child. It's time to go home," Tante Elsa said behind me.

"Yes, Tante Elsa. I'm coming." Before following her, I looked back at the boxcars, but by then they were too far away to see or hear anyone who might be inside.

Chapter 29

Broken promises

It felt harder returning to Châlons, to the pretend life with the Kommandant. I knew it was because of the dead boy with the yellow star, but something else felt wrong.

We returned on a Friday afternoon, and Katarina was eager to go straight home. She hadn't been herself all day, but I didn't know why. I wanted to believe the boy's murder *had* affected her, that she wasn't like the Nazi soldiers. I needed to believe that, but sometimes I wasn't sure.

As soon as we walked through the door of the stolen house, I knew the curtain would rise and my performance would begin. It was always the same; a greeting from the Kommandant, a quick briefing on what we did while away, and then he would retire to his study with Le Soldat Jouet or some other soldier.

But this time was different. It felt like the curtain got stuck halfway open, revealing some ugly truth.

He greeted us rigidly, a dark look passing between them after Katarina told him she had seen Karl the night before.

"Yes, my dear. Karl called me this morning to tell me about your conversation." He had that tone to his voice, the one he always used when he was talking to his soldiers, but rarely used with her.

He turned to me with a look of dismissal. "Run along now, Désirée. You can tell me what you learned after dinner."

I did my little curtsy with a smile and retreated to my room, glad to be away from him, but curious about what was going on between them.

Sitting on my bed, I pulled everything out of my satchel, needing to see the evidence I'd been someone else, someone other than the pretend girl I'd become. It only contained four things; the little doll Grand-Mère had made for me, the old woman's shawl, which still held the faint scent of lavender and sage, a small piece of fading ribbon, and the drawing of my family, now worn at the folds from countless viewings.

I rarely cried anymore, and never during the day, but that day I couldn't seem to hold back my tears. Afraid someone would come in, I went into the bathroom and closed the door.

I sat on the tile floor, leaning against the wall between the bathtub and the sink, sobbing quietly into the folds of the old blue shawl. Through my sobs, I heard voices, not in my head, but seeping up through the floor. It was Katarina and the Kommandant arguing in his study directly below me. The shrillness of her voice cut through the floor, and I heard her anger.

"You lied to us both. You never gave him my letters," she said. "I thought it was because of his school and that awful youth organization you insisted he be a part of, but you lied to him. You told him Leda died at birth, and I was sick with grief. How could you, Anton? You never even gave him a chance to know her. YOU never let yourself know her! Then you and that Möller bitch took her away and kill her. But you didn't have the courage to tell Karl that, did you?!" She was screaming at him, then it became quiet for a while. It sounded like she was crying.

"Karl asked me if you were planning to send Désirée to Himmler's *Lebensborn* program. Is that your intention, Anton? You would take another child from me?"

"No! No Katarina. That was never my intention. She reminds me too much of you, of what our daughter should have been. That's why I wanted her. I thought if I could replace what I'd taken from you, then you'd come back to me. We could be like we were before." He was pleading with her, but I could hear the steel in his voice, and it frightened me.

Their voices faded out of hearing and then I heard the office door close sharply. A moment later, the phone in his study rang, and he answered it with a snarl.

"No! I said there won't be any releases. Send the train directly to the camp, as ordered. Is that clear?" Then the phone slammed down.

I sat on the bathroom floor for a while, trying to understand what I heard and what it meant. I already figured out that he used me to make her stay with him, but I hadn't known why until then.

They had a daughter, Leda. I look like her.

He told Karl that Leda died at birth. That's why Karl always ignores me. He never knew about Leda. But Leda didn't die at birth.

La Dame Noire took her away and killed her.

How old was Leda when that happened?

Old enough that they all think I look like her.

That's why Katarina sent La Dame Noire away. Because she killed Leda. What's Lebensborn?

After a while, I couldn't sit there worrying any longer and had to get up and move around. Tante Elsa would come up to get me for supper soon and I would have to perform something for the Kommandant after dinner, to show him I hadn't wasted my time while in Paris.

The Siege of Paris by the Vikings in 845 was just the thing. The Kommandant liked anything to do with the Norsemen, believing they were part of the Aryan race. So, I figured Ragnar Lodbrok's sack of Paris might help lighten his mood.

213

I didn't have to perform that night because Katarina retired to her room after their argument and the Kommandant informed Tante Elsa he would dine out. So, Tante Elsa and I ate our dinner in the kitchen at the little table.

It was simple food, just boiled sausage with potatoes and cabbage. Tante Elsa had sent Madame Breton home early, so I helped her with the cooking. While we sat together in the quiet house, eating our humble meal, I asked her a question I hoped she would answer.

"Tante Elsa. What does Lebensborn mean?"

I always asked Tante Elsa if I didn't understand a word or phrase, and she would usually answer willingly, but that night I took her by surprise.

She put her fork down, wiped the corners of her mouth with a napkin, then folded it neatly before laying it on the table. She never took her eyes off me the whole time, like she was trying to read my mind.

"Where did you hear that word, child?"

"I heard a soldier say it while we were walking through the palace at Versailles," I lied. I was getting good at lying when I needed to.

She took a deep breath before she answered. "*Leben* means life, and *born* means spring or fount. So, *Lebensborn* means life-spring. But I suggest you not repeat that word again, Désirée. Do you understand?" She had a serious look on her face that held both concern and a warning. I knew better than to ignore it.

"*Ja*, Tante Elsa," I said dutifully, not risking to question why.

"*Gut.* You finish up here, then off to bed with you. I'm going to see if Kat needs anything," she said, rising from the table. Before she left, she reached down and put her hand on my head, gently running her finger across the raised scar along my hairline. Then she smoothed down my wayward curls and said, "You're a good girl, Désirée. I'll be in to say goodnight later."

Katarina came down to breakfast the following morning, dressed and beautiful as usual. Her initial interactions with the Kommandant, though respectful, remained limited and chilly. He could not have been more loving and gracious towards her; standing up when she came in, kissing her cheek, pouring her coffee.

I often wondered what was between them, why she stayed with him, despite what he'd done. I could see her struggle with herself, sometimes loving him, sometimes hating him. But I was just a child, a pretend daughter, and like most children whose parents were quarreling, I stayed quiet and out of the way.

It didn't matter how nice he was, playing his part as the loving husband and father, I sensed something was different, something about him that was harder, like he had done something horrible, and it made me very nervous.

Everything felt wrong, and it wasn't just the argument between Katarina and the Kommandant. There was something else and I didn't know what.

Asking anyone in the house was out of the question. That wouldn't be in character. Désirée, the pretend German girl, never questioned her elders. I thought about asking Madame Breton, but she never talked, except to ask what she should cook, or what they might need from her.

I had to wait until I saw Alex on Thursday, five days away. Those five days felt like forever.

I was sitting on the stone bench under the tree on the far side of the courtyard, pretending to read and eagerly waiting for Alex to arrive. I needed to talk with him about what I witnessed in Paris, about how hard it was to pretend all the time.

The moment I saw him, I knew it was bad. When he walked through the gate, his usual boyish charm was missing, replaced by a solemn face I'd never seen him wear. He came straight over and sat down on the bench next to me, never taking his eyes off me.

"What's wrong, Alex? Something's wrong, isn't it? Is it your family? Is everyone all right?" I asked, keeping my voice and animations to a minimum, in case Tante Elsa or anyone else was listening.

"You don't know, do you?" he asked, his voice low and accusing.

"How would I know anything? You're the only one who talks to me anymore and I haven't seen you in weeks." I worried even Alex was turning away from me. "I'm sorry Alex. It's just... something last week, just before we came back, and I can't stop thinking about it."

He gave me a curious look. "What happened?"

I told him about the buses filled with people at the stadium, and what happened to the boy with the yellow star, and how neither Katarina nor Tante Elsa had reacted at all when it happened practically in front of them.

"They did it here too," he said, giving me a hard look.

"What do you mean? Did what?"

"Last Thursday, the Boches went through the town; factories, shops, homes, wherever they wanted. They took every Jew or foreigner they could find. Men, women, *and* children. Their age didn't matter. If the Boches wanted them, they took them." He looked at me for a moment, gauging my reaction.

"The Boche went to La Maison too, Désirée. Someone told them about the Jews being sheltered there; Madame Jacobi and her children and another family who came a few months ago. They took them... and Rachel... and Janine. Then they arrested Révérende Mère when she tried to stop them."

He stood up and began working, his movements swift and deliberate, the sound of the rake on the stones sharp and harsh.

My breath caught in my throat. I could hardly believe it, but knew Alex would never lie to me, so it must be true. Struggling to hold myself still, to control the flood of emotions threatening to consume me, I wrapped my arms around myself and held on tight.

"Where did they take them?" I asked, though unsure if I really wanted to know.

"They loaded them all into boxcars just outside the train station. The Boches sent those cars away last Friday night to some work camp called Auschwitz. They released Révérende Mère on Monday. Maman said the Bishop got them to let her go."

My tears were unstoppable, and my body couldn't stop shaking.

"I saw them, Alex," I said through my tears. "I saw those boxcars when we arrived from Paris. I didn't know, I didn't know. Who would tell on Révérende Mère, Alex? Who would do that?"

Alex stood up straight and looked around, then continued raking the debris from under the tree, looking at me occasionally. We both knew we weren't totally alone. We had to be quiet and careful about what we said because there was always a guard stationed at the front gate, and Tante Elsa or Katarina were usually inside, but it was hard holding myself together.

"Maman said it was old Sœur Bernadette who told the police about the families living at La Maison. You know how she was. Anyway, it must be true, because Révérende Mère sent her back to Paris. Papa took her to the station this morning. Good riddance is what I say." Then he spat into the bush behind the tree.

"I can't do this anymore, Alex. I can't. It was all for nothing. They said he would leave La Maison alone if I went with him. That's what they said, but it was a lie. Be good and nothing bad will happen, that's what they said, but it was all a lie. I can't pretend anymore, Alex." I was so miserable. All I wanted to do was run away and hide somewhere.

"You've got to. You've got to hold on a little longer," he said, his voice low and almost angry with me. "Listen, Désirée. You have it much better than the rest of us. At least you're not hungry all the time. Besides, this won't last forever. The Resistance is getting stronger, and the Americans are in it now, so it won't be long before the Boches leave for good. You've got to hold on," he said, his optimism recovered.

"Didn't you have lunch? I can make you something if you're hungry." I offered in my ignorance. He looked at me like I'd said the dumbest thing imaginable.

"Wake up, Désirée! Look around! Everyone is hungry except the Boches, and it's getting worse. They take everything they can get their hands on and leave practically nothing for the rest of us." His dark eyes blazed with hatred for his enemy.

I had never seen Alex so angry. It frightened me to think about what his anger might lead to. And I didn't understand why I mattered to him. I was just a girl he knew, not even a relative. Everyone thought I was a traitor. Steigler's girl, they called me. After everything that happened, I felt hopeless, like I would never be free.

He reached out, putting his hand on my shoulder, his anger once again under control. "I'll think of something, some plan to get you out of here. But right now, you're better off where you are. I didn't want to ask, but I think you can help, if you would. You can find out what he's planning." He kept his voice low, looking around to make sure the guard wasn't near enough to hear.

"I don't know, Alex. He never talks about army things when he's at home, and I'm not allowed in his study. Except sometimes he lets me show him something, or he'll read to me in there. Katarina doesn't allow the soldiers in the house unless he's home, so I hardly ever hear anything." I said, but the idea took residence in my brain, followed by terror at the thought of being found out.

"If he finds out Alex, he'll kill me. I know he will. He's done it before. He let La Dame Noire kill his own daughter." The thought of being caught almost paralyzed me with fear.

"Just think about it, Désirée. It's something only you can do because he trusts you now. If he's as careful at home as you say, then he'll never suspect you. In the meantime, I'll work on a plan for your escape." He seemed so sure I could do it, but saw my uncertainty.

"I know it's a lot to ask. You're just a kid, but right now, you're the closest person to him." Alex stopped raking and bent down in front of me to gather the yard waste into a basket. Then he looked up at me and whispered, "Just keep your ears open and tell me what you hear. I'll pass it on. No one will ever know the information came from you."

"All right, but I don't know how much help I can be."

That night I cried more than I had allowed myself to in months, letting the waves of misery spill into my pillow. Afterward, I lay there nursing the sting Alex's words left on my heart.

'Wake up Désirée!! Look around!! You have it much better than the rest of us. At least you're not hungry all the time.'

Suddenly, that truth cracked, and then shattered whatever illusion I had of my life. It was like I had been blind to everything except my need for love, my need to survive. At that moment, the guilt of knowing people I cared about were suffering, while I had everything I needed, added another layer to my pain. It was then I decided to do what Alex asked. It was the only thing I could do.

My hatred of the Kommandant consumed my thoughts. I imagined several ways I could exact my revenge on him. I even considered poisoning his food, but I didn't know where I could get any. Besides, I didn't want to hurt Katarina or Tante Elsa by accident, because to me they weren't Nazis, even though they were German. I resigned myself to thinking of ways to spy on him, despite being terrified of being found out.

I believed I had to do it, no matter how scary, because if I didn't, Alex might abandon me completely. At that moment, losing Alex was the worst thing I could imagine.

Tell me what to do. I pleaded to Maman, to the old woman, to anyone.

It was Révérende Mère's voice that answered me that night. I remembered something she had said the day the Kommandant had taken my fish.

"You need to understand three things, Désirée. Sadness is something you must learn to endure. Fear will always stop you, if you allow it, and anger can both fuel your determination and derail it with recklessness."

I can be brave and strong and clever, just like the old woman said.

I can do this.

I just need to be really, really careful.

Chapter 30

La petite Boche

I was a little over ten years old when I started spying on the Nazis, gleaning every bit of information I could, then passing it on to Alex. I became a child spy living right under the Kommandant's nose.

Alex was right, the Kommandant trusted me. He only saw what he believed I was: a perfect Aryan child.

He never doubted my innocence when I asked him to read to me, allowing me into his study to sit on his lap. While he read, I would look beyond the book he held, and at the papers he left on his desk, memorizing everything. Neither did he suspect I played on the landing at the top of the stairs to listen when they had guests over, or that I would lie on the floor of my bathroom listening when I knew he was talking on the phone in his study below.

I played the part of his perfect little girl, and he suspected nothing.

Pretending was a lot harder than before. I had to stuff my hatred of him deep down inside and never let it show, never let him see how I really felt, because I knew I could end up dead, the same as Leda.

It was even harder around Katarina and Tante Elsa. As much as I hated him, I cared for them, and sometimes it felt like I was betraying them, too. I worried that what I told Alex might hurt them.

Alex never told me if the information I gave him made any difference. Mostly, it was just names of people or towns, sometimes numbers or times. None of it made any sense to me, especially when the things sounded like code names for something else. I remembered everything I heard or saw, and I passed it on to Alex.

It was dangerous, but I did it anyway, because I believed if I didn't, if I refused and let fear stop me, it would be like turning my back on Alex and whatever was left of Désirée, the French girl. I couldn't do that.

From August 1942 to February 1944, my life as Steigler's girl went on as it had been. Katarina, Tante Elsa, and I traveled back and forth between Châlons and Paris, staying a month or more in each place.

In the entire time I lived with the Steigler's, I never had playmates, at least not any who wanted to play with me. Being friends with Steigler's girl wasn't something any local girl in Châlons wanted to do. That was hard for me, feeling rejected by my own people, by everyone except Alex.

Paris was different. In Paris, I was the privileged child of a famous mother, her Nazi affiliation notwithstanding, and that allowed me a certain amount of freedom, at least within the confines of the George V.

Deep in the bowels of the hotel, among the sounds and smells of the bustling kitchen, I found comfort and a little companionship. In the afternoons, I would venture into the restaurant kitchen to be around French people, to listen and watch them while they worked, but mostly to be around the sounds and smells of a restaurant kitchen.

The first time I slipped into the kitchen, the chef spotted me and summarily marched me out to the concierge, telling me to stay where I belonged. I didn't know where that was anymore, but being in that kitchen felt better than anywhere else, so I kept going back.

"I only want to watch," I said when Chef sent me away for the third time and then talked to the hotel manager and Katarina about keeping me in my place.

"What harm can it do for her to watch?" Katarina asked sweetly.

Either by her Nazi affiliation or her charm, Katarina's influence convinced Chef to allow me into the kitchen, if it wasn't a busy time and I didn't get in anyone's way.

At first, the kitchen staff was cautious, most of them treating me like an indulged child of a rich German guest. I usually sat at the table used for breaks and staff meals, where I could bathe in the kitchen's tempo, and make notes in my journal.

Eventually, I became an accepted fixture, with some of the staff even greeting me with timid smiles. It wasn't until the young dishwasher, Marcel, sat down and talked to me that things became easier.

"Bonjour Mademoiselle Steigler," he said, which stung because I hated being thought of as German, but I couldn't tell him the truth.

"Why do you spend time in here when you could play in the park or swim in the pool?"

"I like kitchens and cooking. I enjoy learning different ways to prepare food. My name is Désirée."

"What do you write in that little book of yours?" he asked, looking at me with suspicion.

"Recipes and notes about cooking," I said, opening the journal for his review. The sous-chef, Monsieur Charney, was listening and came over to look at my journal.

All they found were recipes and notes about food, the only things I ever wrote in there. The first were those I remembered making with Maman, then a couple from La Maison and some from Tante Elsa, which were written in German and French. The most recent entry was how to prepare capons for roasting, which I jotted down the day before while watching Monsieur Charney.

"This first one, Cassoulet, is a French country recipe. Where did you learn this, Mademoiselle?" Monsieur Charney asked.

"Maman taught me." By the look on his face, he didn't believe me.

"Really? The famous Katarina Lang taught you how to make Cassoulet?" he asked incredulously.

"No, my real mother taught me before she died."

Before he could ask more questions, Chef called out for him to get back to work. He jumped up, returning to his station, occasionally looking over at me.

After that encounter, it became easier to be there; some of the staff would take a moment to sit and chat with me when they took their breaks. I always chose my words carefully when speaking about Katarina and Tante Elsa, and avoided all questions about the Kommandant. Sometimes Justin, the other sous-chef, would allow me to stand and watch as he prepped for the day's menu.

I became a sort of mascot for some of them, connecting with me as one does with a lost puppy, and that gave me a small sense of belonging.

Others never lost their suspicion of me, never made eye contact, never spoke to me. They were the ones who referred to me as La Petite Boche, though never in front of Chef.

The names they called me didn't matter, because of all the places I could be in Paris, the kitchen at the George V was my favorite.

Chapter 31

Opportunities

I woke to sunshine on my eleventh birthday. It had been three years since the nightmare began, and over two years living with the monster of that nightmare.

I rarely thought of my family, but sometimes a smell or a sound would trigger a memory, some moment from before, and it would feel like being wrapped in a warm blanket on a chilly night.

While I secretly nurtured the memories of my early childhood, I continued creating pretend memories in a pretend life, which was feeling more unstable by the minute.

There was no birthday celebration planned, which was fine. May 15th would never again be a day I wanted to celebrate. Besides, the Steiglers changed my birth date to December 25th when they adopted me. I never knew why, but I didn't mind. It was an easy date to remember, plus I became half a year older than I really was.

May 15, 1943 offered a fresh challenge, but also an opportunity.

The Steiglers were guests of honor at the Saint Etienne Athletic games, being held at the stadium on the south side of Châlons that afternoon. The Kommandant said he wanted us to attend as a family, to show our support for the young athletes. I suspected his real motive was to make sure the local leaders still knew who was in charge.

A few days earlier, Alex told me the Resistance had been growing since the Vichy government established the new forced labor law. Alex also said he heard the Nazis lost the battle of Stalingrad against the Russian army.

All of that was music to my ears. It gave me hope that maybe, just maybe, the Nazis would lose the war and I would be free.

At breakfast that morning, an urgent phone call for the Kommandant sent him rushing out the door. Before he left, he instructed Katarina and me to meet him at his headquarters at noon, so we could drive to the games together.

I hadn't been inside the Bishop's House in over two years and was both nervous and excited about the opportunity this visit offered. The Kommandant had spent more time at his office, rarely working from his study at home, which meant there hadn't been many opportunities to hear anything to tell Alex. This visit was a chance I wanted to take advantage of. If I was very careful and clever, maybe I would see or hear something important, something to help defeat the Nazis for good.

I dressed carefully, making sure my appearance would please the Kommandant so I could distract him. As I looked at myself in the mirror, I wondered if I would look any different if the war had never happened, if my family was still alive and I was still on the farm in the north.

What would Désirée Rondeau look like?

I tried to see Maman's face in my reflection, but couldn't find it. All I saw looking back at me was the Aryan girl I had become for him, the girl I had to be to survive.

"Désirée, ma chérie. Come, it's time to go. Fritz is here to pick us up," Katarina said, gliding into my room. She stood behind me, looking at me in the mirror, straightening my collar and smoothing my hair.

"You look pretty today, chérie. Anton will be pleased. You know how he likes to make a good impression." She gave me a conspiratorial wink in the mirror. "Come, chérie, let's be off to the games. We don't want to keep him waiting."

The Bishop's House wasn't very far, only a few minutes away, but far enough for my nerves to turn my stomach to jelly the minute our car pulled into the courtyard.

I'd become accustomed to seeing the large Nazi flags hanging from every building they occupied, declaring their dominance, but it always seemed so odd to see that huge red flag with the black swastika flapping against the Bishop's House, directly across from the Cathedral Saint Etienne, like good and evil vying for control.

Several cars filled the courtyard and lots of soldiers, which I assumed was normal, but Katarina seemed to think otherwise.

"What's going on Fritz? There seems to be more than the usual activity today."

"Jawhol, Frau Steigler. Oberstleutnant Steigler has a visitor. He would like you to join him in his office," Le Soldat Jouet said as he parked the car next to another large black car with little Nazi flags flying on the front of it.

"Does he now? Well then, we must see who has surprised us today. Come, Désirée. Let's go find Papa Steigler." Katarina squeezed my hand while we waited for Le Soldat Jouet to open the car door for us. "You know the rules, meine Süße. Be quiet and respectful. Don't speak unless spoken to. Hopefully, this won't take long, and we can be on our way to the games."

"Ja, Mama Kat. I'll be good, I promise."

We followed Le Soldat Jouet into the building, then up the curving staircase to the third floor, down a long hallway flanked by countless offices, and ending at the office in the northwest corner of the building. Soldiers were everywhere, working in every office, running up or down the stairs and rushing around doing whatever soldiers do during a war. Every one of them stopped to greet Katarina as we passed.

"Good afternoon, Frau Steigler," they said, with a nod and a click of their boot heels.

"Good afternoon, gentlemen," she responded with a beautiful smile and a wave of her hand.

As we arrived at the Kommandant's large corner office overlooking the River Marne, a shiver rolled down my back. I'd only been there once and had never been back. Katarina said it wasn't a place for children.

"There they are. My beautiful ladies," the Kommandant said as I followed Katarina in and stood discreetly behind her. "Katarina, you remember Oberführer Krögler," he said, taking her hand to draw her into the room.

"Of course. Wilhelm, it's good to see you again. How is Adeline? It's been far too long since the four of us have made a night of it. Is she here with you?" Katarina asked, leaning forward to brush cheeks with the older man.

"Katarina, my dear, you seem to get younger and more beautiful while the rest of us wither with age." Oberführer Krögler looked at least ten years older than the Steiglers but carried himself with the vigor of a much younger man. He led Katarina to one of the two chairs sitting in front of the Kommandant's desk.

"As charming as ever, Wilhelm. If only it were true. But what of Adeline? It would be lovely to see her."

"Regretfully, my Addie is at home, nursing a stomach ailment, not unlike what our Führer suffers from, as I understand. Terrible condition," he said, shaking his head.

"I'm sorry to hear that. Please give her my best when you speak with her."

The older man looked at me with a critical eye. "But who is this little beauty you have with you, Kat? She looks..."

"Come here, Désirée," the Kommandant said from behind his desk. "I want to introduce you to Oberführer Krögler, an old friend of the family. Come and say hello, liebling."

I obeyed, shyly taking his hand and moving to stand behind the desk. "Good afternoon, Herr Krögler." I said, adding a little curtsy. I didn't let go of the Kommandant's hand, which I knew would please him.

"Where did she come from? Surely this isn't the child... well, of course she couldn't be. But what a lovely young girl. She looks a lot like you, Kat," the older man said.

"She does. Anton found her in an orphanage not long after arriving in France. Now neither of us can imagine life without her." Katarina held a cigarette up for him to light for her.

I cringed inside at how deftly she told the truth, without all the sordid details, making the situation sound so perfect.

The Kommandant sat down in his big swivel chair, gently putting his arm around my waist, holding me next to him while he told the story of when he first met me, and how I gave him my fish, which wasn't true. I didn't care because standing there gave me a perfect view of his desk and everything on it. I stood next to him, quietly listening while they talked, keeping my eyes lowered shyly, only lifting them when I sensed it was necessary.

My eyes scanned the papers strewn across his desk, absorbing every piece of information I could find. It wasn't much, just some numbers next to names of things that sounded mechanical and something about the Malice.

It was disappointing I couldn't see anything important looking or marked 'Secret', but it didn't matter. Alex was grateful for whatever I offered.

"So, what brings you to the provinces, Wilhelm? I thought the Führer was keeping you tied to your desk, as many of my invitations as you've declined," Katarina teased. I could tell by the way he looked at her, leaning into her as she spoke, that he was as captivated by her as every other man I'd seen around her.

"My dear Kat, nothing short of duty could keep me from enjoying your charming company. Honestly though, I've had little time for socializing, what with the constant trips to Berlin or Berchtesgaden, and then trying to deal with the idiot bureaucrats in Vichy, I haven't had a moment," the older man complained. "But I'm keeping you both from your outing," he said, rising to leave. "It was delightful to meet you, Fraulien Désirée. I hope we meet again."

"Danke mein Herr," I responded with another curtsy.

"Katarina, it was a pleasure, as always. Please give my regards to your father when you speak with him," he said, lifting her hand to his lips. "It will disappoint Adeline to hear she missed seeing you. Walk me out, Anton," he ordered as he headed for the door.

The Kommandant rose from his chair, leaving me standing by his desk.

"Jawohl, Oberführer," he said, following the man out.

"Stay here, Désirée. I'll be right back," Katarina said, rising to follow the men into the hallway outside the office.

I remained where I was, and even took a seat in the Kommandant's swivel chair, swinging back and forth with my legs dangling from the chair, like a normal child at play. The whole time I was swinging, my eyes scanned the papers on the desk, searching for any additional information to give to

Alex. I didn't dare touch anything, glancing up every few seconds to make sure I wasn't being watched.

I'd just finished another rotation in the chair, having gotten as much information from the desk as I could, when a voice I hadn't heard in a long time spoke behind me.

"Comfortable, Fräulein?"

Grabbing the desk to stop the chair from spinning, I looked up into the face of Hauptmann Stephan Wolff, the one I named Le Loup because of the creepy look he always had. I hadn't seen him since the last time I served at the Kommandant's staff dinner, but he looked the same, just as creepy, just as dangerous. He caught me off guard, and my heart was racing, but I was certain he only saw a young girl spinning in a swivel chair.

"I was just spinning around." I said with a shrug, as if it didn't matter. "We're going to the athletic games today. Papa Steigler is going to cut the ribbon or give a speech, or something like that," I said, tittering like a silly eleven-year-old girl.

I stood up, casually walking around the desk to sit in the chair Katarina had just vacated, trying to stay as far away from him as possible without being obvious. It felt like he was stalking me, like a predator.

"Papa Steigler, is it?" He moved around the desk towards me. "I heard something about that. How fortunate for you, Fraulein Steigler... at least so far."

"Come Désirée. Herr Steigler is waiting. I'm sure Herr Wolff has business to attend to."

Katarina said, taking me by the hand.

As we walked down the hallway, she leaned down to me and whispered. "Stay away from that man, liebling. There's something about him I don't like."

Chapter 32

The Games

I sat next to the window in the back seat, listening to them talk as we rode through the city on the way to the games. After two years, I'd become part of the fabric of their family, their relationship, but it still amazed me how easily they disregarded how much I heard when they talked. They seemed to believe I didn't listen, and if I did, I would forget.

They were wrong.

"Under different circumstances, I would have punched the old lecher," the Kommandant said, grumbling under his breath. "But he said he would work on Karl's transfer as a favor to a friend. At least that's something. You need to work your charm on him when you go back to Paris, Kat. We need this connection."

"Of course, Anton. Don't worry about Wilhelm. Now that we've planted the seed, I know exactly how to handle him. You just need to make sure they don't deploy Karl anywhere dangerous."

"I'm doing everything in my power, but things aren't going well. There may be trouble with Italy soon, as if we didn't have enough to deal with already. I want you to contact your grandfather in Buenos Aires and start planning. If things go well, we can build a glorious future for our family."

Buenos Aires?! That's in South America! I tried to picture where it was in relation to France.

That's on the other side of the world! I can't go there! I would never get back home!

Wait! Does she mean to take me with her?

What will happen to me if she goes without me?

"I've already sent a letter to Father and one to Uncle Fredric," Katarina said. "But I'm not going anywhere until I'm sure Karl is safe. What I really want is to go home, to Salzburg. I'm tired of this constant diplomacy, Anton. I miss my studio, my students, the quiet life I had before."

He took her hand, lifting it to his lips. "I know, my love, but you can't return to Salzburg right now. There are too many reports of bombing raids on Munich, and I won't take a chance of you getting caught up in it. We have time to make our plans. Let's get through this day. Hopefully that pompous fool Klaebach won't make a mess of things again." He kissed her hand once more, releasing it as the car pulled into the parking lot next to the stadium.

Once we'd greeted the local officials in the stands, I asked if I could go down by the field to watch the soccer players practice. Alex was one of them, and I hoped I could talk with him. Katarina gave her permission, promising to save me a seat next to her.

"Hello Désirée."

I hadn't spoken to Annalise since I'd gone to live with the Steiglers, but the sound of her voice brought back a flood of memories of how much the older girl hated me. Time probably hadn't softened her feelings towards me, nor mine toward her. I held her responsible, at least partially, for what happened to Janine and Rachel. Annalise had been close with Sœur Bernadette, mimicking the older nun's every move in her attempt to be the leader of the girls at La Maison. I didn't believe it was possible Annalise hadn't known what the old nun was planning.

"Annalise." I braced myself for the verbal abuse I was sure would follow.

"Aren't you going to take the field like the rest of us? Of course, you're not. Wouldn't want to mess up that pretty new dress, would you?" She sneered at me as she leaned against the fence, stretching in the same blouse and shorts all the other girls were wearing.

"What do you want, Annalise?" I asked, trying to stay casual and nonchalant so I wouldn't draw the attention of Katarina or the Kommandant, who could see me from the stands.

"I just wanted to see for myself if it was true."

"If what was true?"

"If you've really become one of them, like everyone says."

I wanted to scream at her, tell her everyone was wrong, but I couldn't. All I could do was accept the judgement and the sting it left on my heart.

"What difference does it make to you, Annalise? You hated me before any of this happened."

"It matters, because I care about Alex. I don't want to see anything happen to him because of some misguided heroic notion he has of saving someone who doesn't deserve to be saved... So, are you French or are you Boche?" she asked, keeping her voice low but demanding.

I leaned against the fence with my forearms, watching the players practicing. Alex was there, waving when he saw Annalise and me standing together.

"Well, which is it?" She waved back to Alex.

"I'm a French girl, trying to stay alive, like everyone else."

"Right, but you get to do it with nice clothes and a full belly," she sneered, then she moved away towards a group of girls lining up to take the field for the start of the program.

Someone kicked a ball which bounced against the fence and came to rest in front of me. Alex ran up to retrieve it and stopped, bending down next to the fence to re-tie his shoes.

"Hi, Désirée. Did you and Annalise have a friendly talk?" he asked, pretending to ignore me.

"She still hates me. We need to talk, Alex. Something happened today."

"Not here. Don't worry about Annalise. She's one of us. Can you meet me in the little park later?" he asked as he stood up, soccer ball in hand, never looking at me.

"No, not tonight. Tomorrow. I can be there at three."

"See you then." He dropped the ball and kicked it into the air in front of him, then bounced it off his head toward a boy a few meters away.

As I watched Alex run across the field, I worried about what he told Annalise about me. I didn't trust her, but apparently Alex did, and for now at least, I had to accept that. There was nothing I could do but wait and keep pretending to be what everyone thought I was.

I wandered back to the stands to sit next to Katarina and be the dutiful daughter they expected.

Under other circumstances, it might have been a lovely day, perfect for a family outing at a sporting event, but the war and the German occupation had been going on for three years and the toll it had taken marked every French face I saw that day; young athletes and spectators alike.

It was as if they were all pretending to be happy to be there, pretending they wanted to perform for the Vichy and Nazi elite who filled the stands. But I felt the tension, saw the furtive glares of hatred aimed at the French

Police stationed around the stadium and field, ostensibly there to maintain order.

A group of young German soldiers, on leave from the military base just north of Châlons, came to watch the games and cheer on their soccer team while they enjoyed the Spring sunshine. They raucously displaced a couple of families from the first two rows of seats, which earned them a sharp word from the Kommandant about decorum. But that didn't appease the crowd in the stands behind them, judging from the tight-lipped, blank stares I witnessed.

A loud blast from a horn filled the air, signaling the start of the games and silencing the crowd. Then the sound of a drumbeat began and at the far side of the field, two lines of students entered onto the track, walking in step with the beat of the drum. Each line moved in opposite directions, boys going to the left and girls going right, with the youngest leading both lines.

Simultaneously, a guard of French Police and German soldiers carrying the Vichy and Nazi flags marched straight across the center of the field to face the dais, then stood at attention until the procession was complete.

The lines of girls and boys met in front of the stands, turning sharply onto the field, forming uniform rows facing the dais on either side of the guard. When the last students had taken their places in line, the drumbeat stopped.

A few seconds later *Deutschlandlied*, the German national anthem began blaring out of the loudspeakers, bringing the crowd reluctantly to their feet. The German flag guard ceremoniously raised the Nazi flag on the pole to the right of the dais, then stood at attention until the song ended. The Vichy anthem, *Maréchal nous voilà*, began immediately, sung by all the participants on the field (though not very enthusiastically by some), while the French Police raised the Vichy flag.

Once the music ended, the crowd took their seats, waiting for the microphone on the dais to be connected for the speeches that would follow.

Suddenly, a familiar melody drifted over the stadium. *La Marseillaise*, the forbidden anthem of Free France, was being loudly broadcast by some brave soul from somewhere close by. The direction of the sound was confusing, seeming to come from everywhere and nowhere, filling the air with the one melody which could stir the heart and mind of every French person there.

I looked around and saw mostly surprised, then guarded or passive reactions to this overt demonstration of resistance. Some were even indifferent. Only a few old men stood up while the forbidden anthem played; their national pride deeply engrained. Their families pulled them to their seats, obviously fearing repercussions from the Police Chief, who quickly dispatched his men to apprehend the terrorists.

The faces of the students on the field told a different story. Most of them looked straight ahead with blank smiles on their faces while the song played on. They looked like they were all in on a secret, and I hoped the Kommandant and Police Chief didn't notice.

As suddenly as it had begun, the song ended, leaving the officials in charge scrambling to apologize to the Kommandant for the disruption and assuring him of a swift arrest. I sent up a silent prayer that whoever had dared to play that song had gotten away before the police could find them.

Those few minutes ended up being the best part of the entire day for me. Hearing *La Marseillaise* and seeing the reactions of the French people, even though guarded, had been the best 'not my birthday anymore' present I could have wished for. The tune played in my head all day long, sparking a genuine hope that the end was near.

"Did you have a good time today, Kätzchen?" Katarina asked later that night, using the pet name the Kommandant had given me.

Nearly every night since I'd been with them, she would come in before I went to bed to stand behind me at the dressing table, brush my hair (always a hundred strokes) and tell me stories of when she was a famous ballerina or when she was a girl growing up with a famous father. That night, though, she seemed lost in her own thoughts, and her question was just to fill the space. The blue eyes watching me in the mirror spoke silently of unasked questions and decisions yet to be made.

"It was all right. The French boys almost won the game, but the soldiers were older, so it wasn't fair," I offered, testing the waters for her reaction.

"They weren't that much older, Kätzchen. Some of those boys looked younger than Karl."

I could see her mind racing to the obvious conclusion; the Reich was now sending its youngest to war, which placed her son in danger of being called to the front. She shook the thought away, clearly not wanting to consider the possibility that what she and the Kommandant had been diligently working on since she'd come to France might all be in vain, namely keeping their son alive and away from the fighting.

"I wonder, liebling, do you get bored only being with Tante Elsa and me? Do you miss having playmates?" she asked.

I searched her reflection for clues I needed to answer her. Should I tell her the truth or pretend everything was fine? By then I'd learned how to dance around the truth without giving much away, so I gave her what I thought she wanted.

"I never really had friends until I went to La Maison, but that didn't last for long. I like spending time with you and Tante Elsa. You teach me things I wouldn't learn if I weren't with you."

"We've had some wonderful adventures, haven't we, meine Süße? And we'll have many, many more. I can show you the world and all its wonders." She stretched her arms wide, then wrapped me in a firm embrace, planting a kiss on my cheek.

"*Buenas noches, dulces sueños, mi amor,*" she said as she shut the door behind her.

She said the same thing every night. "Good night, sweet dreams, my love." And always in a different language; German, French, Spanish, Portuguese, and sometimes even in English, which she was secretly teaching me. Her use of Spanish that night felt like she had come to some decision about where she intended to go. It felt like Spain or South America was in my future, and that thought sent my mind racing.

I can't go to South America. I can't leave France.

France is my home. I belong here, I told myself, but another thought brought the complexity of my dilemma into focus.

Is France still home for me? Everyone thinks I've become a Boche.

They don't see that I'm still French.

What will happen if Germany loses the war? What if they win?!

What will happen to me?

These questions plagued my mind, as I lay in my stolen bed, praying for answers, for salvation. The only voice I heard was a soft whisper, saying, "You don't belong here."

The following day Katarina and the Kommandant left the house after lunch and weren't coming back until after dinner. Tante Elsa and I entertained ourselves by playing backgammon at the kitchen table while we waited for the strudel to come out of the oven.

I planned to meet Alex at three o'clock because that's when Tante Elsa would go to her room to listen to her favorite program on the radio. Just before three, I asked permission to play in the little park across the street, which she freely granted. I suppose by then they felt this small freedom was harmless enough, given my lack of companionship. Besides, no one in Châlons would dare harm Steigler's girl for fear of severe repercussions, or so Alex had told me.

As soon as Tante Elsa retreated to her room, I grabbed a piece of strudel, wrapped it in a piece of newspaper, and headed out the front door.

"Fräulein," the guard stationed at the gate house greeted me. I thought it must be the most boring job in the world, to just stand guard hour after hour. He paid me little attention as I ran across the street and into the park.

I met Alex at our usual place, on the bench in the center of the park. He was working on his bicycle (or at least that's how it appeared); the chain hung loose around the gears.

"Why does Annalise know you want to help me? Did you tell her about me? She's going to tell someone and then *he's* going to know... and then...." I couldn't hide the anxiety I felt since speaking with Annalise. Fear of being found out was sending me into a panic.

I sat down next to him on the bench, placed the wrapped strudel between us, and took a deep breath to calm myself.

"I already told you. You don't have to worry about Annalise. She's one of us. Thanks for this." He stuffed a small piece of strudel in his mouth.

"How can you say that? She's just like Sœur Bernadette. She probably even knew what the old nun was planning and did nothing to stop her."

I really knew very little of what went on at La Maison, especially since that horrible week when the Nazis raided the house. But my fear of discovery allowed me to cast blame on Annalise for what happened to Rachel and Janine.

Since that horrible day, Alex was careful about what he said. I thought he was being cautious, protecting me from any bad news, but now I suspected there was another reason. Something was going on between Alex and Annalise.

"That's not true, Désirée," he said, his eyes urging me to believe him. "Annalise didn't know what Sœur Bernadette was going to do, any more than the rest of us. It was Annalise who found out and told Révérende Mère. Two days later, the old bat was on a train for Paris. Annalise hates the Boche and anyone who helps them."

"Including me. She thinks you're going to get hurt trying to save someone who doesn't deserve to be saved," I said, echoing Annalise's words.

He shrugged, but I could see the flush of embarrassment creep up his neck. "She worries about me, that's all. Besides, that's exactly why she won't say anything. Trust me, Désirée. Annalise is all right." The blush now reached his face.

I had little choice. Alex was the only person I could trust.

We spent the next few minutes talking about what I saw and heard at the Kommandant's headquarters. Alex listened attentively, then asked to hear twice more to make sure of the details, such as they were. He trusted my memory and never asked me to write anything down.

After we finished with that business, I told him about Katarina making plans to leave, and it sounded like she was planning on taking me with her.

"I think she's going to Spain or maybe Argentina, where her grandfather lives. What am I going to do, Alex? I don't want to leave France, but where can I go if I run away? No one here will take me in. I'm trapped."

"What about Paris? Isn't there someplace in the city, someone to help you?" Alex had never been to Paris and didn't know how huge the city really was. The idea of being alone in Paris terrified me.

"The Germans occupy all the places I know, and everywhere we go, Katarina introduces me as her daughter. Everyone thinks it's true. I don't know if I could trust anyone there."

"We'll think of something. Maybe I can find somewhere no one's ever heard of you. You'll become just another orphan again. Don't worry, petite sœur, we'll work it out. I promise."

That's what I loved best about Alex. He never gave up hope, never stopped fighting for the better life he imagined. He shook the bicycle till the chain dropped neatly into place, then got on, straddling it for a moment.

"Did you like that bit with *La Marseillaise* yesterday?" he asked with a devilish grin. "That was courtesy of some friends of mine. They pulled it off without a hitch and left the police scratching their butts. Perfect. See you Thursday." He rode away without waving, as usual.

Chapter 33

A question of time

Two weeks later, I was back in Paris, sitting at the staff table in the hotel kitchen, wondering if I could trust anyone there, if any of them would help me escape my captivity.

The problem was no one there thought I *was* a captive. What they saw was a German girl who spoke perfect French, a girl who, because of her connection to the Nazis, had more freedom and privilege than their own children enjoyed.

That's what it came down to; I had more of everything, while the French people struggled to feed their families. They didn't know who I really was, and I couldn't tell them. Besides, it didn't matter why or how I was in this fortunate position; that I was with the Germans was a problem for many as the war and occupation dragged on.

"What did you write today, ma petite?" Chef asked as he sat down in the chair next to me while his staff was preparing for the dinner service. He made it a habit to review what I wrote in my journal each day before I left the kitchen. He said it was to make sure my notes and recipes were accurate, but I knew he wanted to see if I had written something bad about the kitchen or the staff.

I passed my journal over for his review and waited for the critique. My notes that day had been on the technique of butterflying a chicken, complete with little drawings.

He smiled and passed the journal back. "I've never had a student so diligent, certainly not one so young."

"May I ask you a question, Monsieur?"

"Of course," he said, though I heard uncertainty in his reply.

"I was wondering, do you know what's going to happen when the war is over?" It was a childish question, but one that had been bothering me for a while.

He stared at me for a long time, dark eyes searching mine. He was gauging his response to match his view of who he thought I was.

"I don't know, nor do I know anyone who does. Predicting the future can be a dangerous thing. Time has a way of changing everything," he said dryly, though I detected a warning behind his words. "You needn't worry, Mademoiselle. I'm sure your mother will always see to your welfare. Leave the adult problems to the adults. Run along now."

It was the only answer he could have given me, but not the raw honesty I sought. Instead, he offered the cautious platitudes adults give to children to calm their fears.

The hollow truth of his words haunted me for a very long time.

"Time has a way of changing everything."

I could feel the change coming.

"Hurry chérie, or we'll be late for class," Katarina called to me, impatiently waiting by the door. She hated being late, especially for dance class.

"Coming!" I grabbed my ballet slippers on the way out of my room.

I didn't really like ballet, not having the same physical grace I saw in the other young girls who attended Serge Lifar's beginning ballet class. But I pretended to enjoy myself because Katarina wanted me to love ballet as much as she did. Sore toes were a small price to pay. Besides, she was happiest when we were there, around Monsieur Lifar and his aspiring ballerinas, which made everything a lot easier.

We arrived at the studio just before class began. I took my place among the other girls in silky skirts, leotards, and ballet slippers, stretching at the barre and waiting for the signal to begin.

Tap, tap, tap and we took our places.

First position. This was the simple part. Tap, tap, tap.

Second position. I was usually doing fine by the second position, except my arms were always too low. Tap, tap, tap.

Third position. This is when I'd usually hear 'Balance Désirée, find your center of balance' as I struggled to keep mine. Tap, tap, tap.

Fourth position. Almost done. Tap, tap, tap.

Fifth position. This was the most difficult position to master, and I was never very good at it. Tap, tap, tap.

Open arms to the side, slide front foot to first position, repeat on the other side. Tap, tap, tap, repeat, and repeat until it's perfect.

I never found the balance they all seemed to understand so well. But I persisted with the same diligence and dedication as the others, though not with the same success. This made me something of an odd character in a place where physical grace was the norm. If anyone had asked, I'd have told them I preferred an apron and a kitchen to ballet slippers and dance class, but no one ever did.

After class, Katarina and Monsieur Lifar stood by the door, talking. They always took a moment to say something to each girl as she passed by; praise, encouragement, advice. By the worshipful looks directed toward Katarina, every young girl there longed to be just like her.

You wouldn't feel that way if you knew what her life was really like.

We usually said our goodbyes after class, then Katarina and I would go somewhere for lunch, but it appeared Monsieur Lifar was going to join us.

"Does he know we're coming?" Katarina asked her friend.

"He knows, but we may find ourselves in the middle of his domestic problems. Are you sure you want to go?" Serge was clearly trying to talk her out of something.

"Of course, I do. I should have gone to see him before this, but, well, you know. Anyway, there's another stop I need to make that's on the way. It won't take more than a few minutes. Ready to go, Désirée?" She tucked a lock of my hair behind my ear with a gentle touch.

"Oui, Maman. Where are we going?" I hoped it wouldn't take too long. I wanted to be in the kitchen when Chef butchered the beef he'd been curing. He promised I could watch him do it.

"We're going on a tour of the Left Bank today, chérie. I want you to pay attention to where we go and how we get there. There will be a little quiz when we get home."

There was always a little quiz.

A short time later, we were riding through the streets of Paris.

The scarcity of cars in such a large city always bothered me. It seemed the average Parisian either walked, rode a bicycle, or took the Metro to wherever they needed to go. *Or maybe they're just staying out of sight until the war is over.*

Our car drove away from the Palais Garnier along the Boulevard des Capucines, west to the L'église de la Madeleine, at the top of the Rue Royale. The impressive church and concert venue reminded me of the photos I'd seen of Greek temples, with its tall, wide columns surrounding the entire building.

We turned left down the Rue Royale, through the Place de la Concorde, past the fascinating Egyptian Obelisk. Across the river bridge, heading directly toward the Palais Bourbon, with its own tall Greek columns mimicking the grander example on the opposite side of the river.

I made mental notes of the landmarks, street names, and general direction, knowing that later I would need to retrace our journey on the map of Paris Katarina had given me.

We turned left onto the tree-lined Boulevard Saint-Germain, traveling roughly southeast for several blocks until it curved towards the east. At an intersection where five streets converged, we turned right onto the narrowest street, the Rue du Bac. By then, I was losing my sense of direction. All the buildings looked the same, and there were no major landmarks for me to remember.

"Number 140," Katarina told the driver as we made our way down the narrow street.

We passed eight side streets before Katarina told the driver to pull over and park across from a large building with a statue of the Virgin hanging over the entrance.

Arched in stone, the entrance held a huge blue door which opened in the middle, but at that moment was closed. A smaller door, cut into one side of the larger door, was apparently the way in. As we parked, two young girls dressed as novices came out and walked up the street.

I knew where we were, or at least I suspected. What I didn't know was why we were there.

"Do you mind waiting, Serge?" Katarina asked. "I won't be more than a few minutes."

"Go on Kat. We'll be fine, but don't be too long. You know how he hates interruptions when he's working, so we need to arrive soon." He leaned back into the cushioned seat and lit a cigarette.

"I'll be right back," she said, climbing out of the car.

I watched her disappear through the blue door, just like the blue door at La Maison, and a chill went down my spine. A million thoughts went through my head about why she would go there, but none made any sense to me. Serge Lifar seemed just as confused about her motives when I asked him, "Monsieur, is this a church?"

"Oui, a church of sorts. This, ma petite, is the Motherhouse for the Sisters of Charity. Around the corner is the old hospital and I believe there's an orphanage somewhere on the grounds. Though why our Kat would come here is a mystery."

I had been with Serge Lifar many times, but never without Katarina. He was an intense man, with large dark eyes that could both frighten and amuse. He was one of Katarina's dearest friends, despite being younger than her, and the Kommandant disapproval.

I overheard the Kommandant tell Katarina that she should spend more time concentrating on her duty to the Reich, and less time with frivolous dancers and artists. She told him she'd do as she liked and see whom she pleased. It was one of many arguments they had, always ending in a truce, which somehow brought them back together.

While Serge Lifar and I waited for Katarina's return, I asked him the same question I asked Chef earlier. "Monsieur, what's going to happen after the war ends?"

He gave me a funny look, then stretched his long legs out in front of him.

"When the war is over, Paris will awaken from her dark slumber. The lights will come on and the people will fill the streets with music. Paris will once again sparkle as the jewel of Europe. It is a day I long for, ma petite."

His vision of the future sounded a lot like his memory of how Paris had been before the war, before the Nazis had taken over everything. He assumed whether the Nazis win or lose the war, they would leave Paris, and everything would go on as it had before the nightmare started.

I didn't think that was possible. Nothing would ever be like it was before.

Chapter 34

The Spainard

True to her word, Katarina hurried out of the blue door and climbed into the car, a little breathless but pleased with herself.

"Not to pry, Kat, but what business could you possibly have with the nuns?" Serge Lifar asked.

It was a question I was dying to ask but would never have dared.

Katarina smiled sweetly. "Insurance, Serge, just insurance. Come, let's not keep the Spaniard waiting. René, Rue des Grands Augustins, s'il vous plaît."

I had no time to ponder what she meant by 'insurance' because the car was moving, and I needed to pay attention. We turned left at the next corner onto Rue de Sèvres, heading toward the river. The street name changed to Rue du Fours at some point, but kept in the same direction.

Like so much of Paris, this neighborhood was a maze of narrow streets webbing off the larger intersections, sometimes six streets coming together at a central axis, like spokes of a wheel. The buildings lining every street were tall and squeezed together, making it difficult to find any distinguishing landmarks. I settled for the street names and what I hoped was the general direction of our journey.

After several minutes, we were back on the Boulevard Saint-Germain, heading east and into the heart of the Latin Quarter. A left turn onto

Boulevard Saint-Michel brought us to the river once again. We were directly across the river from the Ile de la Cité, which had once been the entire city of Paris a thousand years before.

Time changes everything. Chef's words flashed across my mind.

A left turn onto the Quai des Grands Augustins, which was wide and open to the sky on the riverside, brought us to the narrow street we were looking for; Rue des Grands Augustins.

"Park on the Quai. It's only a few doors down and there's nowhere to park down there," Serge said, motioning the driver to a space on the left side of the street in front of a café.

"We may be an hour, René, perhaps less, if we find our host otherwise occupied. Please get the basket from the back for me." Katarina said as the driver opened the door for us.

"Of course, Madame. I'll be here waiting when you're ready."

He pulled out a basket and handed it to Serge, who hefted the basket with a devilish grin on his face, then laughed out loud, drawing the attention of the people in the café.

"What's this dear Kat? More insurance?"

Katarina just smiled and shrugged, lifting her hand for Serge to lead the way. As we followed him down the narrow street, she told me where we were going and who we were visiting. I suppose she thought it important to prepare me, though in hindsight, I don't believe anyone can truly prepare for their first encounter with Picasso.

I don't remember seeing any number on the door, just the word '*Ici*' scratched onto the already marred surface.

Serge's pounding knock brought an older woman to the door. Dressed for cleaning and carrying a broom, she didn't appear pleased by the interruption.

"Oui. What do you want?"

"Picasso. We're expected," Serge said, not quite pushing his way into the building.

"All right, all right. Follow me. But don't blame me if he turns you away. He's been on a rant lately." The woman led us up the curving staircase to the loft on the top floor, grumbling the entire way. She knocked on the door, waited a moment, then opened it, calling out as she entered.

"Monsieur? Monsieur, you have guests. They say they're expected."

From somewhere in the depths of the large room came the response. "If they haven't brought me what I need, I don't want to see them."

Katarina took the basket from Serge and walked forward to greet the owner of the heavily accented voice. "Perhaps you'll find what you need in here, Pablo," she said, handing the basket over to him.

My first impression was that he was short, at least shorter than most men I'd met, and he was messy. His hair was dark but turning gray all over, and it looked as if he hadn't washed it in days. He was wearing a dirty pair of pants and a white undershirt, over which was an opened robe that did nothing to protect his clothes. Splatters and smears of paint in different colors were not just on his clothes but everywhere I looked.

He stood in front of a blank canvas bathed in light from the window above. When he looked around at the sound of her voice, an unmistakable look of surprise lit his face.

"*Hola*, Katarina. *Que sorpresa*. You're the last person I expected to see. Louis said Lifar was coming." He acknowledged Serge with a nod, but stood there staring at Katarina, not moving to greet her, just looking with an intensity that made me uncomfortable.

"Hola Pablo. I've brought you a few things I remembered you were fond of. May we visit with you for a while or are you in the middle of something?" she asked, looking over his shoulder at the canvas on the easel.

"There is no middle. Only the beginning and then the end. This," he said, pointing to the canvas behind him, "is the moment before the beginning. The end is still unclear. Come in and sit. I'm curious why you're here. Has Olga sent you?"

He moved around the sparsely furnished room, pulling two mis-matched chairs out from beneath a small, cluttered table. The only other places to sit were the stool in front of the easel (which he pulled over for himself), on the bed in a far corner, or on a wooden box sitting beneath the opened window facing the street. I chose the box and sat there quietly, listening and observing while they talked.

"No Pablo, Olga didn't send me. But she's still hurt and angry with you, and I don't blame her. I simply came to see an old friend and bring him a gift," Katarina said, making herself as comfortable as possible in the clutter.

"Olga and Marie-Therese should commiserate. Their complaints and demands sound the same."

He searched through the basket, pulled out the bottle of wine, and opened it. Then he looked around the room and found some empty glasses by the sink in the corner and brought them back to the table, along with a bottle of water.

"Art and passion are partners," he continued as if he'd not paused, then he poured wine into three glasses and water in the fourth, to which he added a splash of wine. "One cannot exist without the other. A concept they both failed to understand." He passed a glass to Serge with another nod, which seemed to say that Serge, being an artist and a man, would, of course, understand his point.

"I appreciate your gifts, Katarina, but what really brings you to this side of the Seine?"

I was wondering the same thing.

"Perhaps you've come to tell me you've finally rid yourself of that tin soldier and agree to become my muse at last," he said, turning his intense gaze back to her as he handed her a glass of wine.

"Ah, some things never change, nor some people it seems," Katarina said, smiling at him.

"And who are you, niña?" he asked as he handed me the glass of watered wine.

"*Mi nombre es Désirée, señor. Mucho gusto conocerte*," I said in my best Spanish.

His eyes lit up when he heard me, and then he laughed, a deep rich sound that filled the room. I didn't think he was laughing at me. He just seemed pleased to hear me speak his native language.

"She's yours Katarina? I seem to remember Olga telling me you lost the child. This beauty looks just like you, so I must be mistaken." His eyes scanned my face with an intensity that made me uncomfortable.

"You should let me do her portrait. I've done a few of my beautiful little Maya." He pulled a cigarette from the pocket of his robe and lit it, blowing the smoke toward the open skylight.

"Come, *mi linda*," he said, taking my hand and drawing me to my feet, "look around while your mother and I reminisce."

The room was large, scattered with bits of furniture, and crates stuffed with canvases. Painting of various sizes covered the walls, all of it fascinating. I felt his eyes watching me as I wandered around, looking at the strange images on display.

There was something odd and disturbing about what he created, like he had stripped away all the layers of his subject to get at the essence of what it was. What remained was almost unrecognizable.

That's how it felt when he looked at me, like he could peel away my carefully orchestrated deception and see right into my soul. It was both uncomfortable and exciting at the same time.

The sound of someone thundering up the stairs, shrieking things I had never heard before, caught the attention of the room.

"Shit! Pablo, you fucking bastard!" a woman's voice screamed out.

Picasso simply shrugged, taking another drag of his cigarette. "My weeping woman, Dora, arrives," he said with a look of amusement on his face.

The woman was still yelling as she entered the room. "Pablo, I swear, if that blonde bitch is here, I may just kill her this time!" She halted in her tracks when she saw Katarina, who stood up to greet the new arrival. "You're not her. Pablo, who is this woman?"

"Don't be rude, Dora," he warned, though he seemed to enjoy the spectacle.

"Mademoiselle Maar. It's a pleasure to meet you. I'm Katarina Lang. Pablo and I are old friends. You may know Monsieur Serge Lifar, and this is my daughter, Désirée. We were in the area and stopped in for a quick visit." Katarina's calm grace completely diffused the tension the woman brought into the room. It was a talent I often admired.

"Oh. I thought you were someone else. I'm sorry, Madame." She was still suspicious of our presence based on the sidelong looks she gave Picasso.

"Think nothing of it, my dear. I've known Pablo for a very long time, and completely understand," Katarina said with a conspiratorial smile. "He tells me you're a photographer and doing some interesting new things with the medium. Perhaps you could show me some of your work?" she suggested, skillfully drawing the younger woman into the conversation.

Picasso hadn't moved from his seat the whole time. He just sat back on the rickety stool, smoking his cigarette, and watching while the two women looked through a stack of photos. Then his attention shifted to me once again.

"Tell me niña, what do you see?" he asked, pointing to a painting and an odd-looking sculpture sitting next to it.

"I think it's a bull's head, but it's strange. The metal thing looks like a bicycle seat and handlebars stuck together to look like a bull. But the painting is different. It's like you broke apart the bull's head and then put it back together, but with no soft parts. Only the sharp, angry parts remain, sitting on a table in a dark room."

He laughed long and loud at that, his dark eyes flashing. "Katarina, you may have a little art critic in the making here."

"Yes, she is a clever girl. It's time we left you both to your work. Thank you for allowing us to interrupt your day. Pablo, it was wonderful catching up after so long. Please let me know if I can help our friend. Dora, thank you again. Come Désirée, say goodbye," Katarina said, heading for the door with Serge, who said little the entire time.

"*Fue un placer conocerte, niña bonita,*" Picasso said to me as he walked us to the door.

"*Gracias Señor. Adios,*" I replied, thinking I'd never see the strange man again.

Later that night, when I was ready for bed, Katerina came into my room to say goodnight.

"Did you enjoy yourself today, meine Süße?" she asked, making herself comfortable on the bed next to me.

"Oui, Maman. Monsieur Devaux let me watch while he cut up the beef. He'd been curing it for over a month. I drew pictures, see." I proudly showed her my journal, which was nearly full of recipes and notes about cooking.

"That's wonderful, liebling. Tante Elsa says you're becoming quite a talent in the kitchen."

"Someday I'm going to have my own restaurant, and I'm going to serve the best food to everyone who comes." I'd been nurturing that dream ever since being allowed in the hotel kitchen.

"And you shall, my love. Tell me, what did you think of Monsieur Picasso? Did you enjoy our visit with him today?"

"Well, he was messy, and so was the studio. There was paint spattered everywhere, and they put nothing away. But he was... interesting, I guess. Have you known him a long time, Maman?" I asked settling deeper into the cozy bed.

"We met long ago when I was a young dancer with the ballet. Olga Khokhlova was a beautiful Russian dancer with the company, and she and I became lifelong friends. Olga met Pablo, and I met Anton at about the same time. She fell in love and married Pablo, then gave up dancing to be his wife. Their son, Paulo, is a little older than Karl." The memories showed clearly in her eyes as she spoke, painting pictures of her youth.

"But you didn't give up dancing when you married Papa Steigler, did you, Maman?"

"No, my love, I didn't stop dancing professionally until many years later. Now, let's see if you can show me where we were today. Bring out the map and we'll test your memory," she said, sweeping away her own memories.

I took the map from the side table by the bed and unfolded it on my lap. This was a little game we played called 'Find your way'. Whenever we went anywhere new in Paris, I had to remember how we got there and how we got home, then show her on the map. She said it was in case I ever got lost, I could find my way back, and because it was important to have a good sense of direction in a city as big as Paris. But it was more than that. It was like she was preparing me for something, some eventuality I couldn't foresee. I always played along because I knew it made her happy.

"Ready, set, go!" she said.

Tracing my finger across the map, I started at the hotel, following our path to every stop we made; dance class at the theatre, the church with the blue door, Picasso's studio, then back to the hotel. The only difficulty I had was finding the street we traveled to get to the river by Picasso's studio. The Left Bank was confusing, but I eventually found my way.

"Very good. Time for bed. Good night, sweet dreams, my love."

That night, my final thoughts were about how Chef cut up that piece of meat; where he placed the blade, how he trimmed just enough fat away. I imagined myself as the head chef of my restaurant kitchen, cutting my own cured beef.

The last thing I remembered before falling asleep was Picasso's painting of that strange bull, all sharp and angry.

Chapter 35

Christmas 1943

That fall, the Kommandant received an invitation to attend a special meeting in Berchtesgaden with the Führer and Heir Himmler, *mit Familie.*

Katarina and the Kommandant got into a prolonged argument when he announced his intention that I attend with them.

"Anton, I don't want to take Désirée anywhere near that man. She should stay here in Châlons with Tante Elsa," Katarina insisted, though I could see by the set of his jaw he would ultimately win the argument.

"She's coming with us Katarina, and that's the end of it. We must present a complete family. If Karl wasn't in Poland, it wouldn't be necessary for her to be with us, but since he's unavailable, she will go. I'm sure it will please Heir Himmler to meet her. Make no mistake, Katarina, this meeting could secure our future and Karl's. Everything must be perfect," he said with finality.

She continued to fight with him late into the night, but in the end, she relented. Her need to protect Karl won out over any obligation she felt towards me. When it had anything to do with the Reich, and his future, the Kommandant always won those arguments.

I think if Katarina had her way, she would pull her son out of the military entirely and send him to her family in South America. She talked about it all the time. But Karl was twenty years old and, over the years of Katarina's absence, had become the Kommandant's son, not hers, which made their arguments tinged with bitterness.

Despite Katarina's efforts to convince him otherwise, Karl insisted he do more than push papers in France. The army sent him to Poland as part of an SS command at one of the labor camps. The letters Katarina received from him always made her sad, but she never gave up trying to bring him back.

When we returned from Berchtesgaden in November 1943, the Kommandant completely emptied the study of all his work things, except for what was in the secret drawer. This severely hindered my ability to spy on him. I worried he suspected something, but by some grace I still don't understand, his suspicions never landed on me.

His mood became anxious and moody. He would snarl at his men over the slightest infraction, a behavior that began spilling over into the stolen house. His need for perfection in all things became more and more obsessive.

Alex told me the Resistance pulled off a series of sabotage attacks, killing two German soldiers. The Kommandant ordered the execution of 20 men from the town where the attacks took place. Alex said the whole province was about to explode.

I couldn't help but wonder what would happen if the Resistance came to the stolen house to drag the Kommandant away, like the people did to the king and aristocracy during the Revolution. *Would they drag all of us away too?*

By mid-December, the Kommandant secured Karl's transfer to the Gestapo headquarters in Paris. That Christmas would be the first time we would all be together. Karl would be at his new post and the Kommandant agreed to come to Paris to spend the holiday weekend with the family.

Katarina spent hours with Tante Elsa planning a family Christmas celebration. She wanted everything to be perfect and fussed over the smallest detail. Her nervousness about seeing Karl again became more pronounced in everything she did. Karl was the only person who ever made her lose her composure. She was his mother, but it felt like she was trying to prove that to him.

This family dinner would be the first time in over ten years that Karl would be with both his parents together, and I could only imagine how he was feeling about the reunion. I knew he would find only an illusion of family, held together by hope. Not even Katarina's careful plans could have foreseen the outcome.

I'd only been around Karl a few times before, and each time he made clear his disdain for me and my presence in his family.

"You're just a waste of Mother's time and money," he said.

It felt like he was jealous of me, of the time Katarina spent with me, and angry about the years she spent away from him. Nothing I could say or do would change anything, so I stayed out of his way as much as possible.

Before Karl went to Poland, he was like the other young German soldiers, all tidy in their crisp uniforms, wrapped up in their Hitler Youth and Nazi ideology, sure of their superiority and ultimate victory. But something happened to him in Poland, something shattered his view of who he was.

When he walked into the suite at the George V that Christmas Eve, the callow young soldier had vanished, replaced by someone who had seen, and perhaps done, terrible things he couldn't forget.

Based on how he looked, Karl started drinking long before he arrived. He was well into his cups by the time dinner began. The Kommandant seemed uncomfortable with his son's behavior and tried to persuade him to sit and eat something, but by then, Karl would not tolerate coddling by either of his parents.

"I'm sick of the two of you trying to control me," Karl said, wine spilling across the table as he waved his glass at them.

"I have followed your orders my whole life." He pointed to his father. "Look what I've become. Look Father. Are you happy now?" He held his arms wide, then tumbled into the chair Tante Elsa had moved to catch his fall.

"Come now Karl, have something to eat," Tante Elsa said, filling a plate for him. "You're letting the wine speak for you, and it's not doing you any service."

"I know exactly what I'm saying, Tante Elsa. I've become what they made me. A monster. And this girl..." He pointed at me with a dead look in his eyes, his speech slow and deliberate. "You think she is so perfect. A perfect example of the ideal Aryan child. She's a fake. She's not your real daughter and never will be. She's no different from the thousands of children our fucking Führer orders us to exterminate every day... Humph. I understand now, Father. Auschwitz has shown me the truth... Leda wasn't the aberration. *We* are." He slumped onto the table, resting his head on his arms.

Katarina gasped, clutching her hands to her mouth. Tante Else just sat there staring at him.

"That's enough!" the Kommandant roared, slamming his fist down on the table. "I will not allow such talk in front of your mother."

Karl lifted his head, looking at his mother. "Why, Father? Is the truth too horrible to hear? Are their ears too delicate?"

"Karl, liebling, please. Can we at least try to have a pleasant Christmas together?" Katarina asked, hope clearly written in her eyes.

Karl sat up in the chair, raking back his blond hair with an impatient gesture. I could tell by the look he gave her she was going to be disappointed. He stood up, adjusting his new black uniform, never taking his eyes off her, his expression pleading for her understanding.

"I'm sorry, Mother, I can't... I can't do this. Forgive me. I'll call you tomorrow. Tante Elsa, forgive me." He walked around the table, giving them each a kiss goodbye. He said nothing to me, he just looked at me with the face of someone who had seen death up close, and it was haunting him.

I knew from firsthand experience that discipline and perfect manners were the foundation of Karl's upbringing. His rigid posture exposed the shame he was feeling, shame that he allowed himself to be less than the perfect son his father expected. He stood in front of the Kommandant, clicked his heels together, saluted, then left the suite without another word.

"My apologies ladies," the Kommandant said, grabbing his hat and coat from the hook by the door, "We'll have to do this another time. Désirée, my dear, I know we were to celebrate your birthday tonight, but that will have to wait. I need to make sure your brother makes it back to his quarters in one piece."

"It's fine, Papa Steigler. I understand." It really wasn't my birthday anyway, and I was worried that the things Karl said about me would seep into the Kommandant's mind.

"Should I go with you, Anton? He was so upset, so angry," Katarina asked as she walked him to the door. Her face hid nothing; desperate worry of a mother for her son, sadness at realizing the boy she loved had become a man she didn't know, and anger that she'd been unable to alter any of it.

"No. I need to deal with this alone. I'll be back once I know he's all right. Don't wait up for me, Kat. I don't know how long this will take. I love you." He kissed her deeply, then left in search of their son.

Katarina fell back into her chair, dropping her head into her hands. "What have they done to my son, Tante Elsa? What happened to him?"

"I don't know, liebling. I don't know." Tante Elsa's distress was clearly written on her face. She sat down next to Katarina, pulling her into her arms. "Everything will be fine tomorrow. Karl just drank too much, too fast. He didn't know what he was saying. Tomorrow will be better."

Tante Elsa didn't sound convinced. The shake of her head and the worried look on her face seemed to say she was unsure of what lay ahead for the Steiglers.

We stayed in Paris until the end of January 1944. I expected to go back to Châlons after the new year, but once the Kommandant had gone, it was clear we were going to stay.

"I'm not giving up yet, Tante Elsa. I must at least try to get through to him." Katarina was desperate to repair her relationship with Karl.

That's what she said in the beginning, but after her third meeting with him she came back to the hotel sad and weary, then announced she had done what she could for Karl and for Germany. She spent the rest of the month visiting friends and "tying up loose ends".

It had been bitterly cold that winter and I spent most of January inside; warm, well fed, and miserable. When I wasn't studying, I was wandering through the hotel, searching for something, someone I could talk to, the way I could talk with Alex.

In the entire time I lived there, I never got close enough with anyone to trust them, and maybe that's how they felt about me. No one there wanted to become too friendly with the German girl. They believed I was Katarina's daughter; they had no reason to believe otherwise.

By then I was too afraid to tell anyone the truth, afraid of being hated in the same way I knew they hated the Nazis. They could ignore a German girl, but they would hate and shun a French girl pretending to be German. At least that's what I believed.

I missed Alex desperately and thought about him all the time. Alex was the one person in the world who knew *me*, the girl I used to be, before I had to become someone else. I constantly worried he'd forget about me, forget his promise to save me, to help me get away from the Kommandant. It had been almost two months since I'd seen him, and I knew anything could have happened during that time.

Then, when I thought about never seeing Katarina and Tante Elsa again, it broke my heart. They had cared for me for nearly three years, given me everything. They saved me, and the thought of leaving them made me choke up with sadness. But I knew if I stayed, I would have to accept what I had become, and remain Steigler's girl forever, giving up any hope of being the French girl I'd been before.

I was eleven years old and unsure of my future, no matter what I chose.

Chapter 36

Decisions

We returned to Châlons at the end of the first week of February, and the following day I learned of Katarina's plans to leave France.

"Sometimes I wish we hadn't come." I overheard her say to Tante Elsa, and my heart sank. "I feel like I've sacrificed everything, pretending to support an idea I hate. All to keep Karl safe. I don't know if anything I've done has made any difference, but it's cost me dearly. Hitler will lose this war and take everyone down with him, including my son. Now I've lost France too. I won't be able to come back for a very long time, if ever." She sounded so defeated, and it frightened me.

"Have you decided about Désirée? What you'll do?" Tante Elsa asked.

When I heard the question, my heart stopped, then my mind raced with the possibilities. *Would she leave me behind? Send me away? Take me with her?* Katarina had protected me from the moment she met me. The possibility she would leave was terrifying.

"I can't leave her with Anton. I can't. But where can I send her where she'd be safe from him? What kind of life would she have? You've seen how people treat her now, like she's a pariah. Guilt by association, and I couldn't prevent it. Injured people have long memories. No, I can't leave her, Tante Elsa."

"I know you'll do what's best for her. When will you be ready to go?"

"As soon as I have the documents. Anton said they'd be ready on Thursday. We'll take the train south on Saturday morning and be in Barcelona by Sunday. With any luck, we'll be in Lisbon by the end of the week."

"You must tell her, Kat. She's old enough to understand, and she deserves to know."

It was a week before Katarina planned to leave, and I still hadn't seen Alex. Unless Alex had a plan, I might be leaving France forever.

Despite the chilly weather, I went to the park on Sunday afternoon, hoping he'd be there so we could talk. When he arrived, he wasn't alone. Annalise was with him. They were walking hand in hand, like they were more than just friends. A twinge of jealousy rippled through me when they sat down on the bench next to me. He put his arm around her shoulder as if to keep her warm.

When I told him about Katarina's plans, he almost jumped off the bench.

"No! I won't let her take you! I made you a promise, Désirée, and I intend to keep it," Alex looked at me, then Annalise with eyes that held a thousand silent words.

"A friend asked me to do a job for the Resistance. If I agree, he'll take us to Sézanne, to someone who will hide you until the war's over."

"Alex, no! You said you'd wait until Spring," Annalise cried, clearly distressed at the thought of him leaving.

"I can't wait till Spring, Anna. Désirée needs my help now. Besides, the war is almost over. I'll probably be back by the end of summer," he said, always the optimist, though I don't think he convinced her.

Alex grabbed my hand, squeezing it hard enough for me to feel through my glove. "You are Désirée Pérot. Ma petite sœur. I won't let them take you away and make you into something you're not. You belong here." He was sixteen years old and filled with all the righteousness of youth.

"I don't know, Alex. It's too dangerous for you." Thought of how many ways things could go wrong tore through my mind.

"I'll let you know the plan on Thursday. Trust me, Désirée."

If I wanted to stay in France, to hold on to the girl I thought I was, then I had to trust him, despite my misgivings.

Those last days in Châlons were harder than at any other time. Everything seemed to shift, changing in frightening and confusing ways.

The change between the Kommandant and Katarina only added to my confusion. Their usual pattern of arguing and making up transformed into a tenderness which forced me to believe they would always stay together. Even if she had to leave France, she wasn't leaving him.

Katarina didn't tell me about her plans until Wednesday night. By then I thought she changed her mind and would leave France without me.

She came into my room at bedtime, as she'd done nearly every night, tiptoeing around the room, touching the things I neglected to put away. She seemed nervous, almost shy, as if worried about my reaction to what she was about to say.

"I need to tell you something, Désirée. Come lie down with me, chérie."

I cuddled up next to her, trying to still my pounding heart.

"I fell in love with you from the moment we met. You've been everything I hoped for in a daughter, filling that empty place in my heart with so much... I've tried to protect you, but I fear I've made things worse." She paused, collecting her thoughts with several deep sighs.

"It's time for us to leave France for a while, sweetheart. We'll go somewhere warm, where we can dip our toes in the ocean and play on the beach all day. Doesn't that sound nice?" she asked, as if my opinion mattered.

"I don't know, Maman. I've never been to the ocean. Will Tante Elsa go too? Will Papa Steigler go?"

"No, my love. Tante Elsa is going home to Salzburg on Friday. She says the trip to South America would be too difficult for her. You know how sore her hip gets when she sits too long. And Papa Steigler must stay here for a little longer, but he promised he would join us as soon as he can."

There it was, the basic details of her plan, and I knew she hoped I would be compliant, like I'd been from the beginning. But I couldn't accept their decision of my fate without protest.

"I don't want to leave France. Why can't we stay? I'm afraid if I leave, I'll never come back." Tears ran down my cheeks unabated, soaking her dressing gown.

She held me close, trying to soothe my distress, but I could feel her shuddering breath under my cheek as she tried to calm her own fears. "I know, my love. I don't want to leave either, but we must. I promise we'll come back as soon as we can. I promise."

We both knew that promise was a lie, the type of white lie a parent tells a child, because the truth is far too painful.

All I could do was lie in her arms and cry, totally miserable. Until then, I hadn't considered how Katarina would feel if I ran away. My only thought had been to get away from the Kommandant, from the Nazis. As I released my long pent-up misery onto her silk dressing gown, I knew she would mourn my loss, like she had Leda's, but now *I* would be the cause of her unhappiness. She stroked my back, humming softly until my sobs subsided and I finally fell asleep.

I spent the next day following Tante Elsa around like a sad lost puppy, helping her pack the things to be sent to Salzburg, including the phonograph and box of records. Katarina said we'd be traveling light, and the phonograph would be too much trouble to take with us.

That music had been the soothing balm keeping the illusion of peace alive within the walls of the stolen house. After we packed and sealed the boxes, the house felt eerily empty, like it was done with our intrusion and wanted us all to leave.

After lunch, Tante Elsa and I spent the afternoon in the kitchen baking two big apple strudels from her old family recipe, which she thoughtfully wrote in my cooking journal.

As happy as that last day in the kitchen with her had been, it was a mystery why we made so much strudel. We were all leaving soon and couldn't possibly eat it all. Her motives became clear when Alex arrived at his usual time that afternoon.

Tante Elsa wrapped one of the cooled pastries in a clean kitchen towel and wrapped an old newspaper around that, tying it with a string. She headed for the back door, strudel in hand. "Coming Désirée?"

As soon as we stepped out into the courtyard, she greeted Alex, her tone light and friendly.

"Bonjour, Alex. It's nice to see you again. I wonder if you could help us with something. Désirée and I have made far too much strudel this afternoon. I'm afraid I will become as big as a house if I eat it all. Would you mind taking one, so it doesn't go to waste?" she asked, handing the package of pastry to a stunned Alex.

"Of course, Madame. Merci beaucoup. I'll share it with my family. Merci," Alex said with an expression both surprised and comical.

"One more thing Alex," Tante Elsa said, her voice turning serious, "I want to thank you for being such a loyal friend to Désirée. These past few years haven't been easy for her, or for anyone here, but I am very grateful she's had you. Thank you, Alex. You're a good boy, a good friend. Always stay safe." She left us standing in the courtyard with baffled expressions on our faces.

"I don't know what to do, Alex. This is so hard," I said in a hushed whisper as we sat down on the bench. "I'm afraid to run away with you, and I'm afraid to leave with Katarina. I don't know what to do."

"Well, I do know. You must stay in France. You belong here, Désirée. If you go with her, you'll be giving up everything, giving up who you're supposed to be. You'll be letting them win. I know you're frightened, but you're also a survivor. You can do this." He was so certain he knew best, and I wanted more than anything to believe him.

"Tante Elsa is leaving tomorrow at four, and Katarina says we're leaving early on Saturday. How can I get away, Alex?"

"Don't go to the station with them tomorrow. Make them leave you here. Once they're gone, leave the house like you're going for a walk in the park. I have everything set. Meet me at four o'clock, at the south end of the park. Dress warm, in layers. Only bring what you can't do without, nothing big, though. I'll be waiting next to a white delivery van, the kind the Boche are familiar with, so they won't look too closely. We'll be out of town before the sun goes down. Trust me, Désirée, I know this can work. By the time they realize you're gone, it will be too late. We'll be far away, and they won't know where to look." He gave me a hard stare, his eyes boring holes in mine, like he wanted to make sure I knew *he* was the one person I should listen to, should trust.

I was more unsure than ever, but knew I had to choose between Alex and Katarina. In the end, it was the Kommandant who decided.

By Friday morning, the tension inside the stolen house was palpable. The Kommandant was on edge, and every time he saw me crying or sniffling, he snarled at me. "Straighten up girl. I'll have no more of that."

But by then I couldn't hold on to my mask, my unhappiness was too overwhelming.

I wasn't sure what upset him more, Katarina leaving, the new orders he received that morning, or his frustration with me. I had served his purpose; kept Katarina with him in France. Now that she was leaving, I became an annoyance, a hindrance to the last hours he would spend with her. He lost his self-control with me at the end of our last meal together.

As I was clearing the table of our lunch dishes with tears running down my face, I did the unthinkable; I dropped the half empty bottle of wine onto the table in front of him.

"*Verdammt!* You stupid girl. Look what you've done!" he roared, leaping to his feet, wiping the red wine from his uniform trousers. Then he slapped my face with the back of his hand, so hard I thought my head would fly off.

The blow immediately silenced me. Katarina and Tante Elsa both jumped up to intervene; one to soothe me, the other to calm him.

"Anton, it was an accident. Please. Go change out of those trousers. You've another pair hanging in the wardrobe," Katarina said, placing herself between me and her husband, preventing any additional punishment.

He glared down at me, angry at my imperfection. I wondered if Karl had ever felt the sting of that look.

"Now you have something to cry about," he said, fuming with rage. "As punishment, you'll stay home when we take Elsa to the station. And if you don't stop that crying, I'll lock you in your room." He turned on his heel and marched out of the room.

"I will not allow her willfulness to ruin our last night together, Kat," I heard him say as Katarina guided him up the stairs to change.

"Komm, liebling. Let's get this mess cleaned up before he comes back down," Tante Elsa said as I hurried to clear the rest of the table, including the now stained tablecloth.

"I'm sorry Tante Elsa. I didn't mean to drop it." But a part of me knew it wasn't totally an accident.

"Ja, liebling. I know. Just get these dishes washed and put away while I take care of this." She threw the stained tablecloth into the washtub by the back door, then doused it with seltzer water.

My face stung with a thousand tiny needles, and I knew it was probably very red, but I had stopped crying. He never hit me before, never had to, because I *always* did exactly as they expected, except that day. I couldn't pretend anymore.

After we washed and put away the dishes, Tante Elsa and I sat at the little table sharing the last of the strudel. I allowed myself one last burst of emotion and threw myself into her arms, hugging her as tightly as I dared. I hated letting her go because my heart told me I'd never see her again.

"There, there, sweet girl. No more tears now." She stroked my back and kissed the top of my head. "You'll always be here in my heart, always." After wiping my tears away with one of her embroidered hankies, she tucked it into the pocket of my sweater, giving it a little pat. "You just be a good girl, and everything will be fine. Tomorrow is a new day."

Katarina came into the kitchen holding the stained trousers and carelessly threw them onto the tablecloth soaking in the washtub. She looked at Tante Elsa and me, then straightened her shoulders as if to face one last battle before the end.

"Anton will be down in a moment. Are you ready, Tante Elsa?"

"Ja. We're ready. I just need to get my coat and handbag. I'll meet you at the door." She left us alone in the kitchen.

"I'm so sorry, Désirée. Does it still sting?" Katarina asked, gently touching my face.

"You don't need to be sorry. You didn't hit me," I said boldly, my suppressed anger bubbling to the surface.

She took my hands in hers, bringing them to her lips to kiss. I could feel her struggling to find the right words to say, but it didn't matter, her feeling showed clearly on her face.

"Papa Steigler won't change his mind about letting you go to the station. I'm sorry, Désirée." She looked sorry, her sad eyes searching mine for understanding.

"I've asked him to take me on a drive through the vineyards, after Tante Elsa's train leaves, so we can have some time alone together before you and I leave tomorrow. It will only be for a few hours, sweetheart. We'll be back by seven, before bedtime. All right?"

This was my opportunity to leave, and I believed she knew I would run away. Their drive through the country was her way of giving me a chance, a choice.

"It's all right, Mama Kat. I'll be fine," I said, wrapping my arms around her and giving her a kiss on the cheek.

We walked together to the front door where the Kommandant and Tante Elsa were waiting. He gave me a look that left no doubt what would happen should I shed even one more tear in his presence. I pulled my mask back in place and did what he expected.

"I'm sorry I dropped the wine and ruined your pants, Papa Steigler." The words almost stuck in my throat.

"Let this be a lesson for you. I will not tolerate clumsiness and self-indulgent emotions. Do you understand me?"

"Jawohl, mein Herr." I said, certain it was the last time I would ever say that to him.

"Give me a kiss goodbye, Désirée. Be sure to write as soon as you can," Tante Elsa said, stepping in to ease the moment as she pulled me into a last embrace. "Be safe," she whispered in my ear.

"Merci," I said softly into hers, then she slipped from my embrace, following the Kommandant out the door.

"I love you, Désirée." Katarina hugged me fiercely before she followed them out.

"I love you too," I whispered as the door closed.

Chapter 37

The escape

The chiming clock in the Kommandant's study broke through my immobility. I'd been staring at the closed door for a while, numb with sadness, tears running down my face. The sound alerted me to the fact it was a quarter past three, and if I was really going to leave, I'd need to hurry to meet Alex on time.

Defiantly, I stepped into the Kommandant's study and reached under his desk to release the latch to the secret drawer, the place he kept his secrets, things he valued. I wanted to hurt him as much as he hurt me, so I poured the contents onto his desk and examined everything, committing it all to memory. Then I threw everything into the fire, except for the little key. It was a minor act of revenge, but it felt good. After replacing the secret drawer, I hurried from the room.

I ran upstairs to add another layer to what I was already wearing. Alex said to dress in layers, and it was still bitterly cold at nighttime, so I gratefully followed his advice. I packed my satchel with what I needed, tied the key to my doll with Jean-Michel's ribbon, and tucked it safely at the bottom of the satchel with my other treasures.

Hurry, a voice whispered.

In the bathroom I used the toilet, then washed my face, the signs of a dark bruise blooming across my cheek. Ripping the braids from my hair,

I shed the last vestige of my role as Steigler's Girl, then pulled a knit cap over my wavy curls. My cooking journal got tucked down into the inside of the bag, then I flipped the cover closed and slipped the satchel over my shoulder. I chose my sturdiest shoes and warmest coat, then headed for the door.

Hurry. HURRY. The voice was getting louder.

I checked myself in the mirror above the desk; blue eyes still rimmed with red from all the tears, bruised cheek and wayward hair, bundled up to brave the cold, looking like anyone's child. I prayed I could get far enough away that I could become just another French girl again.

Before I walked out of the room for the last time, I wrote a brief note on the inside of the journal I used for schoolwork:

Merci, Mama Kat ~ Je t'aime, D.

I hoped she'd find it, hoped she'd know.

With a silent thank you and goodbye to the ghost of the girl whose room I shared for nearly three years, I walked out the door.

The house was empty, except for me, but it felt like all the ghosts were making their presence known, finally protesting the intrusion of their space.

"You don't belong here," they seemed to say with each creak of the floor as I ran down the stairs.

"Go now. HURRY!" they shouted, following me through the empty house towards the back door.

I thought out my escape route in advance, knew I had to avoid being seen by the guard on duty. I planned to go out the back, use the side gate which led to an alley, then walk down the alley and around the block behind the house to avoid alerting the guard.

When I stepped out the back door, my heart was racing, the ghostly voices behind me propelling me to action.

"GO! NOW! HURRY!"

I quietly unlocked the side gate, slipping out down the alley before any lingering fear could stop me.

It was a cold but clear day, the type of day that gives you hope the grip of winter is finally letting go. The fresh crisp air cleared my head as I made my way around the corner, my focus now on getting to the park without being recognized.

Be calm. Walk normally, don't run. You're just a girl going home from school.

I kept repeating that, over and over, with each step until finally I arrived at the end of the park. Alex was there, leaning against a tree next to an idling delivery truck. I breathed a sigh of relief.

He's here. I've escaped.

He took one look at my bruised face, and fresh anger flashed across his own.

"Get in. We need to go," he said, helping me into the front, then over the seat to a place where I could hide undetected. "It's just until we get out of Châlons and past anyone who'd recognize you. I'll be right here." He pulled a heavy tarp over my head, concealing me behind crates of empty wine bottles. I heard him settle among the crates behind the driver and pull another tarp over himself. Then the truck started moving, taking me away from the Kommandant, I hoped.

Curled into the small space with my heart racing faster than ever, my mind filled with the possibilities of what could happen, both good and bad. My escape seemed easy, but I couldn't silence the nagging feeling that it had been too easy, that hidden obstacles lay somewhere ahead.

The truck came to a brief stop at what I assumed to be the bridge crossing at the River Marne. He spoke with the guard stationed at the crossing, their conversation brief but friendly. Then we were moving again, out of the city and into the countryside.

"I told you there wouldn't be a problem. I make this run twice a week and the Boche know me. Blind fools love routine." I heard the driver tell Alex. "It's about two hours to Sézanne. You can come out now."

Alex pushed the heavy tarps off and threw them across the crates. "It's clear now, Désirée. You can sit up." When I did, he got another look at my face. "What happened?"

"He was mad about everything. He didn't like it when I cried. Then I spilled wine on his uniform. It was the only thing I could think of to make him punish me, to leave me alone at the house. It was my only chance. He hit me hard and told me that now I have something to cry about." My body shook, my teeth clicking nervously as I recounted the event.

"*Le Salaud*," said the driver.

"What time are they coming back?" Alex asked, his face full of concern.

"Not until 6:30 or 7. No one saw me leave." I hoped it was true.

Alex breathed a sigh of relief. "Good. We'll be safe in Sézanne before they know you're gone."

He reached down next to him and brought out a brown shoulder bag larger than my satchel. "Annalise gave me this for you. She said you'll need it if you're going to help the Resistance."

"What does she know about the Resistance?" I asked, my suspicion of Annalise flaring up once again.

It was the driver who answered. "Anna? She's one of our best couriers. Been running messages between groups for over a year. It was Anna who introduced me to Alex, though I think now she might regret that. She didn't look happy when we left, Alex. I'm Theo, by the way. Nice to meet you, petite sœur." He was an older man, mid-fifties maybe, with dark hair and a friendly manner.

"Merci, Theo. I'm grateful for your help. Alex, won't Annalise need her bag?" I wondered why she would do anything for me.

"No. This was an old one. I had to fix the strap. She has another," he said, then he adjusted his position to stare out the front window. "You're right Theo, Anna was mad at me. But I'm sure she understands. She'll forgive me once this is over." He sounded hopeful, and I felt a twinge of jealousy at the closeness Alex had with Annalise. It was a closeness I imagined but didn't yet fully understand.

"Ahh, *l'amour*. The forgiving is my favorite part." Theo hummed a wordless tune as we drove west into the sunset.

I sat back behind the crates, trying to relax in my new freedom. *Who will I meet? What will happen now that I'm free?* But the nagging feeling in my stomach persisted, the one which always warned me something was about to happen. I told myself it was just nerves, that I'd feel better once we arrived wherever we were going.

I was wrong.

Chapter 38

The courier's mistake

We arrived on the outskirts of Sézanne as the sun was setting. Theo turned the truck onto a side road, then stopped to let Alex and me out. We were going to walk the rest of the way into the town, about half a kilometer. Theo gave Alex directions to the house where we'd meet the 'friend' who would shelter me. It sounded simple enough. Once Alex settled me in wherever I was going, he would meet Theo back at this same spot. They figured it would take two or three hours at most.

Night had fallen by the time we entered the town, the narrow streets settling down for the night with most of the windows shuttered against the darkness. Within minutes of us entering the town, two very large, very mean-looking men with rifles across their shoulders stepping out of an alleyway we just passed.

"Stop right there," one of them shouted.

"Merde! Let me do the talking," Alex whispered.

We turned around and waited for their approach.

"Show me your papers," the man ordered. Alex handed the man his papers and waited calmly for their return.

"You're not from around here. What's your business in Sézanne?"

"I'm bringing my cousin to work in the vineyards. Her grandparents are old and need help." Alex explained. It sounded reasonable enough. I was just a young girl and no threat to anyone.

"Come with us. The chief will want to get your names."

We followed the man down the street while the other man stayed a few steps behind. My heart was beating so fast I thought I might faint, but Alex held my hand, squeezing it for reassurance. He still seemed confident we would make it past this last hurdle.

They led us through a gateway into the courtyard of the police station, where there were two black cars parked side by side. The men herded us into the building and then into an office to stand before the police chief.

The moment we entered the room, I knew it was over.

A Nazi officer sat across from the police chief, and when he turned around to see us walking in, I recognized him immediately. He was Le Charmeur, Hauptmann Rolph Klein, one of the Kommandant's officers.

He stared at me for a moment with a glint of victory in his eyes. Klein was the officer on the Kommandant's staff who caused the most problems, the one the Kommandant complained about the most. I could feel the man's triumph.

Completely terrified, I just stood there, saying nothing.

"Who is this?" the police chief asked.

"They say they're here to work the vineyards. Here are his papers. She doesn't have any,"

"Chief, if I may," Le Charmeur interjected, "I believe this is the female courier we've been looking for. She matches the description, and I received a tip earlier today that the suspect was traveling this way with a male companion. It appears you've captured them," he announced smugly.

I didn't understand what he was talking about. He knew who I was, he knew I was Steigler's Girl.

"Are you sure? She can't be over twelve. They wouldn't use children, would they?" the chief asked, clearly horror stricken, but he ordered the brutish policeman to search my bag.

"There's nothing here but clothes, an old doll and this book," the policeman said, throwing my things onto the desk. Le Charmeur picked up my cooking journal and flipped through the pages. The police chief searched through the shoulder bag Alex had given me, feeling around the on the inside. When he brought his hand out of the bag, it was holding a small, tightly folded piece of paper.

The look of confusion on Alex's face told me he knew nothing about the paper, but he suspected who put it there.

"That bag is mine," Alex said. "I let her borrow it. It's mine," he insisted repeatedly, but the men weren't interested in what he had to say. The chief waved his hand, and they dragged Alex out of the office, kicking and fighting the entire way.

"Hmm. Your guess was correct, Hauptmann Klein. These names have been on our list of Resistance suspects for months. Idiots. Only fools would trust children with such information," the police chief said, passing the paper to Le Charmeur, his interest in me suddenly renewed.

"What's your name, girl? Who are you working with?" the police chief asked me, his tone menacing.

I said nothing, too terrified and confused to speak.

Le Charmeur knows who I am. Does he really believe I'm the courier?

"A fortunate turn of events, Chief," Le Charmeur said, as he calmly put my things back inside my satchel. "Take her to Paris for interrogation. They will get what they need from her there. I will inform Kommandant Steigler you've made the arrest. Your superiors will want to look through these," he said, handing the bag over to the police chief.

"Of course. I'll take her myself. Right away. What about the boy?"

"He was obviously a cover for her. She's the one to question." He looked at me with such satisfaction, and a freezing stab went down my spine.

"Kill the boy, then put the body where they will find it. Let it serve as a lesson to them."

A scream tore from my throat. "NO!!!" Then the policeman knocked me down into a chair to shut me up.

Le Charmeur calmly stood up to leave, never taking his eyes off me. "Thank you, Chief Fabron. You've been a great help." Then he bent over and whispered to me in German, "Goodbye, Fräulein. Frau Möller sends her regards." He left without another word.

"NO!" I screamed over and over until someone slapped me, then tied my hands behind my back and pulled me to my feet. They hauled me out of the office past Alex, while I kicked and fought them, screaming as loudly as I could, but I was powerless to stop them.

The rest happened so fast, there was no time to say anything.

They shoved us out of the building at gunpoint, then dragged Alex to the end of the courtyard by the wall and threw me into the backseat of a car. By the time I could sit up and look out the window, Alex was on his knees. A shot rang out and Alex fell to the ground in a heap, the sound echoing off the walls.

Screaming, endless tortuous screaming filled my ears. Pain ripped through my heart, tearing it to shreds, and still the screaming continued. Then someone hit me hard enough to knock me out and everything went black.

I felt broken, shattered into tortured little pieces reflecting off the puddles on the floor beneath me. The only thing left was the pain, and even that didn't matter, because I knew I would be dead soon. They would kill me, the same way they killed Alex, and then it would be over.

Please let it be over. Please!

It felt like time stopped inside that dungeon, like there was nothing else, before or after. Nothing but that horrid moment, endlessly replaying in my mind as I sat tied to a chair in my wet shift. The monsters kept asking the same questions, over and over, with the same result.

"Who are you working with? Where are they hiding? Where were you going?"

"I don't know, I don't know, I don't know," I screamed at them, but they didn't believe me.

Slap! Slap! "Tell me!" His foul breath felt hot on my face as he snarled in my ear. Then he grabbed the back of my neck once again and forced my head down into the tub of ice water, holding it there until I almost drowned. He'd pull my head from the freezing water and shake me roughly as I gasped for breath, choking, and spitting water from my lungs.

Then it would start again.

I don't know how long it lasted. I'd been screaming and crying for so long my throat was raw and my eyes nearly swollen shut. By then, all I could hear was the tortuous sound of the gunshot that killed Alex, reverberating through my brain, piercing my heart, reminding me he was dead because of me.

Whatever glimmer of hope I might have had evaporated when I heard a familiar voice barking orders at the dungeon monsters, and I was certain the end was near.

"I'm taking charge of this prisoner. Get her dressed. I'll take everything with me. You have the names and addresses you need. Send your report to Gestapo headquarters once you've made the arrests."

My tormentor quickly untied me from the chair, pulling me to my feet. He threw my clothes at me, but I was incapable of doing anything, much less dressing myself, so the garments landed on the floor in front of me. Impatiently, he pulled my clothes on me, pushed my feet into my shoes, then he threw my coat over my shoulders.

A moment later, Karl Steigler unceremoniously lifted me off my feet and carried me out of the dungeon.

"Scheiße! Scheiße! Verdammt! Was hast du getan?!"

Karl was screaming at me, pounding his fists on the steering wheel of the car he'd thrown me into. The meaning of his question barely registered in my rattled brain as I sat next to him, shivering in my wet clothes.

What have I done? What have I done?!

"You stupid girl! She gave you everything, treated you like her own daughter." He was raging with anger and frustration.

And he was right. I made my choice and now Alex was dead. I couldn't go back.

"Scheiße! Why did you run? She would have taken care of you, given you a life you could never have had here. Verdammt!" he roared, shaking his fist in my face.

His anger added another layer to the terror and trauma I had already endured. I expected him to kill me, to lose whatever control he had and just end my life for good. But he didn't. He just kept yelling and pounding his fists on the steering wheel.

"Tell me why you ran away. Tell me damn it!"

My throat was raw and tight. I'd been screaming and crying for hours, and by then I didn't care what he did to me. Alex was dead because of me, and that pain was too much to endure. I lowered my head, letting my tears fall down my face, and I waited.

"Father called after he discovered Klein had you arrested and sent to Paris. He was furious. He ordered me to take you into custody, then put a bullet in your head. Mother begged me not to... Why did you leave?" His tone became quieter, but menacing, and I could feel his barely controlled anger ready to explode again.

"Because I'm French, not German," I said, my voice barely a whisper.

"What difference does that make!?"

I pushed past the pain, struggling to make him understand. My voice choked up with tears as I forced the words out.

"He insisted I be a German girl, and Katarina was taking me away... If I left France with her, I would always be German... I couldn't do that..."

He just stared at me, letting what I said sink in, then with a heavy sigh, he released his death grip on the steering wheel.

"Arggg! I hate this fucking country! I hate this fucking war! And I'm sick of killing children!" He abruptly started the car, then pulled onto the quiet street, heading south into the Left Bank.

It was still dark; the dawn had not yet broken, and the street was empty of all life. He stopped the car in front of the large blue door and turned off the engine. I could feel his conflict, sense his uncertainty about what he was about to do, his hands gripping and releasing the steering wheel in obvious frustration. Then he looked at me, blue eyes shooting daggers of hate.

"Mother begged me to find you, to save you. She's gone now. Father made her leave. Now here we are." He looked toward the blue door, then back at me.

"You chose wrong, girl. What you've done has caused a lot of trouble for all of us. They'll be looking for you, so you better find a deep hole to hide in."

He got out of the car, walked up to the blue door, and rang the bell. He spoke briefly with the nun who answered the door, then he came for me.

"Who'll be looking for me, Karl?" I asked, as he lifted me from the car.

"Everyone. The Resistance, the Gestapo, Mother, Father. Hide, hide until this is over."

Then he handed me over to the nun and walked away without a backward glance.

Chapter 39

Ghosts and silence

"Who is she?"

"I don't know. He just said she needed shelter, and that you would understand. That's all he said. Why would anyone hurt a child like this?"

"Only God knows the answer to that, Sœur. Let's get her upstairs, where we can clean her up and assess her injuries."

The two women gently lifted me from the chair Karl had left me in, one on either side of me, guiding me up a flight of stairs, then down a hallway and into a large bathroom. The younger nun filled a bathtub, testing the water to make sure it wasn't too hot or cold.

Please don't let it be cold.

The other one sat me down on a stool and ever so tenderly began removing my clothes; first my shoes, then sweater and skirt, then my leggings (which I'd soiled during the night's terror), and last, my damp shift. With each touch of her hand, I twitched and shrank away, my body aching with exhaustion and pain, my mind numb with shock and grief.

"It's all right, child. You're safe now," the older nun said. "Tell me your name, dear. What happened to you?"

I wouldn't speak. My throat was so sore and swollen I didn't want to even try. I couldn't talk about what happened, not to anyone. I stood shivering in my nakedness, tears running down my face.

"There, there, child. It's all right. Here, step into the bath. The warm water will ease your pain." She guided me into the tub, the sting of the hot water sending sparks of pain shooting through my chilled body as I sat down and hugged my knees to my chest.

The older nun sat on the edge of the tub, washing me with the soapy cloth, pouring pitchers of warm water down my back. When she finished washing my body, she leaned my head back to wash my face and hair, gently wiping away the tears that wouldn't stop. Touching my bruised cheeks with her fingertips, she probed for broken bones, then swept my hair back from my face, discovering the thin raised scar along my hairline.

"Look at me, child. Can you tell me your name?" she asked as she poured water through my hair and down my back.

I shook not just my head, but my whole body. Terrified, traumatized, exhausted, all I wanted to do was lay down somewhere, and never wake up again.

"It's all right, it's all right. You don't have to say anything."

"Sœur, help me get her out and dried off. We'll put her in one of the novice cells for now. I want the doctor to examine her injuries. This bruise on her stomach worries me."

The warm water had numbed me enough that their touch no longer made me shrink away. I didn't fight them, nor did I help them as they took me from the tub and dried my body and hair. Nothing mattered anymore. I was an empty shell, a dead girl. They just couldn't see it yet.

The room was small; a cot, one chair, a table and lamp. A heavy drape covering the window allowed the morning light to enter the room along its edges. The only thing decorating the pale walls was a crucifix hanging over the bed.

They dressed me in a simple nightgown and laid me on the bed, covering me with a warm blanket. The older nun pulled the chair up next to the bed and sat down, resting her hand on my forehead, her finger lightly tracing the scar.

"Rest child. Try to sleep," she said, stroking my head. "Sœur, please go next door to the hospital and tell Doctor Goffinet I need his help as soon as he can come. Don't give him any details. I will explain when he gets here."

"Of course, Révérende Mère." I heard the door close as she left.

I couldn't sleep, even though I longed for it, for the oblivion it offered. My tortured mind couldn't shut out the memory, the sound of the memory repeating over and over. My perpetual punishment.

The rhythmic sound of the nun's prayers eventually drowned out the gunfire in my head.

"Hail Mary, Full of Grace. Blessed art thou among women. Blessed is the fruit of Thy womb, Jesus. Holy Mary Mother of God. Pray for us sinners, now and at the hour of our deaths. Amen."

A soft knock on the door sent a jerk through me, and I curled up into a tight ball under the blanket. When she stepped to the door, I heard her talking with a man in the hallway.

"...... brought him in a half hour ago. Gunshot to the head. The Police want to call it a murder by the Resistance because the man was Gestapo, but it was obviously self-inflicted. They found him in his car a few blocks from here, the gun still in his hand. He was young, couldn't have been much older than twenty-one. Tell me about the girl. What do you know?"

"Nothing. She refuses to speak, but it's clear someone's beaten her and perhaps worse," the nun said as they walked into the room.

He pulled open the drapes covering the window, allowing in a piercing beam of sunlight, threatening to expose me. I pulled the blanket tighter over my head, hiding from the light.

"That's better. Now let's get a good look at you, girl," the doctor said in a no-nonsense voice, setting his bag on the table.

When he touched me, I screamed long and loudly, tearing my throat to shreds. Flinging myself out of the bed, I screamed and fought, trying to escape him.

Between the two of them, they grabbed me; the nun holding me tightly while the doctor got something out of his bag. "I'll have to sedate her if she won't cooperate."

"Perhaps it's best. She's obviously traumatized. I'll hold her while you get the injection ready."

The nun held my arm stationary with a firm grip while the doctor pushed a needle into it. The pinch and sting of the shot made me jerk away, but she held me until the medication took effect and I relaxed back onto the bed, oblivion finally taking me.

At first, I screamed every time I woke suddenly or if anyone touched me. The doctor said if I didn't stop screaming, my throat wouldn't heal, and I'd do permanent damage to it. He decided keeping me sedated for a few days would help the healing start, both physically and mentally. So, they gave me regular injections of something to keep me calm, wrapping me in a foggy nightmare. That's when I stopped talking altogether.

They brought all my things into the novice cell, everything I had taken with me when I ran away from the Steiglers. It was all there; the clothes, my cooking journal, the doll, and the old woman's shawl, all neatly tucked into the satchel Maman had given me so long ago. I even found the drawing of my family hidden away at the bottom. It was still there, miraculously undetected by the monsters who had torn everything else apart. I knew looking at it would only make me cry, so I left it in place, along with the rest, except for the old woman's shawl. I kept it wrapped around me; the only thing that gave me any kind of comfort.

I had no sense of time, nor did I care. Utterly and completely lost in my nightmare, I hid in the little room with the drape closed; all day, all night, curled into a ball in the corner underneath the old woman's shawl. Even the voices which had always guided me were now silent. I was totally alone.

The nuns would come in to care for me every day, try to coax me out of the darkness. I would let them guide me back to the cot or sit me at the table when they brought in my meals, but I didn't speak. My responses were limited to shakes or nods of my head.

At first, they believed my silence was because my throat was impossibly raw and painful (which it was), but once the doctor declared it was healing, Révérende Mère came into my room to put an end to my silence.

"Doctor Goffinet says your throat is healing well, and you should be able to talk now without pain. What's your name, child? Can you tell me what happened to you?" she asked, sitting down on the cot next to me.

I shook my head in response, unwilling to put words to the nightmare.

"The Gestapo officer who brought you here. Was he the one who hurt you?"

I shook my head again and thought, *Karl didn't hurt me. He thought he was saving me.*

"He didn't tell us anything, except that I would know who you are." She looked at me for a long time before continuing.

"Not long after he brought you here, someone found him dead in his car a few blocks away. He apparently took his own life. Sœur Nadine and

I are the only ones who know he brought you here, and I have sworn her to secrecy. I thought you should know. Perhaps this news will ease your fears."

It didn't. All it did was add one more ghost to my nightmare. Tears leaked from my eyes, and I struggled to hold them back, my throat tightening with the effort. The nun stroked my back, then continued, like she was telling a story she thought I should hear.

"Last summer, a woman came to see me. A German woman, very beautiful and stylish. She didn't give her name, but she gave me an envelope, a donation she called it. Three thousand Deutschmarks, for the children, she said. Then she asked for a favor. She said someday, someone might bring me a girl who will need my protection, a girl of ten or twelve years, with hair the color of summer wheat, and glacial blue eyes, and with a thin scar on her forehead, at the hairline." She waited, watching for my reaction. When I didn't respond, she asked, "Was she your mother?"

I shook my head, closing my eyes against the memories.

She tried to be, she wanted to be, but I ran away. And now Alex is dead, and Karl is dead, and it's my fault.

I collapsed onto her lap sobbing, the sound of my grief leaking from my throat with each shuddered breath. She held me in her arms, trying to soothe my sorrow, but nothing she could do would take away the guilt and heartache threatening to consume me.

"When you're ready, child, come and talk with me. Bad memories fester and grow in the darkness. It's only when we shed light on them, we can beat back the demons. Come to me when you're ready."

I couldn't, wouldn't, talk about any of it, to anyone, ever. I needed to hide.

Chapter 40

Sœur Bernadette

For three months, I hid among the nuns at the Motherhouse of the Sisters of Charity. I didn't speak to anyone, would barely leave my little room except to use the bathroom down the hall. After the first month, they stopped trying to coax me out of my room to join the children in the orphanage next door. I always refused, and they were too gentle to insist I go

Révérende Mère would come to see me every day, just to sit with me, sometimes pray, sometimes talk. She never pressured me to do anything, just offered a helping hand, should I want to take it.

I felt too broken.

Eventually the accusing screams of the ghosts drove me from my room, and I sought some alternate hiding place where their cries were not so loud. I wandered the halls of the residential area, always staying away from windows, always staying in the dark, silently searching for a respite from my torment.

No one knew who I was, no one knew I was there. If I just stayed hidden, no one would find me. But deep down, I knew I couldn't hide from what really hurt me. That pain would never go away, and I didn't think I could live with it.

Then a day came when something snapped inside of me.

Wrapped up in the old woman's shawl, I had wandered the halls since dawn, hoping to distract myself, to push away the fear and pain. There was nowhere to hide from it, the sorrow followed me everywhere. Defeated, I trudged back to my cell. That's when I saw her.

A nun and an orderly from the hospital were wheeling a chair down the hallway and into one of the empty cells. The woman in the wheelchair was old and frail, her face wizened and twisted on one side. Drool was escaping her lips and running down her chin.

None of that mattered. I knew who she was immediately. Sœur Bernadette.

A flash of hatred tore through me like lightning, filling every dark place with a searing need for revenge that left me breathless. It took a minute for the sound of the orderly's voice to register in my brain.

"Girl, come here. Yes, you. I said come here and hold this chair while we get her into the bed."

I obeyed, stepping up to the back of the chair they'd wheeled into the small room. The nun rolled back the blanket, fluffing the pillows to receive the new arrival. I kept a tight hold of the handles of the chair as the orderly lifted the feeble package, depositing it onto the bed. He took charge of the wheelchair without a word of thanks and then left.

I stood there stunned, waves of searing hatred and anger flowing through me.

The nun spent some time fussing over the old woman, who, apparently exhausted by the ordeal, had fallen asleep.

"Will you sit with her for a while? This is Sœur Bernadette. She had a stroke a few months ago and has been in hospital. They needed the bed, so we brought her home to be among her sisters. I fear she doesn't have much time left. Come and find me when she wakes up." She adjusted the blanket once more, then left, closing the door softly behind her.

I was alone with her, and all I could think about was how much I hated her, hated everything. I wanted her dead, as dead as everyone she'd taken from me. Standing over her bed, I imagined beating her until there was nothing left, hurling every ounce of my anger and pain into her destruction.

I didn't do any of that. I just stood there looking down at her and waited.

When she finally awoke, it took a moment for her to recognize who I was. When she did, her one good eye flew open in surprise. Apparently, I was the last person on earth she expected to see.

She tried to say something, but her efforts only pushed more drool down her chin. I left it there.

She couldn't move. The stroke had left her completely paralyzed on one side, and the other was barely usable. All she could do was listen, and I had a few things to say.

I hadn't used my voice in months, wasn't sure if I still could, but my anger was uncontrollable, so I forced the words from my throat, the sound scratchy and harsh.

"I hate you. You're a horrible human being, a monster, just like the Nazis. You killed all those people; the Jacobis, that other family, Rachel and Janine. *You* killed them just as much as the Nazis did. Did you know THAT when you called the Police to tell them about the Jews hiding at La Maison? Did you know they would kill them? They did. He sent them to Auschwitz, along with thousands of other Jews. That's where they kill them. Every day, they kill thousands of people. Karl was there. He said they kill thousands of children every day, and YOU helped them take Rachel and Janine, and now they're DEAD. I hate you. You're an evil, evil woman.

I hope you die and burn in hell forever." When I finished, I was breathless, panting and shaking with rage.

Sœur Bernadette struggled to respond, her wicked eye wide with horror, one arm flailing across her body in a feeble attempt to grab hold of me. I stood out of reach, watching her struggle, relishing her pain. Her body convulsed hard twice, then she fell back onto the bed, her face contorting with a last release of air.

She was dead. One more ghost didn't matter.

I needed to leave. Not because of Sœur Bernadette. They wouldn't blame me for her death. She was almost dead when they brought her in, anyway. I just told her the truth.

I couldn't stay there another moment, and the adrenaline coursing through my veins drove me to action.

As soon as she was dead, I went to get help. It took a few minutes for the house to be alerted to the old nun's demise, but I knew that would be my opportunity to leave. The distraction would keep everyone busy; no one would notice.

I went directly to my room, dressed, and put on my coat, slipped my satchel over my shoulder, and threw the old woman's shawl around me. Then I just walked out.

I walked without direction or destination.; There was nowhere to go, so I just kept walking, and walking, one foot then the other, on and on through the maze of streets. The ghosts followed, whispering to me through the trees as I passed underneath.

"Gone... All Gone... Go... All Gone... Go."

I walked for hours, not caring where I was or who might find me. I didn't care about anything anymore. With each step, the sadness built, layer by layer, until the weight of it was too much. I needed it to stop, to be finally over.

I ended up at the river, exhausted and broken, the weight of my sorrow and guilt unbearable. As I stared down into the murky green water, I wasn't thinking about anything, not my family or Katarina, or even Alex. All there was at that moment was the water, the soft moving water that I hoped would ease my pain forever.

I stood on the edge, my exhausted body swaying with the rhythm of the current. One more step... just one more...

Papa, find me. Take me home, please. I leaned into the watery embrace.

Chapter 41

An unlikely savior

"Stop, girl! What are you doing?!"

A pair of muscular arms wrapped around my waist, pulling me away from the river and stood me against the wall, then shook me by my shoulders.

"Look at me," he ordered. "What were you thinking? You would have dropped like a stone to the bottom with that heavy coat on."

Clearly upset, his brow furrowed with deep lines. He kept his hands on my shoulders, perhaps afraid I would bolt away, then he looked deeply into my eyes, searching for an explanation for my distress.

"I know you!" he said, surprise and confusion flickering across his face. He stood up, nervously looking around at the people walking along the quai. "What are you doing here? Where's your mother?"

I knew he was talking about Katarina, not my real mother, but the answer was the same either way. "She's gone. They're all gone."

"*¡Mierda!* Come with me. Let's get you inside where we can talk."

He took my hand firmly in his and walked me back up onto the street. I went with him willingly, too exhausted to fight. A sudden noise from a passing car made me screech and jerk away, but he held on tight, never letting go until we reached his studio a few blocks away.

No one was there, not the cleaning woman I'd seen last time, nor the crazy woman who charged in while we were visiting. The shuttered windows made it appear as if the space had been closed for a vacation or something. It was tidier than the last time I was there.

He peeled the shawl and coat from my shoulders before sitting me down on a couch with a look that said I should stay put. In the kitchen, he fumbled around a bit, then brought back a bottle of wine and two half-filled glasses

"Here. Drink this. You look like you need it," he said, handing me a glass of wine. He drank down half of his own glass, then sat in a chair across from me and lit a cigarette, inhaling deeply, then releasing the smoke to the ceiling.

"Go on, drink the wine, niña. It will help." He gently urged the glass to my lips.

I took a slow drink, letting the wine fill my mouth before gingerly swallowing. The alcohol burned the tender tissues of my throat on its way down to my empty stomach, where it blossomed into a warm glow, filling the dark places inside. I relaxed back onto the couch and took another sip.

"*¿Qué te ha pasado?* What happened to you? Why aren't you with your mother?" He didn't sound demanding or angry, just curiously concerned.

"I ran away."

"Why?!" he asked, clearly confused why a girl of obvious privilege would choose to run away from her family.

"She's not my mother. I loved her, but I hated him more. I couldn't be Steigler's Girl anymore." The words fell out of my mouth, like dark secrets finally being exposed to the light. All I wanted at that moment was for someone to take away the heaviness, to make all the sadness go away.

"What do you mean, she's not your mother?" He looked concerned, but patiently waited for my response, smoke curling around his head. He picked up a sketchbook and began drawing something while he waited.

It was probably the wine coupled with his cigarette smoke and the hours of walking that let me relax into the cushions, and in that tranquil state I felt an overwhelming need to unburden myself, to tell him my story, all of it, hoping he would believe me.

I started at the beginning and told him everything; my family, La Maison, the Kommandant, Katarina and Tante Elsa, and Alex. I told him about running away with Alex and how the police caught us just hours later, how they found the paper with the names on it and arrested me and then killed Alex. I told him about Karl and the nuns and Sœur Bernadette.

I didn't cry—I'd already shed a lifetime's worth of tears—I just talked, calmly, honestly, and when I finished his expression was unreadable, or maybe by then I was too tired to read it.

Telling my story felt like a purge, slightly lifting the weight of my sorrow. After finishing, I curled up on the couch, pulling the old woman's shawl around me, ready to fall into oblivion.

"*Ay, Dios mío*. What am I going to do with you?" I heard him ask.

"*No se señor*." I said, falling asleep to the sound of his pencil scratching against the paper of his sketchbook.

Chapter 42

Crossroads

I slept through the night, a blissful dreamless sleep, waking up to the sound of his pencil scratching, the morning sun beaming over his shoulder onto the sketchbook in his lap. Still on the couch, wrapped in the old woman's shawl, I was more comfortable than I'd been in a long time, and I didn't want to move. I watched him, his hand moving across the page with an intensity matched by his expression, dark and brooding, and I wondered what he was thinking.

He lifted his eyes, saw me watching him, and his expression changed immediately to something much softer, calmer.

"*Buenos días, querida*. How do you feel?" he asked, putting aside the sketchbook and offering me a glass of water.

"Thirsty. My mouth is dry, like I swallowed sand." I gratefully drank down a mouthful of water. "Merci, Monsieur."

When I realized I needed to use the toilet, I looked around for what I hoped would be a door leading to my relief. He must have sensed my dilemma.

"It's over there, next to the stairs," he said, a smile lighting up his face.

"Merci." I threw the shawl off and ran for the door, the sound of his laughter echoing behind me.

It seemed to last forever; the release was so complete I felt lighter when I finished. I stood at the sink, washing my hands, and looking at myself in the mirror. The girl looking back at me wasn't Steigler's Girl anymore, nor was she the image I always had of myself; Désirée, the little French girl. This girl was older, changed, different in ways I didn't yet have words for. I didn't know who she was, or who she could be, but I saw a spark behind those blue eyes, and that was enough for the moment.

I went back to face the Spaniard.

"Feeling better, niña?" He was standing by an open window, a morning breeze freshening the room of the stale cigarette smoke. I was grateful for that.

Even though nothing had really changed, I realized I felt better, though still sad, still broken, just not as heavy as I was the day before. I returned to the couch and pulled the shawl around my shoulders, hoping for whatever courage it might give me to face what was coming next.

"A little. What's going to happen to me, monsieur?" I needed some clarity.

He took a deep breath, then let it out. "What do you want to happen?"

I couldn't remember a time when an adult had asked me what I wanted. If he'd asked me the day before, I would have said I wanted to die, to stop all the pain and make it go away forever. But right then, I didn't feel that way. I felt like I wanted to give the girl in the mirror a chance.

"I don't know. I don't know what to do anymore." My voice was stronger, but still unsure.

He sat down across from me in the chair he'd occupied all night, as evidenced by the overflowing ashtray on the table between us. Lighting another cigarette, he looked at me in thoughtful silence through the curling smoke, then he spoke in his rich, deep accent.

"A dear friend of mine died a few months ago. The Gestapo arrested him in February, and he died a week later in hospital, before they could send him to die in Auschwitz. *I* didn't do enough to save him. Max was the reason Katarina came to see me last year, to tell me she could pull some strings to get him out of France. He wouldn't go, and I didn't make him go. Now he's dead. I will not let that happen to you." I could hear deep emotions catching in his throat as he finished.

He was an intense man. Everything about him was powerful, despite his stature, but I wasn't afraid of him. Something about him, some magnetism he exuded, made me feel my own power.

He picked up my cooking journal from the table, flipping through the pages, occasionally lifting his eyes to catch me watching him.

"I looked at your journal while you were sleeping. I hope you don't mind. Do you like to cook or is it just collecting recipes and techniques that fascinate you?" he asked, speaking to me like I was a young girl who might have thoughts of her own.

"I've made every recipe in there," I said with a sense of pride, sitting up straighter and looking him in the eye. "Yes, I like to cook. It's the one thing I'm good at, at least I think I am. I wanted to help in the kitchen at the George V, but they would only let me watch. I cooked with Sœur Louise Claire at La Maison and with Tante Elsa and Madame Breton at the house in Châlons, whenever we were there, but that was mostly German food."

"Hmm. And you speak Spanish, if I remember correctly," he said, changing the subject.

"Sí señor. And German, plus a little Portuguese and English. Katarina thought learning other languages was important, so..."

He looked at me for a long time before he spoke again.

"I wasn't much older than you when I knew what my destiny would be. Even as a young boy, I loved to paint, was passionate about it. Painting was all I wanted to do. Then my little sister got sick. I pleaded with God to heal her, promised Him I'd give up painting if He'd let her live. God knew it was a lie, knew I could never give it up. He set my destiny the day Conchita died. I've pursued it ever since. You, niña, are at a crossroads, a time to choose your destiny. Will you be a victim or a victor over what has happened? You get to decide."

I had made a promise a long time ago, to be strong and survive the war, but I forgot for a while, too lost in sorrow and despair, until this strange old man reminded me of that promise.

"Victor.".

"*Bueno.* Then we need to decide where you should go. The war is almost over, but I think it's going to get much worse before that happens. This place is too exposed, so you can't stay here. I know a place where you can stay safe and out of sight until then. Or would you rather I take you back to the nuns?"

I knew it was a challenge. He was testing to see if I was still as fragile as I'd been the day before, or if I could, at my tender age, choose my destiny.

"I won't go back there. There's nothing for me there," I said with fresh resolve.

"*Ay,* niña. You've a fierce spirit. I'll give you that. Are you hungry?"

"Oh, yes." It felt like I hadn't eaten in days, though I knew I must have had something the morning before. "I could make us something."

"No, there's nothing there. Besides, I've something else in mind." He reached for the telephone.

While he made his phone call, I gathered up my meager belongings, ready to repack them into the satchel. Before I did, I pulled out the drawing of my family. I don't know why, but I wanted to show him something to prove my story. Carefully unfolding the paper, I handed it to him. "This was my family."

At first glance, his breath caught in his throat, a crease forming across his brow, then he held the tattered paper up to the light, examining the detail with a gentle but critical eye.

"How old were you when you drew this, niña?"

"Seven."

He exhaled, shaking his head. "Ah, well, your technique is primitive, but this might be the most valuable piece of art I've ever seen. We must protect it. See the creases? They will eventually break the paper. Let me put it in something to keep it safe."

He lay my drawing down on top of his sketchbook, then went to the other end of the studio. After rummaging through a cupboard, he came back with a leather tube, capped at both ends, and a few sheets of parchment. He set it all on the table next to my drawing. Laying my drawing aside, he opened his sketchbook to the last page, then cut it from the book with a decisive stroke of a knife. Bending over the page, he wrote something at the bottom, then handed it to me.

"For you, niña. To remember me," he said with a wink.

It was a drawing of me, lying on the couch with the old woman's shawl thrown over me. He'd drawn my little doll and journal tucked under my arm, the satchel on the floor by my head. I was sleeping, my eyes peacefully closed. At the bottom he wrote, '*la niña dormida*', Picasso 5.1944.

I looked up at this strange old man who pulled me back from the brink of my destruction, and all I could give him was a smile.

"I could ever forget you, monsieur," I said, laying the sketch down on the table.

"Bueno. After all, that is the point." He layered his sketch and my drawing between three pieces of parchment, then rolled them together.

After slipping them into the leather tube and sealing the end, he handed it to me. "Put this at the bottom of your bag, niña, and pack your things. Jaime will be here soon. We'll need to leave as soon as he gets here."

"Where are we going?" I was mildly curious, feeling secure in his company.

"To breakfast, of course. But also, to see a friend of mine who I believe can help you." He patted my knee in reassurance, then explained a few things to me while we waited for his driver.

"While you were hiding among the nuns, there was trouble in Paris, more than usual. The Police arrested several Resistance leaders. I assume they were the names on the paper they found in your bag." He waited to gage my response.

"There are posters with your description all over Paris, asking for any information. The Police and Gestapo are both looking for you as a suspect in the murder of a Gestapo officer. The Resistance would also like to find you. From what I've heard, the different groups are in an uproar over the loss of their leaders. For these reasons, you must stay hidden for now."

This information only fueled my anxiety rather than calming it. "Karl told me to hide."

The posters all over Paris with my description were an unwelcome surprise, and it was frightening to think about what could happen if someone recognized me. So far, the police and Gestapo didn't know my name. I hadn't told them and neither did Karl, but I knew that anonymity wouldn't last.

Chapter 43

Bisabuela

A short time later, we were driving through Paris, the early morning sun at our backs. We crossed the Seine just south of the Eiffel Tower, then eventually drove through the huge Bois de Boulogne Park, where the trees were just filling out with new spring growth. Another bridge, across another leg of the Seine, and we arrived in a modest neighborhood on the outskirts of Paris.

"Park in front, Jaime. I'll be back in an hour," Picasso said as we turned onto a narrow street. We parked in front of the corner house, a pretty, two-storied building encircled by an ivy-covered wall. Whoever lived there obviously cared for the house, though it was modest compared to the stolen house in Châlons.

"Come, niña. Let's go eat something delicious." He took my hand and led me through the gate and up the steps to the front door.

A man in his late forties greeted us at the door, dressed in a gray suit, white shirt, no tie, as if he was getting ready to leave. His handsome, clean-shaven face and dark brown eyes brightened when he recognized his early morning visitor.

"Bonjour, Monsieur Picasso. What a surprise to see you so early in the morning. How can I help you?" the man asked, opening the door to allow us entry into the house.

"Bonjour Julian. You can feed me, and my young friend here. I've a taste for some of Abuelitas' *Bacalao*, if there is any. And I need to speak with you and Lucia, if you don't mind," the artist said, his light-hearted opening suddenly turning serious.

"Of course, Pablo. Come in. Abuela will get you something. I'll go get Lucia. We were about to leave for the restaurant." He gave me a curious look as we followed him through the house.

Picasso patted my nervous legs reassuringly as we waited, seated at a table in the dining room. A few moments later, an old woman with snow white hair and flashing dark eyes came in carrying two steaming bowls of something savory, topped with slices of toasted bread. She said nothing as she served us, snatching looks at the artist and then at me, before retreating to the kitchen.

Our heads bent over the bowls, inhaling the delicious smells rising from what lay beneath the bread. With my eyes closed, I tried to identify the ingredients by the aromas filling my nostrils. Fish of some kind, garlic, onions and peppers, tomato maybe, and oil. It smelled delicious and I couldn't wait to taste it.

The first bite was an explosion of flavor, each one distinct without being overpowering, the combination of ingredients complimenting each other, creating a harmony of taste I hadn't experienced since I was little, sitting in Maman's kitchen.

"Ah, Bacalao. It always reminds me of my boyhood in Barcelona. This, niña, is the best dish Le Catelan does *not* have on the menu. It's reserved solely for the staff and select friends. Eat up." Then he dug into his own bowl with as much relish as I did mine.

"Monsieur Picasso! What in God's name are you doing here with this girl?" a woman's voice asked as she came into the room, pulling her dark hair up into a messy bun. She stood over him with her hands on her hips, scolding him with flashing dark eyes. Julian stood quietly behind her, his own eyes looking mildly curious.

She had caught Picasso in mid-bite, his spoon hovering over the bowl, poised to enter his opened mouth. He looked up at her, smiled, then took the bite, savoring it fully before answering her.

"Bonjour, Lucia. We're having breakfast, as you can plainly see. The Bacalao is delicious, as always," he teased her, winking at me when he took another bite of the stew.

"You know very well what I mean, Pablo. What are you doing with this girl? Why are you here?" the woman asked again, looking me over for visible signs of damage.

"I'm bringing her to you, Lucia, for safekeeping." His voice had become serious, but the woman's posture remained tense.

"All right, I'm intrigued, but first I want to ask her a question." She shifted her dark eyes in my direction. "Tell me the truth girl, I'll know if you lie to me. Has this old man hurt you in any way?"

She was small for a grown woman, not that much taller than I was then, and feisty in a way I'd never seen a woman behave before. I liked her immediately.

"Oh no, Madame. He is a gentleman and was very kind to me."

"Sorry to offend you, Pablo. I can see she speaks the truth, so tell me what this is about. I have work to do, even if you don't. *Dime rápido*," she said, sitting down across from him, her husband standing behind her. The white-haired woman came in with coffee for everyone, taking a seat at the table next to Lucia.

Picasso spoke in Spanish, telling them a simplified version of what I told him the night before, ending with him finding me at the river.

"I recognized her immediately. Katarina brought her to the studio last year when she came to offer help for Max. I couldn't stand by and watch the girl throw herself in the river, could I?" he asked, incredulously.

"No. Of course not. But if this is the girl everyone is looking for, why bring her to me? Is there nowhere else you can take her?" Lucia asked. I could tell she was uncomfortable or anxious. Her eyes took on a darker look than before.

"You know my situation, Lucia. She'd be too visible anywhere around me, and the Left Bank is getting too dangerous with the Resistance fighting the Nazis at every turn. I brought her to you because you and Abuela are the safest place for her. Besides, she's a clever girl. I think she may surprise you." He gave me a smile and a pat on the back.

I presumed that to be my cue to display my cleverness, so I joined the conversation using my Spanish skills.

"If you allow me to stay, I promise I won't be any trouble and will do whatever you ask. I can cook and clean and work in a garden if you have one. But if anyone tries to hurt me again, I will leave," I said, completely serious.

Lucia stared at me, her expression surprised and curious. She looked at her husband, who gave her an affirmative nod.

"All right Pablo, she can stay. We'll see if she has more than language skills.",

I heard reluctance in her voice, but couldn't help releasing a sigh, clasping my hands together beneath my chin.

They both smiled at me, Lucia with cautious curiosity and Picasso with satisfaction. I relaxed a little, relieved they wouldn't send me away. I needed help, and these people felt safe, mostly because Picasso trusted them, and I trusted him.

"Merci Madame, Monsieur. I'm very grateful for your help," I said in as grown up a voice as I could muster.

At that moment, I committed to being the girl in Picasso's mirror; older, stronger, and far less naïve. I would use my experiences and everything I learned to create my life the way I wanted it to be, and this was my chance. At least I hoped so.

Picasso rose from the table, his meal and business complete.

"Gracias para toda, amiga. Tú eres un ángel," he said to Lucia.

"Y tú eres un diablo de corazón tierno," she said, rising from her seat to kiss his cheeks in farewell.

To me, they were both correct. She was an angel and he a tender-hearted devil.

"When you've said your goodbyes, girl, come to the kitchen and we'll talk," Lucia said before disappearing through a side door.

Picasso bid Julian goodbye with a hearty shake of hands, then placed a tender kiss on the cheek of the old woman, thanking her for the delicious breakfast. I followed him out through a side door leading to the sheltered patio in the front of the house.

Another goodbye in a long list of goodbyes I had made in my brief life. I barely knew him, but I'd always be grateful for what he'd given me, a chance to become myself, whoever that may be. I stopped asking 'Why' a long time ago, the question being pointless in a world gone mad, but I wanted an answer from him before he left forever.

"You didn't have to do this for me," I said. "I'm not your responsibility. You could have given me a few francs and sent me away this morning or taken me back to the nuns. Why did you save me? Why didn't you let me fall yesterday?"

He didn't owe me an answer, didn't owe me anything. He'd already given me back my life, but I hoped he would give me this one last gift, his honesty.

Casually leaning against the wall of the house, he took a drag from his cigarette, looking at me with those dark intense eyes, a thousand unknowable memories flashing across them.

"Lucia is right, you know," he said. "I have a terrible reputation with the women in my life, but not with children. I love my children." He took another drag, then threw it to the ground.

"Perhaps it's because you remind me of Maya," he said, looking deeply into my eyes, "or maybe I owed it to Katarina for what she tried to do for Max. Maybe the answer is simply that I needed to prove to myself that I'm not the heartless bastard people believe me to be. All I've done, niña, is open a door. It's you who must walk through it. I believe you're fierce enough to face your destiny. Look what you've gone through to get here. Believe in yourself, niña. Shape your own destiny." When he finished, he pulled me into a fatherly embrace, like Papa would give me, ending with a kiss on my forehead.

I watched from the shelter of the patio as his car drove down the street and disappeared. Sad and nervous, I was also grateful for the door he opened.

I stood there gathering my thoughts, my courage for a few minutes. Inside were more strangers, more challenges I would have to face on my own this time, and it frightened me, but also steeled my resolve to survive.

I took a deep breath and stepped through the open door.

"Come here, girl. Let's have a look at you," Lucia said, drawing me into the kitchen. "What's your real name?" Her dark eyes assessed me and the risk she was taking on.

"Désirée Marie Rondeau, Madame." I wasn't afraid of using Rondeau anymore. It had been a long time, and a lot had happened since the old woman's warning.

"My name is Lucia Laurent. This is my grandmother, Madame de Santo. Take a seat Désirée."

I sat across from them at a small table in the kitchen. Nerves fluttered through me as I wondered what these new people were like and what would happen to me. I hoped everything would turn out the way Picasso thought, but I wasn't sure, so I kept my guard up.

Lucia gave me a hard look. "I heard what Pablo had to say about your circumstance. Now I want to hear your version. First, do you have any family at all?"

"No, Madame. They were all killed when the war started." I knew I should stick to the truth, or this sharp-eyed woman would know I was lying.

"I'm very sorry. That's a difficult thing for a child to go through," she said, her tone softening. "Then the Steiglers took you from the orphanage in Châlons. Why?"

I settled my nerves with a deep breath, giving myself a moment to frame my response.

"I was a gift. The Kommandant gave me to Katarina to make her stay in France with him. I look like their daughter, Leda. He had taken Leda away from Katarina and killed her because there was something wrong with her. She wasn't perfect. I needed to be perfect, or he would kill me, too."

"In all that time, three years, and you never sought help from anyone, not even Madame Steigler?" Lucia sat back in her chair, never taking her eyes off me.

I looked at her for a long time, wondering how to make her understand how it had been for me. Only eight years old when it started, I felt totally abandoned by everyone except Alex.

"Everyone I knew in Châlons was under the Kommandant's control. They were too afraid to do anything. In Paris, everyone thought I was Katarina's daughter. That's how she introduced me to people. The Germans were everywhere we went, and the French people at the hotel were the same as in Châlons, afraid to get too close. I couldn't talk to Katarina because the Kommandant would have known, and then he would kill me for making her unhappy. There was no one, except Alex." My eyes filled with tightly held tears. I knew I needed to answer her questions, but I didn't want to fall apart while doing it.

"I'm sorry about your friend," she said, her eyes reflecting her own losses. "Where did you get the names and addresses that you gave to the police?" she asked with a look filled with pain and loss.

"I didn't know that list was in the bag, neither did Alex. I'm sorry for what happened, Madame. I'm sorry for everything." My control was slipping from me, all the guilt and sadness building up once more.

"Who put it there? Someone did. Do you know who?"

"¡Basta! Nieta," her grandmother scolded. Madame de Santo had been sitting there quietly, her hands folded under her chin, listening and watching the interrogation. It was clear she wanted to guide her granddaughter away from that line of questioning.

"Bien, Abuela," Lucia responded, then she turned back to me.

"Pablo said the Gestapo officer who took you from the Police was Katarina's son. Is that true? Why would he take you to the nuns? And why aren't you there now?" she asked, one dark eyebrow raised.

Talking about Karl and Katarina was difficult. My heart felt like it weighed a thousand kilos and my head ached. I took a deep breath, sniffling back my tears and straightening my back.

"It *was* Karl who took me out of the dungeon. He was so angry. He kept yelling at me, telling me what a stupid girl I was. He told me the Kommandant ordered him to take me from the Police and kill me, but Katarina begged him to save me, to take me to the nuns. I thought he was going to kill me, but by then I didn't care. I had lost everything." The memory was too painful to think about. I had to take a breath.

"Katarina went to the nuns last summer, the day I met Monsieur Picasso. She told Révérende Mère someone might bring her a girl to shelter, a girl who looked like me. Révérende Mère knew who Katarina was, and she knew who I was."

"At first, I couldn't talk because my throat was injured, but I was too afraid to tell them anything, anyway. I stayed in my cell all the time, terrified the Nazis would find me, afraid the nuns would know and turn me in. I never spoke to anyone because I was too sad, too afraid." It was the truth, and I wanted her to believe me, but I could see she had more questions.

"You never spoke to the nuns at all?"

"No, Madame. I never spoke to anyone. After they killed Alex, after everything, I just wanted to crawl into a hole and die."

Tears escaped my eyes, and I bit my lower lip hard to still the quiver, trying to hold myself together. The memory of that night of torture flashed across my mind, bringing with it all the pain and loss. I lowered my eyes, not willing to share that pain with her.

"So, you left the nuns because they knew who were? Or was it something else?"

"I don't know why I left. Probably because I was tired of being afraid all the time, tired of everything. I just couldn't stay there anymore. So, I left." My eyes closed tight as I remembered the look on Sœur Bernadette's face when I damned her to hell.

"Then you ended up at the river where Pablo found you. Were you really going to throw yourself in, or was that his imagination?" Her question took me by surprise, her gaze more intense, and it forced me to think before I answered.

"I don't know. Maybe. I'd been walking for hours, not knowing where I was or where to go. I was so sad and lost and tired that I just wanted it to stop." That was as close to the truth as I could get without breaking down completely, and it seemed to satisfy her.

"Then Pablo decided he should bring you here for safekeeping. What I don't understand is why. It's not like him to do something like this, and I've known him for a long time. Is there anything more you aren't telling me?" She folded her arms across her chest, looking at me across the table, and waited for my reply.

What more was there to say? I couldn't tell her everything. No one knew the one thing she wanted to know. Not the police, or even Picasso. I suspected who wrote those names, but I wouldn't tell anyone, ever. It would only lead to more deaths, more ghosts. I had enough ghosts haunting me already.

I wiped a stray tear from my cheek and told her what Picasso said.

"Before he left, I asked him why he saved me. He said it might have been because I remind him of someone called Maya, or maybe it was because he wanted to prove to himself that he wasn't the heartless bastard people think he is. I don't think that about him. He was kind to me, even though he didn't have to be."

She huffed, shaking her head. "*Increíble.* And no one but Picasso knows you're here? No one saw you with him?"

"No one, Madame. Only him and his driver."

"¡Basta!" the old woman interrupted. She apparently had heard enough and told her granddaughter so. We'd been speaking in French the entire time and I realized she understood us perfectly, but when she spoke, it was in Spanish.

She gave Lucia a hard look. "The girl needs help, and we will help her. She needs a new identity. Think Lucia, for three years this child convinced the Nazis and half of Paris that she was German. I think she's clever enough to become the young French girl that she is. A change of hair color and clothes is what's needed. We can say she's my great-granddaughter, run away from her mother's abusive boyfriend. What do you think, child? Can you pretend to be someone new?"

"*Si, Bisabuela.* I can be whoever you need me to be," I answered in Spanish.

I was going to survive this nightmare however I could, and pretending would forever be a part of my survival. If these strangers would take the risk of helping me, I'd do almost anything to earn their trust, if only I could feel safe.

Chapter 44

A new mask

It was the end of May 1944 when I became Marie Rondeau, a fourteen-year-old from Chartres, who ran away to live with her Bisabuela. Lucia decided the name Désirée was too dangerous to use, so they dropped it for the simpler Marie.

Bisabuela took charge of me, and with her help, a bit of henna hair dye, and a new identity card (miraculously produced by Julian Laurent), they transformed me into the new, older version of me, at least on the outside.

Becoming the new me wasn't as easy as I imagined. I had a lot of practice pretending to be Steigler's Girl, but now the rigid posture, proper use of language and refined manners I mastered were of no use. I needed to learn how a normal teenager behaves, but my sheltered life with Katarina had not given me many examples to follow.

The girls I knew in Serge Lifar's ballet class were all silly, tittering girls I couldn't see myself becoming. When I thought of all the girls I'd known, the one name I didn't want to think about kept rearing its ugly head, Annalise.

Annalise had never lost the hardness forged during her early years on the back streets of Paris, despite the discipline and care she received at La Maison. She wasn't anyone I wanted to be like. I hated her almost as much as I imagined she hated me, but Annalise was the image that kept coming up.

She was smart, cunning, righteously confident to the point of annoyance, a French girl in every way. And she hated the Nazis. She also had a terrible memory for details, always writing things down she wanted to remember. I hated her for that.

It wasn't who Annalise was that I would mimic. It was her mannerisms; a turn of the head, a bored, disdainful look, and a stance that leaned on one hip with hands in pockets. I practiced when I was alone in my bedroom on the second floor, watching myself in the mirror that hung on the back of the door.

At first, I had to stay inside. Lucia and Julian would not take any chances until they were sure they could trust me. I didn't mind; I needed time to adjust to the new me anyway, and to recover from everything.

Once I passed their inspection, they allowed me to go out with Bisabuela to the church around the corner and to the local shops, and eventually to the little park by the river a few blocks away. Bisabuela introduced me to the shopkeepers, subtly making sure they all knew me for one of hers. From the deferential way people treated her, it was obvious they all knew and respected her.

The first trip tested my ability to adapt, to behave as any young person would when being dragged to confession by their great-grandmother.

"Bisabuela! You said we were going to the shops. Why are we here? It's not even Sunday," I demanded, refusing to go inside the church.

"You need to go to confession. It's time you let God take that burden from your heart." She gave me one of her looks, one that said she wouldn't put up with any nonsense, real or otherwise.

I closed my eyes and stood my ground, huffing at her. "There's nothing for me in there."

"Is that so? I disagree. Follow me. I want to introduce you to Padre David, who's the spiritual leader of this community. Pay attention." Then she was climbing the steps to the church, and I had to follow her, but not without a heavy sigh as the door closed behind me.

"Bonjour, Père David," Bisabuela greeted the priest in residence. She could speak perfect French when she wanted to, I noted with admiration.

"Madame De Santo. What a pleasure to see you. How can I help you this morning?" the priest asked, taking Bisabuela's hands gently into his own. He looked over at me, clearly wondering who I might be.

"It's my great-granddaughter, Marie Rondeau. She's just arrived from Chartres, ran away from home. She says her mother's boyfriend tried to hurt her. I can believe it. My granddaughter, Isabella, never had good luck with men. I've brought Marie to you so she can make her confession, to begin her life here with a pure heart. Will you hear her confession?"

It was amazing how she did that. In one fell swoop, she declared my identity, my association, and circumstance to the one person who had the ear of the entire community, thus validating my presence among them.

True to character, I rolled my eyes and huffed at her for exposing me to the priest.

"If this is what she wishes," Père David responded, leaving it up to me whether I wanted to confess.

With another heavy sigh combined with a shrug, I followed him into the confessional. Bisabuela took a seat in the pew across the way to wait.

As I sat in the darkened booth, I wondered what I could say to the priest on the other side of the screen. Surely not the truth. That wouldn't do. Anything short of that would be a lie, and a little voice in my head reminded me to never lie to a priest. Damn.

"Bless me, Father, for I have sinned." I had nothing to offer following that declaration.

"What is the nature of your sin, my child?"

"I hurt my mother."

"How was she hurt, child?"

"I broke her heart when I ran away," I confessed, thinking about Katarina. It was true because I could feel my own broken heart.

"Why did you run away?"

"Because Papa was cruel. He hurt me and I believed he would kill me." This was getting too hard, too real. I didn't want to continue.

"It's not a sin to escape cruelty, child. I'm sure your mother understands why you left. Is there anything else you'd like to confess?" He waited through my silence.

I wished I could forget my sins and never have to think of them again. It was a foolish wish; I couldn't forget any of it.

"No, Père. Nothing," I lied, then I accepted his penance with surly grace, quickly exiting the confessional.

During the following days, I understood what a risk it was for the Laurents to take me in. Lucia kept her distance, uncomfortable around me and not completely trusting me. Then late one night, after they returned from the restaurant, she came to talk with me. I was in bed, but not asleep, when I heard my door open.

"Marie? Are you still awake?" she asked the dark room, light from the hall revealing her in silhouette.

"Oui. Do you need something, Madame?" She could see me clearly, but shadow veiled her face.

"Why did you run away from Madame Steigler? I need to understand why I lost a dear friend because of you." She stood over me, her arms crossed around her waist, like she was holding herself together.

I prayed I could find the right words to make her understand. With a sigh, I sat up in bed and answered.

"I left because I'm French. They tried to make me German, but I only pretended to be what they wanted, so he wouldn't kill me. Katarina was taking me away, and I knew if I left with her, I would always be German and could never be French again. I couldn't do that. If I left with her, I could never come back home." That was everything, the story of a girl trying to survive, and by the slump of Lucia's shoulders, I knew she believed me.

"One more thing. Do you know who wrote the names on that paper?" Her voice strained with grief and anger.

It was the one piece of information I would never give her, or anyone. I shook my head in denial. "I don't know. But if someone must pay for what happened, it should be me. If I hadn't run away, Alex would still be alive, and the other people too. It's all my fault," I said with tears streaming down my face.

She stared down at me for a long time. I couldn't see her face, but I could feel the tension and conflict radiating off her. For a moment, I wasn't sure what she would do. My fate was in her hands, though I thought Bisabuela might have something to say about it. At that moment, I was tired of everything, especially the feeling of guilt that followed me everywhere. I would do whatever Lucia decided.

Lucia let out a deep breath, then sat down on the bed next to me.

"It's a hard thing, living with the death of someone you care about. You have more than your share of that grief already. I'll not add to it." She shook her head and sighed. "There will be people coming in and out of the house at odd times, and I need to be sure you can maintain your new identity around them. No one must know who you were before. Can you do that?"

"Oui, Madame. I can, and I will."

Chapter 45

Making friends

In early June, we heard the Allies had finally come. The British, Canadian, and American armies had landed in Normandy and were fighting the Germans on French soil.

When I heard the news, all I could do was cry. It had been so long, so much had happened while we waited for that moment to arrive. It felt more bitter than sweet to me. I wished Alex had lived to see it, but that was my fault. If I had stayed with Katarina, he would be alive and I'd be somewhere in Spain or South America, living a different pretend life. But Alex was dead, and I would have to swallow that bitter pill for the rest of my life.

My sadness lingered for days, changing into surliness, which wasn't a normal part of my character until then. I didn't know what was wrong, beyond the obvious, and the heightened emotions I was experiencing only made everything bigger and more dramatic than it should have been. Even little things like dropping something on the floor would send me into a fit of tears.

"What's the matter with you, girl?" Bisabuela asked, looking me over with concern after one such fit. "Are you bleeding?"

I looked up, confused. I hadn't cut myself, just dropped a plate, and it hadn't even broken, it just spilled crumbs on the floor. "No, Bisabuela. It didn't break. I'm not hurt, but I made a mess on the floor. I'm sorry."

"That's not what I mean, child. Come over here. Let me look at you."

I stood in front of her, tears still falling down my cheeks. When she squeezed my newly forming and very tender breasts, I couldn't help but flinch. Then she shifted her hand to below my belly, pushing a little and making me squirm. My stomach had been troubling me for a couple of days, but that wasn't unusual.

"You're becoming a woman," she said with a gentle smile. "Your tender breasts and cramping stomach are signs you'll soon bleed like every other woman on Earth. The priest will tell you it's God's punishment on all women for Eve's sin, but that's nonsense. All women bleed each month to clear the way for children, though you don't need to think about that yet," Bisabuela explained, trying to soothe the distress she saw in my horrified expression.

"It usually begins when a girl is eleven or twelve-years-old and continues until the forties or fifties. Soon you'll bleed from between your legs. When that happens, come to me. I'll show you what to do." Bisabuela stroked my cheek, wiping away my tears with her fingertips.

"Our feelings are usually stronger during that time of the month. Don't worry, you'll feel better once it's started."

This new information was shocking. No one had told me anything about this, and I wasn't sure I liked the idea at all.

Why do I have to deal with this too, on top of everything else? Why wasn't I told? It's not fair!

My inner voice continued to complain, but after a while, I stopped. I figured it was just one more thing I couldn't control, so why complain about it?

It wasn't even twenty-four hours later when it happened. I got out of bed, still tired from a restless night's sleep, and I felt the wetness between my legs, dripping and sticky. The bright red stain on the sheets horrified me, even though Bisabuela had warned me it would happen. It seemed like an awful lot of blood, and I couldn't help but think something was wrong. I was standing there trembling and miserable, with blood running down my legs, when Bisabuela found me a few minutes later.

She gently guided me through the steps on how to clean myself and contain the mess that would last three or four days each month. Once I accepted the situation, I calmed down and was even grateful for her kindness. Bisabuela always knew what I needed and never denied her comfort. Besides, she was right. I started feeling better, but I never got used to the mess.

The one advantage to the whole messy business was, I felt more grown up, like I'd suddenly blossomed into the girl I was pretending to be, and it made my life easier in some ways. It felt like being admitted into the secret world of women, one I hadn't known existed. I wondered what other secrets I would learn.

I spent the next couple months in the relatively quiet neighborhood of Suresnes, helping Bisabuela with the chores and shopping, which mostly entailed standing in line for things you probably wouldn't get when you got to the front.

And I began learning a little about the restaurant business from the Laurents, proprietors of Le Catelan, one of the best restaurants in Paris and frequented by the Nazi elite. Expanding my culinary skills became my goal, and Lucia and Julian's talents were the skills I wanted, if I could get them to teach me.

"Lucia? Can I help you at the restaurant? I know a lot already and I promise I won't get in the way." Since my time at the George V, it had been my dream to learn from a professional chef in a real restaurant kitchen.

"Absolutely not! It's too dangerous, at least until the war is over," Lucia said firmly, giving me a look filled with suspicion.

But she was right. It was too soon. My dream would have to wait.

Settling for private lessons on how to make do with what's available when what you want isn't, I learned from Bisabuela, a master of that art. Soon the pages of my cooking journal filled with new information.

"Come with me, Marie," Bisabuela announced one afternoon. "I'm going to introduce you to the young people in the neighborhood. It's time you find your place here."

Camille Dorminy, a pretty 15-year-old, lived around the corner and seemed happy to include me in her circle of friends. Serina was Camille's best friend, and three boys completed the group, Michel, Chaz and Maurice, all the same age as the girls. They all lived in the same neighborhood, grew up together and attended the same school, which had just ended for the summer.

Being shy and unsure of myself, I tried imagining how it had been for them during the past four years, dealing with deprivation, oppression, and hunger.

It didn't take long for me to realize these teenagers had weathered the war resiliently. Their biggest complaints were the lack of food, the intermittent availability of electricity and water, and the curfew. They'd all come of age in an era of uncertainty, and it seemed to give them a careless sense of freedom.

It was music that finally pulled me out of my cautious shell, the music of youth; wild and free. We would gather in an area of common use behind our houses, secure from the streets and prying eyes. Mostly it was just the six of us, but sometimes others would join us. We would talk and play music, sing and dance until someone would yell out their back window for us to be quiet and go home to bed. Then we'd simply move into Camille's or Michel's basement and continue our revelries into the wee hours.

I experienced something during that time that I'd never known before. No one was watching me, no one was controlling me except my sense of self preservation, and so I let myself relax and enjoy my newfound freedom.

It was Chaz Maret and his guitar that really lit a spark inside me. Fifteen and handsome, with dark wavy hair that sometimes fell over his eyes as he bent to play his guitar, his long fingers madly strumming out a popular tune. His voice was clear and strong, with a warm, rich tone that sent shivers down my spine in a good way. He had the longest eyelashes I'd ever seen, and beautiful brown eyes that drew me in, capturing my attention. I loved listening to him play and would sit close, letting my body sway to the rhythms of his guitar, losing myself in the music he created.

"You like him, don't you?" Camille asked me one night while we were sitting around listening to Chaz play.

"I enjoy listening to him, if that's what you mean," I said, trying to hide my blushing face with my hand.

"You know that's not what I mean, Marie. You like *him*, not just his playing."

I shrugged, smiling shyly, not wanting to give her anything to tease me about.

"Well, the good news is, Chaz likes you, too. He's been asking me questions about you. See how he's looking at you, like he's playing just for you, and no one else?"

Camille loved the idea of matchmaking and had set her sights on getting me and Chaz together. It was a mystery to me why she thought we'd make a good couple, but Camille was single-minded. Once she decided something, that was it. Nothing could deter her.

"What questions?" A sick feeling hit my stomach; worry that they would find out, that they would learn who I'd been before, and hate me for it.

"Oh, just the usual; what you're like, if you're really as nice as you seem, do you have a boyfriend back in Chartres?"

I blushed even deeper and had to turn away to hide my face from Chaz, who'd been watching us talk while he strummed his guitar.

"No! No boyfriend in Chartres, and I'm just a girl, like you and Serina. I'm nothing special."

"I don't think Chaz would agree. He has a crush on you, which is amazing! Chaz has never been interested in any girl before. He's always behind his guitar, entertaining us, but also hiding. You've made him look up from that guitar for the first time. I love it! It's so sweet."

I glanced over at Chaz, just as he finished playing, and received the most dazzling smile, which made my young heart skip a few beats as my blush deepened.

It really was sweet. We were both shy, unsure of ourselves, and wanting to please the other. Chaz would save a place for me next to him when we gathered in the evening, and I was always happy to be near him. He never said much, letting his music speak for him, and that made it easier for me. I didn't need to answer a lot of questions or tell him a lot of lies. He seemed to accept what Camille told him about me and didn't pry further.

Ironically, those were happy times for me, despite all I'd been through. But, like everything else in my life, I knew it wouldn't last.

Chapter 46

Shared secrets

By the end of July 1944, the entire city seemed to hold its breath, waiting for the signal the Allies were near, for the moment Paris would finally rise and shed herself of the Nazi bondage she'd carried for four years.

That breathless anticipation infected my new friends with excitement and reckless abandon. No longer fearful of the police or even the Germans, they proudly wore the colors of Free France pinned to their lapels or in their hair. Chaz would play *La Marseillaise* and we all would sing along as we walked arm in arm down the streets of Suresnes. By then the local French Police had lost their resolve and their control, ignoring us and our youthful defiance.

One night in early August, my friends and I were sitting around talking about what it would be like after the war ended. Everyone had a different idea, but it was what Chaz said that made my heart sink.

"Anyone who helped them is in big trouble. I'd like to find that girl who betrayed my parents. I'd like to wrap my hands around her throat and squeeze the life out of her, the way the Boche did my parents," Chaz said, his brown eyes blazing with hatred.

"Who is he talking about?" I whispered to Camille.

"The police picked a girl up last February. She gave up a lot of names of Resistance leaders and underground network workers. The police arrested Chaz's parents. He saw them executed, and it devastated him."

"What happened to the girl?" I asked, even though I knew.

"She escaped. They say a Gestapo officer took her from the police, but she never arrived at Gestapo headquarters. They found the officer dead in his car the next day. Posters went up all over Paris with a reward offered for her capture. No one has found her yet, but I sure wouldn't want to be her when they do."

All I could do was sit there, miserable in my guilt, unable to seek the forgiveness I needed. I could see the hurt, the loss, was still too raw in Chaz, and I caused it. It broke my heart to know that whatever the future held, it could never include Chaz and me together.

Chaz walked me home that night, holding my hand until we reached the back door.

"I'm sorry I got carried away tonight. I don't speak about my parents very often, but all that talk of revenge got me going. Sorry," he said, his eyes seeking forgiveness.

"I'm sorry too... about your family. I didn't know until tonight."

"Don't worry about it. It's just... well, sometimes it's still hard to believe they're really gone." He shrugged, trying to lighten the moment. "Do you want to meet me in the park tomorrow afternoon, maybe take a walk by the river?"

"I'll check with Bisabuela. She needs my help with the laundry, but maybe I can, if I get it done early. I'll let you know tomorrow. Bonne nuit, Chaz." I left him on the back step and went into the house to be alone with my guilt.

Before going up to my room, I went down to the basement to collect the clean menstrual rags I left folded in a little basket on the worktable. The telltale cramping tinge started earlier, warning of the impending mess, and I wanted to be prepared when it started.

The smell of cigarette smoke was in the air, but that wasn't unusual. Julian and Lucia frequently went down there to talk privately with late night guests. I didn't turn on the light, just left the door open at the top of the stairs so I could see well enough to grab my things.

"You're in late," a strange voice said from a dark corner of the room.

"Not so late," I told the voice, startled and searching the darkness for its owner.

He was sitting on the cot in the far corner, beneath the small, open window at the back of the basement. Once my eyes adjusted to the darkness, his form became clearer; long legs stretched out in front of him, one arm crossed over his body, the other holding a burning cigarette, its glow brightening as he took another drag.

"I'm sorry I disturbed you. I'll just get my things and leave." He must be someone Lucia brought home, and I had to be cautious. There'd been several people who'd come to the house since the Allies landed in France, usually at night.

"You didn't disturb me. I was waiting for you to come in."

That was unusual. I rarely spoke with anyone Lucia brought home. "Why?"

"Because I wanted to meet you, talk with you for a while."

Now I was nervous. He had a French accent, but I didn't think he was French. Something about him told me he came from farther away than just the countryside. "Why?"

"I make a point of knowing who I share a roof with. It's a habit that keeps me alive in troubled times. Lucia told me about you when I arrived this evening. I suppose she wanted to make sure I was comfortable being around you while I'm here. She seems to have some mixed feelings about you, but her husband and grandmother both trust you completely. Will you sit and talk with me for a while? My name is Bill, by the way."

I could see him more clearly now. The light of the almost full moon was shining through the small window above his head, illuminating his face. He had a strong jawline, wide-set eyes over a distinctly French nose, straight and a bit too long. His mouth was full-lipped and relaxed, with an amiable smile. I couldn't tell the color of his hair or eyes. Everything in the room was in shades of gray and black, but in that light, he looked like he could transform into anyone and no one.

"All right."

I didn't really believe I had a choice, but I was curious about him and what he knew about me, so I sat down on a stool across from him, then reached over, took the cigarette from his hand, and took a drag from it.

"Do you mind if I share this with you?" I asked, trying to appear as grownup as possible. I could see his eyebrows raise up when I handed it back to him.

"Don't you think you're a little young to be smoking, Chère?"
"Probably."

He chuckled, took another drag from the cigarette, then passed it back to me.

We talked quietly for about an hour. He told me who he was, and why he was there; Captain William Marchand, US Army, imbedded with

General Leclerc's 2nd French Armored Division, who were making their way to Paris but were still some distance away. He was in Paris to gather information for the advancing troops and to meet with the different Resistance leaders to coordinate their efforts. He'd been to France, to Paris, twice before the war, and said France reminded him of his home in New Orleans.

He didn't ask me anything at first. I suppose it was because he had already heard my story from Lucia and had accepted the truth of it. But it worried me he shared so much about himself, information I instinctively knew was sensitive and dangerous. I didn't understand why he was trusting me with his welfare.

"How did you do it for so long?" he asked, after we sat in silence for a few moments.

"Do what?"

"Make everyone around you believe you were one thing, when you were really something else entirely." He was looking at me like he wanted to see inside me.

I wasn't sure if he was teasing or asking a serious question. He was more than twice my age and yet he didn't feel like other men I'd known. He seemed relaxed and curious and spoke to me in a way that reminded me of Alex; sure of himself and his place in the world. His expression, his eyes, told me he needed an honest answer, not for clarity about me, but for some deeper reason.

"I pretended to be what they believed I was, what they wanted me to be. It was the only way I was going to survive."

"Lucia told me you spied on Kommandant Steigler during your time with them, passing information to the Resistance. Is that true?"

"Oui, it's true. But I don't know if anything I told Alex helped anyone. I did it because it was the only thing I could do to help. Alex asked me to help, so I did."

"How long did you pass information to your friend?"

"Since they took the Jews away, summer before last, until last February."

"Sweet Jesus!" he said in English, his eyes wide with amazement.

"Why did you tell me all that about yourself? You must know it could be dangerous," I asked, wanting an equal amount of honesty from him.

He looked at me for a while before answering. "I know your secret. It's only fair that you know mine. Now we're even. Neither of us has anything to fear from the other." He paused, gauging my reaction.

"There's something about you I can't quite put my finger on. You're different from other French girls I've met. You seem older than you are, and what you've been through intrigues me."

He stood up, stretching his arms, then he pulled me to my feet, and walked me to the stairs.

"You'd better get up to bed now, Chère. It's late and we both have work to do tomorrow."

Before I left, he planted a tender kiss on my forehead.

"Good night, sweet dreams, Chère."

Bill stayed for almost a week, slipping in and out like a phantom, unseen and undetectable. He would change his appearance to fit wherever he was going, transforming himself with an ease that both amazed and frightened me.

The Laurents and Bisabuela behaved as if he weren't even there, going about their business as usual, doing nothing to draw unwanted attention.

Following their lead, I kept my same routine of chores and shopping (really queue standing) and visiting with my friends in the evening. Even though the Laurents didn't talk openly about it, a feeling that something big was about to happen filled the house. Bill's presence in Suresnes created a quiet anticipation that soon France would be free. The Americans were here.

For me, it was more a feeling of profound relief. I thought I would never have someone to talk to, who understood what it was to hide who you are. Even Alex never really knew what that had been like for me. He always thought of me as a little sister that he needed to save, never saw me as Steigler's Girl, so we rarely talked about those things.

But Bill was different. He knew what it was like to pretend all the time, to hide his true self. We found solace in each other's company, comfort in sharing honestly for a few moments, unafraid of exposure.

If Bill was there when I came in at night, he'd ask me to sit and talk with him for a while. He talked about New Orleans, and how French it was 'in a Southern kind of way'. I told him about my family and the farm we had, and how Papa made a delicious sparkling wine from the grapes he grew each year. He told me about his parents; his father had died a few years before, but his mother was still living. I told him about the day the Nazis killed my family.

I knew it wouldn't last. Nothing ever did. He would leave and rejoin his army to continue the fight against the Nazis all the way to Berlin, and I would never see him again. At least that's what I thought.

He was packing his bag, getting ready to leave, when I went down to the basement to say goodbye and wish him well. I was going out to meet Camille and the others, but wanted to see Bill one last time before he left.

"Goodbye. I hope you'll be safe wherever you're going. I... I hope... well... Merci, Captain Marchand, for everything," I said, stumbling through my farewell.

He wrinkled his forehead at me. "It's Captain Marchand now? Not Bill anymore? I thought we were friends, Chère."

"Oh! We are. It's just that... I thought... Well, you're leaving, and we probably won't see each other again. I wanted to thank you for being so nice to me, for understanding. It meant a lot to me," I said, shyly lowering my eyes so he wouldn't see the tears that threatened to fall.

"It meant a lot to me too, Chère. Meeting you was a surprise, and a good one," he said, gently stroking my cheek. "I've got to leave tonight, but I'll be back. Maybe sooner than you think. You and I still have things to talk about, Chère. Don't let your friends talk you into doing anything stupid. Things are going to get dangerous around here before it's over." He took hold of my hand, squeezing it.

"I'll be careful. You be careful too," I said, my heart lighter at the thought of his return.

"Good. Wait for me, Chère. I'll come back as soon as I can." He squeezed my hand again. We kissed each other lightly on the cheeks, the way adults do, then said goodbye one last time.

I felt sad, but happy all at once. The thought of Bill wanting to come back to see me was something I never imagined possible. I was just a young girl, far too young to hold the interest of someone like him. But I knew he liked me, felt comfortable around me, and that was enough to ease the pain of his leaving.

As I walked across the yard, heading towards Camille's, I hid away all traces of Désirée, my true self, and donned my mask as Marie, the girl from Chartres.

Chapter 47

Liberation

Bill was right. It got dangerous, worse than dangerous. During the last weeks, small skirmishes broke out all over Paris and the outskirts, citizens rising to challenge the pockets of remaining German forces left behind to defend the retreating army.

Allied planes dropped thousands of leaflets all over Paris, warning people not to do anything that would lead to reprisals by the enemy, urging them to stay calm and wait for the signal to join the march to victory and freedom.

It didn't matter. By then, people were too excited, too angry to hold back any longer. It was like shaking a bottle of champagne, disturbing the delicate bubbles within, and once opened, nothing could contain the precious cargo.

"Come with us, Marie. You can help us build the barricades," Chaz urged one afternoon when they were all planning what they'd do to help the local Resistance fighters.

"I can't. I don't want to leave Bisabuela alone. She gets frightened."

It was an excuse I often used after Bill left, and a believable one. Bisabuela was in her eighties, not much bigger than me and a little frail looking.

Bisabuela was anything but frail. Anyone who truly knew her would know she was fierce and fearless, despite her advanced years. But she allowed me to use her as my excuse for staying inside and close to home during those troubled days. She knew how frightened I really was.

Lucia and Julian were away a lot, trying to hold the restaurant together, to protect their livelihood from any potential disaster. Then the moment arrived when they closed it until things settled down, but even then, Julian stayed there, night and day, guarding the restaurant and grounds with a few loyal men. Lucia would come and go from the house. Sometimes she stayed overnight at the restaurant with Julian, leaving Bisabuela and me to manage on our own.

It was the sound of gunfire that got to me, sending visceral memory shock waves through my body each time I heard it. Dark images would fill my mind, the boy with the yellow star, and Alex, their blood spilling out onto the ground beneath their crumpled bodies. It was more than I could handle, and I hid inside whenever I heard it, afraid of adding to my nightmares.

Chaz would come by to check on us, sometimes with Michel and Camille and sometimes alone, his ever-present guitar slung across his back. He would check the house from top to bottom, making sure the doors and windows were secure, before sitting down with us to share a cup of wine and a bite to eat.

He would play his guitar, serenading us with his silky voice and skillful hands. Bisabuela liked it when he played 'La Malagueña'. She said it reminded her of when she was a young girl in Malaga.

Sometimes his eyes would lock on mine while he played, declaring his feelings through the lyrics. I would shyly close my eyes, allowing myself to imagine for a moment what it would be like to be loved like that. Then the song would end, and I'd open my eyes to reality, knowing I wasn't the girl Chaz thought I was, and never could be. Not for him.

By August 25th, the battle for the liberation of Paris was over. The German military governor surrendered his army to French General Leclerc, and then he instantly became a prisoner of France. All of Paris was celebrating.

I didn't see any of it. All our information came from intermittent radio broadcasts or word of mouth, but even in Suresnes, people were celebrating in the streets, and it was hard not to get caught up in the excitement.

"Come on Marie, come with us, come with me," Chaz urged, trying to get me to go with them to the Victory Day parade down the Champs-Élysées. "The Americans are going to march in formation. Don't you want to see that?"

"No, Chaz, I don't want to go. There will be too many people, and I'm uncomfortable in large crowds."

He sighed, clearly disappointed I wouldn't be joining them in their revelries. I let him give me a kiss on the cheek before he left with the others, and that seemed to satisfy him for the moment. It was hard being around him, caring for him so much, while I kept a dark secret that I knew would crush him.

Later that afternoon, an American jeep pulled up to the front of the house with Bill at the wheel, wearing his US Army uniform, honking the horn madly, waving his cap, and grinning from ear to ear. He jumped out of the jeep and ran to the door, sweeping me into his arms and spinning me around until I was breathless.

"It's done, Chère. They're on the run! Paris is free at last!" he said, setting me back down on my feet. He bent down to give Bisabuela a kiss on her cheeks, greeting her with almost as much enthusiasm. He brought gifts too; a box filled with canned meats and vegetables, bars of chocolate, bottles of wine, and a carton of American cigarettes.

I was never so glad to see anyone as I was to see Bill that day. He came back and my heart was soaring.

Bill was getting ready to leave when my friends arrived back from the 'Victory Day' parade. We heard them coming around the corner, Chaz strumming his guitar and the rest of them belting out the verses of *La Marseillaise*. They marched arm in arm, through the gate into the sheltered patio, to share the day's excitement with me.

At the sight of an American soldier sitting casually with the Laurents, Bisabuela and me, they all stopped short, their music forgotten. Then they all started talking at once, surrounding Bill with their excitement, shaking his hand and thanking him profusely for helping to defeat their enemy.

Bill graciously accepted their thanks, telling them it was the French people who were the heroes. The Americans were simply there for support and to push the Nazis back to Germany. Then he stood up to leave.

"Lucia, Julian, thank you for your hospitality and for your help. Madame de Santo, it's been a pleasure, as always. I look forward to the next time," he said, shaking Julian's hand and giving the women each a kiss on the cheek. Then he said goodbye to my friends. "Messieurs et Mademoiselles, it's been a pleasure to meet you all. Bonsoir. Will you walk me out, Chère?" he asked, taking my hand and heading for the gate.

"You made a big impression on my friends. They weren't expecting to find an American soldier having wine with the Laurents when they came back. You will be all they talk about for days," I teased, as he jumped into the jeep.

"They seem like good kids. Except the one with the guitar. He gave me a look when I asked you to walk me out. He's in love with you, Chère," he teased back.

I shrugged it off, not wanting to think about Chaz when Bill was right in front of me.

He took my hand in his. "I need to report in now. I don't know what my next assignment will be; maybe here, maybe somewhere else, but I'll come back to see you. In the meantime, be careful. I've seen some nasty acts of revenge already, and it may get worse. Don't get caught up in any crowds, okay?" He was deadly serious, and I knew better than to ignore his warning.

"I know. That's why I didn't go with them today. I'm glad I stayed home, otherwise I might have missed seeing you." It always amazed me how easy he was to talk to.

"I would have stayed until you were home safe. I came to see *you*, Chère," he said, his blue eyes smiling and sincere. He started the engine, letting it idle while we said our goodbyes. "Stay safe, Chère. Wait for me." He kissed my hand, then he drove away with his hand raised in farewell as he rounded the corner and disappeared.

The Laurents and Bisabuela had gone into the house, leaving my friends on the patio and, apparently, leaving me to explain the appearance of the mysterious American soldier.

Five pairs of eyes reflecting a thousand questions stared at me when I walked up. They waited for me to sit down and then they all started talking at once.

"Who was he?", "How did I know him?", "Why was he here?", they all wanted to know. Maurice asked if he wore a gun, like John Wayne. Maurice was a big fan of American Western movies. Then Chaz asked, "Why did he call you chère?"

I looked around, smiling like I'd just given them the biggest surprise of their lives. Then I told them about Bill, though I referred to him as Captain Marchand, which seemed to annoy Chaz every time I said it. I told them a basic version of the truth; Captain Marchand had arrived mysteriously one night, stayed for almost a week, then left just as mysteriously. They all knew the Laurents were supporters of the Resistance, so it wasn't a surprise they had sheltered an American. What surprised them was that I had kept the secret.

"I can't believe you didn't tell me, Marie. I see you every day and I suspected nothing!" Camille said, her eyes wide in disbelief. They all stared at me in equal amazement.

"It was a secret. I promised not to tell, so I didn't." But I worried they'd suspect me of keeping other secrets.

I casually reached into my pocket and pulled out three bars of chocolate and a pack of American cigarettes, then tossed them onto the small table. I knew it would distract them for a while, giving me a chance to gauge my answers to their questions. Chocolate had been impossible to get for a long time, and American cigarettes were like gold.

"Oh! Chocolate!" Serina squealed in delight, snatching up a bar.

"God bless America! And their cigarettes!" Maurice declared.

The Laurents had thoughtfully left three glasses on the table and half a bottle of wine, which we all shared. The six of us relaxed in our seats, paired up as usual, and savored the velvety sweet taste of chocolate mixed with the rich, complex flavors of the wine, an incredibly rare treat for the time. Wine and chocolate would become a favorite pairing for me, one I would enjoy many times in my life.

We passed a cigarette between us as they recounted the day's events. Even Chaz took a couple of, which happened only rarely, and only if something upset him. He said little, just sat there absently strumming something on his guitar.

I saw the look Chaz had given Bill and could see his confusion and concern. I didn't want him to worry about me, didn't want him to care about me the way I knew he did. There was nothing I could do to change how he felt, short of telling him who I really was. But I couldn't do that either. I couldn't bear the thought of seeing his hatred directed at me.

Chaz leaned over to repeat his earlier question. "Why did he call you chère, Marie?"

I looked up at him, my eyebrows raised. "What? Oh that. It's just something people from New Orleans call all girls. It's nothing, really." I shrugged, but could see I hadn't convinced him. "He would call Camille or Serina chère, too. Maybe it's just easier than having to remember names." That seemed to ease his mind, and he relaxed a bit, giving me one of his beautiful smiles.

We lingered in that sheltered patio for hours, reluctant to give up a moment of our new freedom. We talked and sang and danced until exhausted, the wine long gone and the chocolate wrappers lying empty on the table. Maurice and Serina were the first to drift away, followed by Michel and Camille. I walked Chaz to the back gate so he could cut across the common area to his house on the opposite side.

"Bonne nuit, Chaz. This was fun."

He grabbed my hand, holding on like he was frightened I would run away.

"Marie, I... well, I think you know how I feel about you. Don't you?" he asked, hope filling his eyes.

"Yes, I think I do, but Chaz, I'm not ready for anything serious. Not yet, anyway." I would have said more, but he swiftly offered his solution.

"That's all right, I'll wait for you Marie. No matter how long it takes, I'll wait for you." He kissed my cheek, then said goodnight, his guitar swinging from his back as he walked across the yard.

I just stood there with my head hanging low,

I wish he hadn't said that.

Lucia was inside, sitting at the bottom of the stairs, smoking a cigarette, obviously waiting for me. She looked up when I came in, concern written all over her face. I braced myself, unsure of what would happen, as I always seemed to be around her.

"I hadn't realized you were so close with the Maret boy," she said, her dark eyes peering at me through the swirls of smoke. "Do you know who he is?"

I sighed, my heart breaking with the knowledge. "I do."

"Then you know you can't let him care for you. That family has been through enough heartache. The only thing you'd do is add to it if he discovers who you are. I would hate to see that happen. For all our sakes."

Her heartache reflected in her eyes, and I knew I was a constant reminder of her loss. I wondered, not for the first time, why she allowed me to stay.

"I know. Don't worry, Lucia. They don't know who I am. They believe I'm just a girl from Chartres, nothing more. The only people who know are you, Julian, Bisabuela, and Bill, because you told him." It wasn't an accusation, just a statement of fact, but I could feel her recoil a bit when she heard it.

She looked at me with a defensive expression. "It was important. I couldn't take any chances and he needed to know the risk. What's going on between the two of you, anyway? Abuela tells me you spent a lot of time with him when he was here."

I shrugged again, needing to make light of whatever it was between me and Bill.

"I guess he needed someone to talk to. You and Julian weren't here, and Bisabuela was busy, so I just sat and talked with him when he asked me to."

"What did you talk about?" She was clearly suspicious.

"Stuff. Nothing really. Mostly about America and what it's like there." I didn't want to talk to her about Bill, wanted to keep my time with him to myself.

"He's too old for you, girl. Get any foolish ideas about him out of your head. Save yourself some heartache." She pushed the cigarette into the ashtray, then stood up and walked up the stairs to the bedroom she shared with Julian, closing the door firmly behind her.

I turned off the light and followed her up to my small room at the back of the house, the echoes of her warnings drowning out all remnants of the day's euphoria.

Chapter 48

Collaboration

During my time with Katarina, I studied a lot, there had been little else for me to do. I studied French history extensively, the era of the Revolution being a time that both fascinated and frightened me.

I could feel the similarities between that era and what was now going on around me. The frenzied excitement at the defeat of a long-time oppressor, and then the transformation of that excitement into an unbridled need for revenge against anyone thought guilty of that oppression.

I knew it was coming, knew the French of 1944 would forget the bloody lessons of the Revolution, or would choose to forget them. Too much had happened.

It was only a matter of time.

'It is for this revenge, this vengeance and justice, that we will keep fighting until the final day, until the day of total and complete victory...'

The newspaper printed De Gaulle's victory speech the day after the liberation, so the entire country could read it. The words seemed to jump off the page, calling for all true French to take up arms in the name of vengeance and justice against the oppressor, and anyone deemed to be a collaborator.

Those were chilling words, a clear warning I wasn't out of danger, nor were the Laurents while I was with them.

The Wild Purification, *épuration sauvage*, began. Forgotten history lessons drowned out by cries for revenge. Someone had to pay for the years of oppression and brutality. Someone had to pay for all of it.

Wild seemed too gentle a description for the savagery the French unleashed on their own people. It wasn't hard for me to imagine the streets of Paris running red with blood and tumbling heads, if the guillotine was still a popular means of execution.

For me, it felt as frightening as when the Nazis had first come to France; that lightning-fast brutality, heedless of what lay in the path.

I didn't have any doubt there were French people guilty of horrible things requiring judgment and punishment. The brutal faces of the French men who had tortured me for hours in that dungeon came to mind. But they would include me among the evildoers, because my actions caused the deaths of too many people to merit forgiveness.

Those were dark times, during those first months of frenzied revenge, and I never strayed too far from the shelter of the house in Suresnes. When I did go out, usually with Bisabuela or my friends, I was always careful to maintain my identity as Marie, and never let my internal guard down.

I would shed my mask and just be Désirée when Bill came to visit, but only when we were alone.

He visited several times during those first few terrifying months, bringing gifts for the Laurents and Bisabuela, and always a little something for me. His company was the only thing I needed. I always felt better when Bill was there; the American Army Captain, another layer of protection between me, and the chaos going on around me. I was grateful for it.

Bill had come by late one afternoon bearing gifts, as usual, and then stayed for supper.

"How are you holding up, Chère?" Concern furrowed his brow as he sat at the kitchen table watching me while I cleaned up after our meal. Bisabuela had gone to the living room to listen to the radio and the Laurent's were at the restaurant.

"I'm all right, I guess. Trying to be anyway."

"That's good. Keep your head down, Chère. This insanity won't go on forever, but I think you should stick close to home until it's over." His worry lines deepened with the warning.

"Tell me more about your farm and your family. What were your brothers like? Did you get along with them?" he asked, changing to a lighter subject.

It never felt sad talking about my family with Bill. It always seemed to be more about sharing my history than re-living terrible memories.

"They were like most boys, I guess. Jean-Michel used to mess up my hair all the time, but that was his way of showing me affection. Jacque was thirteen and looked up to Jean-Michel as his hero, followed him everywhere. They were good brothers."

"I didn't have any brothers or sisters. It must have been nice having other kids around all the time."

"It was." Those were the memories I kept safely tucked away in my heart, only occasionally reliving them.

Bill always entertained us with tales of Army life and how horrible mess-hall food can be, especially if you'd experienced the excellent cuisine of New Orleans. He was funny and easy to be with, always respectful and courteous. Bill was a gentleman in every sense of the word.

I relished his visits and would relive them over and over in my mind. Those were the moments someone saw me, Désirée, and not the pretend girl. Being with Bill felt better than anywhere else.

Bill arrived at the door on a Friday morning in November after the Laurents had gone to the restaurant. With his hat in hand and a big smile on his face, it was obvious he had something on his mind.

"Madame de Santo," he addressed Bisabuela formally, "With your permission, I'd like to take Marie out for the day. I promise I'll have her back by sundown."

Thrilled and barely able to contain my excitement, I prayed she would allow it. I'd been cooped up in the house for far too long, and the idea of spending an entire day with Bill was too tempting to even think about resisting.

Bisabuela stood silent for a moment, looking at him, then at me, then back at him again, her thoughts unreadable. She asked him to sit down, brought him a cup of coffee, then took the seat across from him at the table while I held my breath.

Bisabuela began by giving him a piercing look, the kind impossible to turn away from. "Captain Marchand, I appreciate your courtesy in asking for my permission. That speaks well of your upbringing. However, I take my role as Marie's guardian seriously, and I'm sure you understand my concern regarding her welfare. She is quite young, after all. It is unusual for a man of your age to find interest in such a young girl. Wouldn't you say? So I must ask, what are your intentions regarding Marie?"

Bill sipped his coffee, listening respectfully while she voiced her concerns. When she finished speaking, he looked her straight in the eye, answering her with a level of honesty I don't think she expected.

"Madame de Santo, I understand your concerns. Please believe me when I say Marie's welfare is of the utmost importance to me. I would never put her in danger or dishonor her. My mother would beat me into next week if I ever harmed a woman or a girl. You have my word, Madame, as an officer and a gentleman."

He paused, carefully considering what to say next.

"As for why, I'm not sure I can answer that to your satisfaction. I've been trying to figure that out since I met her. What I *know* is that I care about Marie. She's important to me, and I can't walk away. I want to make sure she's safe and has a chance at life. Given the circumstances, Madame, I'm sure you understand *my* concern." He never looked away from her, never faltered in his answer.

I wasn't sure what the outcome would be, but knew if she refused to let me go, he would honor her wishes and we'd stay home under her watchful eye.

Bisabuela considered him for a long time, clearly assessing his honesty, his honor.

"What do you think of all this, niña?" she asked.

I searched for the right words to explain how I was feeling, about Bill, about everything, but especially about Bill.

"All I know for sure is, when I'm with Bill, I don't have to pretend to be someone, I can just be me, and that feels better than anything else." I needed her understanding and hoped she could see the hopefulness written on my face.

"Very well, Captain. You can take her. I trust you will honor your promise and have her back before dark."

"Of course, Madame. I will return her to you unharmed and unmolested. On my honor. Thank you for your trust, and for the coffee." Bill rose from his seat and reached for my hand to lift me from mine.

"Grab a coat, Chère. The sun's out, but there's a chill in the air."

Chapter 49

A day in the country

B
ill blew out his breath as he leaned forward to start the jeep. "Phew.
I wasn't sure she'd let me take you," he said, giving me one of his
dazzling smiles.

"I'm so glad she did," I said, stating the obvious as I relaxed in the seat
beside him, deliriously happy. I hadn't been anywhere in so long it didn't
even matter to me where we were going, as long as I was with him.

"Bisabuela likes you, Bill. She always says so, but Lucia says you're too
old for me, and I should get any foolish ideas I have about you out of my
head."

"Does she? What foolish ideas would those be, Chère?"

I smiled prettily. "Oh, just the usual. That you're my knight in shining
armor, and you'll ride up on your white horse and save me from the evil
dragon."

He laughed out loud at that. "I'm more of a fast car guy, myself. Never
had much use for horses." His smile was intoxicating.

"But Lucia is right about one thing. I *am* too old for you," he said, his
voice turning serious. Then he looked at me, smiled again and added, "But
there may come a day when that might not be true, Chère."

He drove south out of the city, staying on the smaller roads and heading towards Versailles, which he passed through without stopping. It seemed a directionless journey, like he was driving just for the pleasure of it. I didn't mind. It was enough that I was with him, and away from everything that troubled me. I was happy to let the day unfold, trusting he would make everything all right.

We talked endlessly about everything and nothing, sharing stories of our childhood (mine being limited to pre-nightmare times), and dreams of life after the war. We stopped in a small town to buy bread, cheese, a couple of apples and a bottle of wine from a local vendor. The old man refused to take Bill's money, saying it was the least he could do to thank him for setting France free. Bill just smiled and shook the old man's hand, thanking him, then he left the money on the counter, anyway. Bill knew things were still hard in France, and I never saw him take anything; he was always giving.

It was one of those early winter days, when the sun isn't yet ready to relinquish its hold, and it rises, bright as any summer day, the air crisp and clean, and you can almost forget there's anything wrong with the world.

Bill parked along a quiet country road, forested on one side and a sweeping pasture dotted with trees on the other. It was a beautiful place, a perfect day for being in the country, and I didn't want it to end.

"I love the smell of the countryside. It's so much nicer than the smelly city," I said, taking in as much clean air as my lungs would hold, then releasing it with a deep stretch of my arms.

I jumped out of the jeep, snatched up the fruit, cheese and bread, then headed down the slope to a large oak tree standing at the edge of the pasture. Bill pulled an army blanket and small bag from the back of the jeep, grabbed the wine and followed, joining me under the tree. We arranged the blanket on top of a bed of fallen oak leaves, tossed the rest of our things on top, then stood silently looking out over the pasture, each lost in our own thoughts.

"Want to race?" I asked, smiling up at him, then I took off running down the pasture toward a grove of trees on the other side.

"Hold on, Chère." I heard him call from behind me.

I could hear the pounding of his feet and his heavy breathing as he chased me across the field, catching up just as I made it to the tree line.

"Not fair. I wasn't ready. You got a head start on me." He leaned over with his hands on his knees, winded from the race.

"I needed a head start because your legs are longer than mine. Want to race again?"

"You're on. But I must warn you, Chère, I ran track in high-school and college. I've got some skills. I'll give you a five second start on me, because my legs *are* longer."

We stood at the invisible start line, poised to take off. "Ready. Set. Go!" he shouted.

I started running as fast as my much shorter legs would carry me, counting down the seconds in my head. Halfway across the field, I heard him coming, laughing the whole way. He was hot on my heels by the time I reached the oak tree, and I knew he let me win, but it didn't matter. I collapsed onto the blanket, laughing and catching my breath, the pure joy of that childish moment searing into my memory.

We stayed there the entire day, just the two of us, playing tag and then a game called 'Simon says', that Bill said was a favorite when he was a boy. We explored the deer trails meandering through the forest on the other side of the road, discovering the hidden homes of the forest creatures. The sounds and smells triggered memories of the times I'd gone walking with Papa in the forest by our farm, and how he taught me to always be mindful of the creatures who lived there.

At mid-day we relaxed beneath the oak tree, its golden leaves still clinging to the branches and filtering the winter sunlight. We shared the bread and cheese. Bill opened the wine and poured some into cups he magically produced. He insisted on adding a healthy splash of water from his army canteen into my cup, despite my protest that I was perfectly capable of drinking wine without water in it.

He shook his head. "No, you're not, Chère. You're too young. Where I come from, we don't serve alcohol to kids. You must be eighteen to drink in Louisiana, and in some states, it's twenty-one." He had that *I'm older than you* look in his eye that always made me laugh and roll my eyes.

It didn't matter. The country sunshine and Bill's company were intoxicating enough for me.

It was late when I woke from my mid-afternoon nap. The sun had been slowly making its way across the sky while I slept, and now was getting ready to dive behind the trees on the other side of the pasture. I sat up and stretched, the remnants of a delicious dream still lingering around the edges of my consciousness.

"You look like a woodland fairy, laying there so peacefully with oak leaves in your hair. I wish I had a camera," Bill said when I noticed him watching me. He was sitting back against the trunk of the tree, smoking a cigarette, his legs stretched out in front of him.

"Well, this woodland fairy needs to find some privacy." I jumped up and scanned the area for a likely place to relieve myself. He was still in the same position when I returned.

"I've been thinking about your farm, Chère," he said as I sat back down on the blanket.

"What? My farm?" I wasn't sure where he was going with this train of thought.

"Your family's farm. It belongs to you now. I thought you might want to go back, to go home." He looked at me and waited, openly assessing my reaction to his suggestion.

I closed my eyes and took a deep breath, trying to imagine what that would even be like, being home, where the nightmare started. My head was shaking when I opened my eyes.

"No, Bill. I can't go back. There's no one left to go home to. The village believes I'm dead, buried with the rest of my family. I don't think I could live there again. Not now, maybe never."

"Okay. Scratch that idea. Then maybe you'll consider letting me take you to the States." He waited, allowing this new idea to sink in.

"I can't leave France."

"Of course you can, Chère. You just need to choose where to go. I could take you to New Orleans, to Mama. I know she'd love to have you. You could finish growing up in a safe place, where you wouldn't have to look over your shoulder all the time. You could be Désirée again and have the life you deserve. Think about it."

"How do you know your mother would want me?" It seemed a relevant question.

"I told her about you; what a sweet, funny, smart girl you are, and what a surprise you've been to me. She said she'll write to you, to tell you about New Orleans. Mama speaks French, but I don't know how good her written French is, so I got you this. Hopefully, it will help." He tossed me a small book he pulled from his trouser pocket.

English / French ~ French / English Dictionary, the cover stated in small gold letters.

"Merci, Bill," I said, a bit overwhelmed. I had a lot to think about and more than a few questions.

"Can I ask you something? And please don't make fun if you think it's stupid."

"You can ask me anything, Chère. On my honor, I won't laugh," he said, already smiling.

"It's just that, well, adults make big decisions all the time, and I wonder how do you know if you're making the right one or not? How do you know that what you choose will work out the way you want it to?" I hoped he could give me some secret answer that people learn when they're grown up.

He wasn't laughing, he just looked at me with tenderness in his eyes.

"Ah, Chère, that's the thing about life; there are no guarantees. Most of the time, it's a leap of faith that the path you choose is the one you're supposed to be on. Life is like a fickle woman who'll throw you a curve ball when you least expect it. Sometimes your eyes are open, and you see it coming, and other times she catches you unawares, and the ball wizzes by, knocking you into the dust. Personally, I go with my gut. It's always the best indicator if I'm on the right track." He smiled, patting his flat stomach.

"Well, that wasn't very helpful." I said, smirking at him. "I'm just afraid of making another terrible decision. The last one turned out really awful." I bit my lower lip to keep it from quivering.

"I know you blame yourself, Chère, but what happened wasn't your fault. You didn't betray anyone. It was just one of those curve balls you couldn't see coming."

That subject was going to spoil the day, so I asked a different question, one that had been burning in my mind since morning.

"Bill? What did you mean when you said you *are* too old for me, but that might not always be true? I don't understand. You'll always be older than me."

He leaned back against the tree, shaking his head with one of those *You'll understand when you're* older expressions on his face.

I stopped him before he could say it. "Don't you dare say I'll understand when I'm older. I want to understand now."

"You are such a challenge, Chère." He looked at me for a long time, gauging his response, then closed his eyes while he took a deep breath. When he opened his eyes, I was staring at him, waiting for his answer.

"All right, here goes... I told you about Pops and Mama, right? Well, they had known each other from the day Mama was born to the day Pops died. They were married for over thirty years and had the strongest relationship I've ever seen between two people. When they married Mama was eighteen, Pops was thirty-one. He waited for her to grow up, waited until she was ready and knew her own mind. When that day came, the thirteen years between them didn't matter anymore. That's what I meant, Chère."

His eyes held mine for a long moment, conveying some deeper message I didn't quite understand, but it gave me a warm, tingly feeling inside that made me want to lean into him.

Bill stood up suddenly, pulling me to my feet. "It's late. Time to go. I need to get you home before dark or Madame de Santo will... Well, God only knows what she'll do if I don't keep my promise. Grab your things, Chère."

I wanted the drive back to take longer, because I wasn't ready for the day to end, and knew he had one more thing to tell me. I didn't want to hear it, and maybe Bill didn't want to share it, so we didn't talk until we got back to the city.

Bill drove along the river, then pulled over several blocks before the turn to the Laurent's house and parked the jeep.

He shifted in his seat, then looked at me, long and hard. "I'm leaving tomorrow. I have orders to catch up with the General. I don't know when I'll be back, but I am coming back. Never doubt that. I am coming back." He took a breath, gazing at me as if memorizing me.

"Think about what you want, Chère, where you want to be. Wherever that is, I can help you. Either here or the States or somewhere else, it doesn't matter. I'll be there for you. Please stay safe while I'm gone. Don't take any chances. Stay close to Madame De Santo. I trust her to keep you safe." His face was serious and intense, pleading to be understood.

I could easily have fallen apart at the thought of his leaving, but I put on my bravest face. I knew he would have to leave sometime.

"It's alright, Bill. I'll be fine. Will you be safe where you're going? Will you really come back?" I wanted to believe it, to have that to hold on to, at least.

He took my hand, brought it to his lips and kissed the back of it, holding it there for a moment, his breath warming my chilled fingers. That same warm tingly feeling I felt earlier coursed through me once again, sending little sparks igniting between us. He placed my hand gently down on the seat, then reached up to stroke my cheek.

"I will. I promise. Wait for me, Chère." He started the jeep and headed to the Laurent's.

It was just after dark when Bill parked the jeep in front of the house and helped me out. As we walked to the door, we noticed Chaz standing alone on the patio. He obviously was waiting for me and didn't look happy to see me with Bill.

"Marie? Are you alright?" Chaz asked, worry etched across his forehead.

"Chaz? Why are you here?" He was spoiling my last moments with Bill.

"Hey Chaz. How's it going, pal?" Bill asked casually.

Chaz ignored him, his focus solely on me. "I've been waiting for you, Marie. Is everything all right with your mother?" he asked, reaching for my hand.

I didn't let him have it, slipping it into my pocket before he could touch me.

"I'm fine, Chaz," I said as gently as I could under the circumstances.

When the front door opened, Bisabuela stood there, waiting for me.

Bill stepped between me and Chaz and guided me up the steps to the door.

"Bonsoir Madame de Santo. Here she is, safe and sound as promised. Merci, Madame, for your trust," he said as he brought me up the front steps, handing me over to Bisabuela.

I didn't think Chaz could hear from where he stood on the patio, but I felt the tension in his stance; his arms crossed over his chest, his feet firmly planted beneath him. Chaz was a problem that I needed to figure out, but right then, I didn't want to think about him.

When I looked into Bill's eyes, I knew once he left I wouldn't see him for a long time, or maybe ever again, and I didn't want to let him go. I didn't want to give up the only person who made me feel normal, whole, real, but I had no choice. I had to slip on the mask of Marie, play my part, pretend to be who I needed to be so who I was would stay hidden, and the Laurants would stay safe.

"Merci, Bill, for everything. Be careful, be safe." It was all I could say without bursting into tears.

He smiled, then gave me a tender kiss on the top of my head. "I will, Chère. You do the same," was all he said and then he walked away, tipping his hat to Chaz as he passed on the way out the gate.

I watched from the doorway, struggling to hold back the flood of emotions, until his jeep disappeared around the corner.

"Marie?" Chaz said from the patio.

"Bonne nuit, Chaz. Go home. Marie will talk to you tomorrow," Bisabuela said, slipping her arm around my waist and leading me into the house, closing the door before he could reply.

Chapter 50

Birds, Bees, and Warrents

Bill was gone. There was nothing I could do about that.

Chaz was another thing entirely. I knew I couldn't avoid him or his questions, especially since he was waiting for me outside first thing the following morning.

Bisabuela had explained to him my mother had called, urgently wanting to see me, and Captain Marchand had agreed to take me home. It was a good story, believable even, except I knew Chaz would want more details, and I hated lying to him anymore than I already had.

I crafted a story about my mother and the urgent trip to Chartres. and how difficult the visit with her had been, downplaying Bill's involvement.

"Did she want you to come home? To Chartres, I mean," he asked, clearly worried that I might leave Paris.

"She did, but nothing has really changed. She's still the same, even though she's not with him anymore," I said. All the details slipped neatly into place, adding color and texture to the backstory Chaz already believed about me. "I told her I want to stay here, that I like living with Bisabuela. I told her I hoped Lucia and Julian would take me on as apprentice in the restaurant." Every lie must have a grain of truth.

"Of course they will. Why wouldn't they?" He seemed satisfied, content with my explanation, and he almost let the subject drop, except for his distrust of Bill.

"I just wish Julian had taken you instead of the American. That guy pays too much attention to you, Marie. I don't trust him."

"Why not? He's nice. Besides, it doesn't matter anymore, he's gone. We probably won't see him again." I hoped that wasn't true.

Maybe I should go to church with Bisabuela and light a candle for Bill. It couldn't hurt.

"Well, that's good. He's too old to be hanging around a girl your age." Chaz said, clearly happy to hear the news that Bill was gone.

I wish people would stop saying that!

I was clearly missing something, some important piece of information that would explain why everyone was so concerned about how old Bill was. Fourteen-year-old Marie should have known what that was, but twelve-year-old Désirée did not. I needed to find out what it was. I needed a logical explanation and knew exactly who to ask, Bisabuela.

"... and this is why we guard the virtue of young girls like you, niña. There are men who would steal it without thinking twice," Bisabuela concluded after giving me an all too graphic description of what really goes on between a man and a woman.

"But Bill isn't like that, Bisabuela. He would never hurt me!" I said with certainty.

"I agree. If I had any doubts about him, I would never have let him take you out for the day. But he's not the only man in the world, niña, and you must take care around all of them, including the young ones. For most young men, it takes time, and a diligent mother, to teach them to control their baser urges. That moment of connection between two people is powerful and precious and one should never undervalue it. It's a gift a wife and husband give to each other and to no one else." She searched my eyes for understanding.

"Gracias, Bisabuela. I think I understand now. It's one more thing I need to be careful about. But I know Bill would never hurt me. I know it in my heart."

"You're probably right, niña. Time will tell."

Life went on without him, and I had to wait.

While I waited, the chaos of the *'Wild Purification'* transformed into the *'Legal Purification'*, a much more ordered, civilized form of French persecution against other French citizens deemed 'Collaborators'.

De Gaulle put the government back together, bringing order to the streets and cracking down on vigilante justice. A magistrate would file charges and issue warrants, the police would make arrests, bringing the accused before the magistrate, then they would hold trials, and sometimes, there were executions. It was all very organized, methodical, and relentless.

We read about it in the newspapers, heard the news reports on the radio. It was the subject of choice for everyone. Collaborators: who were they, what had they done, when was the trial? Anyone could fall victim to a vengeful neighbor's accusation. Gossip was currency to the French, and if you had a story to tell, you never lacked for an audience.

It was late December when I saw it, there among the other names of accused offenders, my photo staring up at me from the newspaper laying open on the dining table:

Désirée Pérot (Steigler, Lang), Age 12-15
Blonde, Blue eyes, 137cm
Last seen February 1944, Paris, 1st Arr
Wanted in connection with the unlawful arrest, torture,
and murder of the following French patriots....

The list took up half the column. It was a long list. Most of the names I didn't know, had only heard them screamed at me during that long night of torture. Three of them I recognized; Jean and Genevieve Maret, and Alexander Guerin. The newspaper printed a photo of me that was taken when I was nine after I went to live with the Steiglers. Fortunately, I didn't look like that anymore.

There was only one person I could think of who would add Alex's name to the complaint against me, Annalise. She hated me, but I didn't realize how deep her hatred was until then. I *was* guilty of Alex's death, but this public declaration felt like she was trying to blame me for all the others, for the names she had written and then forgot to destroy. There was nothing I could do to change any of it.

Julian and Lucia had already seen it, and I could only imagine what Lucia was thinking. I tore the page from the newspaper, intending to destroy the evidence of my sin, but I couldn't turn back time, couldn't erase what had happened. So, I kept it, maybe to punish myself because I was too afraid to face the real punishment.

I stayed vigilant in my disguise, slipping ever deeper into my role as Marie Rondeau, never giving Lucia any reason to worry or doubt my ability to remain hidden. I had a lot of practice pretending and a lot of reasons to continue doing it.

Chapter 51

Letters from America

I n the beginning of 1945, two things happened that made life easier; letters began arriving from America, and the Molinaris reopened *Mama Mia's Italian Restaurant* around the corner.

The first letters arrived not long after the new year, delivered by an American soldier who drove up to the house one morning. When I saw the jeep pull up, my heart stopped beating, fear coursed through me like lightning. *Why is he here? Is Bill all right?* A thousand horrible thoughts raced around in my head as I watched him walk up the steps. He was holding a package and smiling when I answered the door.

"Bonjour, mademoiselle. I have a package for Monsieur Laurent. I leave it with you?" he asked in broken French.

"Of course. Merci monsieur, I'll see that he gets it. Merci," I said, taking the package. I wanted to ask him about Bill but thought he probably wouldn't know anything, or even if he did, he wouldn't tell me. He tipped his hat, then left.

I set the package on the dining room table and just stared at it. The name on the label read Julian and Lucia Laurent, and the return address read Mrs. B Marchand, St. Charles Ave. New Orleans, LA USA.

I couldn't open it, of course. Well, I could, but that would be wrong, even though I knew the contents were probably for me. At least I hoped so. I had to wait until Julian and Lucia got home.

It was torture. Every time I passed by, I ran my hand over the top, reaching for some invisible connection to Bill, something to reassure me he was still out there, somewhere.

"What's this?" Julian asked when he came down to breakfast the following morning. "Lucia. A package has arrived from the States. Were you expecting something?" he asked as Lucia followed him into the dining room.

I was waiting for them. The coffee was on the table, the meal was ready to be served, and I didn't want any distractions. I just wanted them to open the package before I lost any measure of control.

"A soldier delivered it yesterday afternoon," I said as calmly as I could manage. "I think it's from Captain Marchand's mother. See? The return address says B Marchand, New Orleans. That's where he's from, New Orleans in America." I sounded like a chittering bird, but couldn't help it. I was eager to see what was inside that box.

"Really?" Lucia and Julian both said, smiling at each other. I confirmed my statement with a wide-eyed nod.

After breakfast, they finally opened it, and I could finally relax, breathe. It felt like I'd been holding my breath since the box arrived, bracing myself for something.

Inside were three boxes nesting together, each beautifully gift-wrapped and labeled, Señora De Santo, M. & Mme Laurent, Mlle Marie. A letter accompanied each gift, written in an elegant, flowing hand.

Bisabuela opened her gift first. Inside was a beautiful scarf with delicate embroidery around the edges. Julian and Lucia received several items; a box of fresh pecans, bundles of herbs in separate gauze bags, and a small bottle labeled Cajun Spice. They both seemed delighted but perplexed by the gifts until Julian read their letter to us.

Dear Julian and Lucia,

Please forgive my familiarity, but I feel as if I know you both. My son, Captain Marchand, has spoken of you at some length, praising both your courage and generosity towards him during a critical moment in time. I find words are inadequate to express my profound gratitude to both of you, and to Señora De Santo, for sheltering my son, undoubtedly at great personal risk. I will forever be grateful to you.

Beau (Bill to most) has mentioned the girl, Marie, and your continued kindness towards her. It seems my son has found another baby bird to help; it was a frequent occurrence during his youth. Should you require any assistance regarding her welfare, please don't hesitate to call on me.

Please accept these small gifts as a meager offering of my gratitude. I thought the herbs and pecans might still be difficult to get in France, and the Cajun spice mix is from Eulaila, our cook, who makes it herself. I hope you find them useful in your endeavors.

Best wishes and many thanks,
Mrs. Beatrice Marchand

"That's interesting. Seems like we all made an impression on young Captain Marchand," Julian said, raising his eyebrows at me, then handing the letter over to Lucia.

"What do you think is in this?" he asked her, picking up the bottle of spice and sticking his nose gingerly over it. "Hmm. Dried peppers and something else. I'll have to think about how to use it."

"Aren't you going to open yours, niña?" Bisabuela asked.

I'd been holding the gift on my lap, running my fingers over the beautiful paper, thinking about Bill and what he might have told his mother about me. *Baby bird, indeed!* I felt a bit wounded at being thought of as helpless. It hurt my pride. I didn't want Bill to think of me as a helpless little bird. I wanted him to think of me as... well, I wasn't sure what I wanted him to think, but it wasn't that.

When I opened the gift, my hurt feelings evaporated. Inside I found two things: a well-read book, *The Three Musketeers*, written in English, and a beautiful peach colored sweater with pretty pearl buttons down the front. I couldn't stop smiling.

"What a beautiful sweater, Marie," Lucia said, gently running her hand over the weave. "The color goes perfectly with your hair. You should write her a thank you note. We need to go, Julian, or we'll be late. Hmm, such a thoughtful gift," she mumbled as she hurried Julian out the door, snagging their gift on the way out.

"I'm going to take these to my room, Bisabuela. I'll be down in a minute to help with the dishes."

"Don't worry about the dishes. I told Estella we'd help them settle in. Come over when you're done."

I rushed upstairs to read my letter in privacy, unwilling to share my reaction to whatever was written there. Bill told me his mother was going to write to me, but I didn't believe that would really happen. She didn't know me, and she lived half a world away. I couldn't imagine she would have much to say to a young girl like me.

My dear Marie,

I feel as if I know you already. Beau talks about you whenever he writes, which is not nearly often enough for a mother's sake. He has shared with me your circumstance and it amazes me that someone so young has the level of courage and resilience you must possess.

I hope you like the sweater. The color should look nice with your hair. Beau tells me it's a beautiful rich auburn. The book is one of Beau's, a favorite from his childhood. He remembered you telling him you would read this story with your father. He thought you might enjoy the English version. I believe he's trying to encourage you to learn our language.

I would love to hear from you, Marie; to hear how you're getting on, what you're doing, how you're feeling. You can talk to Mama Bea about anything, child. I've got big shoulders.

You may not hear from Beau until this horrible conflict is over, but I have connections which allow us to communicate. When last we spoke, he asked me to tell you he is safe and doing well and hopes you are the same. You seem to have captured Beau's attention in a way that is surprising to us both.

Take care, my dear. I hope to hear from you soon.

Sincerely,
Mama Bea

I must have read it a dozen times before I finally put it down. Her words made the time I spent with Bill real again, made him real. I almost thought it had all been a dream, some childish fantasy I made up in my head, that he really cared about me, the real Désirée. Mama Bea's letter brought it all back to life, confirmed it wasn't a dream.

I sent up a silent prayer for Bill's safety, kissed the book I knew he'd once held, then ran downstairs to help the Molinari family unpack.

Chapter 52

Mama Mia's

Mama Mia's opened the first week of February, during one of the coldest winters anyone could remember, and once the doors opened, the little restaurant was never empty of customers.

The neighborhood had waited four and a half years for Mama Mia's to reopen. Before the Nazis came, it was a favorite spot to gather, to share a bottle of wine with friends and a slice of Mama Mia's delicious pizza, served hot from the brick oven in the back.

Bisabuela and I helped Estella and Francesca Molinari settle back into the home and business they'd closed when they fled south at the beginning of the war. Francesca's husband, Antonio, was a prisoner of war along with thousands of other French soldiers sent to work camps in Germany, but she had received letters from him and hoped he would come home soon.

The women were ready to get the restaurant back open, so we all pitched in to help. Julian and Lucia helped get the permits and licenses, as well as the contacts with various vendors. Bisabuela and I, along with Francesca's little daughter, Mia, helped clean the restaurant and put it back in order. That meant sweeping away years of accumulated dust and grime, scrubbing walls, floors, and windows, and making every surface sparkle as if brand new.

Excited to be a part of this new adventure, I willingly did anything that needed doing, with the hope they might hire me to work there.

A week before the restaurant opened, the delivery of firewood arrived. Michel, Chaz and Maurice unloaded and stacked it in the back of the house. We cleaned the brick oven, and swept the chimney of debris, then Estella lit the first fire.

The smell of burning wood and crackling pitch reminded me of when I was little, when Papa would pile up the dead vines and brush, then set it all ablaze. I'd stand next to him watching the fire burn down, his big hand tightly holding my smaller one. It was a wonderful memory.

Once the oven was functioning properly, Estella brought out the first batch of dough, slapping it onto the wooden counter dusted with flour. She rolled out the small ball of dough with a long, tapered rolling pin, turning the stretched dough, then rolling it again, repeating until it had flattened and stretched to the size of a dinner plate. Then she picked it up and stretched it between her fists, until I thought it would break, but she knew what she was doing.

In the end, she laid the dough onto a flour dusted wooden paddle, then spooned a ladle full of marinara sauce on top, spreading it around almost to the edge, then topped it with slices of mozzarella cheese and fresh basil leaves. The first pizza was ready for the oven. She deftly slipped the pizza from the paddle into the hot oven, with the fire burning low but hot at the back. Then we waited.

I'd never tasted pizza before and was impressed by how simple a dish it was, but also by the amount of work that went into making it. From the sauce, which simmered for hours, to the bread and pizza dough, made daily from a starter Estella had nurtured for years, it all took time and a lot of work. She made her own cheeses too, which was a whole other thing.

The pizza didn't take long to bake, and when Estella pulled it from the oven and slipped it onto the counter, bubbly and hot, I could hardly wait to taste it. That first bite was amazing; a crust baked to perfection, tangy sauce with melted cheese and the bittersweet taste of toasted basil. My mouth was burning and deliriously happy. That's when I understood why everyone was so excited that Mama Mia's would finally reopen.

"Please Lucia. I promise I'll be careful. I'll stay in the back, just in the kitchen. I promise. Please, Lucia." I waited in the kitchen doorway, hoping to get an answer before she left for the day. I hadn't asked for anything since I'd been there, had done everything they asked of me. This was something I wanted so badly. It was so close I could reach out my hand and touch it, but I needed her approval, and I wasn't sure she would give it.

She listened patiently while I pleaded my case, sipping her morning coffee at the small kitchen table, watching me from behind the rim of her cup. When she looked at me that way, it always felt like she was trying to see behind the mask of Marie, the mask she helped create. It felt like she wanted to understand the girl beneath the mask, but something always stopped her. She put her cup down, leaning back in her chair and closed her eyes.

I was going to be disappointed.

"I can't think of one good reason we shouldn't allow her to work with Estella," Julian said.

Lucia's eyes flew open, staring at him in disbelief. She could think of a few reasons, her look declared.

"No, really Lucia. It's right next door. She'd be working the early morning shift and only in the back, before opening. Never the front of the house." Julian gave me a sharp look to confirm this directive. "It would appear unreasonable for us to deny her this, especially considering all she's done for Estella already. It will be good training for her. Give her a taste of how hard this really is." Julian had been supportive of my interest in cooking and restaurants from the beginning.

I closed my eyes and sent up a prayer, *Please God, make her say yes.*

I heard Lucia's sigh and braced myself for another disappointment.

"All right, Marie. You can work for Estella, but only in the kitchen and only in the morning. I don't want you waiting tables, understood?" Lucia cautioned me with her eyes.

I threw myself into her surprised embrace, thanking her with all my heart. Her tension relaxed a little and eventually she gave me soft pats on my back before pulling herself away. She would never get too close, never completely let her guard down with me.

The next few months were the happiest I'd been since Bill left.

I worked at Mama Mia's, lived with people who cared for me, had friends who accepted me (at least the person they thought I was), and even though Bill wasn't there, he wasn't completely absent from my life. Letters from Mama Bea kept me informed, kept me connected to Bill through her stories.

I never shared her letters with anyone, kept that part of my life secret, separate from my life as Marie. Marie was who everyone saw, who everyone knew. Désirée could only show up when I was alone in my room at night, when I was reading Mama Bea's letters or writing to her, sharing my own thoughts and experiences.

There were times during those months, I almost forgot what happened before, almost imagined I really was Marie, the girl from Chartres who dreamed of being a chef one day. Almost, but not quite.

I'd been working at Mama Mia's since it opened, working in the early morning when everything was quiet, dawn barely breaking the horizon.

My first task was cleaning out the brick oven. I'd pull open the heavy iron door, a blast of heat warming my face, then scoop out the ashes that had burned down overnight. Once I mopped the oven clean, Estella would slide in the loaves of dough, which had been proofing overnight. Then she would dip her hand into a glass of water and flick the droplets against the hot walls, creating steam which filled the oven, then quickly close the door to keep the heat inside. Soon the kitchen would fill with the delicious aroma of baking bread, warm and tangy.

Once the bread was in the oven, we started making the sauces, which needed to simmer for hours, and then the pasta noodles that would hang on frames to dry. Then Estella would take the batch of pizza dough she'd made the night before, dump it onto the large butcher-block counter, and cut it into portions. I helped her roll them into balls that would become the round foundation of Mama Mia's pizza.

I loved working there. It was easy for me to forget the bad things when I was there. Estella and Francesca were always willing to teach me what they knew about cooking and running a small restaurant, and I was an eager student.

Perhaps if I'd known nothing about fine dining or the art of classic cuisine, if I'd never heard the symphony that plays inside a big restaurant kitchen, music known only to the select few, if I'd never been Steigler's

Girl, I might have been satisfied working at Mama Mia's. The problem was, I lived with Julian and Lucia Laurent, proprietors of one of the best restaurants in Paris, and it was *their* restaurant kitchen I wanted to be in, *their* skills I really wanted to learn.

Julian taught me a few things on his days off. He was always generous and kind, but I wanted to learn so much more. I longed for the day Lucia would finally let me train with them at Le Catelan.

Chapter 53

Youthful indiscretion

On May 8, 1945, the Germans surrendered to the Allies at the US Army headquarters in Reims. Upon hearing the news, the entire city of Paris lit up with excitement. People flooded the streets in celebration of the victory. The world was finally rid of the Nazi menace for good.

I hoped this news would mean a change in my fortunes, and Lucia would finally allow me entry into the kitchen at Le Catelan, but when I asked them a couple of weeks later, after all the excitement had died down, nothing had changed.

"She's too young, Julian. It's still too soon, too dangerous," Lucia told him, avoiding direct eye contact with me. She was never mean about it, just unyielding.

Julian would let me, if it were up to him alone, but they were partners in all things, and his first loyalty was always Lucia. Even though I understood I was young, and it had only been just over a year since everything went wrong... that didn't make it sting any less. I was impatient to achieve my goal.

"Don't worry about it, Marie. Lucia will change her mind. They love you at Mama Mia's!" Camille said after I pouted and complained to her about not being allowed to work with Julian. "Let's go do something fun." She challenged me with a mischievous gleam in her eye.

I was in enough of a rebellious mood that I accepted her challenge, ignoring the nervous flutter in my stomach, the warning sign that something was about to happen. Shaking it off, I convinced myself it was only my frustration with Lucia, and boarded the Metro to the city with Camille, something I never did. Whatever adventure Camille had planned would distract me from my frustration.

Camille was beside herself with excitement when we got off the Metro in the heart of Paris. I was nervous. She had found an announcement about the open house for *École le Cordon Bleu*, which was reopening under new management, and she wanted to surprise me, thinking it was a perfect way to lift my spirits.

"Come on Marie, let's just get the information. It can't hurt to find out."

"I guess not. But I don't know how I would ever afford the tuition. Won't it be expensive? *Le Cordon Bleu* is the best culinary school in the world," I said, even though the possibilities to bloom in my young mind.

"I don't know, but it's worth finding out. Don't you think? If being a professional chef is what you really want to do, why not go to the best school, when it's right here?" she asked as we entered the school on the Rue du Faubourg Saint-Honoré.

A short time later, my mind was still reeling with the possibilities, and more frustrated than ever.

Madame Brassart herself had given Camille and me a tour of the school, graciously showing us around and describing the curriculum to achieve a Grand Diplôme, and the requirements for acceptance into the program. She knew neither of us would enroll, but she was kind and supportive of my interest in cooking and encouraged me to work hard to achieve my goals. "We need more talented women in this field."

"Uggh! I hate not being old enough to do what I want! And I hate having to wait." I complained as we walked back toward the Metro. It was like a tasty bite of something dangling right in front of me, just out of reach, and I wasn't big enough to snatch it. It was so frustrating.

It would be a minimum of three years (Marie was fifteen by then) before I could even consider stepping back through that door. I had to be eighteen, and I had to have a Baccalauréat diploma from lycée, secondary school, which I hadn't even started.

"Don't worry about it, Marie. That time will fly by fast. You'll see. You can go back to school with us next term. God, that will be so much fun. You'll see." Camille chattered on as we walked down a side street.

"Let's stop and have something before we catch the Metro," she suggested as we walked by a small sidewalk café with a few empty tables sitting in the afternoon sunshine. "Get a table and I'll be right back. I need to use the ladies. And order me a coffee and something sweet." Camille headed through the door of the café as I sat down at a table along the sidewalk.

While I waited for Camille to return, I made some quick notes in the small journal I always carried; notes about the school and what I needed to accomplish before even applying to that prestigious institution. I tried not to feel defeated by the obstacles, but it was hard. I knew anything could happen in three years, anything.

When I looked up, I expected to see the waiter, but a man was sitting across the table from me. I'd been so focused, I hadn't even noticed when he sat down. He stared at me, obviously trying to confirm his suspicions, and I knew I only had a matter of seconds.

I recognized him immediately. He was Jean Pierre, the waiter at the George V, who had routinely served Katerina and me during our time there. He knew me from the kitchen too, when I would sit at the staff table writing in my cooking journal.

Merde! My journal. I quickly schooled my face and controlled my breathing, trying not to panic.

"I wasn't sure, but now that I get a good look at you, I'm certain." He glared at me intently, his breath reeking of stale wine. "You're that little Boche bitch from the George V, the one the police are looking for. You used to write in that little book of yours, always spying on us." His voice was low and menacing as he reached across the table to grab my wrist.

I pulled away before he caught me, standing up abruptly, then snatching up my things. I yelled at him as loudly as I could, "Eww! You filthy old man! How dare you touch me! Stay away from me, you old lecher." I hurried away just as Camille was coming out of the busy café.

Oh, God! He knows me! Oh God! I need to get out of here! I thought as I ran across the street.

Camille called to me, "Marie? Wait! What's wrong? What happened?"

I could hear the man yelling, "I know who you are! They'll find you! You can't hide forever!"

My God! Oh my God! I was panicking, not sure of what to do, but knowing I needed to get as far away as possible. I kept moving up the street, kept my head down, trying to control my fear, my breathing, not knowing where I was going. Then something solid blocked my path, and I felt powerful arms grab my shoulders.

"Whoa! Hold up, little lady," said the American soldier in English.

I tried to squirm out of his grasp, desperate to get away.

"What's this, Sargent?" I heard Bill's voice ask as he walked out of the hotel entrance and approached the soldier. "Marie? What are you doing here? What's wrong, Chère?" he asked, pulling me to the side, concern etching across his face when I looked up into his eyes. He bent down, holding me by the shoulders, scanning my face for the reason of my distress.

"He knows me, recognized me from the George V. He knows who I am," I whispered, trying to hold back the flood of tears.

Bill stood up and looked over my shoulder, searching for the threat. I could feel his body tense when he found it. He spoke to the soldier standing next to him.

"I know this girl, Sargent. That guy over there is harassing her. Do me a favor, Luke, take care of that for me, and keep it on the down low. I'll take her home and then meet you back at HQ in a couple of hours," Bill told the soldier in English.

"No problem, Major. I'll take care of it," the soldier responded with a smart salute.

Camille caught up just as the soldier left, clearly concerned but also surprised at the sudden appearance of Bill coming to my rescue. She immediately started in on a string of questions, but Bill cut her off.

"Be quiet, Camille. Come with me, both of you. I'll take you home." Then he led us to a jeep parked not far down the street and helped us into the back seat.

I couldn't speak, couldn't do anything but sit there next to Camille, who kept staring at me with a million unasked questions. She was dying to know what had happened, but I couldn't tell her. I could barely think beyond my need to escape, to hide. My heart was beating out of my chest, and it took every bit of control I had to stop the shaking that threatened to send me running again.

"Who was that man, Marie?" Camille gently asked. "Why did he say that he knows you?"

"Please stop talking Camille. Please," was all I could say.

We pulled up in front of Camille's house a short time later. I remained in the jeep, staring straight ahead, unable to look at my friend, afraid she would know me for a liar and a fake, and maybe even worse.

Bill helped her out of the jeep, then stood in front of her, still clasping her hands. "Listen to me Camille. If you care about Marie, you won't say anything about this to anyone. Do you understand me? If you care about her at all, you'll forget this ever happened," Bill said, worry written all over his handsome face.

Camille just nodded her head silently, her own worry showing, but she accepted his instruction and told me she'd talk with me later. I watched as she went into her house, giving me a final wave goodbye.

A few minutes later, Bill and I were walking through the Laurent's front door.

Chapter 54

Confessions and choices

"**C**aptain Marchand. What a surprise to see you. Come in, come in." Julian greeted him with a friendly handshake. Then he took one look at me, slumping onto the sofa in the front room, and his smile faded.

"She's been seen, recognized," Bill said as Lucia and Bisabuela came in to greet him.

"What?!" Julian and Lucia said in unison.

"Where? When? Who saw her?" Lucia asked, seeking the pertinent information.

All the adults in the room shifted their attention to me for the answers. I had no choice but to confess my foolish inattention to our mutual safety. Still shaking, I pulled myself together to answer them.

"Camille and I went to the city, to the open house at *le Cordon Bleu*. I just wanted to see it, to find out if I could go there to study cooking. After our tour, I was sitting at a café writing in my journal, waiting for Camille. I thought I was being careful... but then he was there, sitting across from me. He was a waiter at the George V. He called me the little Boche bitch, said I used to spy on them, and that the police were looking for me. I think he was drunk. He tried to grab me, but I jumped away from him, called him an old lecher, and shrieked at him to leave me alone. Then I ran."

My heart was still beating hard and fast. I could feel the fear flowing through me as I recalled the hateful look on the man's face and the panic I felt when I knew he recognized me.

"Right into me, thank God," Bill added. "I got in last night and was on my way to HQ with my Staff Sargent when she ran into us, literally. My Sargent went to handle the man with as much discretion as possible, but quite a few people were around. I'm not sure yet how much they heard him say. Then there's Camille. She will have questions, even though I've asked her to not say anything about it, for Marie's sake." Bill was already thinking about what repercussions might lie ahead. He scowled up at the ceiling, breathing hard.

"Merde!" Lucia yelled with a look in my direction that spoke volumes. "Did he see you at *le Cordon Bleu*? Is that where he spotted you? Does anyone besides Camille know you went there today?" she asked me, demanding all the details.

"I don't know where he was when he saw me. Suddenly, he was there in front of me. Madame Brassart knows we were there. She took us on a tour and had us sign the guest book," I confessed, finally realizing the magnitude of that mistake.

I'm so stupid! I never should have gone! Why didn't I wait! I screamed inside my head. *I've ruined everything!*

"Merde!" Lucia shouted to the ceiling.

"Even if he spotted her at the school, Lucia, I can take care of that," Julian said calmly. "I'll give Elisabeth a call tonight, thank her for her kindness to the girls today, explain how thrilled they were to see the school, then give her another opportunity to convince me to teach a class for her. That should mitigate that problem." Julian was always very calm under pressure.

"All right, Julian, that will take care of Elizabeth, but we still need to figure out a safer place for Marie to be. Suresnes is obviously too close to Paris. People saw her too often with the Lang woman. They will remember her," she argued. She couldn't look at me, and I didn't blame her.

"I agree. But let's think about this, figure out a place that's best for her. We knew the risk, Lucia, the moment she arrived, and we took it. Are you now willing to pass that risk on to someone else? Someone who won't consider what's best for her? I know you Lucia, I know you'd never want that."

Lucia looked at him for a long time, shook her head, then sat down in the corner chair, covering her mouth with her hands, and closing her eyes.

Bill was pacing the floor in long strides, smoking a cigarette, his face lined with worry. Bisabuela sat next to me, holding my hand, the one that wasn't clutched against my mouth, trying to hold back my tears.

I was a bomb with a lit fuse, sitting in the middle of their living room, ready to go off at any moment, and I didn't know how to stop it.

Bill suddenly stopped his pacing, his back to us, his head lowered. "Shit. I thought I had more time," he told the empty dining room in English.

"Captain?" Julian was the first to speak.

Bill turned to face us. "It's Major now. Battlefield promotion," he stated flatly. Then he kneeled in front of me, taking my hands into his. He held them firmly but gently, capturing my eyes with his.

"Look at me, Chère. I told you I would help you, be there for you. Wherever you want to land, I will catch you. Do you remember?"

I nodded my response, biting my lower lip to keep from crying. I knew what was coming.

"You need to choose now, Chère. There's no time to waste thinking about it. I thought we'd have more time, but now we don't. Will you stay in France, or let me take you to Mama? If it's here, I'll make sure you're safe, some place where they've never heard of you, some place the war didn't touch, if there still is such a place in France." He let me sit with his words, with the feeling radiating from his hands.

"Ah Chère, I think you know what I want you to choose. You could be happy there with Mama. You could grow up without being afraid. Trust me, baby girl. I won't ever let you fall." He squeezed my hands in reassurance.

"Why does it matter to you, Bill?" I asked.

He looked at me for a long time, his eyes pleading for an understanding he wasn't sure of himself. "It just does, Chère. It just does. I can't let this war destroy the rest of your life. I won't let it."

I sank into the cushions and slid my hands out of his, wrapping them around myself. Bill sat back on his heels, waiting for my decision. They were all waiting, like a collective holding of breath, wondering if the bomb would explode or defuse.

A million thoughts raced through my mind, retracing all the moments that led me to this one momentous choice. Would I stay in France or go to America? Would I give up trying to get back to the Désirée I'd been before all this, the French girl Alex believed I was?

When I really thought about it, I knew she was gone; bit by bit taken or destroyed by the Nazis and finally shattered into nothing the moment they killed Alex. Only a ghost of her remained, the memories of a lost childhood in the north of France. The girl I'd become since then was just an illusion, living in a temporary state of grace, another mask disguising the emptiness behind it.

I didn't know who I was anymore. I'd been pretending for so long that nothing about me felt genuine. There were bits of me in every pretend girl, but mostly I became what the person in front of me thought I was. That was how I survived.

I wanted more than that, more than just a pretend life that someone or something could snatch away in an instant. I didn't want to hide anymore. Then I heard the rich thick accent of Picasso echo in my mind, reminding me it had always been my choice.

'You are at a crossroads, a time to choose your own destiny. Will you be a victim or a victor over what has happened to you? You get to decide.'

I opened my eyes to find them all watching me, waiting. Lucia was in the big chair in the corner, Julian perched on the arm, both their faces expressing a mixture of emotions. Bisabuela was still beside me, my protector, my guide since I'd been there, quietly waiting to see if she needed to step in should my choice be to remain in France. And Bill, still sitting in front of me, his eyes full of tenderness and hope.

"It will never be over for me... the war, I mean. It will never be over if I stay in France."

I reached out my hands to Bill. "I'll go Bill. I'll go with you to America."

A collective sigh went through the room, extinguishing the fuse. I couldn't help but feel the sting of it. The danger was passing. I would leave, and Lucia was relieved.

Bill pulled me to my feet and wrapped me in his arms, sheltering me from that hurt. "Thank you, Chère, for trusting me," he said, placing a kiss on my forehead.

The rest was just business. Bill, Julian, and Lucia discussed the details of my escape from France. I'd done my part, chosen the direction. Now they were going to decide the rest.

Bill would whisk me away on a flight to London using diplomatic papers (whatever that meant), then we'd take another flight to the States and that would be that. Lucia would create a story to explain my departure to my friends and the neighborhood at large. Julian would cover my tracks with Madame Brassart at *le Cordon Bleu* and create a new identity card for the new me.

My thoughts were no longer required. I was only thirteen, after all. But I had lived the past year as a girl of fourteen/fifteen, with all the personal freedom that age would allow. I didn't want to go back to only being thirteen, and I told them so.

"Can I at least be fourteen?" I interrupted when Bill gave Julian my new name and age; Désirée Gautier, age thirteen, May 1, 1932, Sedan, France. The date wasn't even right.

Both men looked at me and firmly said, "No."

It was disappointing, to say the least.

"You're thirteen, Chère. Be thirteen. Think of it as having more time than the rest of us," Bill said, stroking my cheek tenderly.

I released a sigh, rolling my eyes at him, showing my displeasure, but also my acceptance. I *was* thirteen, but sometimes I felt as ancient as Bisabuela. Well, maybe not that old, but older than I really was.

"I've got to get back, Chère. There are things I need to do, people I need to talk to. I've got to work a little 'Marchand Magic' to pull this off without a hitch. Pack your things and be ready for me in the morning. I'll be here to get you by seven." Then he bent down and kissed my cheek, said goodbye to the others and hurried out the door.

The three of them had made their plans and left to execute them; Bill to do some 'Marchand Magic' and the Laurents went off to take care of their parts. I just sat there on the sofa, overwhelmed, frustrated, and sad. Every emotion hit me hard as I thought about what had just happened.

"Are you all right, niña?" Bisabuela asked, still next to me on the sofa, occasionally stroking my head or back. She was the nicest old woman, always so kind. I knew I would miss her, like I missed Tante Elsa and others. Some women have that effect, they just know how to nurture.

"I'm fine, Bisabuela, just tired and sad. I wish it had been different. I was happy here, more than anywhere else since the beginning. I wanted this to be real. Sometimes I even thought it was. I'm sorry for everything." Tears were freely running down my face by then.

She pulled me into her arms, holding me against her bosom until my tears slowed to a trickle. "Dry your tears, niña. You've nothing to be sorry for. You're on the path you must take, and my heart tells me you will live a full life. Sometimes we must let go of the things we cling to the hardest, to make room for what we need." She released me and dried my damp face with her handkerchief.

"Was it hard for you to leave Spain, Bisabuela?"

"Of course. It was the hardest thing I've ever done. It was like ripping out my heart. But I was already an old woman by then and had a lifetime full of memories to take with me. You're young, niña, just beginning your life. Take the good memories with you and leave the rest, then go make new ones. Trust in yourself, always listen to your heart," she said as she gently placed her hand over the spot on my chest, my heart beating powerfully beneath her fingers.

Chapter 55

Goodbyes and beginnings

I hate goodbyes. They always feel permanent. Most of the time they are, and the day I left France was no exception.

I spent my last night sitting alone in my room, thinking about everything; every choice I made, or someone had made for me, every person I cared about and had lost or was about to lose. Everything. Most of it had been beyond my control, most of it had been circumstance, chance meetings, other people's choices about me and for me. But I couldn't escape responsibility for the choices I made on my own, and those were the moments I grieved the hardest about. Regret is a heavy burden for a young girl.

I thought about all the what ifs. What if I hadn't gone to Paris with Camille? What if Picasso had taken me somewhere else, to someone else? What if I had never run away from the nuns? What if I'd left France with Katerina? What if Katarina had never come to France? What if I hadn't gone fishing with Alex the day that I met the Kommandant? What if I had simply died with the rest of my family in May 1940? What if the war had never happened at all?

As I examined the possibilities of what a single change in any of it would have made, I understood the obvious truth; every step and stumble in the past five years had led me to this moment. It had all led me to Bill.

I didn't know what lay ahead for me, hadn't ever really known, but I trusted Bill more than I trusted anyone. I trusted he wouldn't let me fall.

Before dropping off to sleep that night, I said a prayer.

Please God, don't let the ghosts follow me.

There was nothing left to say. We had said it all in one form or another. Julian, Lucia, Bisabuela and I sat quietly at the dining table, sipping coffee, thinking, waiting.

My suitcase and satchel were by the front door, awaiting departure. Lucia re-styled me to a more age-appropriate look, and Bisabuela seemed reluctant to let me go.

Marie Rondeau had already left, and soon she would fade from memory, leaving little or no trace of her existence. I'd already pulled on my new mask.

When Bill arrived, we had no time for long goodbyes, thank God. It was a quick farewell, good luck, brief hugs and kisses and I headed out the door, my hand held firmly in Bill's.

I was leaving France forever. I knew I would never come back. An enormous lump settled in my throat as we drove away from the house in Suresnes. It has never gone away.

Two days later, Bill and I were in a cab pulling up the driveway of a big white house in the Uptown District of New Orleans. The cab stopped in the driveway next to a large round portico leading to a door flanked by tall multi-paned windows on either side of it. Bill paid the driver and collected our bags while I waited on the step, my nerves fluttering in my stomach.

"Are you ready, Chère?" he asked, squeezing my hand to reassure me.

That warm tingly feeling I always got whenever I was with Bill flowed through me, filling every empty space. "Oui. I'm ready Bill."

He lifted my hand to his lips, kissed it tenderly, then led me through the door.

"Mama?" he called out as we walked into the house. "We're home, Mama. I've brought Désirée home."

End—Part One

Cast of Characters:

Désirée Marie Rondeau – (Desi) 8-13 years old

François and Claudette Rondeau – parents

Jean-Michel – brother 15 years old

Anna – sister 14 years old

Jaques – brother 13 years old

Yvette – sister 12 years old

The Old Woman – Madame Elise Montclair du Châlons

Henri Pérot – friend of Jean Michel

Père André – Catholic Priest

Janine – Romani war orphan 10 years old

Margot & Jon – war orphans 6 & 4 years old

Rachel – French/Jewish war orphan 9 years old

La Maison de la Charité in Châlons:

A school/orphanage for girls

Révérende Mère – Sœur Valarie

Sœur Marguerite – Staff, teacher

Sœur Louise Claire – Staff, cook

Sœur Anne-Marie – Staff, teacher

Sœur Bernadette – Staff, teacher

Annalise – resident orphan 12 years old

Sylvie – resident orphan 11 years old

Karin – resident orphan 9 years old

Giselle – resident orphan 8 years old

Châlons en Marne:

Joseph-Marie Tissier* – Bishop of Châlons

Père Phillipe – Catholic priest

Dariel Guerin & wife – Groundskeeper for Cathedral

Alex Guerin – son, 12 years old

Robert Guerin – son, 2 years old

Monsieur Breton – Pharmacist

Madame Breton – daughter to pharmacist, housekeeper

Juliette Breton – granddaughter 12yo, student at La Maison

Monsieur Denier – Baker/Owner, boulangerie

George Denier – son, 12 years old, friend to Alex

Nazis in Châlons:

Oberstleutnant Anton Steigler – The Kommandant

Leutnant Fritz Bruener – Le Soldat Jouet

Frau Möller – La Dame Noire

Hauptmann Rolph Klein – Le Charmeur

Hauptmann Stefan Wolff – Le Loup

Katarina Lang Steigler – Ex-Ballerina, wife of Kommandant Steigler

Karl Steigler – son, Leutnant in German Army

Leda Steigler – daughter, killed by the Kommandant at 3yo

Tante Elsa Lang – Katarina's aunt

Paris:

Fräulein Heller – Tutor for Désirée in Paris

Serge Lifar* – Director, Ballet de l'Opera de Paris, friend of Katarina

Pablo Picasso* – Artist, friend of Katarina

Olga Khokhlova* – Picasso's ex-wife, friend of Katarina

Elisabeth Brassart* – Proprietor, Le Cordon Bleu (1945-1987)

Suresnes:

Julien & Lucia Laurent – Proprietors of Le Catelan restaurant

Bisabuela, Madame de Santo – Grandmother to Lucia

Camille Dorminy – 15 years old neighbor

Serina – 15 years old neighbor

Michel – 15 years old neighbor

Chaz Maret – 15 years old neighbor

Maurice – 15 years old neighbor

Captain William (Bill) Marchand – US Army, Intelligence

* Denotes actual person living at the time.

Acknowledgments

As anyone who has ever attempted to write a novel will tell you, despite the long, lonely hours it takes to put the words on the page, it doesn't happen in a vacuum. There are many people to thank for their wisdom and support in getting *Désirée's Story* out into the world.

Thank you, Shari Evans, who led the Kingston Writers Group for years. Your steadfast support has been invaluable. And thanks to all the members I've connected with over the years, for your insight and critiques. Many thanks also go to the Kitsap Writers Critique Group; Archie Kreager, Roland Boykin, Michelle Van Berkom, Kristina Anderson Younger, Jerry Hall, Mikko Azul, Paul Hathaway, Meghan Skye, Evan Harris, and Jeanne Lewis. They generously contributed their expertise and support to this project and helped me become a better writer in immeasurable ways.

Sincere gratitude goes to Trent Shadburne for the original art created for the covers. He captured my vision exactly with his beautiful imagery. Anna Shadburne made the words visually express the feeling I was seeking. Thank you both so much.

My deepest thanks to my family and friends for sticking with me on this journey—I know it has been a long slog. To my wonderful, brave beta readers who offered their keen insight to help me improve this story; Susan Sanders, Deb Smith, Gale Smart, Janice Cespedes, Jessica Kirchhofer, Lindy Bryson, and Vicki Schiller, who encouraged me to pursue this quest. I couldn't have done it without your support, dear friends.

To my sister, Waaknee Lerner, who brings joy to my life every day and who never gave up on me. Thank you. My children, Bliss Ogilvie and family, and my son, Diego Moreno, deserve equal praise. Your support means the world to me. And a heartfelt thank you to my husband, Robert, who continues to give me all I could ever need or hope for after forty-plus years of marriage. Thank you, my love.

Finally, I owe so much to Desi, the woman who gave me the inspiration for this story. Her willingness to share her long-held secret prompted my unquenchable thirst to find the answers. Desi never shared more than a few remarks about her early life, but what she shared made me want to dig deeper into the realm of possibilities; how a young child could survive WW2 and make it to America. I like to think that the story I've written would please her. Thanks, Desi. You will live forever in my heart, *ma Belle-mère*.

Denise

About the author

I began my writing journey in earnest after retiring from a long career as a financial officer. Throughout my life I've been an avid reader and daily journaler, so when I retired, I decided to spend my free time writing the type of book I wanted to read. I dedicated months researching the historical context of this story and then years honing my skill to tell it.

I live with my husband and sister in the woods of the Pacific Northwest nestled along a quiet little bay. My love for reading remains unquenchable, and I channel my passion for storytelling into writing stories of hope and resilience, while enjoying quality time with my family, friends, and fellow writers.

Connect with me on:
Facebook @DeniseMoreno
Instagram @driesaumoreno

Made in the USA
Columbia, SC
29 November 2024

47856337R00226